THE

FELL

ROBERT

JENKINS

RedDoor

Published by RedDoor
www.reddoorpublishing.com

© 2019 Robert Jenkins

ISBN 978-1-910453-74-2

A CIP catalogue record for this book is available
from the British Library

Cover design: Rawshock Design

Typesetting: Westchester Publishing Services

Printed and bound in Denmark by Nørhaven

For my parents,
For my children,
And for Donna. Heroes all . . .
Non illegitimus carborundum

One

I see a man hanged himself once, in the trees back of the lido late in that first burning summer after the little circus stopped coming to town with the tattooed Jewish trapeze girls, and after they stayed away it was like loneliness came in their place and later on people would say they had the sight and we should have known.

That summer was like living every day in the embers of a big and hungry fire that burned for ever and sucked all the air out of everything and every breath scorched your lungs so you breathed shallow and it was that same summer my friend Snotty Nosed Chaves went drowning in the canal after he jumped in for a swim and couldn't climb back out because the sides were steep and sheer and too high and nobody knew. He was no great swimmer and the water was deeper and blacker than it looked and colder too. And that same summer a woman commits suicide down the road walking in front of a train and they raised the fences after that. They said the devil was on the whole neighbourhood that summer. It was airless and breathless and long and hot and perfect but for the flying ants and the dying. They said there were demons over us all like a cloud of flies and some Baptist preacher did the rounds preaching on street corners and even knocking on doors like they used to in the black and white days, but my dad said it was nonsense and he wasn't scared and he forbade me to be scared too.

I was scared anyway. He said people die when it's their time or if they go early it's on account of they make mistakes or get bitten by plain bad luck, like the kid did in the canal, or had no job or good woman or man in their lives, or got betrayed or just lost in the fog of it all. He told me I could pray if I wanted but best not to any god in particular. Hedge your bets, he said, and don't be scared. No god listens to chickens he said. Chickens don't have a god. Chickens just get fried he said.

But people dying is an unpleasant thing and by all accounts from what I observed a very random thing and I was properly scared if I let my mind go there. Death was just too unpredictable and always very personal and as ugly as the flying ants that covered everything like tar and drowned in their millions in the cool water of the lido. Every morning we scooped them off in big nets on long poles before the customers came and everyone came there that summer because there was nowhere with cooler shade or sweeter water and it was everyone's wish all day and all night just to submerge their super-heated bodies in those cool holy waters.

It was my dad cut the hanged man down. The shrill screaming whistle that broke up the air hurt my ears. One whistle blast, the first one, led to others as people joined in the panic. It was like a horde of cicadas from hell were let loose in the still and perfect summer afternoon. Blowing whistles was the alarm signal at the lido and my dad was foreman. It was grown-up professional lifesavers doing something when nobody knew what else to do. They all had shiny chrome whistles and that whistle was authority.

That noise made my spine almost hurt and lit me up with excitement. It was a pure shiver-making, knee trembling adrenaline kick. It meant the ordinary and peaceful was gone and something bad and exciting had come. There was a pause when the lifeguards and swimmers all looked across the water at each other like time and gravity and everything just stopped. I swear I could see their eyes clearly from halfway up the shallow end where I was, which was a long way. Fear and panic. When those things are in someone's eyes you can see it a mile off. Then someone was running fast and I realised it was my dad.

That pool held one million and two hundred and fifty thousand gallons of water. That's a lot. My dad said it was one of the biggest in the world but I don't know if that was true or he was making his job out to be more important than it was, but he ran a full hundred and fifty yards and straight into the small copse before the fence just past the deep end. The deep end was fifteen feet deep, I don't know what that is in metres or yards, but it's deep. You won't hit your head on the bottom even if you dive off the top board, which is pretty high. He ran straight past me and I was shocked at his speed and the power of his body in a fast sprint. I'd never seen him go like that before. I half turned away as he almost hit me. He sure wasn't going to go round me at that pace. His bare brown feet struck the ground and lifted again like an Olympic sprinter with dust lifting from every footfall. He was wearing little swimming briefs in a spotted print like a leopard and a washed-out orange tee shirt with LIFEGUARD right across the chest. One day I wanted one of them shirts. People respected a man who wore one of them shirts and they were always sun warmed. You could pick one out of the drawer in mid-winter and hold it your face and feel the sun on it. They *radiated* summer and that's a magical ability. They even smelled warm.

He went so fast he was almost in flight, his feet hardly touching the ground at all and his arms pumping and boy could he run, and he jumped clean over a lazy swimmer who climbed out

3

of the water like a fat old seal in the sunshine and was stuck on his fat stomach trying to gain his feet, and he cleared him easy. Other men joined in the race and everyone still in the water and on the side stopped their playing to watch and slowly gather to see.

I went after him. I tried to make my feet strike the ground like his, lifting them the very instant they touched the ground and flicking them up behind me and raising my knees high like he did. I was trying to make dust fly. I was slow compared to him but there was a satisfying flick of dust behind me and I looked back and see it and heard it slide under me.

Other lifeguards ran too but not like him. Mostly they ran to be second at the event, to witness history, but he ran to change it. I could tell.

I saw him slow as he passed the first whistle-blower who was pointing and speaking with his voice loud and panicking and his face filled with fear and my dad kind of bounced and pivoted around him hearing all the story he needed, then went into the copse past the pool. I saw him climb a big old mossy oak tree. Just a glimpse through the heavy foliage.

I ran harder but I was so slow and I hated being slow. I wanted to see why my dad was climbing trees. He climbed easy and seemed to almost swarm it like he was rippling up over it and climbing it like a wind climbs a hill. I saw him in those glimpses through the trees and he was fast.

I got there late but soon enough to see a big man, fattest and palest I ever seen, fall to the ground and my dad jump down beside him. The fat man crashed but my dad landed light as a cat. The fat man was so pale he was like a fat and dimply human-shaped candle that had softened in the sun and lost its intended shape. His skin looked like it was made of candle wax too. Old candles starting to yellow. I saw candles that colour at my nana's funeral. They didn't look good on a human being and death close up is not like in the movies. Death close up is a cold and heartless hard bastard. Everyone should hate death. There ain't no sweetness in death.

The man was in swimmers and now he was laying in the dry leaves and acorns that had been there since autumn and winter. Beside him was a rope and noose and I could see how he had tied its bitter end onto the lower limb of the tree and slung the noose end over a higher branch then climbed up and done the deed. His white foot had a cut where bark had opened the soft skin. There was moss under his finger nails where he'd scrambled up one last scramble and blood and skin under his nails too like coils of fine cotton, and deep scratch marks all round his throat where he had fought the choking and tried to take back the hanging and changed his mind or maybe the horror and pain of if made him fight or he saw Death and realised what a heartless cold fucker he is, and I heard my dad say that and he never swore before and I didn't understand it at first but hearing it made the whole thing even worse. I could see where my dad had cut the rope to fell the man. I knew he had a knife, he always had a knife, even in his swimmers. An old liner lock knife, smooth handled and razor sharp. Older than me. It wasn't a weapon, it was a *tool*. And it was a *Live* blade. A Live blade is like a razor.

The oak was an easy tree to climb even for me and I was no shaved monkey. It was one of the best trees in the whole wood for climbing and always made you feel good even when you was a bit tubby and not much of an athlete like me, but I wasn't going to climb it ever again. Not after this day and there weren't no smudge stick witch or bells and blessings could bring it back clean.

5

The man wasn't looking too flash and people gathered and looked on with stillness and frowns, but my dad had pulled the noose loose and was pounding the Waxman's chest and giving him *artificial respiration*. He wasn't going to quit on him. He was sweating and hitting the man's chest really hard so I thought he'd break it and then rocking on it with all his weight, pushing it down and letting it rise.

Another lifeguard, Mad Louis, joined in and took over the chest compressions while my dad breathed into the man's mouth, and after a long time the Waxman suddenly vomited right up over my dad's face.

And he breathed.

At first not the healthy breath that comes with life, more a rattling feeble kind of sound that didn't bode well, but breathing is breathing and for sure it's better to rattle than nothing at all, and he was breathing and in a few minutes the breathing settled into a shallow rhythm.

My dad and Mad Louis rolled the Waxman, who was now tinging pink like he was outbreaking in roses, onto his side. This was the *recovery position* and now they would *monitor* him. I'd read the book in the lifeguards' hut. I knew this stuff.

Around the man's neck a redness and blackness and mauveness appeared as blood went to where the noose had been. He looked real bad and real sore, and where he had clawed himself started to bleed little fine rivers and many nights after I dreamed bad dreams of fine white coils of cotton skin grown huge in focus and lacy rivers of deep red blood.

A slender good-looking woman with a real short French bob handed my dad a towel and helped him wipe his face clean of sick. She kind of tended him. She was in a flowery bikini and looked fit and taut like there was no fat anywhere on her body.

When the ambulance came and carried the man away, my dad walked through the small crowd to the pool and one or two people patted him gently on his back and others just parted for him to pass. Other people gathered up the rope and policemen came to take such things away. I saw them all but nobody bothered my dad. They just watched him quietly like he was kind of risen above other people that day and people did right by recognising it without saying a word. He passed me without speaking.

He walked for a bit, head bowed like a prize fighter and a hero, then dived into the pool, tee shirt and all, and swam all the way to the shallow end without once coming up for air till he was over halfway. Then he broke the surface gently, almost tenderly and without a ripple, and swam the rest of the way in a slow breaststroke. He had a good stroke with no screw kick or anything. Some people thought he had been coached to swim in proper lessons, but he learned it from his brothers in the canal and just perfected it. He read books on it.

People still watched him. He leapt out of the pool with ease and didn't need to use the steps and walked back down its length to the lifeguards' hut. In there he wouldn't be bothered. It was Staff Only. It said so on the door in bold letters. One of the best things in my life was I was allowed to go into that hut and other kids were jealous. It was a special privilege. There wasn't much in it, a kettle and a couple of hard chairs and a table all stripped of paint and a kind of bed-cum-couch for first aid. There was a big first aid kit and a Minuteman resuscitator and a refrigerator. There was a window either side of the door, but they were small and shuttered so only splinters of light came through and it was always golden light, always warm, and dust always floated and drifted in the beams and I could watch dust like that all my days. The room had some tall lockers and a sink and smelled of aftershave. It was always cool in that hut because the concrete walls and concrete flat roof made it like a bunker, and just along from it was the first of several big old fat fountains whose water drifted in mist across the concrete and faded peeling paint and cooled even the hottest noon day. It felt safe and manly and strong.

I knew some things for sure that day: I knew I'd always remember when I saw a man hanged and brought back alive, and I knew I would never understand how a man would want to die in such a way on such a sunny day by a perfect blue sparkling swimming pool or abuse a fine old Oak climbing tree. It was a living day, not a dying day and I knew a grown man should have known that. I also learned that day that dead people don't look good, not like in the movies, and there ain't no peace in it. The dead might be still but the living are frenzied and furious and broken by it and afterwards their new shape is nothing like it was before. And I knew for sure that the dead do come back.

For a moment there by the pool in the fine sprayed mist of the fountains as the heat shimmered and people drifted away I wanted to be righteous. I wanted to be a hero and to live a hero's life. I decided I would strive to rise to that challenge and try to be pure in thought and deed and save lives. It was settled. My road was made and I made a solemn pledge and an oath to be righteous and pure for ever.

A suntanned brown girl in a pure white bikini, older than me but not quite a woman, ruffled my hair and smiled. She had green eyes and fair hair bleached almost white by the sun. She knew I was the *saviour's* son, so in some way I was kind of holy and special. She acted like that, like touching me was somehow touching *him*. I smiled up at her in gentle humility because that seemed to be the appropriate thing to do. I knew the look to make. Like a kid in a Jesus movie they showed in the youth club at the Baptist church. She touched my face with her finger, brushing a strand of hair from my eyes. Her finger was delicate and her nail very white against her brown skin. She smelled of perfect coconuts. I did The Lamb of God look. I was righteous and pure.

She had the most glorious titties I had ever seen, really ripe and full and straining at my face. I could actually see her nipples outlined under the thin cotton and I think I smelled them too and felt them alter the fabric of the air just there in front of me, so my face tingled and was heated up. It was the same as an electric charge you get from one of those alien metal zorb balls in the fairground only it was zapping me straight from her nipples. I reckoned I was seeing the best little titties in the Western world right there an inch in front of my face. I wanted to touch them and it was almost impossible not to lean forward and just open my mouth like I was taking holy communion, but I resisted. Resisting such temptation was what a hero would do and also she was pretty strong looking and would likely knock the shit out of me if I touched her uninvited, and I was glad I was wearing shorts and not just little swimmers and I resolved right there and then to one day get me a pretty golden girlfriend with titties just like hers. A real genuine wahine from Hula-Hula Land. And I swore another oath as I watched her walk away and she was as perfect from the back as she was from the front.

After the shock wore down, which was quicker than you might think, that day got perfect again and just the same as before except for being a little subdued and quiet because a lot of people went home early, and for another few hours that day stayed perfect as a picture. There were a lot of perfect days that summer.

The pool was edged in concrete terraces where people could sit and sunbathe or eat their sandwiches and ice creams or sip coke from cold glass bottles. There was grass growing up through cracks in them terraces, and the painted edges were peeling and faded and patched with lichen which flaked and powdered under the lightest touch. I sat around on one of the higher steps until most of the people drifted home and I watched the evening settle on the big old pool and the holy water was stilled. The air was always perfectly still in them nights and there was a silence like in a church. It was still warm and the terraces still gave off heat from the sun. The last people filed home tired and relaxed and some were red and sunburned but they looked at ease with everything, like for once the buzzing was stopped. In the lowering sunlight I could make out flying bugs and dust and pollen and soon birds dipped onto the surface of the pool to drink, just flicking over it without even breaking their flight. It was the same every evening because just as people went away nature reclaimed the lido and nature didn't mind me watching.

Lifeguards swept up and emptied bins and some were smoking and the smoke curled like genies lit blue by the sun. I promised myself that one day I would smoke like them and make blue genies. It sealed the relaxing moment. Everyone moved slow and lazy and no one was rushing to be someplace else because no place else was better.

Every night just before lockup I grabbed a snorkel and mask and went searching for money and jewellery that people lost in the water. Signs everywhere said DON'T LEAVE YOUR VALU-ABLES UNATTENDED and some people were so worried about leaving their valuables unguarded that they put them into the pockets of their swimmers and forgot them. Swimmers only have shallow pockets so there was always something to be found and sometimes I got riches and I was like a treasure hunter, which was my dream profession and still kind of is. I had a nose for where the loot would be and knew how to get the right angle so the low sun would reflect on anything shiny. I was good at it, better than anyone else, and if someone lost something like a ring or gold necklace and knew they'd lost it I was always the one they'd ask to try and find it. If I couldn't find it, it wasn't in the pool, simple as that. If someone reported a loss my dad would always point them in my direction and I was proud to be the finder. If they didn't report it though, it was finders keepers unless the person who came the next day to report it was a nice old lady or a poor guy or something or it was a wedding ring or locket with a baby picture. I always gave that stuff back and the rest I kept.

But it was a lean night. Just a few coins and a rubbish necklace not worth keeping, so I left it on the side. I dived down to the bottom again in about seven feet of water, not deep enough to have to clear my ears but deep enough to be cooler water, and I was planning on just chilling out down there for a while because I could hold my breath a full three minutes but Mad Louis suddenly appeared next to me on the bottom. He had a mad bulging-eyes look and he ambushed me like a shark. He was properly mad, which is how he got his name, and more like a small kid than a grown man. He ripped off my mask and launched me straight up like a rocket, driving off the bottom with his feet so one second I was looking for sunrays to light up lost gold and the next I was out of the water and spinning in the air. He was strong and explosive as mad people often are.

In my slow-motion somersault I saw my dad and other life-guards laughing and getting ready to jump in. This was the best of every day, when everyone would wash off the dust and sweat and sun and have some fun, and if Mad Louis was in the water, throw me around until I was sick.

I hit the water with no grace or style whatsoever and stung my back real good but I didn't make a fuss. My dad made a rule that went however much it hurts or annoys you, always come up smiling, so I came up smiling and Mad Louis threw me again but more gentle this time. He knew I took a stinger the first time and wasn't going to let up but never wanted to hurt me either.

Then the peace was all over everywhere as the younger lifeguards hit the water all around me and shouted and laughed and wrestled. The older lifeguards just slipped into the water at the other end and swam gently to cool off, not wanting to draw attention from the youngsters because they didn't want to wrestle. My dad could have wrestled but he wasn't of a mind to, so he kind of positioned himself between the two groups and everyone left him be. He just swam off the day without going far or fast and he was still brooding over the hanged man, I could tell, and when I thought about it it was right to still brood because it was a dark thing had come to pass and my dad had brought a man back from death and Death don't like being cheated.

I got out of the water after a while because I was being used as a ball and it was tiring, then soon after most of the lifeguards and other staff had gone and just my dad, Mad Louis and young Davy Crockett were left. They called Davy 'Alamo' because he had the same name as a cowboy who died in the fort there in a war against the Mexicans. Actually he wasn't really a cowboy, he was a *frontiersman*, which suited Davy even more because that was exactly what he was in his own way and in our time.

When we were alone Louis and Davy made me spar and throw punches at their upheld hands and duck their counters and move my feet and bob my head and they said I was a boxer and my dad scoffed and said I was a cardboard boxer and they laughed and said I would be a champion one day. Then the men robbed the café and shop. My dad had cut a master key from a blank one night in winter and after Davy locked up the gates we helped ourselves to choc-ices and ice-cold Pepsis. I never took anything from the store because I wasn't allowed to steal, but they took what I wanted and gave it to me. It was a *perk* of the job. Every job has to have a *perk*. The old-time lifeguards all talked about perks and spent a lot of time looking for them.

The night watchman wouldn't arrive for another hour and we'd always wait for him so my dad could hand over the keys and report that everything was fine. You heard him coming through the iron gates, so we never got caught in the shop, and my dad loaded his bag with sweets for everyone at home and wrapped choc-ices in sheets of newspaper so they wouldn't melt too fast and locked up the shop again. It was the once-a-week treat and he made sure nobody ever took too much. Just a skim, a taste and somehow it always tasted better when you didn't pay for it, so the ice cream was just a little bit creamier, the chocolate a little more chocolaty and the Pepsi a little cooler with bubbles that popped gently in my mouth. Even the water beaded on the bottle more perfectly when you didn't have to pay.

Davy sipped his Pepsi and smoked a hand-rolled cigarette so the smoke drifted around me and tasted damp and sweet. It was laced with old rum and went by that name. He made the others smile by blowing smoke rings right over my head so I was like a saint. He'd changed into a washed-out tee shirt and faded and torn blue jeans that were real old and threadbare and patched on the knees and crotch. I liked them and wanted a pair just like them. Maybe I would smoke Old Rum too once I got started on my smoking career. A man could do a lot worse.

I never knew where Louis and Davy lived but they never rushed there and when they went out through the gates at the end of the day, it was always with something like sadness and it came on us like mist and it was like they knew all this wouldn't last. Both men moved slow and confident so every part of them was relaxed and easy and they moved with a kind of natural rhythm. They didn't so much walk as stalk across the shimmering ground. They were very different from each other, but that one thing was alike. I practised their walk when nobody was around to see and you have to half shuffle and roll your shoulders too like you're dancing a slow dance with an invisible lady and just move real easy and calm like a cat on a hot day. You *slink*.

Mad Louis rode a massive old Triumph with an upswept exhaust spotted with clumps of rust in small flowers. Sometimes he took me on the back and it was like flying. I'd perch up behind him, hold round his waist and he'd slalom all over the deserted road between the lido and the highway. I could feel the power of the big engine right in my stomach and even when he went fast I always felt safe.

I wished we could all live at that lido, the lifeguards and my dad and me and my family, because when I was there I was never lonely or afraid and I hate being lonely and was always afraid outside of them gates, but inside the rusty wrought iron gates the world was perfect. There were no gangs or vandals or druggies or drunks and no one trying to put the bash on anyone. They wouldn't dare – my dad and Mad Louis and young Davy Crockett banned anyone who caused trouble or even looked like trouble and nobody would dare take them on because they were bosses amongst men and they said it was a family place, and so it was.

But it was more than just safe, it was deep everlasting peace. Or so I thought in the days when I believed in such childish things.

My dad said the 'Dhammapada' could have been written right there at the lido. That's a book by the Buddha that Davy read and onetime he gave my dad a copy after. Davy said you shouldn't kill things but sometimes killing people was OK because they could come back better and more 'elevated and enlightened'. He said killing people was sometimes a righteous favour, and Davy wasn't a liar.

Then too soon the sky was deepening its blue and it was getting towards dark and the watchman came in through gates that were squealing tired and old with exactly the same tune they did every night and I heard the engine far away through the trees and the dusk as he pulled his old car safely inside. The noises drift low through the evening, and hiding our loot in an old Gola sports bag, we went. My dad always took one last look over the water every night the same and I thought then he was just checking everything was OK, but really he was searing it into his memory so he'd never forget because he knew it wasn't for ever and it wouldn't ever be better or more perfect and he didn't want it to end.

The watchman was nearly two hundred years old. He always gave me a fruit-flavoured hard lolly which I think he stole by the handful from the shop at night, so I reckon that shop must have made a loss every summer. His name was Bill and he chained and padlocked the gate behind us and locked the old lock like he was nervous of intruders and would spend the night in the lifeguards' hut, doing a round of the fences every hour or two and using a key chained on a post every here and there to turn in a big black box he carried on his belt that told the bosses he had done his checks. It seemed like a nice job. He had a small mangy black dog called Blue and a big lunchbox and long silver torch and always some fruit cake in tin foil and I reckon he slept most of the night. If anyone broke in he wouldn't be able to chase them away because he was too old and he wouldn't frighten them off because there was nothing even slightly threatening about him or Blue except Blue's yellow rotten teeth that might poison you to death if he bit you, but who would break into a swimming pool in a forest?

Mad Louis kicked his Triumph alive and revved it, destroying the peace with rattles and thunder and choke choke choke and then he revved it again and again until my dad was pissed off, then he laughed as he rode away. Davy threw his duffle bag over his shoulder and strolled into the woods, taking the long path to town. Most nights he liked to walk and only accepted a lift if it was raining hard. He turned briefly before the trees and nodded to my dad, softly saying 'good job today', and kind of saluted with a smile and a flick of his right hand. He had a really good smile. My dad returned the gesture and Davy turned again and was gone in the fading light. The forest just seemed to envelop him and dandelions floated around his footfalls and tiny bugs glinted silver around his head, and in the haze he vanished and I was left alone with my dad and he was colder when we were alone so I was never fully at ease, and I think he wanted to walk that path with Davy or ride out with Louis but instead he had to take me home and be a father. I think being a dad wasn't his natural element, which in my book made him even better at it than if he had been a natural born dad. He had to work at loving me and still I was loved, so he did good and I knew it was true and he was sad as he watched them go and told me softly to get in the car.

It was getting late in the season and soon the lido would close and the gates would be locked for winter. The lifeguards would all go away as they did every year and my dad and me would be lonely again. It was always this way and in the weeks of winding down, a heaviness settled on us. Right then I wasn't sure if that was the reason he was sadder than other days or if it was the hanged man or both, but I knew afterwards that it was more than both those things and he couldn't name it and neither could I, but I think right then he sensed and knew real bad things were coming and he couldn't see their shape yet nor smell their breath.

He wiped some dust off the wing mirror and winked at me, which was rare because he never looked my way much, and I climbed into the hot car. It was a Singer and a rust heap that he worked on every weekend. It was a major job keeping it running on no money and even the seat belts didn't work so there was a scarf he used to tie me in my seat. My dad was a man who loved a routine. He loved to make lists and write on things in heavy indelible pen and he tied me into that seat just the same way every day.

Outside the lido and the trees and peacefulness and perfect nature, the city was on you straight away and the pace of the roads and closeness of the buildings was tight in your face real fast so there was no time to prepare for it and it was always a shock. Fear spiked up in me every day the same and my Spidey senses lit up because it felt like threat was everywhere and dusty mean-eyed people stared at me for no good reason as we passed. Dusty roads replaced the fine sweet dirt of the forest, which was a real forest but I guess if you were a woodsman you'd call it a copse. It was the last outpost of the great ancient woods that met the city to the east and it was ringed by roads and derelict buildings, so just a narrow track linked it to the greater wood and I thought that link, thin and winding as it was, kept it alive like an umbilical cord. If we had driven east we could have gone a lot of miles under the trees but we never went that way. We headed instead straight towards the baking hot city and there was no tree nor grass nor flowers that way for a long long time. My dad tuned us in to *Listen With Johnny* where Elvis was falling in love, and the city through the dust was mellow yellow in the evening light and my fear was getting smaller as the music filled me up even though we were heading deep into the concrete and tarmac towards home. Home was good and the fear in me had no reason to be and each day once I was over the shock of leaving the lido and seeing all the hard concrete and hard people I just took on a different skin and rolled with it and the fear died down as the music came up and I saw the city dust and the city people dancing that special city dance and it was OK.

I kept my head down because my dad was brooding and he was dangerous when he was like that and I was looking down at my worn-out tennis shoes and right then I was surprised at how worn out my pumps had got. They had been white once and in my mind they still were, but the canvas was grey and dirty and there was grass stains and the rubber toe cap was slit and the canvas was fraying and I must have been looking pretty intently because I saw a lot of detail. My dad saw me looking down and I felt his hand on my neck, hot and strong and calloused, just briefly touching me and it sent a warm shiver though me because a touch was so rare and even a brief one was something good and he looked brown and lean and hard. His dark-blue polka-dot shirt was all open at the chest and it clung to him and he wore a small gold cross nestled in his chest hair and I saw him how other people saw him and he smiled and that was all.

He was like a lion and when people saw him like that they knew they were looking at something properly dangerous and my dad could smile at you and somehow make your blood run cold and a shiver dance right through you. It was all in the eyes and the corners of his mouth and something in his energy. Every night I went to bed convinced that nobody would kill me in the night except maybe him, so every night I said, 'Good night God bless Dad, see you in the morning' and wouldn't go to bed until he said the same thing back because he was a man of his word and if he said, 'Good night, see you in the morning', I knew he wouldn't kill me in the night, but I had to get that promise or the night was long and full of demons. My dad didn't hate anyone or anything and wasn't a trivial man but I knew for sure he could and would kill anyone and destroy anything without even losing a minute's sleep over it. Not a minute. Unless he gave his word. He was a man of his word.

Two

The bad things I knew were coming came fast and things went very bad as that summer ended with my big sister getting into trouble with the law and in the end it changed the world for ever so that summer ended true to its vile nature. *Vile*, that was Lilly's word for it. She was always saying it was too hot and too many bugs and unnatural happenings and people being taken from their beloveds for no good reason. Vile she said, simply vile.

Lilly is a hottie and never did wear many clothes and was always showing her legs, which were lean and shapely and went on for ever, and the shape of her breasts under real thin cheesecloth or thin cotton tops with little embroidered flowers on them which she put there herself. She had them perfect little titties that were just stuck on and followed you around the room. She didn't need a bra and never would. She was my sister but I'd be lying if I said I never noticed. Lilly was skin and bone and tits and legs and an elegant neck and perfectly shaped elf-like face. She never owned much but looked really good in whatever she wore and could make anything look good and straight out of Paris, she said. She had that real special beauty and would have looked good in a potato sack if that was all she had to wear and even ladies' make-up was damage. In spring and summer she would make tiny wild flowers into tiaras and wear them in her hair. She had a perfect little nose and lips like peaches and her eyes were shaped like big almonds and deep green with tiny brown, grey and blue flecks running through them as if glitter had been sprinkled on moss.

Lilly was beautiful for sure and in another world she would have been a model and walked the catwalk or been in magazines or movies, but no scouts or movie directors came to our part of town and there were no fashion shoots and she didn't care because she trusted the universe and she was a lot of fun. She would practise talking like one of those black and white movie stars and walking with a book balanced on her head, her chin poised upwards just a touch to keep the book flat. She made me sit in front of her and watch her feet and each one had to tread in direct line with the one behind so she kind of snaked and slinked a perfect line with perfect poise.

Sometimes her friends joined in and tried it too but they weren't as good as her and I would be the judge. I would sit in a forest of bare suntanned legs and brown feet with brightly painted toenails and short shorts and perfect little boobs. Sometimes I could see right up under their tee shirts to the brown rounded underpart of their globes and I think they knew but didn't mind and it was idyllic and perfect.

Lilly always won. To the other girls it was a game to pass a warm evening but for Lilly it was passion. She turned heads everywhere she went because she had that deep grace and one day, she said, grace would carry her out of Dodge on a great white stallion. Lilly only owned one book and it was called *Anne of Green Gables* by Lucy Maud Montgomery and it was tatty and yellowed with furry pages but she loved it and carried it almost everywhere.

Sometimes she would call me Gilbert, and she would be Anne with an E, and sometimes when the world was getting hard for her Green Gables was her world of escape. We didn't have a garden but there was a yard out back and my mum had big plant pots full of soft grass and pretty weeds and she was proud of them and sometimes put in seeds but they never amounted to much. My mum came from a place where people used pretty words to describe everything, so the bush was a forest, and there were meadows in place of paddocks, and dells, rises and mounds and no weeds or scrub but wild flowers and evergreens and mist and twilight and a dawn chorus and her voice was like a thrush's song at sunrise.

Lilly tended that soft grass and made out the pots were part of a glorious garden from France and she told how the flowers would brighten up the old place when they came and she said it in her Anne accent and I believed her. She read that book aloud every night even though she knew it by heart, and when she was being Anne she used a real old accent and drawled her words and sometimes made out to be Marilla and sometimes she spoke to mum and called her Marilla instead and then mum would call her Anne, or Lilly would call me loud and drawly and I would be old Matthew Cuthbert and she herself would be Marilla and then little Jasmine from next door would be Anne. We just rolled with it and were so used to it, so it was like second nature and always made us laugh and sometimes we would stay in that world the whole day long and fall asleep safe in Green Gables and she would stroke my eyes and I would cuddle into her and feel her warmth and the scent and the flavour of her warm soft skin, and the hairs on my arms would stand up she was so magnetic.

Lilly was also what some people called volatile and one sad evening late that vile summer I got home still damp and smelling of chlorine from swimming at the lido and imagining being a hero and looking forward to the lollies in my dad's bag and she was already arrested and cops were in the house.

She'd been caught in the shops with a friend who was stealing a lipstick, which was real stupid because she barely had any lips, and when they went onto the street the cops were there and stopped them. It turned out Lilly didn't steal anything and didn't know her friend did either but she took exception to the cop bullying her and accusing her. She stood her ground, which she was always wont to do, then she got angry when he manhandled her friend and first got righteous and indignant, then got volatile and stabbed him in the neck with her metal nail file. She was always doing her nails and people said she could have made a paying job of doing it for other people and it was my fault it cut him so good because I sharpened that nail file to a razor's edge so she had a self-defence weapon. It was a dumb-kid thing to do one evening when we were bored and she was worried about men following her and being inappropriate in the city and I wanted her to be safe. I used a whetting stone my dad kept in the cellar and gently brought the edge alive and if I hadn't done that things would have been very different for sure.

The cop didn't die but he bled a lot and they took it personal and made a major fuss. It was the dumb sort of thing any teenage girl might do and she just lashed out and it was bad luck that she was holding her nail file. It could have been a handbag if she owned one, or a newspaper if she ever read one, or a hairbrush or cheese sandwich for that. But it was a nail file and sharp as a razor and it was the most exciting thing that ever happened to that cop and the worst thing that ever happened to Lilly or any other person for that matter.

That night when we got home the whole street was watching for us. People were outside in the last of the daylight and the moon was up but the sun hadn't fully sunk and it was still too hot to rest indoors, and I see them people looking and whispering and worried. Lilly was already a hero because nobody in my street liked the cops and stabbing a cop was considered a righteous act.

Straight away before we even got to our door and before I knew why the cops were in the street I could tell from my dad's face that this was not good. He smelled trouble and he hated trouble like a bull terrier hates a cat or a rat.

As I got out of the old Singer, Fat Vinnie the Samoan gave me a thumbs-up and a really knowing slow nod of the head. He never said much so a thumbs-up was almost a French kiss from Fat Vinnie. One of his older brothers, the sixth or seventh one, nodded, too. Nobody was smiling though. They all knew that Lilly was going away for some long time even if I didn't know it right then.

In the house my mum was crying and looked like all the suntan had been washed away and she'd got suddenly old and thin. Even her skin looked thinner and grey than it had that same morning and I realised for the first time ever that old age, like death, could come on really fast and without warning and it's a callous evil bastard second only to Death himself.

My dad went into the house in front of me and I could feel the mean in him as I followed in his icy and fiery wake. He was holding things inside really tight. He spent a lot of time and energy keeping calm and making sure our world was as peaceful and perfect as he could make it, but he worked so hard at peacefulness because really he was afraid of how good he was at war and chaos and havoc. I always knew, I could sense it and every living thing could sense it. Even bugs didn't bite him. I swear it.

He sent me up to my room without speaking a word, just shot a look. I went up but didn't go to any room and I sat with little Jasmine, perched on the top stairs. My mum looked after Jasmine most nights until late because her daddy was away and her own mum worked long shifts, and little Jasmine leaned into me with her eyes big and fearful and dark hair dropping in waves right down her back and I put my arm around her. She was wearing a brushed cotton nightie and the Donald Duck slippers she inherited from Lilly and they were too big but she didn't care. There were a lot of cops in the hall and they all watched real cautiously as my dad passed through them into the living room. Every one of them was much taller and wider and younger than he was and every one of them was scared. I looked down on them and they didn't know it but they were huddled liked frightened sheep and you'd have to be a dead man not to feel the danger that clung to my dad. In the short walk past them my dad saw every one of them and read their faces and eyes. They were weighed, and they knew it.

Then a couple of minutes later he walked back out of the living room and opened the street door and waited and the cops filed out leaving just a sergeant and one other. He sent the cops out without a word just the way he had sent me to my room and they actually went. They didn't even look at the sergeant for orders.

I heard the old policeman tell the story of Lilly and when he was done my dad spoke real slow and low and sounded every letter of every word, 'Is the policeman OK?'

The cop nodded then and in the calmest of voices my dad said, 'Good . . . that's good . . .' Then he said, 'Lilly's a minor and she can't be interviewed without an adult present. Where is she now?'

The cops said something I didn't hear properly and my dad said, 'Is she OK?'

Then the cops said something else and my dad growled in a voice that sounded like a rumble so deep I felt it more than heard it, 'If she's been hurt, touched or messed around, it's on you. *Personally* . . . you understand?'

He told my mum to stop crying, that it would be OK, and his voice was gentle when he spoke to her and he went outside with the cops in tow and when he left, my mum tried to be strong and for a moment she smiled at me and tried to brave it out and she took up a tea towel to dry some dishes but then she slumped and I was afraid for her, and Jasmine and me ran downstairs and hugged her and Jasmine cried and went and got *Anne Of Green Gables* like the book could heal even this.

On some sunny days we would go to the park and there was a weeping willow tree and in one corner of the small field the grass was wound up with camomile and we would have a picnic there and my mum would play catch with Lilly and me and dance and laugh and she was fine and fragile like a sparrow and her bones were delicate as lace and she was like a movie star and her arms reached me wherever I was and however far away I was and she was stronger than an oak tree and her spirit was everywhere just like it was made of the air and wind and I was always safe because she made me safe like she was everywhere and everything and even if she was nowhere to be seen she was with me, but right then with Lilly taken away she was lost and it was like evil had come and was too big and all over her and bad men had cut into the oak tree and she was cut through and she clutched her belly where Lilly and me were grown and she felt the great pain, and I knew it was just beginning and there was nothing I could do, so I marked my dad's words and tone so I could practise them later and use them one day, *On You . . . Personally . . . you understand?*

When my dad got to the police station he found Lilly with a black eye, a broken wrist and forearm and a split lip. She was shaking scared and I heard him say she was like a leaf. *Shaking like a leaf.* They wouldn't let him bring her home. He went to bring her back and I could tell he really thought he could work it out but they let him see her then locked her up and he never did bring Lilly home. Not ever.

Lilly got ten years in in a Juvenile Detention Centre, which is like a kids prison. Ten years is a longest time for anyone but for a fifteen-year-old girl it's for ever and I kept repeating the number and thinking of them years stretched out ahead. Not one day of those ten years would be easy and I knew it would change her for ever and she wouldn't be my Lilly when it was up. The truth is it didn't go so easy for the cops either, or my dad or any of us, and it went even worse for Mad Louis and Davy Crockett. That stuff is far back in the mist but it matters.

Three

After Lilly's misunderstanding my world became a bleak and twisted fairground ride and I was the smallest weakest person in it and then time just took a different shape and I couldn't tell you how long any part of it took to go.

I was crying all the time and I had been that way for a while, not wailing like a baby or sobbing like a sissy but enough to make everything look blurred and misty, and seeing the world through tears had become so normal I forgot what edges looked like and I lost weight too, which would have pleased my dad if he had been around to see it.

People kept telling me everything would be OK and had been telling me that for a long time, but it wasn't OK and wasn't going to be and only a fool would think otherwise and I knew that much for sure. Something was broke and wasn't getting fixed and sometimes that's just a fact of life.

Even my feet had taken to feeling strange, so the ground under me was unreliable like it lived and moved and was treacherous so I was sea sick most of the time and living on a big orange jelly like old ladies make. My palms sweated sometimes without warning and I was hoping every day that I'd become numb and hardened but it seemed that wasn't going to happen anytime soon and panic lived just an inch from my nose and there was always a little part of my brain or mind or soul that said, *Hold on, hold on, this will pass.* Trust your voices my voices told me and I did and in time the voices said, *See, hush now hush now*, and nobody told me I was leaving until men I didn't know took me to the airport.

I broke down and cried on the way because we went past the gravel road that lead into the trees and then to the lido. I couldn't help it and caught a few sobs and let my forehead bang on the window of the car and the trees were full and the road snaked into them so familiar that it called to me and beckoned me and I knew there would be lifeguards there readying the pool for the new season, hosing it clean, painting the places it was peeling the worst and playing football or sweeping the terraces, and I hoped they wouldn't break up that lichen too much because it was fine as lace and twice as pretty. I would know some of those lifeguards but some would be new and wouldn't even know how good it had been before. They just wouldn't know and that was heart-breaking because things forgotten are worse than things never having been and forgetting is up there with Old Age and Death in the trinity of evil.

I'd never gone straight past the lido before in all my life and it pulled my guts out to go straight past it now, and it was like walking right past love and not stopping and love not seeing you and I was looking at a cemetery where everything that was or could have been was stopped for all time and grown over and even the names had worn away and faded already. I'd seen cemeteries like that. I closed my eyes and hoped when I opened them I'd be back in the lido sweeping the winter leaves away and sanding the rusting legs of the lifeguards' watchtowers and sniffing up the scent of Old Rum. I would be listening to the men laugh and seeing them smoke and sweat and work and smelling the paint and disinfectant and chlorine.

When I looked again we were still on the highway and I caught my breath in a hiccup. The rest of the journey was so hard I chewed my lips until they bled and peeled tiny bits of flesh off them with my teeth and I couldn't help it.

The airport was big and busy and the two men with me were quiet the whole time. They thought they were special agents or SS but they were just social service lackeys and I didn't call them nothing and didn't even speak a word.

One big man stayed with the car and the other big man chaperoned me through the crowds and sat me down. He never took his hand from my shoulder until we sat, then he sat between me and everyone else like I was dangerous and the crowd needed protecting. He never took off his sunglasses either and he never smiled at me or spoke much and when he did speak he put on a fake deep voice, I could tell. I reckoned he'd never seen titties in his life unless they were in some sticky magazine he kept under his bed at his mummy's house along with his fake gun and chest expander and he probably broke sweat every time he passed a primary school and I could tell.

As I was sitting waiting to board the plane a bigger boy came and sat next to me and the big lackey scowled at him but the boy just smiled at me and ignored him. The boy was older than me and looked real confident and smooth and I could tell this was his kind of place just as the lido was mine.

I was holding an envelope with the name and address of my destination printed on it and the boy just reached out and took it from me and read it and passed it back and I was too tired and weak to resist. Then he struck up talking about aeroplanes and he sounded like he knew his stuff. He was tall and lean with ginger hair and was nice looking and I could tell he was very rich. He was wearing good clothes and proper brogue shoes shined up so you could see your face in them and their pattern was real holes and deep not just patterned on the surface like the ones in the Number 10 Discount Shoe Store. He looked like the cleanest, most soaped kid I'd ever seen and he even smelled of soap and he held out a wrinkled paper bag full of Rhubarb and Custards. At first I didn't dip, but he shoved it at me harder so I took one and it tasted good but it's juice kind of stuck in my throat.

'Best Rhubarb and Custards in the bloody world, eh?' He smiled and I nodded. 'Mum gets them from a shop in the city. By the *quarter* if you don't mind!' He laughed. 'I'm sure she pays in coppers and pennies!'

I reckoned he was called Rupert or Sebastian or something like that, not that I'd ever met a Rupert or a Sebastian. He was going *long haul* and told me all about the best planes to fly in. He must have seen I was teary and assumed I was afraid of flying because he went into a big talk about how planes want to stay in the air and all the *physics* of it.

He was smart and I didn't know what he was talking about but the essence of it seemed to be that I shouldn't worry because there was a very high probability that the plane wouldn't be crashing today. He said the best planes are jets but if you're flying props, singles are pretty good, but twin prop aircraft are dodgy because balancing the two engines is a real skill, you have to *feather* it, and if one engine dies it's a *battle royal* . . . so whenever possible, avoid twin-props. *Feather* it . . . I didn't know much at all about planes but I knew there were no feathers, so I just nodded and I wanted to ask him what exactly is a *battle royal* but thought I should probably know already, so I said nothing.

His plane was called a few minutes later and he said goodbye and offered his hand and I shook it. He had a firm cool grip and wore a long stripy scarf even though it wasn't cold and a posh-school uniform with a multi-coloured stripy blazer and grey slacks and them deep shiny brogue shoes and he was movie-hero stylish like a ginger film star and I liked him.

'Time flees.' He looked at the lackey then back to me. 'Be staunch fellow traveller,' he said, and patted my shoulder, looking at me hard and deep. I hadn't said a word the whole time and for all he knew I could have been a mute or deaf. Then he took a colourful marbled notebook from his inside pocket, unsnapped an elastic band that was wrapped around it and scribbled a note the way a doctor writes and put it in the bag of sweets and handed them to me. 'Keep these. For your journey. I have about two thousand of them in my luggage.' Then he walked away and was lost in the crowd.

When he was gone I pulled the note out. It had an address on it in the smartest part of the city and his name was Hamish Taunton and underneath was scrawled *Non illegitimus carborundum*. I didn't know what it meant and put it back in my pocket and I reckoned I could like Hamish Taunton if I ever had a chance and I could be his friend.

The big lackey suddenly smiled like an idiot does when he realises he actually knows something and he told me his name was Mr Lore and it sounds like *law* then spent the next twenty minutes sitting there at that airport lying to me about how lucky I was to be going to such a lovely place, and he didn't know shit. He'd never even been there, he told me that straight off, and even if it was Shangri-La all I wanted in the whole world was to be home and for it to be months and years ago. He was trying to be nice and I didn't like it and he was angling for a Rhubarb and Custard and he wasn't getting one.

Then the idiot lackey stood up and nodded to me. 'Time to board,' he said softly. It was the first genuine gentle thing he said all day and right then I almost bolted, but his hand fell heavy on my shoulder and I knew I was getting on the plane like it or not. I hated him but right then I wanted to fold into his chest because in that final parting he was all I had from anywhere near home and I knew I should have bolted long before and hid out and been like smoke and now it was too late.

We walked for a couple of minutes and down some stairs into ever more smaller and narrower places where eventually through big windows I could see huge jet airliners, some new, some older, all belonging to different airlines. They were like great shining manta rays and dolphins and there were jets with two engines and jets with four and I guessed Hamish Rupert Sebastian Taunton was on one and for a moment then I slid outside my own self-pity and wondered by what miracle something so big and heavy could actually fly and physics or no physics it didn't make sense and it was science and sorcery. Their tails were all painted differently and it looked like a hundred different companies had aeroplanes on the tarmac in a magical banner parade.

Then the fake man idiot lackey gave my ticket to a young woman in a uniform and she smiled at me and he patted my back and at the same time shoved me through the gate and it wasn't until he lifted his hand off my shoulder once and for all that I realised how heavy he had been on me.

My sudden lightness made me stagger for a step or two, then the sweep of people carried me along and onto the tarmac and I'd expected to walk through a tunnel and straight onto the plane, but it was a lot lower budget than that and I was outside in the fresh air and we walked across the tarmac with yellow lines to keep us from straying and an airline security guard was walking me towards my plane and I felt sick and for the first time I was afraid of flying, and it wasn't a jumbo jet or even a jet of any kind, and it was dwarfed by the other planes on the tarmac and looked puny and weak or a toy or maybe through another eye delicate, graceful and elegant. And it was a twin-prop.

Four

The light was different from home and more stark and more white and I didn't expect that and the sky was more blue and the sun itself looked hard and spiteful and full of needles. There were other colours, the green was greener, and flowers breaking out along the fence line were startling like everything was overfilled with the sharpest hardest colours and everything was super-defined. They would have looked amazing in Lilly's hair but by the fence they were just lost hope. Even the concrete ground was cleaner and newer and harder and more concrete and it wasn't cracked and lined with lichen and weeds and life. It was all too clean so I felt grubby and dull and greasy and oily.

I followed a big fat man as we filed towards the small air-port building and I tried to stick my chin up and be brave and because I didn't know what else to do I just followed the crowd. I dug the envelope out of my shirt and waved it to dry the sweat off it. I didn't have inside pockets.

The airport was no bigger than a large house with a small coffee shop and a giant metal sculpture of a horse made entirely from rusty horseshoes. It was clever but weird and out of place because an airport should have had an eagle or something with wings and a horse sculpture belonged in a bus garage or rail station. There were maybe seventy people coming off the plane or waiting for a plane or meeting loved ones and I just let myself be swept along and followed people to where our bags were already arriving on two trailers pulled by a quad bike. I was no longer in my city and not any city and I had never been in a small town before and already it made me nervous. I had never seen a quad bike either.

The lady who met me at the airport was short, fat and very round. She had short red hair with purple streaks over auburn and black and mauve and orange and yellow clothes all flowing like a torn-up tent and from a distance she looked like she was a little fat fire ball, and I was the only kid there so she made a thundering beeline for me.

Her shoes were orange and her ankles flopped down over them, and over her knees was another fold of fat. Her dress was too short and low cut so when she walked or bent over I had to look away. She was wearing pink lipstick badly applied, so her lips looked really fat and round like a goldfish. Maybe she applied all her make-up with a baseball bat. Smear and whack. She was the extreme opposite end of the woman scale to my sister Lilly.

I prayed to sweet Jesus Christ, *Don't let me ever see her in shorts. If I see her in shorts I will be gay straight away. Please Sweet Jesus please don't make me gay* . . .

She was sweating and flustered and pale and pasty. Her skin was dimpled and a bit mauve like her clothes and hair and she was born angry and I could tell.

When I handed her the envelope I'd been given that morning she huffed and put it away with the small placard with my name on it. 'You're late!' she barked and I said sorry like I was guilty and it was my fault and I could control the airline's timing. She turned on her heel, a movement that almost made a hole in the polished concrete ground, flared her skirt, and walked too fast to the car park hurrying me along and making no allowance for the weight of my case which I was struggling with. Then she stopped and huffed at me again and took my bag without a word and just threw it in the back of her jeep like it was rubbish. I understood that she wasn't into collecting me and I wasn't welcome and it made me feel even worse that she had tossed my case into the car like it was weightless. It held everything I owned but she heaved it in next to old burger wrappers and an empty KFC family bucket. By the time she fired up her engine I guessed we weren't going to be friends.

For the next twenty minutes she told me all about how busy she was and how little time she had to be picking up boys like me and how inconvenient it was that I was late and I didn't say a word back and she said she taught maths when she had time which wasn't often nowadays, and I hate maths with a headache.

She was a bad driver too and she should have been flogged for the way she missed chances to go or waited too long or went too soon. It didn't seem possible that just a few hours on a slow twin-prop plane and the world could be so different.

The roads seemed wider and there was much less traffic and fewer people and more space. We drove past the football ground, its floodlights on even though it was still just daylight, and we passed a movie theatre with giant gold and black posters on the walls advertising *Metropolis* by Fritz Lang and *Night of the Hunter* and smaller colour posters on its windows advertising the movies showing and I was relieved then because they were the same ones showing at home and at least we were in the same century.

There was a Burger King and a surf shop and a KFC and holy Golden Arches and a shop called Gourmet Burger, and cafés and bars lining every clean road. We went all the way up a shopping street where every shop had hanging baskets full of flowers outside, which were being watered by some kind of automatic waterer and it was funny because people were having to dodge getting wet even though there wasn't a cloud in the sky, and I laughed and the purple lady almost laughed, too, but stopped herself just in time. People were drinking coffee and beer outside the pubs and bars and cafés and they looked like the people at home but richer and older and whiter.

There was a cathedral that the lady pointed to with pride and it had a stunted tower you could look right through like they hadn't ever finished it and it looked like it had no soul and only a gutted skeleton and no magic. She told me a cathedral meant this was a true city and I thought maybe she could read my mind, but I knew it was just a small town, cathedral or not.

The trees were big and healthy and there was no graffiti and no litter and no beat-up cars and no boarded-up shops and it was unsettling and like nobody really lived there and it all looked shiny and all around were high forested hills. It was 'pleasant', and 'pleasant' isn't good.

Then we were leaving town and driving away from the waterfront and already I was missing it because I was dreading the next bit. Back in the town there was a marina with yachts and I'd seen them as we came in to land and there were tourists and maybe there was hope, but as we went further from town it was all locals and they looked stern and jealous. They didn't smile and didn't ignore us either. They scrutinised and they judged.

The woman nodded to the right of the road we were travelling on and told me to keep away from that side of the road because over there led to the bad side of town. Lincoln Valley, Victory, and Terri Terri, and she said decent people called it the Bronx. I reckoned that's where the kids like me would be if they were here at all and where I would find some friends and I made a note of the route.

'Keep away from there, do you understand?' I nodded and when she looked at me to make sure I understood, I nodded again more keenly. Her eyes were narrowed and mean and she didn't believe me and I nodded harder because she wasn't looking at the road and she really needed to be and she was proper scary and she liked scaring me and did it well.

We snaked a few left and rights, always too sharp and badly timed and fiercely braked and then we were alongside Cutter College and I knew it was Cutter College because a huge sign carved in stone shouted it out.

The fat purple lady told me several times that she was the Assistant Principle and Director of Boarding, which was why she couldn't teach maths any more and some other stuff I just tuned out and I could tell she was real proud of her titles and maybe just a little surprised. Everything she said, even nice stuff, sounded like it was a threat. Her name was Ms Biggs. And she emphasised the Ms . . . MZZZ Biggs. Like it was important. It's not important.

The college wasn't a college, it was just a high school like any other and was a big creamy coloured building with a long set of steps up to a central tower with a clock over it and in front of it all was a football field with posts.

Mzzz Biggs swung the car up the driveway so we could get a better closer look. She pointed to the clock, beneath it were the words *Tempus Fugit*, which she told me means Time Flies. It doesn't, it means Time Flees. I looked it up later. When you think about it, it's quite different. Hamish Taunton knew that.

Behind the school were more high and well-wooded hills and it would have a been a good place for a fortress, and she gunned the jeep on lurching so I nearly hit the windscreen. The road narrowed and snaked and rose higher and higher and in time she did a hard right down a short steep lane and pulled up in a small carpark over-roofed with thin branches from webs of trees, and dark and mossy it was too.

There was a big oblong building made of concrete and steel sitting high on that hill in them tall trees and the day I first saw Feallan House I thought I'd fallen through a hole and landed straight in hell. Close up it was two oblong wings joined in the middle by a huge square block like a giant brutal khaki green butterfly.

Broken lettering on the wall hung and limped out the words FEALLAN HOUSE. Looking at them I could see they had been grand once and some had blue and maroon enamel still in blackening brass frames. The S in HOUSE was upside down, the U was also upside down. There was only four letters left in Feallan, spelling FELL but there was a black stain on the wall where the others had once been.

The building looked like a cross between a military bunker and a mental hospital. I've never seen either but if I had Feallan House would be like them. It was neglected but seemed to have embraced neglect and was proud of it and it had a presence like it was aware I was there and it was examining me, which kind of spooked me because concrete and steel can't do that, only maybe it can and it does and on that day it did and I had a feeling the building was approving of me. It was broken down and unloved and defiant. We belonged together.

Ms Biggs turned off her engine and we sat as the metal sang a little and pinged as it cooled. She looked warily at the dark building and seemed to breathe deeply for a moment like she was composing herself.

'Welcome to Feallan House.' She smiled evil and sneering again and she was like a huge giant toad and I was a fly and she said it *Fear-lan*. 'Get your case,' she barked and she levered herself out of the jeep and it took her three goes to make it and I did as I was told and fast too and I made out not to notice her fatness. She watched me struggle with the case but didn't help me then led me through a heavy half-glazed door and into a dark corridor.

Feallan House was dark and cool with the kind of air that sits right on you. It would be cold as the grave in winter and I could feel it. There was a deep red vinyl floor and it was dull where it could have been polished and shiny and the walls were lined with old black and white and yellowing photos of boys going right back in time, what looked like a hundred hundred years, all staring right at me and speaking in whispers. They looked as defiant as the house itself and they were asking me if I was defiant too.

There was a trophy cabinet and a dead solid door with a brass sign that read HOUSEMASTER.

Ms Biggs rang the bell and it was opened by a small pinched-up woman. Her hair was short and shapeless and dull blonde, cut like a boy, and she looked tired pale and mean. She didn't smile. A couple of boys passed behind me but didn't stop or even look my way and I only knew they were there because I sensed it and felt them pass. They could be living or dead, I couldn't rightly tell.

Ms Biggs pushed me gently forward. 'This is Mzzz Russell. She's the housemaster here, and she'll take care of you.' Then she smiled at the pinched'up woman and said, 'All yours.'

'Hello Miss,' I said polite as you like and she twisted her mean little mouth and tilted her head.

'Mzzzzzz.'

I nodded an apology.

Then Mz Russell made a silly *I'm thrilled face* and she and Mz Biggs walked out to the Jeep, speaking in whispers and leaving me alone with my bag in my hand. My fingers were going numb and I realised I was gripping way too hard, so I put the case down and was careful not to scuff the unpolished floor and I was reluctant to let it go because it had been my mum's, and she never went anywhere with it but still it was something from home. I saw a boy halfway up the red stairs just sitting on a stair in the shadows with his knees under his chin and his elbows on his knees and he looked small and shifty like a criminal pixie. He was wearing glasses and they caught the light and reflected in two speckles like crescent moons each facing away from the other.

He knew I was seeing him and he smiled.

'Good day to you,' he whispered low so nobody would hear except me and with no sign of sarcasm. 'Welcome to the Otherworld! I see you met the Mzzzes? Ms, when made into Mz is a lesbian thing. They're lesbians. There's a lot of them here at college. All fat too. Or real skinny like bones. Corpses.'

'Hi,' I nodded and my voice was croaky and then I was aware how dry my throat was and I couldn't remember when I last had a drink of anything.

He stood up straight and fast like he was startled then sort of slimed and drifted and weasled down the stairs. He was so light and skinny he wouldn't leave footprints on a beach. He held out his hand.

'I'm Humphrey . . . Hummfree, not Hump-free. It's got umphhh . . . in the middle . . . H.U.M.P.H.R.E.Y Hummfree.

Can you spell? Don't matter if you can't, I can teach you. Grammar too. But you can call me Hummer if you want, for Humphrey. It's pretentious. It's my name though. It's got umphhh . . . Call me Hummer?'

I nodded, I got it, I shook his hand. He gripped me firmly and his hand was cold and bony hard. 'I'll show you round, shall I?'

'I think I have to wait for Ms, Mz Russell.'

'They'll be ages. They're lesbians. They're probably out there kissing and doing it . . . Do you want to watch? We can see from the laundry window.'

I didn't want to watch.

'She's a science teacher . . .' He nodded wisely as if that explained everything.

Mz Russell returned almost straight away and as she approached Humphrey whispered in my ear, 'I bet she has lipstick smudged round her mouth from sucking Mz Biggs' dick.' And he slipped back into the shadows until all I could see was that pinprick of light in his glasses as he became still and silent again.

I didn't want to look for smudged lipstick but I couldn't help myself. There was no sign of any lipstick, her own or Mz Biggs', and if they had kissed she would have been smeared for sure because Mz Biggs' lipstick was just about molten. Mz Russell had thin hard lips, not lips at all really, just a mouth, and the more I looked the more pinched she was, like life was a bad smell and all the moisture had been sucked out of her. She wore a light blue shirt like a man, all buttoned up to the neck and straight black slacks. Her shoes were black and shiny with little bow tassels, proper girls shoes and they were the only sure sign she was a woman except her titties, which were real small and

43

high up little golf balls. I reckoned she wasn't nearly as old as she wanted to be but was born as old as she was right now.

Mz Russell looked closely at me like I was a specimen in her lab. She looked cold.

'My name is Ms . . . Mzzz! Russell. SuZanne Russell. Not Susan, Su-Zanne. Emphasise the Z. Zzzanne. Make sure you get that right. It's not Susan. OK? It's got a loud firm solid Z in the middle. A big Z . . . It's not common. Say it, no don't bother. You'll call me Mzzz Russell. Hump-free hiding up there will show you around and help you find a cube.' She said his name the way he didn't like. 'Are you tired and hungry? I don't care if you are . . . You must be tired and hungry. Dinner's at six. There are sheets and blankets and a pillow waiting in your dorm. The other boys and Hump-free will show you the ropes. Any problems you may see the duty supervisor. Hump-free will introduce you . . . Once you've settled in we'll talk.'

She stepped past me and pointed to a sheet of paper taped on the wall and traced the wording with her finger. I noticed her nail was bitten down low. 'In the meantime . . .' Then she read aloud as she traced the words as if I couldn't read myself, 'We care. We support you. You are safe. You are important and you are valued. All the boys in *Fear-lan* House are equal . . . That's our charter.' She said it all in the same tone and with the same gentleness that she might have said a pound of carrots and a turnip. Then she sighed, 'Now don't bother me and you might just survive the year. You will be homesick, it will pass, you will be afraid, it will pass. I am here for you, so if you need me any time knock, but if you knock you'd better be bloody dying because if you're not, I will kill you.' And she smiled and I think she made a joke but I wasn't sure, so I didn't smile back and she huffed, 'If you break my rules or bother me, you won't make it past a week and you won't be going home, you'll go somewhere else. Somewhere horrible and further away. You won't like it. Which suits me just fine.'

And without a smile or a blink she went back into the room with HOUSEMASTER in brass on a plaque and slammed the door. I relaxed and breathed, but just into that breath as suddenly as she slammed the door she jerked it back open and made me jump and stiffen and from the corner of my eye I saw Humphrey had started to rise and then dropped again like he had been shot. 'And whether I am or am not in fact a lesbian, is none of your business,' she said, and she was gone in a crashing of the heavy door into its heavy jamb. Then again she jerked it open. 'And lesbians don't have dicks. As a matter of fact, neither does Hump-free. Nor balls.' And she was gone again.

Humphrey smiled and re-emerged from the shadows. 'Bloody lesbo witch! Hysterical. She likes you. Looks like you're all mine for now, New Blood!'

'Don't call me new blood . . .' I sounded meaner than I meant to.

'Sorry . . . Be friends?'

Humphrey took me upstairs to find a bed and stow my clothes, and the stairs were wide and long, turning on each level and on each level was a doorway to the dorms. Humphrey said boys could sleep wherever they chose so long as there was space but most boys our age were on the top floor, so we kept going up and on the next flight up Humphrey took my case without asking and carried it easy and he surprised me. At the very top of the stairs a fat puffy round man with a clipboard and half-rim eye glasses stood watching us come and he never said a word and sloped away before I got to say hello.

Humphrey watched him warily and whispered, 'I'll introduce you to Big Ben. He's head boy of the whole house. He's been Year 13 twice, he's very nearly nineteen years old. And he isn't very, well, *smart*, but he's OK. A good sort. He'll look out for you right . . . that was Mr Swindell.'

The windows were big and wide open but everything seemed dark like all the light was somehow soaked up and couldn't get free, and I wasn't even making a shadow.

Old paintings hung on walls covered in dust and along the tops were cobwebs. They were boring and faded and clumsy save one and that one painting was deep red like blood with a kind of cross like Jesus died on just off-centre and the words *Non illegitimus carborundum* painted across the bottom.

I stopped in front of it and searched inside my pockets for the bag of sweets, then I read the note, comparing the words and they were the same. Hamish Taunton knew this place.

Humphrey was staring hard at the bag of sweets, 'Rhubarb and Custards?' He was almost drooling. I offered him the bag and he took one, and one for later, and one for the morning, and I let him.

I asked him but he didn't know what the words meant. The painting was old he said and as far as he knew it had always been right where it was like it grew there on its own accord, then he led me through a heavy timbered fire door with a small wired glass window set so high that I couldn't see through it unless I was on tiptoes. The door closed itself behind us and we turned into a small sitting area. On a vinyl bench seat was a folded sheet and a duvet and pillow and pillow case, and Humphrey told me to pick it up because it was mine.

On each dorm there were half a dozen rooms for Year 13 boys. 'They all have their own doors 'cos big boys have privileges, you'll have privileges one day. You see,' Humphrey said proudly. 'We all will.'

The dorm was long and narrow and dark with cubicles off left and right and each cube was tight and had a curtained window and two beds and they were poor and neglected and rotten and stank even though every window was open wide. The beds were a mess and every mattress I could see exposed by dishevelled sheets was sagging and torn open. Curtains were hanging unevenly at the windows and some windows had no curtains at all, other windows had curtains drawn closed, and it made me sad because closed curtains on a sunny day means someone died.

Humphrey told me to pick a cube and that any bed without blankets and sheets on was free to use and he recommended a couple and told me the names of the boys I'd be sharing with as if I'd know them already. There wasn't much choice because most cubes were fully occupied and between each cube was a partition that didn't quite reach the ceiling and the ceiling was dull grey and covered in flaking paint and there was mould and strip lights and half of those had no bulbs. Over each bed was a square reading light fixed into the wall, and this was a poor poor place boys were making home, like little mice in cozy little mouse holes.

At the far end of the dorm was a cube with a spare bed and clean and tidy it was too, but sitting on that spare bed were four marionettes and I had never seen marionettes before and one of them was white-faced and black-haired and he wore a three-piece suit and he was smiling, but as I stepped into the cube he looked up at me and shook his head slowly and I knew not to sleep in that cube for sure and I stepped out again and Humphrey didn't even see it move.

Halfway up the length of the dorm on the other side and buried in the gloom was another cube with a single made bed and it was tidy and unnaturally clean and there was a teddy bear on the pillow and copies of story books on the single shelf over the bed. I said I would make up the other mattress and Humphrey looked proud as punch and said it was his cube and he would certainly be very proud to have me as a roomie and it was clean and homely and with story books and a teddy bear and that was all. Humphrey was all lit up and proud and ran to find Big Ben.

Five

Big Ben was big as a giant and so big he shut out what little light there was. He was near seven foot tall and broad too, and I'd never seen anyone so tall and so broad. Usually tall people are skinny but Big Ben was all muscle and I reckon he was nineteen years old and had size twenty feet. He was wearing a basket-ball singlet which was too big for him. He had tattoos on his forearms and chest and he didn't look like no schoolboy I ever imagined or saw before.

Ben stared down at me while Humphrey stared up at him and back to me like he was watching a vertical tennis match and Ben reached out and shook my hand. His hand was a gigantic bear claw and swallowed mine and half my forearm too. He had a big man's grip and a real deep voice. 'Welcome to Feallan House. We call it Fell. The sign says Fell, so it's Fell. Actually, *we're* Fell . . . If you're solid you get to be Fell . . . that's us. If you're a wanker, you get to be fucked.' He seemed to ponder a moment. 'Call it Fell I reckon . . .'

It seemed complicated and important, so I nodded and made sure he saw me. His head was twice as big as mine and I thought Big Ben was going to be a retard like most really big people, but he sounded normal even if he didn't look too normal and he looked like he should be wearing animal skins and carrying a stone axe. 'Once you've unpacked, Hump-free Buttoncock and I will show you round and tell you the rules. It's all pretty simple. Rule 1 is don't get caught. Rule 2 is if you do get caught keep your mouth shut. After that it don't matter much. There isn't really a rule 3 . . . You'll fit in just fine. I think. If you don't, who fucking cares. Are you sure you want to share with this snivelling little fuck?'

Humphrey ignored the insult like it never was and helped me unpack while Big Ben just stood and towered and examined everything I took out of my case. He took a shirt from where I laid it down and unfolded it and studied it, folded it neat as a pin and put it back where he took it from and never said a word, then a minute later he handed me a pair of my own pants. 'I've been in Fell four years. I came in Year 9 . . . I'm Year 13 now. That's four years, right? Five?'

I nodded. It was five years, but fuck, who would argue?

'I fail every year but they keep me for my basketball.'

'I've been here more years,' Humphrey put in, looking sad.

'How? You're younger,' I asked.

'I came as a preppy. I was seven. The only one.'

'His mum and dad are dead,' Ben said without emotion. 'Finished? You ain't got much, eh? Lots of shit. We'll borrow you some stuff if you want. You're gonna need winter warmers come winter. Come on, we'll have a tour. If you see anything you want just tell me and I'll get it for you.' He looked happy at the thought. 'You're eyes are a bit red. Been crying? I cried too when I came here. I'm on a sports scholarship. Basketball. I fucking hate basketball.'

Then for no reason I could work out Big Ben shoved Humphrey onto the bed without any effort or threat at all and Humphrey flew but bounced back all in one well-practised move.

The dorm was joined to another by a toilet and shower block, ten toilet stalls, ten shower cubicles and all of them smelling of piss. Deep red curtains provided some privacy in the showers but they were hanging off and sagging and low half doors on the toilets lent privacy but anyone could look over. There was a long stainless-steel urinal and half a dozen hand basins in front of a long mirror but it wasn't glass, just very reflective metal of some kind so I could see my reflection but not in real detail. Everything looked bomb-proof but still damaged and I reckoned damaging it must have taken real effort and imagination and planning.

All the dorms were the same as mine but maybe even more worn out and a few boys were laying on beds playing games and reading or sitting two and three on a bed talking and everyone said hello and seemed nice enough. Nobody made smart remarks to me and everyone had a smile and I wasn't sure if they were being nice because they were nice or because Big Ben was telling them, 'Say hello. Be nice. Smile. Take your hand off your cock . . . Wash it. Don't shake his hand . . . wash that hand! Be nice. New boy on the dorm.'

'They have to be nice to me too, right Ben?'

'No Humphrey,' Ben said gently. 'They can fucking rape you for all I care.'

'Who would rape that runt?' a voice called from a cube somewhere and someone else replied 'I will . . .'

Big Ben chuckled. 'There you go Humpy . . . You scored.'

Faces blurred so even though boys said their names and some even shook my hand, I didn't register any of them on that first night, and every time someone shook my hand Big Ben muttered, 'Wash that, he's a wanker . . .' and the boy nodded sadly in agreement.

Big Ben told me he would look out for me and as head boy of the whole house it was his job and he was proud to do it and he promised I would be safe most of the time and not battered or robbed, mostly, and no one would smart mouth me usually and if I was battered it was just horseplay, if I was robbed it was just borrowing and if I was smart-mouthed it was just banter, and I understood. 'But!' he said turning to me, 'if anyone touches you, you know, in that way . . . lovingly . . . tell me and I'll break their fucking arms. If you want. If you like it and it's OK with you then it's OK with me. I ain't judging.'

I nodded. 'Thank you.'

'Don't thank me . . . I'm just a jealous fucker!' He slapped me on the back and nearly knocked me down. 'Mostly the staff leave us alone, except when they give us shit. Ain't no staff here with anyplace else to go. They're all broken down and beat or plain lazy. If you don't show them they won't look, they just want to get through like we do so they ignore us and let us do whatever we want, except when the headmaster makes them do their little purges. If they say anything to you, just roll with it, it's a game . . .' he said. 'Just watch out for Swindell.'

'Why?'

Humphrey whispered that we had met Swindell already and Big Ben raised his one very long eyebrow. 'He's a drunk and a dick and likes to be a bully. He's also the cherry picker for the headmaster. It's ugly. But you're past the cherry stage, I reckon, that's one of the good things about being a teenager, and he's easy to manage really. He's been a tutor here since Adam was a wanker and he's stale and mean and bitter. A drunk's a drunk. But . . . he's a fuck off good trumpet player and when he practises it's like fucking amazing so we keep him, eh Hump-free? He also fucked his neck playing footy so he can't look round too fast. Makes life a bit easier! He loves to wrestle. Don't wrestle him. It's pervy and he's good.'

I asked him what a cherry was and he laughed at me. 'Kids . . .' he sighed and Humphrey nodded wisely and I decided it wasn't good and not something to aspire to and something I should probably know already, and I nodded wisely too like the penny just dropped.

Big Ben left us after showing me the common room which was on the ground floor and huge but drab and empty and broken. There was a tiny TV and a pool table with peeling cloth and no nets under the holes and a half-broken table tennis table and nothing at all of colour or warmth. There was a tuck shop with nothing in it.

I went back upstairs to my cube slow as a weary old man and I wanted some time alone to make sense of everything and get a handle on the day but everything was noise and there were boys everywhere and smells of deodorant and aftershave and stale food and that piss and sweat and everlasting farts.

I stood looking out of the window for a while trying to figure the shape of things and get a hold on the panic in my belly, because I was in it for real and no one was coming to save me and I didn't even know where I was and I was in free fall and my gut was empty and that empty is frightening and it becomes a real solid thing and people say emptiness is just empty, but it isn't, it's solid and heavy and dead. There was hardly no remembering in me of what happy felt like and I was struggling to care and fighting to care and fighting to remember what caring felt like and I knew I didn't matter so much any more. I was just a refill in an empty bed and I could dissolve into the mattress like so many other boys before me and no one would care and neither would I because everyone was gone and I was fading into grey.

Behind the house steep wooded hills were scarred in places from old landslides so you could see the light clay earth. The trees were big and heavy, some swaying gently and others fixed like paintings and softly out of focus. In front was a small wood of tall mature trees that sloped down to the college and from my big arched window I could see a concrete path wind its way down steps towards the school and to its right another path made of dirt, a shortcut trod by boys tramping down through the years and it must have taken decades to tread it out, and the foliage curled over it in a long arch and if you weren't in exactly the right place to see it I reckon it would be invisible.

I could see the ocean beyond the town and if I looked real hard I could make out the long straight lines of the lazy swell as it rolled towards the beach like vapour trails on the sea.

My cube was getting dark even though the cicadas were still rowdy and bell birds were still chiming and I lay down on my bed and buried my head in the pillow. It was lumpy, so I punched it about to soften it up and it smelled stale and musty and tasted worse, and suddenly I was crying and all the loss came over me and I couldn't close my mouth and my face was stiff and I clawed my eyes when I thought of my dad and mum and Davy and Louis and my sister Lilly and the terrible terror that comes with knowing you ain't seeing someone again never. I cried so deep I thought I might not breathe again and noise wasn't coming out of me and I was swallowing the noise and it was making me rigid and choking me and I knew I wouldn't be seeing the people I loved again because some of them were gone from the world and how can that be, and I was standing right in front of me and I couldn't get a hold of me.

I managed to close my mouth and compose myself and a few minutes later I stopped being a baby and just shook and vibrated and my eyes ran like a leaking tap then I got that under some control too so I was just sniffing snot.

When I looked up from my pillow there was an audience. Humphrey was stood at the door of the cube with a whole load of other boys just standing and watching in silence.

'That was intense . . . epic . . . but crying won't do any good,' one boy said and I could hardly make him out in the twilight, just a silhouette. I got up from the bed and wiped my eyes and face.

'Just saying. It don't help,' he said, and there was no mockery or teasing in his voice and he sounded concerned and frail and the group of boys looked at me without words and it was like being watched by a flock of gulls.

'It's dinner time in a minute,' the same boy said and as my eyes adjusted I saw he was a freckled ginger kid and pretty fat, and that's not an easy road in a boys' school, and he looked like he was going to cry too and maybe that's why he sounded afraid and maybe once one starts it opens the floodgates.

'I said I would tell him. Not you!' Humphrey protested. 'He's in my cube!'

'I've told him now,' the ginger kid said and walked away and the others went too, dropping into single file as they sloped silently out and left Humphrey with me. He looked fidgety and awkward. 'It's dinner in a minute.'

I nodded and wiped snot from my nose, there was a lot of snot, 'Got it. Thank you.'

Humphrey studied me then nodded. 'Thank you. Do you require a hanky?'

I didn't, but he gave me one anyway and I kept it and I have it still.

In the right time I was told the history of Feallan House which was passed down through the older boys to every new boy once they were accepted into the family, and they told that for a hundred years Feallan House was the outsiders' house, and amongst the worst and most wild a club was made and those boys were called The Fell and sometimes The Slaugh, and unique in boarding hostels Feallan would take any boy from anywhere and social agencies had forever used it like an orphanage or unofficial lock-up where boys could be sent and forgotten until they were boys no longer.

Fell boys had been close right from when the Word was with God and tightly bonded as a fist and hated by outsiders, but we didn't care and we got our strength from each other and adults ruled the days but the children of Fell held the nights. Over more time I got shown places and told secrets that were precious to this boy or that boy and the best was how to get onto the roof through the upper bathroom where there was a trap door in the ceiling. It was high so you had to get a chair or a leg up and once it was open you had to reach up inside and grab the lowest rung of a rusty metal ladder and haul yourself up hand over hand because the sliding part of that ladder was padlocked and that lock was proper. Once up past the hatch there was a box room with a proper big door and through the door was the roof and sky and free air, and on the roof I heard gentle music and harps and the sound of peace and the sky was waiting and that was sacred.

The roof was covered in old asphalt and small pebbles and you could see across all the town to the ocean and mountains so that for a brief time the tightness in my chest eased off. Kids had carved their names and dates on the blacktop and some were really old so I would sometimes sit and trace their names with my finger and wonder what came of them or where they ended up. They were all gone though, and that was almost certain.

I knew if I was going to survive in this dark I had to drive out all memory of the light and every day I looked for ways to get harder and I showered in cold water and refused to recall the names of my beloveds, but light is a magical mystery thing and even though I tried to stop it and I tried to turn away, little specs still got into me a splinter at a time, always uninvited and unwelcome and always when I wasn't expecting it. Light is like that, it sparkles and startles and won't be ignored and leaps at you like sparks from a spitting log.

At first I didn't like those sparks because there is nothing as painful and treacherous as hope when you're really genuinely hopelessly hopeless, but a boy called Johnny took a liking to me and he said *Non illegitimus carborundum* was the last words of the Christ and meant looking for the sparkles and holding on to them for all you're worth, and he said I needed to appreciate the moments of light and I should seek them out because they were mine and secret and personal to me. Life can be shit, he said, but we mustn't make it shittier. Don't look for shit he said, shit just is. Let there be light he said.

So the roof and sky and me became close and faithful buddies and some nights I even slept up there huddled in a rough old blanket.

One time I watched a bird rise in stuttering flight like it was dying upwards, coughing upwards on billows of invisible smoke chasing a bug that was sparkling in the sunshine. It rose and fell and swooped beneath me, above me, beneath me. The bug glistened on and off and made the bird work hard. I didn't see the kill but the bird wheeled away and settled on the grass by the trees looking real cagey and protective and hunched, so I figured he got that bug. It was a beautiful and graceful dance and even if it ended in a death it was a beautiful and graceful killing.

There were rabbits and hedgehogs in the long grass and rough ground and possums in the trees and when they thought nobody was around they would emerge, and everyone was sworn never to kill any of them, and they never saw me on the roof but I could watch them. Some days and good days, ducks would turn up and wild geese, and from the roof if you were quiet and still you could see them all exploring and foraging and peeking from the trees. Sometimes big overpainted butterflies, broad as your hand, would dance awkwardly in the sunshine and seeing them always caught me out and made me laugh. How can a butterfly be so big and painted like a paint factory had exploded all over it fly too? Sometimes I think God must have been on acid.

One late afternoon across the houses and trees towards the town I saw roller pigeons, a flock of eight, chasing around and flipping and dropping. After that I saw them many times and sometimes they came right overhead and I craned my neck to watch them and whooped and shouted at their brilliance. I knew they were rollers because a kid at the end of my street, my old street where I used to live in my living life, used to keep them with his grandad, and I swore one day I'd have me a whole loft load of rollers and I'd make the loft myself and I even got to imagining the drawings.

At night I'd get myself to sleep by working out the plans for that loft and I'd breed the best and bravest rollers, not the show rollers because they're really just tumblers and can't fly. I'd breed them to roll backwards in tight backflips so they'd go down and down and my rollers would pull out of the dive just before they hit the hard dirty ground. That's how I got to sleep. I could feel them in my hands, warm and soft and trusting against my chest. Pigeons are special. They aren't like other birds, they have character and personality and get attached to you, and they are more like mammals than birds, and rollers aren't really homers because they love to roll not navigate so they never go far. And when I couldn't sleep even after I had built that loft a few times, I would imagine each bird and name him and smile at his character and he would coo me to sleep, and sometimes I could hear Swindell practise that trumpet low and soft like I never knew a trumpet could sound and I loved those nights when his drunken breath kept me company, and maybe he was just like one of us but grown saggy and left behind and bitter and lost.

Then on colder nights when the season turned and the night air got in through those big windows, a bigger, older boy would come in through the darkness, barefoot and real quiet, and nobody would ever mention it in the morning. You knew he was there because you could sense him and smell his deodorant or hair gel and you could pick out his footfalls and other boys would slide over and make space in their cribs.

Six

No one came to my bed right off and I almost got to be jealous of the boys with a bed buddy. They were younger than me though, so easier I guess, and they were prettier too.

It didn't happen to everyone. Humphrey never had one, or the fat ginger. Then Johnny came and Johnny was a boss of the boys and he liked me and he was tall and lean and tanned brown and was a great shot with a rifle and he always looked good. He hunted wild pigs and deer and even giant Himalayan goats and boys said he could shoot better than perfect. Sometimes he brought his rifle and cleaned it then hid it in the back of his wardrobe behind his number ones where he had a hiding space. He had hunting knives too, a skinner and a sticker in old leather sheaths, and they were long as my forearm and sharp enough to cut the air. That's what Johnny said.

First off he was nice to me and talked soft, using my name a lot, which startled me and felt good, and sometimes he came to the dorm during the evening when we were all in bed and lounging and waiting for lights out when it was still light because night hadn't fully fallen and he'd playfully bash a few kids and eat some of their sweets and give me some. He would come into my cube and sit talking on my bed and leave again then one night he came and stayed and it was different. It was late in the evening and he sat into the dark and chatted like any other time and then he said he was cold and asked if he might just slip in beside me like a mate keeping warm, and I shoved over for him and as his cold body touched mine it was like I was alive again and it felt good to have a human being that close. He had a torch and we read a magazine about underwater diving and talked about nothing much that first night and the same for a lot of nights after that and Humphrey in the next bed would talk too and Johnny would tell him to shut the fuck up and laugh. It wasn't like it was a secret and it wasn't dirty or strange and everyone took no notice and everything just carried on, and when I looked again it was natural and normal and nice and right.

Sometimes the touch of another body saves your life and gets you through and it was just a cuddle for sharing warmth and company. We didn't call it a cuddle though, and it wasn't a golden wahine in a white bikini in the sun by a sparkling pool, but you can't always be picky and everyone needs touching sometimes.

Johnny started to come when others were asleep and it was so dark I couldn't even see him and we just kind of spooned and he would kiss the nape of my neck before I fell asleep and it wasn't bad stuff and it wasn't sissy. It was just a sleep buddy and a tender friend and when day came he was always gone and nobody ever mentioned it.

Sometimes he kissed my eyes and nose and he gave me cigarettes and sometimes a little weed and then he kissed my mouth and one time he showed me pictures of his girl naked and we jacked off together and it was messy and funny. Johnny challenged everyone to cock-fighting bouts and some boys went head to head with him like they were hung with blades, but he always won because he said he was blessed with a sabre and everyone else packed penknives and toothpicks and he was always hard. I never fought him nor anyone else that way. Just saying.

Humphrey told me the best technique to keep him away was to wet the bed, just a little bit, a squirt. Humphrey did it when he was a preppy and nobody wanted him as a bed buddy after that. Humphrey was looking out for me in his way but I told him it was just company, but I was lying because when I was in Johnny's arms it was the only time I wasn't afraid and I loved him in those nights.

Provided nobody told tales or made a fuss it was nothing to fuss about and no one was getting harmed and maybe someone was getting saved, and Fell House wrapped like a fortress around us and it was better than being diesel-pumped or bed-flipped. Boys who made a fuss or told tales got both and I see a kid getting diesel-pumped for telling and he got done in all quarters, which meant every limb. He was pinned down on his belly and had books and wooden blocks put behind his knees and in the crooks of his elbows, and boys pumped his ankles against his arse and the books behind his knees stretched him so his knee joints felt like they would burst open and all his ligaments stretched and that went on until he went through the laughing and into the crying then the screaming and the fainting. That boy had both elbows dislocated that night and put back by Big Ben and he walked OK a few days later but couldn't run properly for a season and picking his nose was a problem for weeks and he didn't even wank right that whole year, but his mind was subdued and his manners more compliant to the code.

Some nights boys got bed-flipped. They'd be asleep and someone would pin them by gently stretching their sheets and covers over them and tucking them in really firm and tight and suddenly a whole heap of boys would descend on them and flip their mattress up into the air and over like a pancake so they were underneath it and they would crash face down on the bed boards, then the boys would all pile on top of them and jump up and down. It was inherited and tradition and if you wanted to tell tales you could tell Big Ben and he would fix it, but never tell an outsider, and that was our code.

Occasionally someone would take a dump, a big steamy stinking pile of shit, and catch it on paper then put it outside Ms Russell's door and decorate it with flower petals and berries. They'd smear shit on door handles they knew staff would use and they'd wait until they knew the staff were asleep and run through the house screaming so everyone woke up and came out bleary-eyed and put their hands in the shit.

One boy was famed for wanking eleven times a day and had a proper calloused cock and produced semen by the pint and pretty much had a production line going and every little swimmer went through a staff keyhole.

We would trigger the fire alarms and the horns would scream two-tone so loud it made you sick and dizzy and nobody could turn it off except the firemen. Those firemen arrived in a speeding truck and you could tell they were bored and desperate to save someone and they wanted us to burn just a little to justify their existence because in this town of Cutter nobody and nothing ever needed them.

I liked those men, they looked resigned and patient and they understood. I swore that someday I would get a proper blaze going just to give them something to fight because a man needs something to fight and I vowed that when it came it would be biblical and I made an oath.

If you hit the alarms a few nights running Ms Russell and the other staff just looked more and more ragged and exhausted and it was a joy to behold, just like Baby Jesus was to the shepherds.

The lead fireman was a nice old man and he would chastise us gently as we lined up on the quad in our pyjamas or wrapped in blankets in the dark all in our year groups and quiet and perfectly behaved. A few boys wore bunny rabbit onesies with big ears and a little white tail. An Asian kid was a tiny four-foot-nothing tiger.

I think that old man was so nice he would have *died* to save us but he was never going to have to do that because we could evacuate the whole house from sleep to year group lines in under two minutes. In fact one night we evacuated five minutes before the alarm even triggered and as we stood there in the dark, if Ms Russell stared at Johnny he would stare right back with his chin down a little and his eyes up, and always in boxers or a tiny towel that hardly made it round him and was always split from his navel down so you could accidentally see everything you shouldn't and you couldn't help but look. Sometimes he would get a hard-on and stand in front of her not talking or even looking at her, real proud and innocent like he didn't know, and she would flush and blush and scuttle away. Johnny could get a hard-on at will, which was a rare and precious gift and it was always the fireman's cue to leave and they left smiling and every year the boys sent them a crate of beer at Christmas.

Ms Russell liked Johnny despite herself and Ms Biggs liked an older boy called Leon and the women liked those boys even when they knew they shouldn't and hated us more because of it and because they couldn't help it. The boys joked that one day Leon would take one for the team by sleeping with Ms Biggs and it was money in the bank. He would need to take a miners' lamp and sandwiches and someone would have to belay him in but he would do it for us and everyone said so.

Leon was made a bit like Johnny but older and madder and leaner and badder and calmer. He was pretty and well shaped and he hunted too and was better than Johnny because he had no sense of self-preservation, and he played football sometimes and was very good. He was angry with the whole wide world but he hid it down inside himself so he could seem cool like ice, but I knew underneath that ice was something real frightening and he and Johnny hung out together a lot and when they were together it was dangerous water and nobody was safe.

Whenever the mood took her Ms Biggs would get Leon to go to her house and move furniture and he would wear tiny shorts and a singlet and go quietly to his duties and some days when he was younger and just a cherry the headmaster would have stuff to move, too, but nobody joked about those days and nobody said a word.

The headmaster of Cutter skulked and sifted around the school grounds all day and half the night like he was looking for something but had forgotten what it was, and he wasn't so old but wasn't ageing well. He was a drunk and gouty man and he carried that lingering scent of alcohol on him and the cow-eyed look of someone who wanted you to know he was *oh so tired* and *oh so committed*.

Even though he had a name we just called him Sir, or Headmaster, and he liked that best of all. Behind his back we called him Jac, which stood for Just Another Cunt but he never knew and we didn't tell. He limped because of his gout or because he thought it looked distinguished, and went to assemblies wearing a black robe like an old-time schoolmaster or demented vampire and he looked proud in that gown but he was Jac and that was all.

At special assemblies he wore medals won by someone else and he bought them in an antique shop and was known to swing both ways and have an inappropriately keen liking for thin boys from the Far East and they were real young and some boys said they had seen him.

Leon came to my bed one night and whispered in my ear that the headmaster had asked after me and Leon gave me a chocolate bar and told me if I was sent for I should smear it on my arse and legs and the headmaster would be disgusted then and send me away as dirty and he told me keep it under my sheets so if Swindell came to inspect me I could do the same. He said it was the way with new cherries even if I was a tad over-ripe and it felt good he was looking out for me.

Leon said the headmaster was just like all the teachers in Cutter and riding high on the crest of mediocrity and he said they all worked and lived with no fire or passion or soul about them. He said they had dead fire in their eyes and smelt of damp ashes.

I was nervous after that but the headmaster never did send for me and I didn't eat that chocolate bar and kept it safe just like Leon said, *for insurance.*

Swindell came by the cubes most nights and just looked at us one by one like he was gauging our weight, but mostly he spent his time wrestling with kids younger than me and sometimes he sent one of them cherries for special tutoring with the headmaster and I was relieved he never picked me and grateful for that blessing and I was real glad I was over-ripe.

Seven

The weeks and months blurred into each other like drops of water in the sea, so I didn't know what month it was or when one ended and another began and I didn't care and days could pass real quick or so slow it was a month between sunrises and them nights were longest of all and all time was lost.

Beyond the town was the port and on a good night and the right tide you could see ships lit up and ranked in the bay waiting to come in and load or unload and they were a comfort and I was desperate as a moth so any light was a welcome light.

Sometimes a shrill whistle would ring out to let the men in town know that there was a ship that needed more hands to unload and the casual longshoremen and stevedores and any other men without regular work would gather and wait to work the twelve-hour shifts. That whistle call would drift over everywhere, and everyone would know and the men with regular work would take comfort knowing they didn't need to go. Some ships would be so pressed to turn around it was like every man in town was crawling over them and the cranes dipped and rose and dipped and rose like giant rusted dinosaurs with hundreds of blazing eyes. When my confidence came better I would sneak out when the sirens went and I would go down there to the water and take my blanket and nestle into the dunes and watch and listen to the music of metal and engines and work and gulls and gruff shouting and the sea lapping and laughter, and I would smell the diesel fumes and tobacco smoke and ocean and I would sleep in dreamless peace those nights in the dunes and wake covered in dew and my lungs clean and fresh. One morning when I woke on the dunes I saw Leon alone on the foreshore just standing and if he ever saw me he didn't let on. I think the dawn foreshore was like his rooftop and he stood watching the sun rise without even moving or breathing like a statue made of icy stone.

There was a telescope in the house and I scrounged it and from my window I could turn it to the sea and spot the small yachts bouncing from wave to wave rushing in past the sea wall to beat the seas into safe harbour on a windy day.

Johnny could sail and fish and knew the ropes and he taught me knots. He said one summer he would teach me to sail and that sounded spectacular indeed and something to look forward to. A man who can sail has the whole world to see. He swore it as a promise, '*Promisi, promii,*' he said.

Johnny was always making up Latin and because no one in the whole fucking world knows Latin he got away with it and even the Classics teacher would nod in admiration and agreement like she knew what he was saying.

Johnny said Ms Biggs was *lesbianus clositania*, and he was the cockiest boy in the whole world unless he was with Leon and then he was rightly more cautious.

On a bad day, when the mood took him Johnny would spear tackle me or throw a football in my face real hard when I wasn't looking and for no good reason. It always hurt because he had a good arm and it was always a sudden and short-lived thing and I got used to watching for them moods. I didn't like him at those times because it was like he hated himself and everyone else too and especially he hated me and he was searching for reverse and to ruin the tenderness, and I just sat on my bed and waited and took it. There comes a time when you're getting hit when you've been hit so many times either inside or outside that you just stop reacting and flinching and feeling, so all the shouting and telling and whipping just washes over you and all the slapping and punching just washes over you and that's where I was, soft and swaying and dead like a curtain in the wind just moving so and so and so and I felt good afterwards if there were good bruises and cuts. Stroking a bruised face or touching a cut lip with my tongue was satisfying and I felt alive and fulfilled but that isn't love at all really.

The only person who could stop Johnny's rage was Leon and he did it without a word and just the slightest shake of his head and Johnny always did what Leon said and straight away.

Leon had hunting dogs and they were three finders properly called bailers and the bailers were scruffy and lean and they picked up the scent of prey then chased it down and kept it in one place snapping and barking and harassing it but not going in for the kill and they waited there for the holders. And he had two mean holders. Them holders were brutal war dogs and looked like something from an old-time engraving from ancient England and he said their names were Crib and Rosa. Leon had their picture on his wall like they were family and the only time the ice thawed and his eyes got soft was when he spoke of them dogs.

Sometimes Leon and Johnny tired and filthy brought back a pig or deer they killed and it would be strapped on the back of Leon's old truck and they skinned and butchered it at the back of the house and they would BBQ it up for everyone and hose down the blood. Leon kept that old truck hidden in a back lane and went hunting and did just about whatever he wanted provided he stayed the right side of Ms Biggs.

Fattus Bitchus Johnny called her and told tales about how one day surf lifeguards had tried to refloat her when they mistook her for a beached whale and he swore that for a whole hour they kept her blowhole wet before they realised it wasn't no blowhole, and Leon would smile at them stories, just a little.

Johnny laughed and jiggled around doing the 'fat bitch' dance and mimicking fucking her and he was really good at it too and one night right in the middle of the jigglebug dance a new boy arrived and he was fatter than any kid had a right to be and fatter than Ms Biggs too and so fat he silenced all of us and when he first walked in sweating and hauling his suitcase Johnny just froze mid-jiggle. 'Call me Moby,' the boy said. 'Is that your real name?' Leon asked. 'No,' Moby smiled. 'But I'm real pale, real ugly and fat as a fucking whale . . .'

Leon smiled. 'You're going to fit in just fine Moby.' And Moby did fit in just fine right from his very first day. He laughed harder than anyone else laughed when Johnny did the fat jiggle and though he was real fat he wasn't the least bit self-conscious about it. He had ladies' titties and puffy nipples and some boys would make him get them out and put a bra on him to practise taking it off for when they got themselves a wahine. Sometimes they'd fondle him there too, just to see what it felt like, and he was cool with it and only occasionally did he lamp someone right in the mouth and he was a big kid so when he swung and connected it double hurt.

Some nights he would do the dance of a thousand veils for the whole house and strip right down to a leopard-skin thong someone gave him once. There was a kid from Korea who was polished on the oboe and clarinet and he would play a dance and

Moby would wiggle and jiggle and we would laugh so much we cried and I held my guts because they ached so much I thought I would die. Things improved when Moby came to the house. I really liked Moby, we all did.

Moby was floppy and always puffing and sweaty and his toes frothed a bit. There were other fat kids in Fell, but Moby was way bigger and more girly than all of them and it could have made him a target but he owned it and never got bullied.

He also had a world-class party trick. Moby was mortally allergic to shellfish but passionately in love with their taste, and periodically he would acquire some and take us to the hospital and sit on the grass verge outside the door to the Accident and Emergency room and then eat them shellfishes and savour every mouthful and smile and whisper, 'Take me in fellas . . . I am about to expire!' And he would count down as the experience came upon him and he would bloat up and his lips and eyes would swell and his breathing would become all strangled and he would fix us in his narrowing eyes and we would rush him inside and leave him there with the empty wrapper on his lap as his life hung in the balance and his skin changed and he sweated and panted like he was breathing through a straw. It came to pass that the nurses became angry with him because it was so dangerous and his tolerance was on the slide so they said he would die if he carried on, but Moby was heroic and he did so love shell fish and with an unnatural passion too, and he accepted that one day they might kill him and so be it. No kid with that kind of commitment and passion will ever be a victim. He was a legend. And he could shimmy for Jesus, too.

Leon said he was an inspiration and would be remembered fondly, which is how people remember hard times and raucous children and mischief and he said nobody smiles when they

71

recall a scholarship-winning kid and nobody remembers the name of the kid in Billie the Kid's class who was real good at algebra, or Bonnie and Clyde's Assistant Principal, or whether Jessie James could recite the periodic fucking table, and best of all, Athletics Day was coming and that day, according to all legend, according to all history and myth, was all ours. And Moby was running the hurdles.

Eight

Leading up to Athletics Day we were up before dawn every day to get some running practice in, racing round town in little mobs and with mini races taking place all the time and the sports captains had note pads and started to decide who would do what events.

I was chosen to swim the fifty-metre crawl. The other boys were not great at swimming so it made me look awesome and they were proud of me and I puffed out my chest and pretended my dad could see me training and I heard him say I was doing real well and he told me to go hard, and I pretended my mum was sitting watching and smiling and nodding to me. Johnny patted me on the back when I was getting dry one day. 'Make us proud,' was all he said but it made me feel ten foot tall and I was back at the lido and my dad was watching and he was proud and I could smell him and feel his warmth like sunshine came right out of him, and he was smiling.

The pool was on the other side of the school grounds and every day I went there to practise and the water was cold and green and filthy and not like any pool should be and the first wetting always took my breath away and I trained so hard I got up a sweat despite the cold. I climbed the fence and hammered out lengths three or four mornings a week and some evenings too. I'd swim a width, jump out, do ten press-ups and dive back in and swim a width, jump out and do ten press-ups, and back in and sprint and out and press-ups and in and sprint, and do the whole thing again and again until I was near sick and always my dad urged me on.

Other boys came with me and made me the swim captain and coach and we'd skulk through the grounds in silence and slip over the fence like ghosts in the dark, proud and determined and slight as shadows in the night, and by the big day we were ready like marlins.

It was tradition for Fell boys to shave their heads for Athletics Day, not an all-over cut but in patches and parts and varying lengths. There were boys with half their heads shaved, some with extreme mullets, some with cheques and squares and others with bald pates like monks. One or two just had clumps missing like they were afflicted by some awful disease. All morning before sunrise the shavers were going like a prison barber shop. They shaved a boy called Tommy with the most carefully cut giant F. Tommy was the best guitar player in the house and he could have been the best in the world but couldn't play an F. He could play as well as a professional if the song didn't have an F and he was sensitive about that and didn't like to talk about it. He wrote most of his own music and it was pretty good but kind of missing something, and after Tommy they turned their eyes and razors on Humphrey. He made out to try to run away and shinned up a tree but he enjoyed us shaking him down even though the fall made him limp a while. When the barbers were done he looked like a skinny kid from a work camp. They left one clump of hair randomly on the back of his head and dressed him in stripy pyjamas and called him *Rabbi*.

As the sun rose we face- and body-painted ourselves in deep red, like blood, and black and white which were our house colours, and we helped each other do it and some boys took a lot of care and some were striped and some were spotted and some were dark and some light. Some were more red and some more black and some were exactly half and half but everyone was painted and there was a kind of symmetry and sense to it and we all looked different but we all looked alike. We were a wild tribe straight from the darkest lost forest and we banged drums and upturned bins and one boy played bagpipes and I never was so proud before.

Moby destroyed them hurdles and on the day he did it in ladies' underwear but halfway he tore off his bra and went 'au naturale'. We pelted him with prawns and he knocked down every hurdle in his lane and the lane beside it and face-planted on the second last, got up, stumbled across two lanes and crashed their hurdles too and finished the race a full minute behind the next slowest, and went back on his hands and knees to collect up them prawns and became an even bigger legend. We all ran to him and cheered and mobbed him chanting 'Well done Fell!' over and over and he danced until he dropped sweaty and heaving for breath like an asthmatic albino seal on a parched and scorched icy beach and an ambulance took him away. A song was made up for Moby and sung by us all that day.

Halfway through the day we all went to the pool and the water had been transformed into perfect sparkling blue and the chlorine was so strong it made spectators cry and eye glasses melt. The crowd packed onto the concrete and we smashed everyone and won everything. I won my race and didn't take a breath the whole way, but the teachers with the timer watches said it was too close to call and they gave it a draw and my dad nodded from that crowd and he looked proud and we both knew I won fair and square. In under an hour we were back on the sports field with trophies and bragging rights and I felt like a champion and was treated like one. A champion amongst men.

I saw the headmaster standing alone at the college doors and he looked down from the top steps and even at long distance I could see he looked wistful and sad and jealous and I knew in that moment that he would have to destroy us because he couldn't be us and couldn't control us and in the end he would do anything to end us because his big swollen drunken head couldn't abide not being part of us and we had what he never had, which was belonging and brothers and potential and renown.

We beat the field that day and carried each other shoulder high all the way back to the house just as the sun started to drop and the air filled with pollen and bugs and the cicadas were calling our names in perfect choirs.

I was itching from all the hard sharp grass and the long ears we had been resting on in the shade and my nose was sunburned and lips dry and throat raw but none of it mattered. We were tired and hungry and thirsty more by emotion and victory than exercise or effort and it was a day to remember for all my days.

We snaked up through the trees singing and laughing and we saw Ms Biggs, Swindell and Ms Russell had beat us to it.

The doors were locked and bolted and the good day when we were normal noisy kids was over and in that instant we remembered we were not normal noisy kids and all our actions through the day would be repaid.

They made us wait outside until they were ready and Ms Biggs was inside smiling out through the glass looking sweaty and tired and flustered and dimpled like half-set jelly.

They made us hose each other off and as we stripped down Swindell called out of the upper windows making comments to the younger boys about their dicks while the women watched. Then Johnny started washing boys real seductively and the adults were disgusted and looked away. Big Ben and Leon didn't wash or strip and they just sat on a bench and looked up at the windows and the adults let them be.

When they finally let us in we rushed up the stairs noisy and dripping wet to get towels and get dry so we could get back down to a dinner we were starving for but when we reached the dorms boys stood in silence looking at a huge and terrible mess. Russell and Biggs and Swindell had been in every room and searched everything and tipped out everything and turned over everything and taken down and ripped up every photo and tossed every item of clothing into a heap, and they made us put everything back except the photos and used a ruler and a tape and made us do it military style and they stood over us like fascists and made us know this place was not for ever and it was not ours and they had the power and we shouldn't ever forget it and our dinner was cold now and the night dark. Only Big Ben and Leon's rooms were spared and Big Ben had nothing anyway and Leons dog photo was left intact, but in silence he took it and down and ripped it up so he would be like us and he dropped the rippings on the fat lady's fat feet and she didn't even look down.

Then in the middle of our desolation and loss Moby returned from hospital looking tired and pale and everyone cheered him and Moby rose to the chant and clapped his hands two times and sang out, 'If you're happy and you know it, clap your hands,' *Clap clap*, 'If you're happy and you know it, clap your hands!' *Clap clap*, and he stripped off his clothes and marched naked through the dorms repeating it over and over until a hundred boys marched behind him and everyone joined in and we clapped and sang and rose up our noise and we were raucous and stole back the night and we went to dinner and ate big and feasted like kings and warriors and champions and we didn't care one bit if the food was all gone cold.

Nine

I found a boxing gym on the wrong side of town and started going there whenever I could and sometimes I went every day and I was getting stronger, using weights and running, and I was feeling good and eating well and the fear was smaller by daylight and the people in that gym were healthy in mind and body and practised the sweet science and welcomed me, and I was at peace there and being there was like being underwater and it took me into a better place and all around me was decay but in the chaos I was thriving, and I was sharpening and slowly I was becoming live as a razor, and I was respected in the house.

Then without any planning or deliberate tactics the war turned our way and greedy boy-hating Ms Biggs had her heart broken into a million splinters and it was joyous to behold.

Flavoured condoms arrived in the sexual health clinic in town and a good number of boys hanged them condoms from the ceiling over their beds and sucked them at night like everlasting sweets. Strawberry and banana were favourites, and every few days Ms Russell went round removing them and every time she did someone went to the clinic in town and came back with fresh boxes and hanged them up again and you could tell she was disgusted and it disturbed her and then a ladyboy from Thailand got caught stretching one of them condoms over a frozen banana and using it to pleasure himself in the night and it was Ms Russell that caught him cold in her torchlight and right there and then she gave up and out of the blue and with no warning she fell on her sword and left the house. Next day, seeing Biggs weep openly and almost tear her clothes in despair at losing her friend was the icing on our cake and we rejoiced.

Ms Russell went to somewhere in Eastern Europe and last I heard she was kicked out of a Romanian orphanage for being too cruel. I think that was a lie.

New housemasters came and went as fast as teaching staff in the day school and we hardly noticed, and stopped counting or learning their names and just rolled on day after day and nobody made a difference. We had a still where we brewed Navy-strength eighty proof gin sweetened with real juniper and herbs, and in the woods behind the house a couple of boys grew cannabis, strong and evil and oily, and holy powerful and perfect too. The seedlings were raised in wardrobes under lights rigged to burn all the hours and those wardrobes were proper hot boxes. The dried leaves were rubbed down and sold around college and town and the oil hardened into resin was sold by the ounce or gram or just roughly rounded into a ball and sold in a tinny of foil and the profits were pooled so we all had some money and for a while we were kings of our own cartel and one boy wrote to a famous man in Colombia but he never wrote back.

Slowly, over time, Fell House became just about adult-free and the inspections and tossing of our things became less and less until one day they stopped.

Girls were smuggled in at night and we gave the girls false names so nobody could spread bad rumours about them and nobody except one or two boys knew their true identity but nobody cared.

Valerie was the favourite and Valerie was a brunette-streaked strawberry blonde and her hair was long and frizzed out and she wore faded torn jeans and a cotton blouse and a knitted cardigan. Her titties never saw a brazier and pretty perfect they were too and her abdomen was teak and her backside was perfect full moons. She wore a scarf which she pulled up over her face and you could just see her perfectly straight nose and brilliantly lit eyes in the half dark of the house. The scarf was fine silk and all the colours and she looked beautiful and mysterious moving like mist without making even the slightest sound as she tiptoed barefoot to whichever boy she favoured on any given night. She kept a lot of boys happy and she said my time would come and I hoped she was truthing. The younger boys would press their faces against the windows to watch for signs she was arriving and try to pass her on the stairs to catch her scent which was always heady and soapy and perfumed. There was something heated and lovely about being so close to a real girl who really did sex. Her promise that my time would come made a vibration in my stomach. Valerie.

Summer and autumn faded slow and winter came bitter and freezing like stormers in the night, and the school let us freeze, removing our heaters so the dorms frosted over and windows iced on the inside as deep as the outside and we were frosted like the old-time boys and it made us proud.

The trees became long skeletal fingers all knuckles and nails and at night the moon never got above them and in the day the sun barely showed through their raggedy thorny crowns. Snow fell first on the high ground and in the mornings the rising sun lit the western ranges and they were crested white like sleeping dragons grown old and wise in the darkness and lit bold golden and pink in the dawn.

Each nightfall the supervisors locked up their doors or left completely to sleep somewhere else so it became us and the ghosts of those who went before us and nobody else and those ghosts were sometimes loud and disturbing, running through the house or crying in rooms where no living boy was present, so sometimes the house was alive with the dead.

We hung flags and banners in the big common room and cleaned it up and mounted animal skulls high on the walls and it took on the face of a great hall and the room used by Valerie was made like a Bedouin tent, candle lit and draped with fabrics and carpeted with rugs and lavalavas. It was scented with flowers and incense and cleaned and freshened every new day, but disease crept into the edges of the house and one day a kid got real sick with fever and with no one to call for help a boy named Doris danced a shaman ritual for him and he was healed in three days. After that we did a lot more shaman stuff and put animal skulls on the trees and wrote mumbo-jumbo curses on the walls. One kid even reached out to a school in Haiti but they never reached back, and really, fine as it sounds, it wasn't always good and some nights you had to do the suck on the bong or swallow the gin just to get through.

Ten

The winter nights were so cold pretty much all the boys slept two to a bed or heaped nasty old grey woollen blankets on top of each other and snuggled right down under their weight and we tucked each other in tight and once I got warm I forgave those blankets their scratchiness. Those were deep-freeze nights and it was the coldest winter for a generation and it was deadly over the whole country, and outside Fell it was so cold old people died in their own homes so we didn't complain.

We said we were heroes for doing it so tough but we knew heroes are most famous for falling and dying and even Gods get nailed to trees, so long term we were proper fucked. We said every pirate knows he's going to hang one day and that knowing never did stop men becoming pirates and sometimes women too and we said how you end isn't as important as how you live and saying that made us stronger but not one bit warmer.

We had a big winter solstice party and lit a bonfire that came a bit out of control and danced around it drunk and stoned, and like ancient people all painted and wild, and cold from the night or scorched from the fire or both. Then we walked the hot coals to shamanic chanting led by Doris and Moby and burned our feet and some boys couldn't walk for weeks.

When spring started to come things should have lifted but for a while it just got darker and colder and I knew then the seasons within Fell moved different from the rest of the Earth and it was so cold I started to worry that the world wasn't turning at all and there was talk of sacrificing someone to the sun and just when we thought it was as bad as it gets in all the chaos and coldness, a boy from Korea fell down hard. He was nice kid who was in his last year of school and he had been in boarding in one place or another since he was five years old and it was suddenly over and he'd been summoned home unexpected.

One morning really early, I woke and didn't know why, and that's an uncomfortable feeling. Maybe it was whispers and vibrations or echoes or something else but somehow we all woke at the same instant and before I realised we were all awake I lay there wondering if some part of me was especially cold or some noise had startled me or there was an earthquake or invasion or civil unrest or I needed to pee. Then I realised others were awake and there was movement around me everywhere like something was stirring Fell's cauldron and I was compelled to follow everyone else in silence and we were all looking at each other and wondering why we were awake, but we were called and we all went.

That morning with the ground full of frost and the sun still only threatening to rise cold and faint, we woke as one living body and found the Korean boy hanging from the tree behind the firepit. He was a long thin pencil hanging down in the grey light like rags, a charcoal thumb smudge on paper, like he never did live in the first place. It made me shiver to my soul to see it. We stood in the cold and silence as more boys came without anyone calling out or hollering and with those more boys came torches and I saw the frost under the hanging boy was burnt yellow by his piss. His bowels had gone too. The torchlight showed up his tongue swollen right out of his mouth and his lips puffed

and huge, and blood under his chin where he had bitten something, and his eyes, big big like a bug's. Wide open. Too wide.
Wide open but dead and empty and shuttered from within and
he was dead but there was no peace and no god in it and no
glory. It was just a horrible wasted mess and there was no hero
to save the day because the day was lost before it was begun and
his was the death that comes in the nightmares of the most lost
and lonely demonic nights and it was pity and pity and pity.

Leon was only wearing grey flannel track pants in the cold
but swung up a branch easy like a chimp and checked his pulse,
but took his hand away real fast when he felt how fully dead he
was. Then he looked down at us, staring into the torches with
his breath shrouding him in clouds, and we knew it was all done.

Johnny whispered 'turn off the fucking torches' and they went
out instantly all as one, so we went back into the dull grey dawn
light and we were loster than before. Johnny and Big Ben and
some other boys took his weight and Leon cut him down and
they hugged him close to them as they lowered him softly to
the earth.

His name was Sun.

Sun never harmed no one and he was a good boy and he
glided through life with grace and dignity and a sense of calm
and sadness like he had seen it all before, but whatever he saw
in that last night was too much and it led him to the most terrible and sorry deed. He had poise and grace and light and god
should have let him live.

We said there was a Summer Land out beyond this life and
in that land the dead wait in the meadows and foothills of great
mountains, keeping a fine campfire burning and waiting for their
people to pass into that world from this world and they would
greet them and welcome them when they came, holding them

tightly in their arms, and when they were all together once again they would cross the mountains into the next world which is the warm and sweet world that every great teacher and prophet promises, and I could see the long dead waiting by them fires, watching the newly dead come, hesitant and confused, walking the path towards their own special fire where their loved ones and lovers waited smiling and offering them safety and sense because the newly dead are confused and scared and lost. But not for long, just until they find their people or make a new fire and settle in to wait. To the living, the dead might have gone years before but in the Summer Land time is different and even if they wait years it seems like a short time to them so they are never lonely for long. That's what we said. And in that land the dead aren't mutilated and damaged by life or age or the nature of their going. They are beautiful and strong and glow like they are newborn and the Summer Land is a good place and a place of life and re-joining and a place of love and hope. If you were a good person.

If you were not a good person there is another land and that's a land wasted and lonely and cold where the punishment is solitude for ever. Aloneness. Isolation. Shunning. In that land there are no campfires and all are ignored by God and there is no hell worse than being ignored and shunned and lonely.

Leon said it was so and Doris thought long then agreed. A boy from an Arab land called Majid, who we said was a Bedouin but he probably wasn't, said it was *Maktub*. Which means '*it is written*'. And Majid knew these things because he watched for signs in all things and read the clouds and spoke of spirits he called *Djin*, which are like smoke in the night. So it was that we knew the afterlife was real and for someone like Sun it was a good place and we would meet him again and he would tend the

86

fire until we found him there. It was not yet, because it was not our time, but in all the schemes and twists and turns of the all the worlds it would be soon enough. But it didn't make anything easier. Not a thing.

We were silent for the longest time and the day passed without me seeing it. Probably none of us did.

Later that same day after the ambulance drivers and police people and adults who expected and demanded a proper mourning and grief and shock had all left and gone home Swindell passed us as we sat in silence on the quad, and looked up at the overcast sky and smiling he said, 'Sun won't be rising today boys . . .' And he giggled and nobody reacted and we didn't even flinch and it was like we never even heard him even though in my belly something froze like ice and our silence was solid as a granite wall and my bones were cold like stainless steel and that day that stupid man sealed his fate, and everything he had done before, however mean and nasty, paled away. That day the man was dead and didn't even know it.

We said we would give Sun a powerful funeral with a war chant and sad songs and we would tear our flesh and pull out our hair in grief just because we needed to and so he could see how much we loved him, but Sun didn't get that either. His body was taken away that day and shipped back to Korea where he would be buried their own way in his own homeland by people who never did want him since he was five years young. Sun was like all of us, lost and pretty much alone and clinging to each other and to Fell and reassuring each other that we were family, but right then it felt false and our loneliness was right there in front of us made huge and ugly by stalking mocking death. Majid prayed in Arabic every day in the house, and again at the mosque in town, and he was peaceful in his sadness and strong and after he did that I thought the call to prayer that drifted from the minaret and could be heard if the wind was right or the daybreak air was very still was just about the sweetest and most beautiful sound you could hear on a lonely dawn. It was a call that said awake, awake and take note, light is coming, light is coming and the light will triumph over darkness again, see it and rejoice, and I wished Sun could have heard that call from the minaret just one more time.

Some boys played sadly on the piano and strings and wind instruments and one boy played the flute and when he did that I saw fairies running through a bluebell wood, and another boy greeted sunrise and sunset with a cello and it was beautiful and deep so I felt it in my chest, but my nights were haunted by face-less terrors and the call of the owls and witches and my night-time soul lived in valleys deep and dark and I could hear the cello even when there was nobody awake to play it, and its ech-oes reached right through the house and into my soul like unbid vibrations and shadows came into the dorms and I stayed still so the shadows wouldn't find me out. I spent whole nights awake and barely breathing and pleading for spring and then a point came each night as morning got nearer when I knew if I stayed in bed I would be swallowed up into the deepest darkest hell, so I got up fast like my pillow was full of electric shocks and went straight outside and smoked two, three, four cigarettes. The doctors tell you cigarettes kill you but on the underlip of that dark valley sometimes they save your life and in the shadows I could smell the smoke of others too and some of that smoke was a hundred years old.

One night I woke up and took an axe from the broken-down woodshed where we stored our moonshine and started at that tree, but the axe was blunt and I wasn't even bruising it. I swung and sweated and swung and cried once the rage took hold and the tree stood taunting me and mocking my efforts.

Leon and Johnny and Big Ben came sleepily and took the axe off me, then they sat with a whetting stone in the moonlight and oiled and waxed the blade like Vikings before a raid, honing it till it was a razor glinting in the silver night. You could hear its tune change from a blunt dead thing to the song of a sharp and cutting wind, ringing like a sword drawn from a sheath. They worked the edge hard at first then slowly and lovingly and even the noise of the whetting stone changed and we took it in turns to strike and strike and strike without even a word being spoken or noise being made except the noise of metal on wood, and that big tree came straight down a natural avenue between other trees and over the next weeks we cut the bastard into matchwood so it was like it had never existed at all and one day it would be forgotten and that was a justified and righteous curse.

Eleven

The spring midday sun was soon warm enough for tee shirts, but each night the cold came back nasty and jealous and reached into you as soon as the sun dropped, and several nights brought snowfall and it was heavy and perfect and brought silence and peace and quiet. Even the spiders that infested the house and wove scraggly webs all over the windows abandoned us and went to ground and built tiny night-time igloos around the dead flower beds, and every day that snow melted except for in the deepest, darkest back streets and most nights it came again.

We gathered and smoked the last of the potent stinking holy weed, weeping softly as it disappeared, and spent the evenings huddled under blankets listening to other boys play musical instruments or watching them put on short plays and dances and play games. 'One Thousand and One Nights' was the best because it had glittery golden cloth and jingling bells and special scenes with Moby or Valerie.

Some nights I walked alone in the cold and dark and watched people through the windows in town. Every second Friday there was a salsa party in the back room of a big tavern and I watched the ladies swirl and men turn and it looked exotic and everyone smiled in that room and even if it was cold outside they looked like they were sweating up good. One day I'll learn to dance that way and buy a Cuban hat and a white singlet and shoes with pointed toes. I had seen some of them people around town, working in the supermarket and discount bulk warehouse, and I knew one woman worked in the mussel factory on the waterfront because I'd seen her smoking outside. The people in that mussel factory wore white overalls and white boots and blue hairnets and woollens and ear muffs and it was a noisy, deep, chilled satanic hell hole on the fringe of a great ocean of no compassion, but on the dance floor every second Friday the smoking woman lived large and burned with red hot Latin passion. When I saw her dancing it was like her feet were on fire.

That next Saturday Johnny took me on the back of his dirt bike and we rode the back alleys down to the massive long wide town beach and he made me stand in the middle of the great desert of sand and wait and he sat on a dune and smoked, and I just stood where I was told all alone on the huge beach and waited because he said to do it and he was the boss so I did it and felt stupid. Then the wind blew the dry sand along the beach and the tops of the low waves were clipped back, so I was silent and struck by the natural sounds of wind and ocean and the noise of sea birds protesting, and slowly there came a sunset so perfect I couldn't speak or think or take my eyes off it because I didn't want to lose it and not long afterwards the sky darkened and the colours muted and blurred together into night. The sun sank away behind the range in the west but Johnny motioned to me to stay put and minutes later the sky erupted in such colour it was like the noise of an orchestra and streaks ran from some point invisible past the mountains. First the sky lightened again then tinged orange and into pink and red and mauve and it just went on and on and spread and stayed like that with small clouds backlit and edged with fire for another half an hour. There were only a few people on the beach wrapped warm against the murderous wind and all in the distance but they stopped dead and even men who had never noticed the sunset before stopped and watched and I think the word is 'beheld'. We 'beheld' the sunset and I heard violins rising to the challenge of the sky and I was stunned.

Johnny said it was the best medicine for morose boys and he took me there many times after that and showed me many special sunsets and some nights, just sometimes, the sun set and moon rose opposite him at the same time, which you wouldn't think was even possible, night and day all together so the sun was just over the western range and the big full lady moon was risen over the eastern range, and if you found yourself standing right between them with the ocean in front of you and the palms behind you, you could reach your outstretched hand towards the moon and the other towards the sun and feel all the energy particles of the universe run right through you. It was a mighty and powerful thing and freely available without penalty to the poor. Johnny would stand with me on them nights and reach out both his arms then we would whirl like dervishes and fall down together and make a small fire of driftwood and fir cones and watch the flames and not talk, then ride back home on his noisy motorbike.

One night from the roof I saw a shooting star and knew it foretold good things were coming and I told Johnny and he said it was probably space junk, but I knew it wasn't. It was bright as a flare and came right overhead and just dissolved right in front of my face so you could almost hear it fizzle and pop and it made me feel right as rain.

That was about the time I got my first ever letter from Lilly saying she was struggling with the rules and some of the prison people but she said she was doing good and learning woodwork and weaving. She told how she made a small stool for sitting on and wove string and coloured thread back and forth to make the seat, and she described it in real close and fine detail but didn't send a picture. She said she wanted out of that place because the people were mean and always sore at her for even little things and we would be together soon if I would just wait and be patient like she was waiting. She said she would come one day and it was a promise and she swore we would be together again and a family again and all sit around a great table and eat cakes.

Lilly wrote she was allowed visitors once a month and on the back of her letter drew a map for me in case I ever could get there, and even wrote the bus routes and times. She had the neatest handwriting so it was like reading art and I could picture her perfect long fingers holding the pen and making the words.

She said she was sorry for all the trouble that came about from her actions and she asked me to tell her what happened after she was took away because she wasn't getting any visits and had been moved to another jail far away, and to tell it as I saw it not as the court said or the newspapers, but I didn't feel inclined to write about it so I told it to Johnny and he wrote it down so I could send it. I showed him a photo of Lilly in her crown of flowers and a tie-dyed little tee shirt that ended midway down her body, and denim cut-off shorts and he said writing her would be one of the greatest pleasures of his life even if the tale itself wasn't such a pleasant one once it was unpicked and put down and she was a convict and all. He kept looking at that photo though and I think he fell in love right there.

We spent all night writing that letter and I read it back over and over but Johnny never once got cross or impatient. Then Johnny called a council of older boys to get an opinion and they sat around at dawn and he read it aloud to them as they smoked and drank coffee and ate toast and then Leon said to wait before

I sent it because he wanted to hear it again at night since it was a thing of gravity and significant significance and he said they needed to talk it all through.

It went this way:

Dearest Lilly

Thank you for your lovely letter. I very much enjoyed reading it and especially the chains of flowers you drew all down the margins. It actually smells of you, which is perfect.

You should know this letter is written in my good (older) friend Johnny's hand because I could not bring myself to write the story and preferred to speak it to him. But he is as discrete as he is handsome and mature and he will write only my honest words which I will check when I read it before it is sent. [Johnny added that bit]

The first thing I have to say is that the stool you are making from pale wood and coloured cord and flax sounds beautiful. I can see it in my mind and know it will be fine and strong, as you are. [Johnny helped with that bit too]

I hope you are in good health and this letter finds you in good spirits despite being in that place full of evil bastards and lesbian whore guards, and I hope you have made good friends as I have myself. [Johnny]

The other thing is that you must not take on board any sense of responsibility for what happened after your incident with the police. [Johnny] *You know the big stuff but you need to know that it happened the way it happened is all, and it was all adults who knew what they were doing and if they didn't know then they did it anyway and you are not to blame.*

I saw Mum and Dad were very sad all the time you were on remand and they couldn't get you home. They were always talking about what they were going to do when you came home. The places we would go and food they would cook. Then when you got the long sentence, everyone was shocked and there was a lot of anger, not just from Mum and Dad but everyone. Even Fat Vinnie and his brothers smashed up a police car and the cops were still in it! (But they got away). I don't think the cops chased them too hard because the only thing more dangerous than chasing them was catching them! Anyway, they did some other stuff too and didn't get caught once. A crowd got drunk and burned down that courthouse too.

Mum and Dad just kind of sat a lot and thought about a lot of stuff and after a while they went pretty quiet. Mum cried most days. Sorry to say all this and I hope it doesn't hurt you too much? If it does, just stop reading and go to the last paragraph – after the chain of flowers Johnny drew back for you (he likes art). [Johnny added that]

It was maybe a few months after your sentencing that Mad Louis was riding his Triumph through The Elms when the police stopped him. It was the policeman who grabbed you and hurt you and who you hit with the nail file. According to what people said after, Mad Louis took exception to the cop and told him so and asked how comes he was on the street and free without even so much as a scar and with a medal and commendation and a pretty little girl like you was locked away for all her youth?

The policeman must have said something but some say he never said anything at all and Louis just got madder and madder, but whatever the truth is Louis got very mad and the policeman put his hand on Louis.

The policeman said he wasn't the judge nor jury and you were volatile and a danger to the community but it wasn't his place to comment and would Louis please calm down and show his motorbike driver's licence. Louis never did have any kind of licence, not for a car or bike, and definitely not for the 9mm automatic he offloaded into the policeman's face. He pretty much killed him on the spot, then chased down the other one who was with him and executed him too.

Mad Louis wasn't so mad and definitely wasn't stupid or simple and he knew this was all too much to pass and by the time he calmed down he knew it was a bad scene and people passing had seen and he couldn't shoot them all. I heard he said the Triumph had made him free and it was also the thing that brought him down because every witness would remember the bike and that would lead to him.

Louis went back to his apartment and by all accounts he locked it up in a barricade and got out all his guns.

Davy Crockett was at our house with Daddy when the news came in from neighbours that Louis had done the cop in, and Davy and Daddy knew he would go to ground and Davy rushed out saying he was no way going miss his Alamo! When I heard that cop was dead I have to say Lilly that I got to tingling all down my back and neck like I was plugged into the mains electric. I felt the air in my chest and it felt like a relief. Like a weight was gone and in my head I could hear the Irish jig music the Lennons play at parties. Daddy didn't look so happy though and he swore and cussed like I haven't heard before, then he took off after Davy.

By the time they got to Louis' home the police had tried to storm it but given up because Louis shot them up and down, so the cops were holding people back with a cordon and Louis had shot down four more policemen. He hadn't killed them, just wounded them is all. He's a real good shot Lilly so he could have killed them if he had meant to. He had a rifle with a scope and pump shotgun and his 9mm, so it was harder not to kill people than to kill them, and he was doing them a humanitarian service by missing if only they would see it.

The police had that cordon halfway up the road each side of the house and front and back and they evacuated people from their homes. Davy got arrested by armed police just as soon as he arrived and they made him lay down in the street and Dad stood at the cordon and tried to talk Louis out by shouting from the cordon tape because the cops wouldn't let him inside it. Then Louis called to Daddy, and Louis said he was done and wounded and Daddy just walked straight through that cordon and it was like he was invisible and magical and the cops missed him completely and didn't stop him and he walked right up to the door and Dad and Louis were talking and laughing through that big door and Louis pointed out to Dad that to shoot someone is serious, to shoot a cop is very serious, but to shoot a cop in the face who is in uniform and going about his rightful duty is kind of game over. Satisfying as it may be.

Daddy told him if he would give himself up it wouldn't be so bad, he would go to jail for sure but he would take him Mum's fruit cake in prison every week, and Louis said fuck, he might as well shoot himself as eat Mum's cake every week.

It turns out Louis was mortally badly wounded in the first attempt the police made to storm the place and by the time Daddy got to him he was pretty done for and he wasn't in no shape to make a break for it. He started to open the door to get closer to Daddy and there was shots and Daddy got shot down right there on the door step of his friend and afterwards the cops said it was Louis done it but we all knew and everyone *knew it was a cop bullet that got him. Louis fired back and tried to pull Daddy into his place to make him safe but the police opened up again and Louis stood over Daddy to keep him safe and made a stand and they shot him all up and down and he died right there. He was a real-life hero Lilly, and people are singing his name in the pubs and school yards, but it was just awful and I would have run to them Lilly and made a stand too but I was pulled away by people and they wouldn't let me break free and I couldn't do anything.*

I dream of him sometimes, throwing me in the air in the lido. I miss him a lot. I can feel his hands on my ribs. I miss Daddy a million times more. Daddy got shot for being righteous and helping those in need and he was always looking to help people and he was a good man Lilly.

Davy took off to Africa but went to Iceland first with a blonde woman to dive for seaweed, and some seaweed is very rare and worth a lot of money. He had a job waiting in Africa for a republic fighting rebels who wanted to overthrow the government or maybe it was the other way round and he wasn't sure.

But I guess you want to know more about Daddy. The truth is Lilly, Mum and Dad loved us very much and probably too much and we are blessed for that. [Johnny]

After you went away Daddy would come to me when I was trying to sleep and I was in your old room and in your bed and he read to me and told me stories and Mum would come and snuggle up.

Then not long after Daddy fell down Mum got to not wanting to be alive anymore and not seeing the sun or sky, and Old Missus Kitzman from next door tried to help but couldn't and then men came and took Mummy and they took me and they closed up the house and that's the all of it.

Maybe I will remember it better later. I know we will hear from Mummy one day, but I don't know for sure. I think the government and cops won't let her contact anyone and Johnny says that's normal in these circumstances.

I am fine and well. I miss you very much.

All that happened would have found a way of happening and was really nothing to do with what happened to you. People make their own choices [Johnny] and at least the evil cop now has face like Swiss cheese. [Johnny]

I miss you Lilly and want to see you every day.

Your little brother, always, always. Love, until all the seas run dry.

XXX.

Twelve

Old Missus Kitzman from next door offered that I could stay with her but the authorities said she was too old and she looked frail and worried and her face was lined like twisted bedsheets. On her forearm was a line of numbers in blue-grey ink that the *shmutsik* Nazis tattooed on her when she was in the camps, and she was the oldest person you ever met and maybe she had been made ancient by bad people. She was tiny and frail and spoke English Yiddish in a way you had to hear a thousand times before you understood, but she had a grip like a wrestler and Old Missus Kitzman could grip and scrap and spit swear words in all God's languages but couldn't run for shit being so old and if I ran away she couldn't catch me and she never had a phone to call for help and that's the reason they said she couldn't care for me, but she was stronger than any man living and a real-life Yid-disher saint and she told me that herself and she called me little *pisher* boy and I loved her.

When my dad and Mad Louis got shot down on that black smoke day she was the one pulled me into her little round body and kept me from seeing and kept me from running to them and kept the cops from shooting me too and she took me home and her grip on my wrist made my hand go blue and cold and nearly drop clean off.

After that my mum got lost and looked startled the whole time like she was seeing things no one couldn't see and she gave me holy beads made of black wood and silver and she wrote me two prayers on a slip of paper and one was a 'Hail Mary' and one was the 'Our Father'. Then the men took her away from me then and I fell into all the loss and death like my mum did, only she never could come back and she went to a place I couldn't go and couldn't even visit. Once you fall into death like she did, there ain't no ladder or a knotted rope or no light.

*

After Johnny read the letter to the others again that night there was silence and just some heavy breathing and a lot of smoking and they were looking at each other a lot, then Big Ben took the letter and read it through again then scratched his head and said, 'Fuck. That's hardly a fucking pick-me-up, eh? In my opinion don't send that. Send her some flowers and a card telling her you love her and miss her and will visit her in the holidays . . . . She's in fucking jail, mate. She already knows shit's happened . . . this will make hard hard reading.' He opened a bottle of whisky and swigged it before passing it round.

Johnny wanted to send the letter because he said Lilly needed to hear it all so she could *process* it, and he was happy to write to her often.

'You're just saying that 'cos you got writer's cramp scribing it all out!' Big Ben spat and he sounded angry, then he looked at Lilly's picture for a while. Everyone was silent and thoughtful and passing the letter carefully from hand to hand looking at it and dwelling on it and passing her photo the other way and looking hard at it and dwelling on that too. It was serious business and there were five or six faces wise in the candlelight all contemplating on the gravity of it.

From the darkness someone put their hand on my shoulder, just resting it there.

'Do you know what I think?' Big Ben said again, still looking at the picture then handing it back to me real gently. 'She's lovely,' he whispered. Everyone just looked at him waiting and he drew really deeply on a cigarette and blew a huge smoke cloud through his nose and mouth together. 'I think . . . you shouldn't send this letter, your sister Lilly is teetering on the narrow bridge between not much and a bit less, and she don't know which way to go.' Big Ben lit another cigarette from the butt of his dying one and blew the smoke over all of us then with great gravity he added, 'I think, we should break her out.'

Nobody else said a word and he had said a very big thing right there and we all just let it sit because there was nothing to be added. It's a dangerous thing to give an idea like that life by saying it aloud and Ben had done just that and given it life and now it was alive it would have to be dealt with and that would be big indeed. I saw Leon's face in the golden candlelight and he looked deadly serious, cold, thinking deep about a plan and everything behind him was black so he was all the world right there and Johnny was beside him and half his face was in shadow and half in light and he stared straight ahead to some point a thousand miles away.

We were on a new and unknown path and the silence that settled over us was like a heavily pregnant rain cloud and we drank whisky and smoked another round then I went to bed dizzy and wobbly and all my balance was gone. I wanted to be a hero and save my sister but I couldn't see how we could break her out, and Ben and the other boys went to bed without saying no more or telling me the plan.

'Don't send it. Not yet,' was all Ben said, which was pretty much an order, so I put the letter under my pillow for now and looked at Lilly's picture before I closed my eyes. There was a lot I couldn't tell Lilly in a letter and I didn't want to tell the boys, not even Johnny. You can't tell someone that what they done killed the people they love the most and you can't tell someone that her mum cried until she was a wraith and you can't describe what a broken heart does to someone and how you see it broken on their faces and see your beloveds become less and less each day and each minute and just fade away, and some things are better put from your mind until they fade into black and white then you hope they lose all their edges and shape and the feelings just bleed out with the colours. That's what forgetting must be like. Like photos left too long in the sunshine. You hope for forgetting and dread it at the same time.

Thirteen

Two strange things happened next.

First a boy from China who never said much to anyone went and found a radio in the roof space. Just above the top dorms were crawl spaces so tight only the skinniest kids had a hope of exploring them and you also had to be brave because it was pretty claustrophobic and you had to come out the way you went in because there was no room to turn, but he was into caving and Chinese virgins and he went in with a head torch and not a word to anyone and came out with an old valve set all covered in dust and dead and cold. Boys gathered around it in wonder and fascination and tried to work out what it did, but when it didn't work straight off they drifted away. I'd seen its like before though and I took out every single valve and cleaned them with a cotton cloth torn from a pillowcase and went deep into its sockets with a toothbrush and I went into every inch of that old valve set like my dad did his rustbucket Singer and I tweaked it and tightened it and cooed softly to it, encouraging life. When it was plugged in again it lit up like a copper and bronze skyscraper and once it warmed up it tuned itself in like some invisible hand played its dials, and at night when the air was clear it picked up a faraway radio show and at first the voices were scrabbly and scratchy but just like an old car, the more it ran the more it remembered, and pretty soon it was making music.

Some of us started to listen to them shows at night and it was reassuring and settling and I looked forward to the dark then, because the radio picked up shows better in the dark, and we gathered around it like it was a campfire and it was mysterious for sure but radio always is.

Real late some nights we picked up Woody Guthrie on a show called *Oklahoma* and we didn't know right then how far that signal had travelled, but it travelled worlds.

Second strange thing was a few days later our latest Matron, whose name nobody bothered to learn, got two new beds ready for two new boys and it wasn't the time of year for a new boy to arrive and we were getting two.

The first was a big solid unit called Kellen. He was a boxer and a southpaw, which we saw straight away when he worked the heavy bag hanging from the rafters on the ground floor, and pretty much straight away we called him Lefty.

Lefty watched me walk across the quad one afternoon and called me to wait up. He was like a bear. 'You move like a fighter, Cuz,' he kind of growled and I knew to be careful because he might be spoiling for a scrap and he was way too big for me, but it turned out he was just being friendly and reaching out. Everyone was careful around him because he had scars on his belly where he had been stabbed and shot and when he was asked about them scars he shrugged it off and said it was an operation, but you can tell the difference easy and if it was an operation it must have been carried out by a cobbler. He also had mean fast hands and a warm smile and he tilted his head when he spoke to someone and if he didn't know them real good he kept a distance that was just a little more than an arm's length. I knew it because my dad taught me the same and he called it the fighting distance, and Lefty kept it good and I had never seen anyone else doing it so I knew right then Lefty was the real deal.

After that we would play-spar and he would roll and slip my punches and I would do the same for his and he slowed his down so I could evade him fully and he made me feel real good. He trained every morning and night and we skipped and slipped and rolled and jabbed. I'd been doing my own boxing but he took me straight to another level and had bigger expectations.

I took Lefty to the Lincoln Valley Boxing Gym and presented him to Coach Petey like a trophy and was pleased when I saw how impressed Coach Petey was. Lefty was my find and I done good.

The other new boy was called Tawhaki, after the god of thunder and war, and he came a week or so after Lefty and later than expected, which is common with thunder, so his bed was robbed bare by the time he arrived and Matron never made it up again. We called him Fucky and he didn't mind. He was quieter and more reserved than most kids, just like thunder is before it rumbles, but his smile could melt ice and his nature was real good.

Soon as the boys saw him they liked him and he had a light and magnetism that made you want to be close to him, so by the time he had unpacked his single Surplus Store kitbag we had made his bed up again all neat and tidy and fresh and he never said nothing but nodded thanks, which was enough. He was very fast and very special on the football field so the school took him in despite him having some bad history. He was smart too and Big Ben said he had a high degree of native cunning and he was real handsome and like Lefty he took the weaker and younger boys close and he needed to care for someone because maybe he had lost everyone, and he put that care anywhere it was needed and I knew that much straight off just by intuition and instinct.

Tawhaki and Lefty were good to call friends and I felt I was rich as a king to know them.

A while after they arrived, Big Ben called a council and we discussed again his idea to break out Lilly. It was important that we had a goal even if that goal wasn't so realistic, so I never made a complaint but I didn't get my hopes up either. It was a dream and having a dream and a plan counts for a lot.

Lefty and Tawhaki were invited this time because they were straight away trusted and invited to join us in our deepest circle of trust. Lefty came along but just like thunder, Tawhaki was nowhere to be seen, and at that meeting Lefty listened for a while then shook his head sadly and said, 'I been in a place like that one and there ain't no breaking her out from the inside, you gotta break her out from the outside. Ain't easy but you boys might be in with a shout . . . being majority white and all . . .' Everyone just stared at him until he picked up again 'Sometimes an inmate gets a day trip or something, or gets an invite to a wedding or funeral or day release or something and that's when you can make your move, but if the someone is inside the wire that someone ain't gonna get broke out like they do in a movie . . . I mean sure it happens but not so much and sure not by you . . . us. That's adult work, you gotta have resources.'

Johnny leaned in and watched him for a while waiting for more words of wisdom but Lefty stayed quiet and just looked into a candle flame.

'Do you know this place where Lilly is?' Johnny asked.

Lefty shook his head. 'I don't know that particular place but they're all the same pretty much. I might be able to find out more. Maybe. I can ask some people. My family populate a lot of correctional institutions. We're frequent flyers you know?' He sounded wise.

Johnny looked at me right in the eyes then and said, 'I say we can do it, one way or another. One day. She deserves us to try or she's there for years. Years!'

'It would be heroic!' Big Ben said and when I heard that word rumble out from his giant frame and sit there in front of me in the darkness like a neon light I knew it was meant to be and it was more than a dream and we would make it real.

Johnny came to my bed that night and we sat under the blankets with a torch and a black-covered notebook and pencil and we decided to make a list of essential things a hero must earnestly do, but in truth we didn't know what to write or what makes a real-life full-time professional hero so we gave up and made a list of people to kill instead. We put each name in a column and beside it the preferred means of their demise and kept it safe and it was sacred.

I told Tawhaki of our plan and asked if he would join us and he smiled and declined and said he was not a hero, he was God, and it was different. But when the day came to break out Lilly, he swore, he would rumble for me and shake the earth and the walls and that was enough.

A week later a kid called Carlos came to Fell and Carlos was a cripple in a wheelchair and almost deaf too and sending him to Fell was about the cruellest thing anyone could do because apart from everything else that was wrong with the place there were so many levels and bumpy slopes and stairs and we decided right away that he must have properly offended someone in some power somewhere or finger fucked their pigtailed daughter because just to get to the house there were about two hundred steps through the trees and then all the stairs in the building, so he was truly in trouble, but if he had offended the world so much and so grievously he was one of us and Carlos was our real-life hero from day one and he was accepted into The Fell before he even heard its name. He wouldn't take help getting up the steps at first, and spent hours bumping up one step at a time, and didn't trust anyone or ask no favours, and he worked out by bending down each side and reaching from his chair just to pick stuff up because it trained his abs like a body builder and he did chin-ups with the chair strapped on so he was weighted down, and he had a torso shredded and ripped like a pro fighter.

Carlos was always tired because everything he did took a lot of energy and hard work and he got sick for a few days because toilet anxiety got him like it got us all when we first arrived and it was a real bastard, so you just sit there and can't do anything because there are hardly no doors on the cubicles and everyone passes and asks, 'How's it going?' *How's it going?* They're just being polite but that's a damn mean question to ask a kid straining and embarrassed with a freezing cold stone numb arse and bowels filled with concrete and Carlos had it worse than most because just getting from his chair to the pan was an epic battle and again he wouldn't take help so he struggled and crashed and bashed and his chair would spin away and then nothing and he would just sit and all the world would go by and *How's it going?*

Carlos wasn't too smart and he made up a world of stories claiming he wasn't always in a wheelchair and everything anyone did he done it better before, and nobody ever shot down his claims or made mockery of him and we just let him have it.

Carlos said he could swim all the way across Lake Cloudy on one breath and dive down in the middle and pick up rocks from the darkest deep, but that lake is five miles across and a mile deep so we knew he wasn't truthing. He swore to all the gods and crossed his heart and then high-fived me like he'd proven something beyond all doubt. Then a while later he lit up like an electric light and started on about how before he got twisted he was a runner and so fast and long winded he won the 10,000 metres but done it so swift that after that they named it the 10,000-metre dash, and he swore it and high-fived again.

That year there was a teacher in school who taught social studies called Mister Solomon Sesay and Carlos told him one day how he had won that race and swum that lake and Mister Solomon Sesay said he knew already because he had been at that stadium and seen it and the whole class believed him and I think Carlos believed him, too.

Mister Solomon Sesay was on the edge of being mad and nobody on that edge ever comes back and I was lucky to know him before he slipped over into that deep and terrifying pit. He was tall and strong and blacker than anyone I seen before and handsome with tattoos and marks on him and he spoke in strangely clipped English so I could mostly understand him but not always and I trusted him on account of his colour because being black made him an outsider like I was. He said he was from Africa and Africa is beautiful and is called Paradise, and he told me that.

He didn't teach much social studies, whatever that is, but I learned about beekeeping and how to woo a woman in French and even one day he showed us how to sew up a wounded baby goat. I would have said kid but you would have thought I meant a schoolboy and he wasn't that mad yet.

At first I thought he was wasting my time because, seriously, who keeps bees and who cares, but he took us to a hive back of the school and those bees were watchful and keen to sting and the idea was so strange I had to pay attention and soon enough I

110

knew about bees and Mister Solomon Sesay was certain knowing bees was more useful than algebra, and skinning a goat was more useful than the periodic table, and he was right on both counts and he was the best teacher I ever knew.

Mister Solomon Sesay was also a kendo master who twice a week, or three times when work let him and he could make it to the dojo, dressed in black armour, a mesh mask and, as he put it, thwacked the living shit out of white people with a bamboo sword. It didn't sound very samurai, but one evening I sneaked out, borrowed an unlocked pushbike and went to watch him train in the local dojo and it was fully scary and noisy and skilful too. I hid in the corner shadows by the door so he wouldn't see me and planned on watching for just a few minutes and getting a burger and banana milkshake on a slow ride home but stayed two hours and it was worth it every minute. It made my skin break out in goose pimples the way they leapt across the mat into each other with total screaming commitment to the attack.

I decided I would learn kendo one day, maybe when I started salsa and learned the tango, and Mister Solomon Sesay was the closest thing I ever saw to a living, breathing samurai, so I decided to ask Mister Solomon Sesay what it is that makes a man a hero and maybe I would tell him about our mission to break out Lilly.

Everyone thought he liked me the most of all the boys but I knew he didn't like me any more or less than anyone else but he had that quality of humanness that meant he didn't really dislike any kid enough to be too mean and he didn't take anything too seriously, and if he didn't like kids he would have left teaching all together and gone and walked the samurai path or sat under a tree or something.

The flip side of that coin is that he didn't much like any of us either and one day he confided in me that he saw us all as frogspawn. Ugly and slimy and living in a messy glup and even if we made it to our fullest most perfect potential all we were going to be and all we could hope to be was fucking frogs. I spent a while after that trying to work out what the most majestic heroic noble frog would look like and it was kind of disheartening.

I didn't tell him right off about Lilly but I told him a few of us had been talking at night and we had tried to work out a hero's path that would suit all heroes from all times and would he perhaps suggest what a hero was and how to live like one full time and walk the earth as one, and I asked him most politely so he smiled and ignored me completely and gave a lesson on Lucius Anais Seneca who said, 'misfortune nobly born is good fortune', which made me think Mr Lucius Anais Seneca had never really had shit dealt to him, and William Shakespeare, who wrote 'nothing is either good or bad but thinking makes it so . . .' So I knew he had never seen Sun hanged under the winter tree with shit and piss running down his young legs and his beautiful sweet tongue that had never kissed a girl he loved hang massive and blackened. Mister Sesay's attempts to make me appreciate philosophers failed and I decided I wanted to line them all up and execute every fucking one of them and after the lesson he asked me if I had enjoyed it and I said no but thank you and I left and he didn't even give me a detention.

I actually learned things from him without even realising it, which is a rare thing in any school day, and sometimes I wasn't quite sure exactly what I had learned but I could feel a kind of waking up in my head like little electric pulses firing off and bits of my brain lighting up and trying to make sense of his lesson because some part of my mind kind of grasped it and the rest was flopping around trying to get a handle on it. It was like a neon light was flickering deep in my brain trying to fire into life, flicker flick flicker, flicker flick flicker, a moth zapper on a warm night zinging and zapping the nocturnal beasties, and that means you're learning. Or dying maybe, if you're old or a moth in a zinger.

I told Mister Solomon Sesay one day that I wanted to execute all the fucking philosophers in the universe and I actually said the swear word too by accident and I was expecting a detention for my honesty and for swearing but he said that was fine and he said, 'The purpose of my classes is not to change your mind on such matters. The purpose is to help you understand and explain *why* you want to act so . . . and give you the tools to present your argument in an academic fashion so that should you ever manage to *execute all the fucking philosophers* in the universe, you will know why you have done so and be able to rationalise your actions. Have a good evening small puny boy. And do not swear in my presence again, or I will take your tongue for a trophy.'

I liked that, it made me shiver and I bit down on my tongue just gently to feel it and appreciate it, and he smiled again when he saw me do that and Mister Solomon Sesay might not know what a hero was but he knew how to make a man value his body parts.

Then one early morning I finished up training in the Lincoln Valley Boxing Gym and I unwrapped my hands and went to put on my old sweatshirt and an envelope fell out of the hood. It was sealed up and folded and had Mister Solomon Sesay's writing on it and it said '*small hero*'. I looked around quick but the teacher wasn't to be seen and inside the sealed-up envelope was a note neatly written and I couldn't figure how anyone could come into the gym with all of us training and leave a note and get out and not get seen and all them eyes and all them people and only one little door and even smoke and mist gets seen and Mister Solomon Sesay had done it and the note read:

Heroes tilt at windmills, for sometimes windmills are giants.

I read it again and again and I think Mister Solomon Sesay was fully mad then and I decided not to ask him again.

That night I struggled to sleep and was listening as the branches of trees scratched the windows and a dripping tap somewhere in the building bounced and by some marvel of vibration made a noise everywhere despite its smallness. I listened as the breathing of boys stroked the air and even the house itself seemed to creak and inhale and exhale in slow deep night-time breathing. It was steel and concrete and just like a drum and I came to know where each noise originated from and it was like living inside a living thing and I could hear the whispers of the Marionette kid who didn't have to share a cube because nobody would sleep near him. He never spoke much except through his marionettes which he had dancing all hours and some nights he cooed to them and hushed them to sleep and some were proud and some were restless. Some nights he put on a show for everyone and them marionettes were called names like Marmaduke Much and Mournful Mary, but mostly he stayed to himself and deep at night you could sometimes hear the tip-tapping of their tiny demonic feet as he made them dance and dance and dance but tonight he was murmuring to them and hushing them. He was a small, scrawny moon-faced kid and he was weird as fuck but I wouldn't say it aloud and neither would anyone else and everyone called him Ems and mostly didn't talk to him at all and he could silence a room and scare the shit out of Geronimo just by looking round the door, and I really liked him.

And I could hear Carlos humming along to his transistor wireless solid state radio soft and sleepy. He was attached to it like nothing else and if it wasn't in his sweaty calloused hand it was tied and taped to his chair or snugged deep in his undies and it was precious more than gold to Carlos. It wasn't bulky fixed furniture like the big valve set and it could tune in to lots of stations.

In time I came to covet and borrow that radio because Lilly said in her letter that she liked to hear night time rock ' n' roll shows and with that radio I could snug down in private under my blankets and listen to them same shows and think of her in her cell listening too and I would be listening with Lilly and could almost reach out and touch her.

That transistor wireless radio was a cool green hold-in-your hand Westminster Solid State, and made in Japan I reckon, with the tuning dial on the front and the volume on the side and the on/off switch on the top. All over the front were little holes to let the music out and a plastic lanyard to loop over your wrist so you wouldn't drop it and the lanyard had a copper-coloured metal swivel connection so the lanyard wouldn't twist and break. They had thought of everything and it was a marvel of creative design. It had FM and AM and a pull-out aerial so you could get even faraway stations.

I lay beside Carlos some nights and we listened together and on nights when there was really clear air I heard Russian and Chinese and Korean fishing boats talking and laughing late at night and they weren't close even though they sounded close but their signals can bounce off the atmosphere and come back to Earth and get picked up, so they sounded like they were in the bay but they could be a world away trawling off some wasted desolate shore or far away at the other Pole. And Carlos pretended he knew what they were saying and interpreted for me and I slept easy those nights.

There was even an earplug so you could listen in private.

Carlos said he kept that Westminster safe most of his life that he remembered and he wouldn't trade it for nothing. He dribbled a fair bit and sweated a lot and had a small flannel rolled up that he used to wipe the radio dry and clean if it got really bad. He would hold the radio really close to his face because his eyes weren't so good and his hands would shake as he tuned it because doing small things with his hands was hard and the smaller the thing he tried to do the more he shook and trembled, but he wouldn't take help and Lefty said it was heroic and Lefty was right.

One day I saw a radio just like it for sale in town but it was big bucks and no way could I afford it and I promised myself I would steal it soon as a chance came up and I told Carlos my plan and told him I was covetous of his Westminster and he nodded and said wisely, 'You need a transistor for sure . . . But not mine. I need it much as you do. We'll go and get the one from the shop. Mustn't forget the batteries. They use batteries. For now why don't you just use the valve set?' He kind of slurred at times and his words were all full of spit and split up with big breaths so he said it like *whydonchaya . . . just . . . use the . . . valveshet?*

But the valve set was too big to listen to in private and had become the meeting place for everyone with no sleep, and it was pretty to look at once the valves lit up because one side of the case was broke away and you could see the valves alive and lit in the dark, and come 11pm it would play Woody and Cowboy Country and some old prison blues always on that same setting and just after midnight when the show wrapped up it popped and died just like that. The valves warmed the room a little and it looked good on its table and I'd never had furniture before, but a big valve radio is impressive furniture fit for a rich man and I would even dust the valves, but you couldn't snuggle down with it and listen in private and hold it in your hand or close by your heart so the next week we got me the hold-in-your-hand transistor radio from the shop in town and batteries too.

Fourteen

The radio raid was a spectacular success and too easy by far and if I wasn't so strong willed and morally well adjusted I would right there have become a professional thief. We planned it loose and worked it looser and we went into the store separately with Johnny and me going in first and making straight towards the radio aisle and Lefty and Majid entering a minute later and going to the other side of the shop. Lefty looked suspicious on account of being black which drew the attention of the salesman and I stuck the radio down my jersey while Johnny liberated a packet of batteries and all the while the man looked hard at Lefty who was doing nothing wrong but browse, and he looked with contempt and terror at Majid as he browsed electronic components and timers and wiring and spoke Arabic and smiled kindly.

The lesson there is a good one and clear: If you're going stealing or doing anything illegal or any time you want to get away with something, always whenever possible take with you the darkest blackest kid you can find and preferably he should be real black, big and tough looking and poor, though to be fair I reckon any black kid would do, even a choirboy. And if there's no blacks to hand, take an Arab. If you're an Arab, don't smile and don't look at electronics and timers and if you're black maybe definitely just stay home because you're getting the blame whatever happens and whoever does the deed. I knew then that black people are a godsend for white criminals. White criminals should pay them just to hang out. If I ever do a serious act of wickedness or deal dishonestly, for sure I'm going to have me a black fella right there beside me. It might not be heroic but it's a way to stay out of jail and that's called a *compromise*.

The radio was perfect and soon as it was in my hand I knew my hand had always been waiting for it. Once the batteries were carefully inserted it had a healthy, living weight and it tuned into about ten different channels and the sound was very good and clear. Sometimes the channels came and went but if one went you could find another one straight away and most of them were in English or Spanish. Carlos bent over it and showed me in great loving detail how to use it but it was pretty simple. You just turned it on and wiggled the dial, and Carlos loved my radio almost as much he loved his own.

My radio was a Sony and made in Japan but still good quality despite that and had a chrome front cover and the rest was deep rich brown plastic and it was plush. It had the same ear-plug arrangement as Carlos's Westminster but mine had two earplugs coming off one lead so you could listen with both ears or share the music with a friend provided your heads were close together.

I loved the feel of turning it on as it popped its little hello and then voices came and music and you never knew what you would hear first so it was like a lucky dip at the fairground and I was connected to the whole wide always-awake world and every voice was personal and it was uplifting and a night-time reassurance and satisfying and it healed a lot of loneliness.

Even though I had that plush Sony I still gathered with the lonely boys at the valve set to listen to the *Woody Show* and we would sip whisky and I would look at the faces of my friends all lit warm golden and they looked perfect and pure and a man with a valve set will always have friends and good company and that's for certain. But it was good to snuggle into bed afterwards and listen in private to my Sony and Lilly was listening, too.

One night we were sitting doing lots of nothing and Leon was cleaning his rifle and Johnny was tending his nails with an emery board and Lefty and Majid started on about how sinful stealing was and they felt guilty about aiding in my possession of the hold-in-your-hand Sony and maybe I should take it back and they started softly praying at the same time, both mumbling hushed and private words in the dark of the lamp, and they heard each other and eyed each other shifty, and then they were praying against each and laying their words over each other, and Leon dropped a bullet in the breach and put the muzzle of the rifle on them and I think he would have done it and they knew and they went straight away quiet and they never said it was a sin again and I got to keep it as mine for all time.

Fifteen

It was a Friday night and late and when I settled down Humphrey was still awake but before I could ask him if he fancied next day at the beach he fell asleep with alarming speed and abysmal manners. He never seemed to care that he was alone and never seemed to need to talk and I wondered if that meant he was stronger than me.

I was still getting comfortable when Moby showed up in the dark like a manatee and told me his grandma and family were coming soon and maybe even this Sunday and would I like to have lunch with them? I accepted with genuine gratitude as good etiquette dictates and straight away I was wondering what I would wear and if it was clean because I would want to make a good impression and my own mum wouldn't want me looking tatty or unkempt and there might be cake. I like cake, and bread and butter pudding too, and that was the kind of thing a grandma might bring, or heavy fruit cake maybe even with icing and cherries or marzipan, oh god let it have marzipan, and maybe sandwiches and egg and bacon pie. A scotch egg even. And the rolls might be dusted with flour and filled with egg mayonnaise with sliced cucumber and all those things came straight to my mind in the single blink of a hungry eye and my mouth watered.

When I accepted his invite Moby smiled broad and sat heavy on my bed so I rolled towards him and he rolled me away again and we talked about what we would eat and what we would do and where they would take us and he chuckled deeply. He had a giant mega extra pack of coconut and raisin cookies and we ate them all as we laughed and imagined the feast the family would bring. Fried chicken too! I really liked Moby and his family and his fat and bearded grandma and her baking and I knew she would be fat and bearded because all the best grandmas are. I told him Leon and Johnny were hunting the weekend and maybe if his folks did arrive on Sunday we could ask them to save some pig or deer meat and we could bring it to our picnic and I told him I was insufficiently resourced to buy offerings and Moby said no matter, but I said I would go walking in the woods in the morning and would look out for berries and nuts.

Sometimes I felt morally obliged to partake of nature and walk in the hills and sometimes I went on long walks far from the sea on the high paths, and those paths were densely forested and wild. I read books on walking in nature and surviving the wilderness. A few miles in as the terrain got higher and harder the walking tracks gave up and looped back towards the town and only logging and hunting tracks continued up through fire breaks and down through ravines and old log slides and I would walk there sometimes and be alone in all the world. It was Woodsman country. There was no town for nearly two hundred miles and no sealed roads except the highway which wound its way through the whole range to the ferry port and on that highway were spotted tiny settlements hugging the coast where small-time fishermen brought in their catch, or mussel farms and fish farms filled the inlets. Inland of that road, there was just forest and tracks and disused abandoned gold mines where broken dreams hung like low clouds and it was wilderness and I knew exactly where to seek nuts and berries and even wild grapes and peaches.

It was pig and deer country and Leon and Johnny spent just about every weekend hunting and tracking up there. The pigs were legendary and black and hairy and big as ponies and tusked and wild. Some weighed over 400 pounds, with thick black coats of hair like steel wire and yellow eyes like crocodiles and Leon told me so.

I invited Moby to join me but Moby shook his head and said nature was his sworn and mortal enemy, and he picked some belly button fluff from his deep dark navel and sniffed it, rolled it and flicked it in my face and left.

After he left I had trouble tuning the Sony transistor because all the signals seemed broken and wavering and in the dark the dial was sometimes hard to read but eventually I settled on a channel with some sad songs and folk songs and a pretty girl with a guitar. Then as I drifted a little and felt my eyes grow heavy Lilly's voice crept from the radio. It took a few words of her voice before I realised it was really her and my tired mind found the recognition.

Then it was shocking and glorious and wonderful and I didn't understand it at all. It jolted me awake and wide awake, too, and alarmed me, so I stiffened and almost sat up. She was singing like she always loved to, her voice a perfectly pitched bell as she sing-songed my name. She told me not to worry so and then as I lay still she settled me like she always did. 'Don't fret so much little brother. It will be all be resolved in our favour darling, now listen and sleep and I will read to you . . . your favourite . . . you will be my Gilbert and I will be your Anne with an E. Now listen and stop your sadness . . . *ANNE OF GREEN GABLES*, chapter one.' Lilly breathed deeply and I heard her giggle just a little like some exciting mischief was upon her and I laughed, too.

Lilly stole a copy of that book from the public library from before I could even remember and it was dog-eared and yellowed with its clear plastic cover cracked and torn, but she taped it up a hundred times so it weighed heavy and the pages turned stiffly. Sometimes she read it to Jasmine and me and sometimes she thwacked me about the head with it. I reckoned she didn't need to read it because she must know it off by heart but she read slow and with her special voice like in the pictures, and without due regard for decency or decorum someone settled on my bed and I peeked out of the bedclothes expecting to see Johnny or Humphrey or Moby again but it was the weird kid with the marionettes. He sat pale white and slight in the dark just looking at me and one of his marionettes stood on my bed in the crook of my knee tapping me with long pale white wooden fingers. The kid just looked and I looked back. He was in brushed-cotton bunny rabbit pajamas. I passed him the spare earpiece. 'Anne of Green Gables . . .' I said, and he slipped into the warm beside me without a word.

The marionette was always well dressed and usually wore a dinner suit but tonight he was in silk pyjamas and a fancy dressing gown and he climbed off my bed and sat on the floor with his legs crossed and head bowed and he smoked a cheroot through a long cigarette holder. He didn't feel the cold or fear the dark but he looked lonely as a graveyard's stone angel so I felt sorry for him then, but he was a sickly pale, cold fucking scary presence. 'Is he going to sleep there?' I hissed and I heard Ems voice properly for the first time ever when he shook his head slightly and whispered back like a small child, but low and hushed and with every word perfectly sounded, 'They don't sleep, not softly like us, not peacefully. There is no calm repose. See . . . their faces are tense, screwed up, frowning like they're holding back a scream . . . a long terrible scream . . . But they don't scream . . . they take our screams and swallow them up.' I wished straight off he hadn't said a word because now I had a shiver and he smiled and the marionette turned its head to look at me, white faced with a red spot on each cheek, and nodded. I shivered more. 'Don't be afraid. They are our friends. We all need friends . . .' and the marionette bowed his head more deeply as the boy lay down beside me and got comfortable. Ems smiled and I knew we were friends and I was glad of that because he was properly fucking fucking scary.

'Anne of Green Gables . . .' I said again and helped him place the spare headphone into his ear as Lilly continued her story. I wriggled deeper into bed and my sheets were so cold they felt wet through, so I stayed still as a rock and they got warm quick.

I slept warm and peaceful like I used to when I was young and I woke alone but all my limbs and muscles had been drained of fear and dread and tension. The Sony had been turned off and I guessed it was Ems and was an act of kindness and it preserved the batteries.

It was Super Saturday like every Saturday is and the light was grey and cold and it was still Dark O'Clock and I knew dawn was sneakily coming but it was still a way off and all the world was cold and held its breath waiting for the new day. It's an evil time to be awake, and not yet day and no longer night and like no-man's land in time and nothing holds sway in that time, not good or evil or living or dead, and maybe once, in the long long ago, something cold and hungry and merciless came in those grey hours and hunted the warm furry creatures that became us over millions of years and we still have that memory hidden deep in our souls and it makes us fear and be sad for no good logical reason.

But those hours are different if you mobilise and act and turn the tables, so I rolled out of bed light and easy and got dressed quick against the cold and pulled on the warm camouflage clothes Johnny had gifted me when we first met and belted on a knife. The clothes were soft to the touch and comfortable as a glove but warm and tough and according to the label designed to wick away your sweat.

In a pocket was an old chocolate and oats and dried fruit EatMe bar, which is about the best fast nutrition you can get into an active body and it says so on the packet and I knew Johnny put it there on purpose as another gift.

Then it was time to walk the tracks into nature and find berries and nuts and fruits, and I was summoned and there is no other word for it, and the trees called me to come visit and I went.

Sixteen

I walked straight out of the house and into the woods then I walked two hours or more and still it felt like the sun hadn't risen and I had never been in the woods in such early light and I didn't know trees and bushes and earth made noise like breathing, but it does if you can hear it, and it was a watercolour world.

And soon I was lost and after soon I was in trouble because I wasn't *Oh dear I'm lost, let's follow this track and this sign with a walker and a cyclist on it* lost. I was *I am going to get fucking eaten alive and raped by fucking mutants and never fucking seen again* completely lost.

So I cried.

I stood still for maybe even ten minutes and my breathing settled and my sweat froze. Two goats straight from fairy tales walked past, just stroking the bush ahead of me, then two more. They weren't farm goats or zoo goats from a petting zoo. They had thick wiry fur and short horns and looked perfect in the forest, with keen confident evil yellow eyes with black coffins in them and one had blue eyes and that was more evil, and they had a sense of ancient peace and there was nothing about them to snag on trees or scrub and they even had shorter legs so they passed under the denser higher branches not even bothering to hide from me or look nervous, which was a grievous insult given my place on the food chain and it hurt my pride.

In the books they say walk downhill, keep the moss on one side of the trees, look for the sun and line it up with your watch, but it's all bogus and bullshit and sitting down and screaming and sobbing is just about as effective. The forest can be so dense and dark and the coverage so complete that you can't find your way unless you're an expert and not just any expert but an expert in this kind of forest. I came to ravines that were sheer and deadly and there were vines and creepers and this was real ancient forest where people were out of place and in this forest you could be lost for ever just a hundred steps from your own back porch.

I yelled and hollered and howled but nature soaked up my voice and nobody came, so I walked on and this is a mistake, it says so in the *Woodsman's Bible*, Version 4. Stay where you are, it says, and wait to be eaten alive and raped by mutants.

Then the light mist became a heavy mist and it was wetter and colder and the heavy dense woods beat me up and whipped me and stabbed me and tripped me up. Walking for pleasure is an undeniably effeminate and elderly person's pastime but this was different and I knew I would die of wilderness poisoning in the arms of a heartless bastard called nature and that's a bitter pill to swallow, so I walked for survival and life, and that's manly.

Then I got a lucky break and by no skill on my part came out on a rocky clearing over a river and the sun was on the river making it a silver-blue and green ribbon below me and the river was noisy and I whooped and laughed and grew cocky again real quick. The mist was cleared over the course of the water where the sun had burnt it away so all the trees lining the river were blurred-edged and soft, their colours and lines all running into themselves, and the river was molten metal running fast over black rocks. The sun on my face as I stood on the edge of the outcrop was warm and welcome so I stood awhile and soaked it in and composed myself.

I decided to walk the river downstream like the *Woodsman's Bible* says, but first I needed to climb down, which wasn't so easy but also not a rope hard climb. I got low and took my time, stopping here and there to check the route and make sure I kept control of all my limbs. Slowly slowly, three points of contact (*Woodsman's Bible*).

When I got the river's edge I knelt down and drank deeply and it was the coldest, freshest, most pure water I ever drank and near enough killed me by freezing my internals. I rejigged my clothing to get comfortable. I could breathe freely and realised I had been holding my breath for hours and that must be a world record, and I washed my face and hair, splashing the cold water over myself.

Then from my kneeling I saw an old man.

A way down the river as it twisted through the rock and ramparts of soil it bent hard into an S and on the opposite bank an old man sat on rocks with his bare feet in the shallow water's edge and all around him were silver glinting objects. His trousers were rolled up almost to his knees and a pair of boots were on a rock beside him. He didn't see me and was too far off for me to make out clear detail but I knew he was old because he had that old air hanging about him like old people sometimes do, and he didn't look like a mutant. I could tell he was smoking because there was a light blue-grey cloud of soft tobacco smoke over him.

I was drawn to him like dust gets drawn to a shiny surface just seconds after you polish it.

I edged along the river and was glad of the sun. People think misty forests are romantic and artistic but let me tell you they are not. Not when you're wet and lost and cold and the forest is full of spiteful snagging bastard bushes which rip you to bits because all the beautiful mighty trees were logged out a hundred years ago. And there's a lesson I learned right then, and that's once you cut down the mighty, the great, and the heroes, all the spiteful little nasty stuff gets out of control and spreads until there is nothing but the same nasty stuff everywhere and people think it's a forest and call it a forest but it ain't a forest like a forest can be and once was and nobody knows the truth because all the mighty trees are gone so people have nothing to compare to. You can put all the effort and light and love you want on that stunted spiteful snagging weedy shit and you won't never grow yourself a great giant noble tree.

I hated it and despised it and hated that I had been beaten up by inferior flora and if it was high and dry summer I would have lit a bush fire and burned it all down to ash and then concreted over it and made it a dead and soulless car park.

I picked my way along the river until the old man was clearer then I saw he wasn't alone. There was a girl behind him almost camouflaged against the trees and she was pretty and slender and dressed in a floral summer dress. The dress she wore was so sheer it was see-through in the light and she was lean and firm-looking and I could see the shape of her legs and high bum and breasts. She radiated and I couldn't stop looking at her and she was kind of dancing behind the old man and around him on a sandy beach left in the bend of the river by higher water. She moved so light she hardly touched the ground and her toes were long and she rose up on them like a ballerina. I could swear there were butterflies around her shoulders and head but it wasn't the season for butterflies so maybe it was just midges in the light, but she looked like a real-life fairy girl and it was the first time I ever saw something so magical. She shone and I heard her laugh like a tinkling bell as a bird swooped down to skim the water and somersaulted and dropped again over and over and she danced gracefully and didn't see me because my camouflage was so good against the earth bank. I could see her skin was impossibly white like silver, and white gold like the sun was always on her but never burnt or browned her, and her laugh was pretty and tiny tinkling over the harsh noise of the water.

I moved to see her better and she saw me, froze and said something to the old man and he looked up straight at me, and I was no longer camouflaged and then I was really uncomfortable because I felt like I was a peeping Tom even though I was still a good hundred big paces away.

I raised my hand in a lazy wave and I could see her relax and she waved back. Then the old man waved and called out but I couldn't hear what he said over the noise of the river and the distance. I tilted my head and shrugged so he knew I didn't hear him, then I picked my way a bit quicker towards them and I kept smiling broad as an idiot so they knew I was friendly and I think right there I was in love.

Seventeen

I walked strong and staunch as I could and soon I was directly opposite the Fairy Girl, and the old man stood up and seemed to unfold to his full height and as if by magic he looked younger.

The river was narrower there and shallow, running fast over flat golden-brown river stones all polished smooth and worn looking, but the water was not even knee deep by the looks of it. We were only ten paces separate and I loosened my jacket as the man called me over. He had a pot boiling over a wood fire in a natural pit with damp logs round it and I could smell wood smoke and coffee and the last hints of sweet moist tobacco. The Fairy Girl just glided from behind him and tiptoed into the water, going stone to stone to halfway then outreached her hand and long slender arm. Her arm just seemed to reach right across the water and she smiled at me. 'Stay on the stones, the water's deeper than it looks,' she said. Her voice was soft and perfect and the water didn't seem to go round her ankles but through them as if by magic.

I took her hand and an electric charge ran through her to me and she guided me to the other bank, stepping around me and then behind me lightly, and putting her hand on my arm she guided me to the man and I hadn't seen whiteness like her skin except on statues. Her skin was so perfectly delicate and her eyes so lighted I could hardly breathe and couldn't look away and couldn't look straight at her either.

'You're lost.' The man offered me an old enamelled mug of black coffee and I took it even though coffee wasn't my drink and he knew I was lost because he was a wizard and he had that wild and weathered look wizards have. His hair was straggly and grey and long and his nose thin. Maybe he wasn't so old but time hadn't written kindly on his features and his lines were deep, but he had a big smile.

'I've been slaying boar.' I tried to sound like it was no big deal and something I did every day but knew I sounded stupid as soon as I heard the words leave my mouth and the fairy girl laughed gently as she stroked the man's grey curly hair and I could see it was black once. He looked past me and all around. 'Really? Did you leave him on the hill?' and the girl smiled kindly and nudged him to be silent and spare me.

She whispered at me 'You're the *hunter* . . .' She looked happy enough in her face but there was a sadness over her and I could see it in her eyes and wanted to look deeper but I had to look away because it isn't polite to stare and not safe because she was a being from another world and staring at her might strike me down.

'Slaying boar . . .' the man repeated back at me in a similar voice I had used and he laughed like she laughed, gently and not like they were mocking me, so I wasn't offended and I nodded.

The girl danced a pirouette like a kid more than a ballerina, 'And now . . . you're lost?'

I nodded. 'And now I'm lost.' All I could do was sigh it off and be honest and I was looking dumb as a post and the girl was lovely as mist over a meadow in the morning.

She said, 'But now you are found! And we will keep you . . . safe.'

The Wizard stepped closer to me and helped me out of my jacket, saying it would dry better on the rocks, and with a stick he rolled some more wood on the fire so its flames licked up smoky despite the dampness of the timber. All around the fire, hemming it on every side, were more small logs, which is a woodsman's trick to dry out damp wood before you feed it to the fire. In the wilderness fire is life, the *Woodsman's Bible* tells you so.

The flames were too hot to get real close to and my jacket was steaming off its dampness in seconds but I got as close as I could and could feel the heat getting into my knees and ankles and chasing out the gripping cold. That kind of cold gets you really deep and makes you feel old, but fire is a miracle of healing.

'Sit . . .' said the Fairy Girl and I sat straight away on a rock by the fire where her long finger pointed and it was like a spell was upon me and she knelt and undid my boots and soon I had no jacket and no boots or socks on and she had half stripped me and I had let her and the spell meant I couldn't resist her and she was graceful and beautiful and as lithe as a sliver of moonlight. I saw she wasn't wearing a bra and tried to catch a glimpse of her boobs and not to at the same time because the *Book of Cool* tells us you should never be caught trying to see a woman's boobs, and she saw me and smiled, turning her head away and her big watery eyes down and didn't cover herself and I didn't turn to stone or fall down dead, which could have happened had she not been so merciful.

The Wizard smiled kindly. 'Have you panned before?' He picked up a battered silver metal bowl, which from a distance had gleamed like silver dollars but close up was dulled and dented and bruised, and went to the waters edge with it and crouched. I wasn't sure what he meant at first but understood he had changed the subject to save the girl from my clumsy perving and I was ashamed as he scooped up sand and gravel from the river bed and swirled it with water in the pan. He knelt and studied it then swirled again in smooth practised circles so the water and the lighter sand and stones slopped gently over its lip, and the fairy girl tiptoed around the flat stones. 'For gold . . . Panned for gold? Marvellous stuff, so pretty,' The Wizard said.

He had my interest. 'Do you find much?'

He looked at the girl then back to me. 'No. None! Never! Not a bloody spec! But it's an optimistic way to spend a day out by the river.'

'Why don't you fish? That's an optimistic way to spend a day by the river too,' I said.

'True. Perhaps. Do you fish?'

'Sometimes.'

The girl spun towards me. 'Are you as good at fishing as you are at slaying boar?'

'Don't tease him . . . come and see,' he said, and I went with him along the river bank to a shaded bend and with his hand and silent gestures he slowed me and told me to go slow and quiet, then he pulled me by the arm into a crouch beside him and pointed into the water where it was running faster and clear and green right under overhanging bushes whose roots were poking out of the bank where the river was eroding the earth. At first I saw just water burbling and noisy and pure and cold but then I saw in the reeds under the bank a beautiful fish, long and stripy like a tiger, and muscular and thick so it looked like a single long muscle, all power, all primal and earthy and ready as a coiled spring and so still in the fast waters.

'You see Mr Trout?' he whispered and I nodded and hardly breathed and I had never seen a fish like this fish and he seemed to be made of water and diamonds and rubies and pearls, and the Wizard edged forward slowly and entered the water downstream of the fish without seeming to move or disturb the surface so it didn't even ripple as much as it would if a single raindrop fell onto it, and he crept into the stream and reached down, slow, moving with the soft current and his eyes unblinking, and came to the trout from the rear. The great fish was pointing upstream into the current and holding in one spot with barely a pulse of its tail and had no idea the wizard was behind him because all its attention and focus was forward and all its hopes and optimism was forward – and whoosh! Quick as a cat the wizard stood up holding a fish that was longer and thicker than his forearm and all its world was changed and never in a million years did it see coming or imagine this event, and that's how death comes more often than not.

He came to me with it like it was precious and fragile. 'Rainbow trout.' He smiled and carried the fish with me towards the girl, who swooned over it.

The great freshwater fish was beyond beautiful. It shimmered with all the colours I could name and some I can't describe and it was perfect. Every scale was carved from pearls and pure paua and shimmered electric and neon and rainbow upon rainbow. It gaped and looked shocked and I could hear it calling out in panic and I wanted to put it back in the water.

I had never fished, in truth and it wasn't something I got to do in the city but never could admit it and I had never seen a fish look as beautiful and alive and perfect.

The Wizard smiled, holding him towards my eyes. 'Perfect.'

I nodded.

'She is,' the girl whispered. 'Praise the perfect lady fish!'

Then the Wizard crouched and lay the fish on a flat river stone and killed it with a single sharp blow with a stick and I was shocked by the power and precision of that blow so I stepped back a pace. Maybe I jumped a little and I don't know if the girl gasped or I did but for sure one of us gasped and maybe it was both of us and I felt something inside me jump with horror and recoil and protest, for it was a terrible deed and so unexpected that I was shocked and hurt and grabbed the fairy's hand in mine or maybe she grabbed me.

The Wizard held the fish before my eyes again and I saw its colour going away and its electricity fade until it was no more than a shadow of dirty muddy brown. The day darkened.

I had seen death in the Hanged Man and in Sun the Korean and seen its shadow move in the streets and follow me but I never seen life end so deliberately before me and never saw all its hope and potential and energy fade so fast.

The Wizard said, 'We will eat him for lunch . . . but you see pup, when you pan you hope for gold and wealth and new clothes for the ball, but when you fish, if you are lucky and favoured, it ends in death . . . and there is no good death. I hope, I really really hope, you are hungry.'

But he knew I wasn't hungry enough to warrant the killing and then I was ashamed.

'It will feel worse when you slay the boar, I hope,' the man said. 'It should. The boar will run, it will fight, it will be afraid and then angry, and eventually when it's exhausted and worn down it will scream and make its stand, and it will be overwhelmed and torn and then it will be spiked, screaming, panting, slayed, but not bowed. It will not be a quick or kind or honourable end. There won't be glory. So, yes boy, if you're a good person you will feel worse.'

'Feel much worse, my dear. Much worse,' the Fairy Girl echoed.

I already felt worse.

The fish tasted better than any fish I ever ate and I could actually taste its life on my tongue and although we ate only small it seemed to fill me up because maybe its life set my senses alive. The fish meat tasted like summer and honey and pure and clean and lean and we ate without words, but I reckon we all thought the same thing and felt guilty because of it. We ate the all of it, everything, every scrap, and sucked and licked our fingers then the tiny bits left over and the skin and bones were thrown into the river and flowed away into vanishing like the fish had never even existed and it was too quickly gone and I said to myself, A life, any life, should leave more of a mark. I also knew life should be remembered, so I promised the fish I would remember him and I do.

The Fairy Girl washed her hands in the river and rinsed her mouth, then kissed the Wizard on the mouth and me on the cheek and I was sure with the touch of her lips that if I never saw another girl I had seen the perfect woman and felt her perfect lips on my imperfect skin.

Her hair flowed long and copper red and blonde depending on how the light caught it and her eyes were blue and green and sparkled like the river stones on the bottom of the stream. She wasn't so much older than me I reckoned. Old enough to be a woman but not so past me in years I couldn't catch her up one day and make her my own. I watched her move and I was looking at a magical and mystical being and I swear her feet didn't even touch the ground when she walked and there was something serene about her that made me feel content and peaceful and safe.

The Wizard smiled and his hand went onto my back in a fatherly way like I hadn't felt in a long time and he passed me my jacket as rain started to fall and the mist of the forest crept down over the river.

I followed them back from the river and along a path that rose to higher ground and into a shallow cave where we sat and watched the mistifying of the day. He said the rain would pass soon and he would get me back to a path that would take me home. He didn't ask me about myself and he didn't say much about anything else, but I seem to recall that I said a lot about everything and most of it was just blabber and when you're in love you do that kind of thing and I was very in love and I wanted to ask the Fairy Girl her name but it didn't seem right and I didn't want to be too forward like some kind of Romeo. The *Book of Cool* says be patient.

With the rain and mist the air temperature fell quick but the Wizard had brought logs and embers and the Fairy Girl brought kindling from the river fire and in seconds we had another fire to sit by right in the mouth of the cave. The smell of pure fresh woodsmoke mingled with the damp earth smells and I could smell everything perfectly and like I was smelling it for the first time as it interwove with the perfect scent of the girl's skin and hair. There is something primitive and satisfying and ancient about sitting sheltered and watching rain fall, especially when it falls on a river and you can see how cold the world is but you have a warm fire. Fire and water and rain and mist and smoke are the ancient perfect things that take your mind from anything else and just hypnotise you and keep you locked right there in the very moment of their constant new creation and I knew it before I knew it. I sat there with a wise old wizard and a beautiful young fairy woman and the fire and the shelter and couldn't figure why people had ever stopped living in caves.

I had two cigarettes stashed in a plastic bag wrapped up in a rubber band and we shared them both in the best smoke anyone ever had. We told funny stories and laughed as we picked our way through a box of raisins I found in another pocket and we were like kings and queens.

And then I saw my first wild, living, breathing wild pig.

It passed through the trees just across from our shelter and it was magical like everything else there that day. He was huge and powerful, so much more than I expected, but low to the ground and with compacted muscle and tusks with yellow eyes and thick black hair. The girl held her finger to her lips as I caught my breath and she whispered in my ear like a serpent, 'Seeeee him! Seeeee what you have come to kill, boarssssslayer . . . The thrill of the hunt is the chase not the kill. The chase is life and all the excccitement of life and all the fun and energy of life. The kill is the end of life, sadness, colourless, the end of the heartbeat. The heartbeat is the most beautiful sound in all the world, the sound of the world itself. A heartbeat . . .' And the pig was gone back into the mist and trees, beautiful and primal and masculine and dumb and simple and I wouldn't want to see it killed and wouldn't kill it and wouldn't eat it neither and I swore a solemn oath. It was too real and alive and too important and ancient and pure.

When the rain stopped we headed up a path I would never have seen if I was alone and the Wizard and the Fairy Girl both put on long thick woollen jumpers and she tied her hair up and walked ahead stroking the bushes as she went. Her jumper reached the hem of her dress midway down her thighs so it looked like she wore no dress at all. Her thighs were strong and perfectly shaped and her calves were like teardrops and she wore army-style combat boots only half laced up.

I was expecting a long and hard journey like the one that had got me to the river, but we were back on the path real quick because I had walked circles and figure eights in my confusion and lost isn't about distance and you can be lost in your favourite armchair in your own front room and I learned that later and lost isn't about place but time and mind and I learned that later too.

We came around a tight bend and jammed into the trees was Leon's truck and close off we heard voices and dogs and I said this is my friend's truck and I offered them a ride home but the Wizard said no and he shook my hand and left me there. I sat on the tailgate of the truck like a half-drowned Buddha and before she vanished into the trees the Fairy Girl turned and smiled and she blew me a kiss and the Wizard laughed and walked ahead.

When no one could see I reached up and caught that kiss and she turned again and caught me in the act and her features were perfect and hair red and waves of bronze and her legs bare and her dress pressed down under the woolly sweater and her boots all muddy and she looked cold and red-cheeked and knock-kneed and perfectly pure and she smiled, saying, 'My name's Melody . . . Melody Grace, by the way . . .' And I shivered at the perfection of it. Melody Grace. Melody Grace happens to be my favourite perfect lady's name and it was spring rain and summer sun and winter snow and everything perfect and right and magical in the whole wide universe and all the bells of all the world chimed her name and she was gone like mist into the forest and then I breathed.

*

Leon and Johnny were back shortly after with the dogs yapping and a big boar roped on Johnny's back with its mouth held open with a stick and its head up over Johnny's like an ancient war helmet. Johnny was sweating and bent under its weight and it was one hell of a pig but only half the size of the beast I had seen. Its throat was a torn wide slash of flesh and blood and its tusks white and mottled yellow and its eyes stared black and red and its face was messed-up raw.

Leon had Johnny's backpack worn on his chest and he dumped it before helping unload the boar, then straight away he locked up his short-barrelled rifle in the truck and they looked me over and in that way experienced woodsmen know. They knew straight off I had got lost and started talking about me like I was invisible and they mocked people for getting lost and they were mocking townies as if being from a town was a crime, and even the dogs ignored me.

The hunters dried down the dogs with old beach towels and checked them two or three times for wounds but they were all good and they put the dogs in their cages, then they loaded the pig on top of the dog cages and lashed it down and got back in the truck and still they never spoke to me and I just slid in beside Johnny.

Leon tapped a magic tune on the steering wheel which he always did to ensure a first-time start and turned the key in the ignition one click, waited for the coil light to go out and tapped the tune again then turned it another click and the truck rumbled into life as the rain started to drift down again and the boys started laughing but I said nothing. We lit cigarettes before we bounced back down the track. I was wet and cold and starting to feel the tiredness and hunger so I leaned into Johnny and wedged myself between him and the door and footwell.

It was less than a mile when we passed the Wizard and Melody Grace and I strained to see her and my heart leapt when she came into view so I actually felt it in my chest and I wasn't expecting that and had never had it before. They stepped aside to let the truck pass and Johnny looked to the couple who looked away.

'They were at the river,' I said and wished I hadn't straight away.

'What river?' Johnny studied me hard. 'There's no river for about twenty miles, no way you could've walked to the river and back today!'

That sealed it for me. Magic had happened. 'There was a river.'

'Ain't a river . . . So, they your friends?' Johnny grinned at me. 'Buddies?'

I shrugged. 'Just people.'

Johnny laughed. 'You keeping secrets?'

'No . . .'

'That's Dirty Dick Dave and Twenty,' Leon said and he had slowed down as we approached so we kept pace with them a while. When she realised we were looking Melody Grace dropped her head even more and I knew the couple were uncomfortable being shadowed by the truck and I would have been too.

'What kind of names are they?' Johnny asked.

'Dirty Dick Dave and the Twenty Dollar Whore,' Leon whispered like they might hear him and waved grudgingly as we crept past, but neither the Wizard nor Melody Grace waved back.

'So . . . what kind of names are they?' Johnny asked again.

'Accurate adjectives buddy . . . Dirty Dick Dave will put his dick in anything and fuck anything with a pulse however filthy, so his dick is a miracle of fucking science just by staying attached to his scrawny body, and Twenty will do anything with anyone for twenty bucks. She's a boat's girl mate. Do the whole crew in a night. She is pure oxygen to lonely desperate and pitifully impoverished men . . . . Especially fishermen. Twenty bucks and you can spit roast her.'

I was sick. He was a liar and it turned me mad.

Johnny said, 'Have we got twenty bucks?'

I could feel Leon's words distorting the air and I wanted to kill him right there and then and I was a bomb about to blow and was sick right in my stomach, not because she might be that thing he said but because someone was saying it who couldn't see she was a fairy girl and I was trying to get my knife and stab him right in the neck and filthy mouth but I couldn't get it because I was too jammed tight between the door and Johnny, so I just wriggled and squirmed.

Leon said, 'I'm hungry and tired and I'm not fucking nothing that cheap and neither are you two! Your cock'll fall off! I know it . . . Mine will. We're not Dirty Dick and our dicks will not survive. Heard it happened to a fella a few years ago after a trip to Thailand. His name was Phil, now they call him Phillis. Silly-Phillis . . .'

I couldn't find words and couldn't get my knife but there were tears running down my face and they were for rage and sadness that someone could say such things and even if she was the Twenty Dollar Whore I didn't care and I didn't care one bit and I would kill anyone for her and even myself.

I choked like something was in my throat, so Johnny looked at me and studied me a bit and seeing something was wrong he frowned and brought his face close. Sensing my trembles and seeing my eyes and cheeks wet with crying he wiped my face without speaking and then I got my hand on my knife and straight away his arm went across mine and he turned to Leon. 'Just fucking drive,' he said. 'And shut up.'

Leon didn't know nothing about what was happening beside him but he drove on faster, revving the truck and blasting the horn.

Johnny didn't let me go for a good while, he just whispered in my ear to be 'shhh now, shhh . . .' like I was a horse and he wiped my face more.

In my soul or my gut something was deeply wounded and I loved Melody Grace even more than before like she was an injured bird and my dad always fixed up injured birds and made them well and sent them back to fly again and I didn't understand how Leon could be so wrong and mean and there was a knot inside me and I didn't even want to look at him or breathe the same air as him and I sat with my forehead against the window waiting to get home.

A couple of times Leon spoke to me but Johnny always took the question like I was a mute and eventually he told him I was asleep and I closed my eyes to help the deception and Johnny kept his hand on me and I didn't make no sounds.

Halfway back home we pulled into a forest layby to skin and butcher the pig and there were big steel bins in the layby just for that purpose because it was a hunters' route and it's no good burying guts because Johnny said nothing ever gets buried and stays buried. Johnny said the bits we didn't want would go in the bins and get collected and even the skin would be minced and fed to cage-reared pigs, the sort people buy as bacon. I didn't like the idea of cannibalistic pigs and my face must have given up my doubts but Johnny was certain and swore it and said the heart and brains and liver and kidney would go to the dogs and we would eat the rest.

As the boar was prepared and reduced to steaks and joints and ruined into parcels of meat I kept looking up the road in case Melody Grace came walking past, and Johnny whispered to me that she would be walking a good hour unless they had a car hidden up there.

He put his arm around my shoulder like a big brother would if I had one and he sighed and whispered, 'You like her eh? So she's a whore, so what? She's still human, still a woman, still got a heart beating in her chest. If you like her you like her. It ain't no perfect world. I once liked a chick who was a vegetarian. How fucking sick is that?' He held up the blooded skinning knife. 'And don't be so sore with Leon. He was only talking shit. He liked a girl once and she didn't like him back so he says shit and sometimes he doesn't like the fairer sex. Makes him feel better to say mean shit. Like he ain't missing nothing.' And he took my knife from its sheath as he spoke as easy as taking a lollipop off a toddler and slipped it in his belt. 'Don't blame him for it.'

But I couldn't tell him that I didn't like her, *like* was too weak a word, I was in love, proper love, and it was a curse for sure and all the alarm bells were sounding in all my body because woman love is a dangerous thing and not something anyone wants because it brings pain you can't control and it's a one-way ticket to an unknown country full of earthquakes and volcanoes and woe and you walk that Romeo walk all alone right into the mouth of grief and hell and destitution and loss itself, and I heard grown men say so. Leon had already forgotten Melody Grace and he and Johnny were talking about cooking up the pig for dinner and how best to sear in the taste and I was properly glad of that diversion and we drove home slow.

The temperature was dropping even lower and smelled of snow and Leon reckoned there would be a drop after dark and

146

it would be the last snowfall before spring woke up properly and when he said that stuff he was usually right.

I was dead tired and my gut was twisted tight, so that night I kept my oath not to eat of the pig and I was in bed while boys were eating and talking round the firepit on the front quad. I could smell the pig fat even inside the house and the boys were making a big hoo-ha about the pork and filling their bellies in the dark, which would usually lull me off good but I couldn't stop thinking of Melody Grace, and I wanted to run into town just in case I might catch a glimpse of her but it was dark and freezing and flurries of snow were starting to build up and look in from the window frames so I lay still and kept warm and planned our wedding and named our children.

Eighteen

When I woke it was quiet and still deep night. The glow of the flames from the firepit had stopped lighting the north windows orange and although I was instantly wide awake I could tell it was a long way from morning.

It was darker in the dorm than usual. No one was reading by torches and no one burning a lamp and I was startled by the solid blackness and I stared hard ahead, knowing for sure there were things in that blackness – doors, beds, cubes, walls, living sleeping boys and mice and frozen marionettes – but I couldn't see them. I thought maybe I needed to pee, and as soon as you think that you need to whether you needed to or not, so I got out of bed and pulled up the blankets behind me so it would be warm when I got back in and braced myself to go pee and it was cold as ice.

I stood in the passageway that split the cubicles east to west and knew directly in front of me, maybe twenty or so steps, was the fire door with a meshed glass panel, but however hard I stared all I could see was blackness. It was as though my eyes were closed and I was staring against my own lids and I reached up and felt my eyes to make sure they were open and I couldn't even hear boys breathing or muttering or snoring in their sleep and you could always always hear that.

I walked to the windows and wiped a hole in the condensation.

The sky was clear and there was light snow on the windows and there was a moon and stars outside and as I peered out I could see all the marvels of the night sky but the light of them stars and that moon just bounced off the windows like they were mirrors and didn't penetrate and I knew at least there should be enough light to cast shadows and shapes, but on that night there were no shadows and it was the blackness of a sealed and windowless vault.

I walked like a zombie with my arms outstretched so I wouldn't walk into the fire door but I still walked into it too hard and had to fumble to the bathroom feeling my way along the walls and had to guess where to aim my pee. White flecks swimmed across my vision and floated like fireflies but they were in my eyes or brain or nerves and outside of me there was no light, no sounds, no world at all it seemed, and then I knew he was there before I saw him, and I stared into the blackness and then I saw him slowly like he grew his shape from the darkness itself and a pale kid with a long face and long hair emerged, not living and solid but a reflection held and suspended in the air right before me, and only he was lit and his light didn't spread so I saw him but nothing around him and if I hadn't already peed I would have peed myself then. As he came clearer I saw his face was banged up and bruised and cut all over one side and all smashed on that side so he looked raw and torn and he looked wet too.

I reached for the door handle to open the bathroom door so I could get away and stepped to go through it all at once but the door slammed shut and I crashed straight into it and bounced off and I was trapped and my breathing was shallow and I just stayed against the door for a while not wanting to turn and face him and not able to escape.

'Can you see me?' the ghost asked and he reached out and his hand was on my shoulder and he turned me gently to face him and I saw him clearly and he was a boy like me but not like me no more.

I tried to open the door again because I was needing to run but it opened just an inch and slammed shut again and it took all my strength and heroic instincts not to fall down, and just breathing was hard because something gripped my lungs and my heart was racing and I knew if I fell down I might never rise again because down was so dark and deep. The ghost leaned closer, too close, so that I turned my face from him. 'Can you see me?' the boy ghost asked again. 'You can, can't you?'

'Yes . . .' I think I mewled.

'Don't look away. Tell me . . . How do I look?' He sounded just like any other kid before a night on the town. He was older than me and his words were well spoken but he was still a kid.

'I don't see my own face, you see? In mirrors or the glass . . . I see how I was but not how I am. How am I?'

I didn't want to tell him he looked so banged up and ugly. 'You're not very clear, not well defined . . .'

'You can fucking talk!' the ghost scoffed, and he laughed. 'I mean, do I look good?'

'You're dead . . .' I said.

'But . . . I remember . . . the front field. Football. The boys . . . Do I look good?'

'You look . . . like a ghost. Good for a ghost though . . . And bruised and cut.' I pointed to his face reaching out then pulling my hand back and I realised one eye was out of its socket. 'Am I going to die? Have you come to take me?' I sounded pathetic and hated my voice and its tremor and I was trembling and it was in my voice, and my toes and even my ears were trembling.

He smiled ugly. 'Do I look like a fucking bus driver? No. You will get there when you get there. Or here when you get here . . . or whatever. Not sure. So stop shaking, you're an embarrassment! Man the fuck up.'

'Why are you here then?'

'We're always here,' he said. 'I'm . . . Sam. Why am I fucking here? Are you serious? Is this a fucking philosophy class? Why are *you* here? Prick!'

'You're a ghost?' I mumbled.

'So it seems. Big fucking deal. And you're a chicken! Look at yourself, all goose bumped. Cluck cluck, fucking cluck. Fuck . . . And don't mumble.'

He stayed there right in front of me looking me over with contempt and I didn't know what to do or say next because nothing prepares you for your first close-up and personal ghost encounter. Then he said, 'I need you to do something for me. We, from the other side, need you to do this. You have been chosen . . . a message, from the dead to the living . . . Will you? Will you?' He moaned and his voice drifted. 'A messaaaaage . . .'

I nodded and was excited and I was chosen and Sam looked me up and down and smiled widely. His smile was crooked and showed the teeth in the bashed side of his face were smashed and bloodied and on the same side of his face his eye hanged loose like the socket was smashed, not dangling but loose, and he must have died of them wounds and I was sorry for him as I was afraid of him. The eye didn't see me, so whatever had done that to him had blinded that eye and smashed his handsome face and it must have been brutal and violent and painful and he was disfigured so his echo wasn't pure like it should have been and I felt pity and loathing and then shame for my loathing.

'I will . . .'

He came even closer so my face chilled. I was trembling less because the pity and shame forced down the fear. 'Are you sure?'

'Of course . . .'

'You swear?'

I swore.

'On your eternal soul?'

I swore on my eternal soul and he nodded slowly and thanked me.

'Go to the headmaster, whatever his name is now . . . at assembly, whenever assembly is. Will you?'

I nodded again.

'Promise me? Promise an old Fell boy. A Fell boy like you. It's important?'

I nodded more. 'I promise. Of course I will. I swear.'

'Stop fucking mumbling! Go to him in his gowns and finery. And tell him . . . tell him . . . he's an ugly bloated boy-fucking cunt.'

The ghost just stared at me in all earnest sincerity for a few more moments then laughed and laughed and laughed clutching his belly and the air swirled and the door threw open so hard its wire mesh reinforced glass pane shattered and hanged in its frame like Sam's eye, and he was gone and so was my pity and back was my terror as the air around me erupted in the violence of his leaving.

I ran to my bed in the solid blind darkness and hit every object and bounced off every wall in my panic and I dived under my covers and realised I was frozen and sweating too. My heart was beating so fast it was a constant vibration and I was scared to my core so I quivered like a leaf.

A little later Johnny came to me and I felt the weight and pressure of a body sitting down and at first I flinched away thinking it was the ghost come to my room and I reached out timid and blind in the dark and my hand touched a living shoulder and Johnny took my hand to his face and I felt his features, his chin and cheek and nose, sharp and straight and proportioned and alive and I was so relieved that it was him and he was a living person that I almost cried. He took my hand to his chest and he was cold as marble so when he slid under the blankets I shivered even before we touched.

In the complete dark all there is, is touch and scent and sense and the soft sounds of breath and then my ear went against his chest and I heard his heartbeat and it was like Melody Grace said, the sweetest sound in all the world, and I told him what she had said and I listened to his chest and stroking my hair he whispered, 'If you put your ear to a stag's chest after a good shot but when its heart's still beating and it's dying and you listen you hear the heart beating and when it stops it's like all the good in the world stops too. The girl you met in the forest is right. It's like God dies with the end of the heartbeat, again and again and again. You never can get past that silence. It's an awful, awful silence. I hate that silence when the stag dies.'

'Why kill the stag then?'

'I guess . . . In the end it tastes so fucking good.' And we slid deep under the blankets. 'And once you done it once, the rest is easy. That's why they blood hunters young. By the time you know how fucked up you are, you're fucked up.'

We warmed quick and wriggled with the simple joy of heat and in the darkest cold desert of yourself, if by some miracle you come by the warm touch of a human being and their scent and breath, even if it's stale and too sweet, you cling to it, savour it and wrap yourself in it, milking it for everything and every second and you hope with all your strength it won't be taken away, and heaven is company and touch and a heartbeat and a breath and heaven is when you're not alone any more. Johnny hushed me and kissed me and I tasted him and he tasted me and he wanted me that night and I let him have me all, and afterwards I told him my true-life ghost story and he shushed me and didn't believe me and I could tell. I didn't talk a single word more because I was scared of the ghost and scared of what I had done and because when the demons are roaming in the night you don't want them to find you and they find you by the trembles of the air when you shiver or speak. I held on to Johnny and he held me back and being together made us stronger and braver and I was in a boy's arms but as I drifted to sleep Melody Grace's face was there right in front of me, elflike and smiling. When Johnny and me kissed goodnight I was kissing her lips but I didn't tell him and I was truly grateful for his arms and legs and love.

*

Snow came all night and stayed for many days and nights but it was good snow and deep enough to close us all in so all we had to do was read and trudge to the dining hall and play cards, keeping warm as we could and riding a sledge and anything else that would slide.

Over those frozen days I built a pigeon loft on the roof out of old wooden pallets that someone had safe-stored behind the bike shed and chicken wire I stole from a garden shed in the lane at the back of Fell, and it would hold ten pairs of pigeons and I lined it with layers of newspaper and grey prison-issue blankets to keep out the worst cold. Long ago the bike shed roof had been given shiny new iron over the torn-up old stuff that had worn paper thin, so I stole that old rusty iron from underneath the newer stuff and used it to weather-tight the loft. I got Humphrey and Lefty to help me lift and carry and spent two days banging nails and sawing planks with frozen hands. I stole hinges from windows in the house to hang the wire mesh door and nailed those windows so they couldn't be used but wouldn't fall out neither.

When I was done it was the finest and proudest pigeon loft in Cutter and maybe the county and we all reckoned honestly it looked even better than the pictures in *Ditchfields Little Wonder Book* number 16, but maybe we were being biased. I had a loft and it was good and I made it and I even thought to bang in nails so I could hang up a torch and light up the dark and not everyone would have thought of that. Everyone who helped me carved their names in the wood and thought it would last for ever because no one ever came up on that roof except us and it was sure solidly built. Even when the snow blew near horizontal it didn't get inside and I thought maybe you could live in it with the birds themselves, just about.

The third day just about every boy in Fell found their way onto the roof to see it and even the farm boys with good building skills said how good it was and all I needed now was the birds.

The freeze wasn't letting up so after another day inside I went to town anyway, slipping and sliding on the black ice. Town was a half-hour walk and on the ice it took a lot longer, but I'd watched the flock of rollers over the town a hundred times from the roof and mentally plotted their movements and had a picture of their roost within a couple of streets down near the port and knew that's where their loft must be. Whoever owned them had bred them good and I could tell they were full-blood Birminghams, which is rare thing. If I could find where they lived I might get their owner to let me have a pair and I'd even be willing to work off their price if he had jobs about his place that needed young hands. In my mind it was all planned out, even what I would say when I knocked on his door and what they would be called, and I would clean his car and split some wood for him because he would be old and tired, and I could look for Melody Grace too while I did the commute back and forth.

Every second of every minute she was in my head smiling and staring at me with those watery eyes and it was perfect and agony all at once because there was no escape. She was the shadow that followed my thoughts and came in my dreams and not knowing her more and not having her company made a terrible nagging deep inside me.

School closed because of the snow and ice and we built the biggest snowman ever and encased some poor kid in it for long enough to nearly kill him and had snowball wars and sledged and rolled down the hills.

Moby's family never did come to take us for lunch, not Sunday or any day, but he stayed optimistic and later I stole a fruit cake in a box from Quick Save Grocery and took it to him when I got home and we dressed up smart and laid a table, invited friends, and ate it with steaming hot cups of English Breakfast tea and I stole that too, not because I liked it but I couldn't reach the hot chocolate.

Every day I walked the streets and the alleys around the port and docks and marina and around the town and all the way to the beach. I nearly froze to death and never saw no pigeon lofts but I got to know the town pretty good and better than a local.

I found about twenty bars and two brothels and a fish restaurant and a dozen coffee shops. There was a cool magic-trick store in a narrow street next to a Cuban café that sold drugs wrapped in tinfoil and gave me a bowl of hot spicy soup to warm me up and some crusty oily bread every time I passed. There was a real fat guy played guitar in there who looked like a fat Cuban Santa and he always jumped up when I passed and called me inside in Spanish or Cuban or Latin and grinned wide as he ladled soup into a big old bowl, making me sit down and eat as he played guitar for me and sang. He told me his name was Riel and he had a powerful sense of kindness about him so he was everyone's favourite fat Cuban Santa. There were always people in that café and when I told Johnny he said the café was that way day and night and a genuine bonafide community hub. One day I want a café like that and will paint it terracotta and pastel blue and maybe one day I could run away and hide out with them and be a Cuban. They were real nice people, as criminals and gangsters and illegal immigrants usually are.

Out back of the café was a boxing ring and speedballs and bags and Cuban boys trained and sparred and there was a lean mean gangster called Jesus and he never said much but he was important and he looked dangerous and handsome and the other Cubans honoured him. Some of them boys were good boxers and real natural and they moved different to Lefty and me and their feet were like dancers feet and they threw punches from all angles and fast. There was a couple who dealt drugs but not to the other boxers. One of them came over to me one time and held up a wrap but the fat Santa Riel said something in Spanish and smacked him with a soupy wooden spatula and the boy turned on his heel like a wriggly dancer and walked away laughing. I liked that café mucho and thought it would be good

157

to train there sometimes, maybe when I got a bit older and more experienced. The older fighters were prize fighters who did their fighting for money, and some who were nearly twenty or even older had about a hundred fights under their belts because they were fighting for rent money whereas Lincoln Valley was just for amateurs and we fought for glory.

A few doors down was a Mexican café with killer hot bolillos and the sweetest churros you ever tasted and that was on their sign outside and they were open all day and all night too. In the next street was Skinny Joe's fried chicken shop and its smell filled the whole street and just walking past made you greasy and the fattest islanders hanged out there and Joe wasn't skinny. I reckon eating must be big business but hard work because most of the people working in those houses were lean and trim and most of the people eating in them were not, and that's being polite. When the wind ripped through the streets and banged the shutters I thought maybe I could have a good life in a café and you could never be lonely in a café especially if you had a family running it. That soup in little Cuba was the first time I ever ate in a formal restaurant setting and it was a real pleasure and something to do dressed up with a lady. I thought maybe I would take Melody Grace there for lunch and for dinner and on special occasions to La Gourmandize French Café where all the waitresses were pretty and the maître d' was like a Parisian beauty from the black and whites. French music played there and the pretty waitresses smiled and I don't know the French language professionally but it sounded pretty as the ladies.

Despite the ice inside the windows and the deathly cold air that was nearly solid in my lungs the cherry blossom tree just before the woods was starting to bud and that meant spring was properly in the mind of the earth and soon we would be browning on the beach and swimming in the sea, so we stayed cocooned and patient and positive, and finding the cafés had comforted me and knowing people were awake and talking and laughing all night long meant there were no more nights as dark as before or as lonely and never would be again.

Nineteen

When the snow cleared up, the sludge came and the weather-board houses looked as sad and miserable and broken down and peeling as old people alone in a park. Then the streets flooded as the drains got overwhelmed with the melt so I got wet feet for a few days and still didn't find where the rollers lived or catch any sight of Melody Grace.

Two Saturdays later, spring was on the world properly and Johnny and me posted the letter to Lilly. It had gathered a lot of dust and we added a little extra note from Johnny because he said he felt for Lilly like I felt for Melody Grace, which I doubted sincerely because what I was feeling was not a common thing but I didn't say nothing against him because he sounded serious and you should never question someone's love declarations.

That same day Johnny and me went on his dirt bike to the beach at sunset so we could talk about love and practise dancing without anyone overhearing us or watching. The sun set in the spectacular and dramatic way that was its habit on that beach in those days so people were looking up trying to work out its light and every night it was different and startling in some way that it hadn't been before. Before the sun even set it was shrouded in clouds of golden orange and red molten gold and copper tsunamis rolled under and before it in all the stages of heating and cooling, and colour was poured across the sky all at once and it made me frown and be dismayed that it was so beautiful and so fleeting, and I felt the infinity of space and atmospheres and clouds and all the magic of it and I was uplifted. I wasn't godly but I hoped there was a god because only a really creative artist of a god would invent that kind of ending to the day. He or She or It or Them was saying, *Look, whatever else is going on in your fucked up little ant lives, look up, look up and rejoice! See what I done . . . Fucking get a load of this antpeople! Am I God or what?*

Sunset was a final kiss of a day lived right through and a reminder before the dark came that the dreaded sorrow of night would pass and these colours would come again and again if you only looked for them and looked up. And we were brave then and danced and leapt around like fools bathed bronze. We danced until it was all so blue dark we couldn't see a thing except the pale yellow crescent moon and a bright white star swinging below it. There was a unicyclist riding circles below the dunes where the sand was firm like stone but we lost him sometime after sunset which was just as well because Johnny said he was going to punch him on principle. Johnny would have lost that fight though because I'd seen that man walking tightrope on a line between posts on the top of the sands and doing handstand and practising some kind of martial art, so he might have been carny weird but he was no clown and would have cut my Johnny down.

When we got home Moby was once again doing the dance of a thousand veils and getting his boobies out, which he was starting to enjoy a bit too much, and we got drunk on whisky a boy brought from home. Two big bottles of expensive single malt and one of them was Irish and it damn near killed me and I could feel brain cells dying and I liked it. Valerie came too and made Leon and Big Ben and Johnny all happy one by one.

She offered to make Lefty happy too but he had Jesus (Jewish Jesus not Cuban Jesus) and that night as Humphrey snored and smacked his lips she came to my bed with Johnny and he left her with me. It was my first time with a real lady and I tried to resist because I wanted to be with Melody Grace and I wanted to be faithful and I was really scared and didn't know what to do, but Valerie told me it was OK and made me be still first then tremble and it was life changing and much better than doing it to myself by a million miles and afterwards I knew there was no way I could have stayed faithful and I wasn't proud to know it.

Valerie was the real thing for sure and I could tell you what she did and how but that would be wrong and compromise her modesty and suffice to say I was shattered and remade and shattered and remade several times in just a few minutes and when she left I had this violent twitch in my right leg that wouldn't let up and my hands had felt the most perfect things and shapes and textures, and I had smelled and tasted pure heavenly honey. I never knew a lady's skin was so soft and so firm and so shaped and so warm and so perfect. The shapes I had looked at and admired for so long were just a taster and the touching and the scent and the feel and the privilege of her sharing her body and mouth and juices with mine took me to a new place and I couldn't even imagine that place before. Even the feel and smell of her hair and the little noises she made were unimaginable and it was like everything made sense and I knew that God had made something even more special than sunsets and it was called Sex and I was saying over and over, 'Holy Fuck! Thank you Jesus, thank you God, thank you Jesus, thank you God', and after she was gone I kept laughing and I had bliss because everyone knows if a man can fight and fuck he has all the world and I looked over at Humphrey and he had one eye open and a thumb up. His other hand was busy. Then we smoked wrapped in blankets by a window wide open to the night and I wasn't afraid that night and nothing banishes fear in the dark like sex and sex is perfect and you can't do it too much and that's about all the sex education anyone needs. I don't know how many girls like Valerie there are on Earth but for sure the world needs more and if you told me making love with Valerie or Melody Grace would be my death one minute afterwards, I would still do it, and happily, and so would any man.

One day soon after sexnight, Humphrey returned from a weekend home and brought me two of the finest plumpest and healthiest looking Blue Checker racing pigeons you ever saw. He lived miles off-grid and on the lane to his place was a pigeon fancier and Humphrey cut his lawn and sanded his deck and promised to keep his little demonic sister away and the man had paid him out with the two birds in a little crate so they wouldn't bounce around.

I ran them up to the roof and one by one took them out and nursed them and they were fine and strong and firm and real prime. You could tell they had been handled before but not much and their eyes were lit up bright and their hearts were pounding and racing but they weren't panting or stressed and I put them safe in the loft. I sat watching them for hours every day just making soothing sounds and getting in with them so they knew I was their friend and feeding them just a little and not too much. They weren't rollers but they were mine and no one but me was allowed to touch them, but I let other boys come and watch and there was something soothing and relaxing about them and even boys who thought keeping pigeons was a crazy old man hobby got some peace from them including Leon and he believed every animal lived in order to be killed.

One evening Leon came up on the roof with his rifle and scope and got a bead on the rollers over the port hills and didn't tell me what for. I knew he wasn't going to shoot them because he was a real responsible gun handler and wouldn't put a shot blind over a town and I thought he was just practising tracking them across the sky, but he watched them patiently until they were gone home and like the hunter he was he managed to follow them all the way down. He didn't say nothing to me and he had been quiet since the hunting trip and hadn't mentioned Melody Grace once or said sorry for offending my sensibilities and I knew when he came back a day later with four young squabs straight from the rollers coop that this was his way of making amends and I never said a word. I just took them in gently and gratefully and he knew all was good again.

The four babies took a lot of attention because they were real young and one boy gave me a sheepskin to line their box but in the bitter hours of night I kept them in a shoe box in my bed and put them out once the sun had risen and we stole them some feed and each day the birds got stronger and shone brighter. A lot of boys helped me because Johnny said it takes a village to raise a pigeon.

We planned Flight Day for two weeks later and a whole group of us agreed we were going to meet up on the roof with food and beer and wine and whisky and cigarettes and maybe some weed and bread and cheese and malted oat crackers and water wafers and anything else we could steal. The boy with the cello said he would join us and play music to uplift the soul and we would let the two adults have their first short flight and let the babies watch. We decided the adult birds would know where home was by then and they could have a wing stretcher an hour before dusk so they wouldn't go all day and not come back.

I figured if we left it late the coming night would reign them in naturally. Johnny said he would bring the rum. He was drinking a lot of rum lately on account of being a pirate and he had an eye patch too which he only wore when the rum was flowing.

For many days then there was peace and even the nights were quiet and the radio played crooners and faraway noises from the ghettos and boulevards and alleyways and nightclubs. I was a wisp of breath and nothing more and on some nights all I could see was Melody Grace's perfect watery eyes looking at me from within my own closed lids.

Twenty

Come Flight Day we were all nervous in case we lost the Blue Checkers and I called them Bertha and Billy and I was most nervous of all and felt sick.

Usually I would feed them in the morning with good grain from an old tea tin which I rattled before I opened it and added a little grit and I always picked it all up after so they were used to eating up good and quick, but I hadn't fed them that whole day long so they were hungry and I figured I could open up the loft and let them fly and they would do a few circles and come right back when I rattled the tin. They would go right high and see the sun just short of setting over the bay and tuck their wings and come on home and that was the whole of the plan.

There were ten of us up on the roof just waiting and watching, including Carlos who we had to prise out of his chair and haul up through the hatch and then link ropes to drag his wheelchair up the outside of the building at the back because being away from that chair made him real angsty, and we had a bottle of whisky and a big jug of cheap rum and some smokes and cheese and bread so he settled with a few swallows of hot rum and we stayed close to him because the roof had a natural gentle slope into gutters and we didn't want him rolling off. There was nervous chatter for a while then it settled and I knew it was my time and I felt nervous like it was me myself going to fly. I explained to the boys that the birds we were about to fly were Blue Checkers and not rollers so they wouldn't be doing any showy aerobatics and the boys nodded silent and expectant.

I went into the loft quiet and soft and Bertha and Billy were easy for me to gather up and bring out and I whispered to them that the pressure was on and I whispered more and asked them to fly beautiful and put on a fine show for the boys and to please come back. The baby rollers were getting big and watched and cooed so peaceful and deep.

I took the Checkers to my face and nuzzled them and in that lowing light their blue was lifted up so they glowed and I loved them even more because I knew I might lose them for good when I sent them up.

I came out of the loft and stood looking at the sky. There was maybe an hour and a half of light left. I felt Johnny's hand light on my back in reassurance and Leon picked up the rifle and checked the scope so he could track them if they headed off. He winked at me to reassure me he wasn't going to shoot them down and I knew he wouldn't even though he was a natural born killer and that's what Johnny said he was and Johnny knew all about NBKs. Johnny kept his hand on me and those were precious minutes. Sometimes a hand on your back just makes you tingle and shiver and grow into the other person so you become two, three, four people strong. That's how a single person can be an army.

I held onto Bertha, passed Billy to Johnny, and he kissed his beak gently and at the same time we raised them up high and opened our hands, giving them just a tiny shove upwards so they had to fly or fall.

They fluttered clumsily like they'd forgotten how to fly and for a moment they dropped, then with a flick they were up and up and they flicked their wings and went up and in silence up. We cheered and whooped because we had been holding our breaths and not moving and they went up and up like they were stirring up in a cyclone and they were magical against the reddening darkening sky and got tinier then lit up bright as the low sun lit their bellies so they looked like fireflies. Past them in the sky I knew the first stars would soon break night and I thought for a minute they might fly away into the Milky Way.

Suddenly Leon swung the rifle barrel across the sky in complete silence making everyone look to what he had seen but I couldn't see anything at first then I picked out a bird hovering and holding in one place, tiny and dark it wheeled and froze, wheeled and froze, and how Leon knew it was there was a miracle. Leon always took aim through his scope with his free eye open and narrow and watching and he had seen the hawk when it was just a spec and he watched it now through his scope. He whispered to me, 'We sent them up too soon . . . Hawk's still flying . . . Bring them home . . .'

And straight away I crashed into the loft, grabbed up the feed and lurched back out and I rattled the feed tin and raised it up above my head, shaking it and rattling it and banging it and holding back the urge to call and shout and scream because I knew they wouldn't hear me or know me that way. It looked for a few long seconds like they were heading off and I felt my heart sink and then the hawk rocketed up towards them and over the top of them and turned over to strike and I thought Leon would fire but he didn't and the pigeons broke apart from each other and dropped like stones and rolled over and over head over tail heading straight back towards the safety of the loft, tumbling all the way like the best rollers ever bred even though they weren't rollers. The hawk seemed confused by their lack of grace and order and the lowering light benefited Billy and Bertha and the hawk went for one then the other and locked onto the one to the left and I couldn't tell whether it was Billy or Bertha but the hawk was close and getting closer, then the pigeons suddenly stopped tumbling and cut and swerved and twisted cleverly so they came together and seemed to fly belly to belly, then weaved in and out platting the air behind them so the hawk didn't know which to strike and we all breathed faster. They confused that hawk and flew with instinct and skill, so they raced towards us and I swear their eyes were big and round as dinner plates and someone cheered in a half-choked way and both birds skimmed past me and into the loft like living bullets and I thought they would kill themselves hitting the mess but they pulled up hard as the hawk pulled away and hovered high above us and he looked down and marked our spot and Leon watched it the whole way, his movements smooth and fluid and his breathing level, and there was ice to him but he didn't take the shot.

Humphrey said, 'Shoot it Leon!' His voice was trembling and he clenched his fists.

But Leon just followed it with his rifle, his eye glued to the scope and his voice low and distant and full of depth, and it sounded strange, like the voice wasn't coming from him at all so it made me look at him and not my birds: 'Can't shoot it, scrote-boy. No. Safe. Shot. The bullet could fall anywhere. And when you kill something you give it the chance to come back as something better. Something greater. That creature . . . look at it . . . it can't come back better. Look at it! It's pure pure perfection. Shit . . . I couldn't kill it . . . I mean I could, I'm good enough. But I couldn't. It would be wrong . . . a late hunting hawk . . . cheeky, and clever too.' He breathed softly as it circled, 'Namaste . . . Namaste . . .'

169

'What does he mean?' Humphrey whispered to Johnny in a voice that instinctively mimicked the spirit-filled tone of Leon, 'What's Namaste?'

'Nothing . . . He's being profound.'

'Is that swearing?'

'No, that's profane, but it's the same shit.'

Leon looked at Johnny and laughed then he relaxed the rifle. 'Great pigeons . . . feed them extra!' he said and he left the roof.

Quietly everyone followed him and some patted me on my back like I had done something special or trained the Checkers to be so good at defensive flying and I wished I had because I could be rightly proud of such a thing but I had done nothing. Still, I was proud of my pigeons and they lived, which was all and was enough. The boys squeezed Carlos through the hatch and lowered his chair again without asking me to help and when I was finally alone in the dark I went in and stroked the pigeons, settling them and soothing them with a firm but soft hand and deep gentle cooing. They were hot and panting and glad of me and I cried because I thought I'd lost them and I was relieved and they cried too and told the squabs all about it and it was the best first flight they could have had because now they were as scared of losing me as I was of losing them.

After that I went to the roof every morning and every night and sometimes I skipped school and spent an hour or two during the day just handling my birds or watching them and talking gently about my day so they got to know me really good and knew what made me tick, and I could still get into town and look for Melody Grace and I looked late into every night without luck and I told my birds everything and they said they would look for her too, every time they took flight. Then one perfect fairy-tale evening just as night fingered across the sky and settled over the town and the lights of the houses and docks and ships lit up the dark sea like winking sparklers I saw her riding an Italian Vespa scooter. Her Vespa was decorated with painted flowers and lots of headlights and a long aerial wagging behind her and her tiny dress let her legs be shown as it blew in the wind and I swear I could see her knickers and her legs, and she wore high ankle work books and she wore an old army khaki long coat and it was torn and half open and loosely belted and a silver basin helmet with her red hair streaming behind her. I saw it all in an instant and I saw everyone look at her as she passed because she looked like a goddess streaking and falling straight from heaven and in that instant I saw everything and I chased her like a fool, with her red-lipsticked lips big as buses in my mind, and I ran behind her like a dog chasing a postman. I ran until my lungs were burnt out and she was so far gone towards the waterfront I had no idea which way to go but I could smell her scent in my nose so I sniffed the air and there was soap and perfume and roses and oil and engine and I knew she was still in town and real and that was a million bucks. I had hope again and if she rode that route once she might ride it often, so I resolved I would be waiting on Johnny's dirt bike next time and I would catch her or at least follow her so I would know better where to look in future and I had a good feeling about it and it was a good day and I had a plan.

The next week passed with no more sightings and all I did was get chased by cops who knew I was too young to road ride and the bike was illegal. They never caught me because they were fat and slow and dumb and I was fast as a falling pigeon and sharp as a chasing hawk. A truck driver offered me a ride in his cab and a hamburger (with double fries and a large shake) and all he wanted in return was a blowjob but I politely declined and took off.

Then days became weeks and maybe months so time seemed to claw its way through a spring marked first by the brilliance of buds breaking like fireworks along the branches of the cherry blossom trees then by heat and light and the greening of the trees and a thousand thousand flowerings but no more sign of Melody Grace. The birds flew every day and the squabs became strong adults and the flock was born and took shape and flew in perfect formation and I watched them in proud awe like they were my own much-loved children and if I had a house and a kitchen with a fridge I would put their shit on the fridge door like all proud parents do.

Lefty and me spent more time at boxing because the fighting season was coming and he was lined up to fight fifteen bouts ending in the Golden Gloves and Nationals and I was helping him prepare. Boxing is a solitary game so it's good to have someone to do the hard yards with, Coach Petey told us that all the time. 'Train together, work together, win together,' he said. We made sure each other were eating right and staying on the straight and narrow and sleeping well and sometimes we shared my cubicle when Humphrey was away, which was nice and we would talk about old-time fighters and how to hit the power line.

I still listened in to Lilly on the radio but she sounded far away and some nights she didn't come through at all. Whenever I got money for a stamp I would write her a letter but hardly ever got one back and the ones that did come got shorter so they were just notes and they got less talky like she was running out of words. Johnny was concerned at what he said was her *inappropriate brevity* and each time after a letter came he would get deeply thoughtful because time was passing and she was languishing and life was too short for that and it weighed on Johnny and me and we spoke again of breaking her out because words are powerful and once you say things out loud magic comes and those words get a life of their own and we hoped that by saying it we would make it manifest and be conjured.

Then Big Ben got a basketball scholarship letter for a college he never even applied to and he was sent there early to get his fitness up even though he was fit as a butcher's dog and he was leaving for ever and I never let on but the night I heard I picked my palm till it bled and I cried. Humphrey must have told him because next night he brought me a bottle of bourbon and a basketball vest that fit me like a dress and told me the college he was heading to and promised to write. He was no letter writer so I knew he was just saying stuff to ease the pain but I said I would look him up there sometime, and I hoped I would.

He sat close to me that night as we drank and mumbled in the darkness. 'This girl, Melody? I see Melody, I think it's her, parked along near the Big Red, you know, the red Big Red Liquor store?'

I didn't.

'Opposite the diesel silos down by the logs and trucks . . . over across the road. Look there.'

I had seen the diesel tanks on the way to the beach. They were huge and peeling and rusty and ranked up in rows on a slip road off the highway and there was a log park and massive container parks between the highway and the dock and the fish factories. The trucks would refuel from those tanks and some tanks were close to the water and ships would use those ones, but I had never looked around much or took too much notice because it was like a wasteland and industrial. I nodded and Big Ben smiled and it made his giant bulk seem vulnerable. 'Look opposite the tanks and you might get lucky.'

I nodded again and leaned into him and his arms just folded over me.

'And when you go to break out your Lilly, I will be there with you. I swear.' And I knew he meant it but I knew he wouldn't be and that was OK.

We drank that whole bottle and fell asleep on the floor covered in blankets and so drunk the morning was a dreaded and sand-dry painful place where regret stood over me like a giant masked sweaty Mexican wrestler dangling his privates in my face and a hammer pounded in my head so I thought I might be brain damaged for ever.

I had dribbled down my chin and wet myself a bit so there was a little circle on my pants and I needed to run to the toilet and pee but every running footfall burst in my head and my head throbbed like a big bass drum was being played right in the back of my skull and someone was clapping cymbals in my temples, but if I could spend every night drunk and snuggled up with a good friend I knew I would.

Once I got cleaned up Lefty took me for a run to punish me and make me sorry for drinking. 'You jus rooned three days of hard work!' he said, 'so we gonna run till you got no pook lef.' Lefty always trained and even ran with a gum shield in. He believed it made him used to it but it was a strange and unusual habit and I didn't argue, instead I suggested we ran to the water by way of the port road and diesel tanks, which was a good long way for a hungover trot, and Lefty was impressed and satisfied with such penance.

The cottages Big Ben mentioned were once waterside weatherboard fisherman's homes but land reclamations back along had pushed the water and beach back and now huge diesel tanks and container yards and the log park crowded across a road officially called a highway which was really just a busy as hell narrow little road. Them cottages were mostly red-stickered, which meant they were condemned and nobody was supposed to live in them, but they had all the magic of the waterfront that had been stolen and were a hundred years old and sweet and powdery as Turkish Delight and they were all out of place now and dwarfed by industry and machinery. They shone out like pearls even though some townspeople said they were slum huts and should be pulled down and plenty of people lived in them still and I reckoned they must be pearls, too.

I stopped running to look at them and Lefty thought I was taking a breather so he ran on and said he would pick me up on the way back. At least I think he said that, the gum shield made it almost impossible to understand him once he was breathing hard and drooling so I nodded and stretched as he ran off into the slatey haze.

There was a no-budget backpacker's all painted like a gypsy caravan and next to it was a grassy lot where just a redbrick chimney rose high from the earth with no walls around it and beside that was a doss house place for smack addicts and then a poets' café and a row of rundown old shacks that seemed empty, and further along there was an old abandoned chapel which slumped bad and ugly and sad because on one side its piles were broken and rotten and sunk. There was a high loose bank behind them that rose to a steep hill and the hill had slipped in the past and there were gaps along the way where cottages had been swept away by slides and time and dust and now a beaten-up car yard took up a long gap. Dead opposite where I stood was one cottage I couldn't see clear because it was behind a tall fence and the fence was covered in thick ivy and climbers with big clutches of small colourful flowers hanging off it like bunches of grapes.

I skipped across the road once the traffic showed me a gap and peeked through the tall solid gate. It didn't look like anyone was home so I slipped through and walked around. It was perfect and small and cute and although there was hardly more than walking space between the house and fence it was planted in wild flowers and overhead there were strings of fairy lights and colourful cotton flags. There was a table and chairs at all four corners of the house and the windows were tiny and divided up in even smaller squares and on two sides were white painted French doors. It was all white with pastel-blue window frames and a red iron roof. Behind it there was a path cut into the steep bank and from there I could see the roof was made up of a hundred pieces of rusty tin iron in a patchwork quilt and round back in the lee of the hill was the tiniest veggie patch you ever saw.

It was like a fairy cottage where everything was smaller than usual but enchanted and I knew for sure it was where Melody Grace would live. Some kind of magic was holding the steep hill at bay and a big tree leaned towards the roof but had only slipped so far then been held by a special spell. I wanted to look through the windows but didn't want to be so rude so I slipped back out and closed the gate and ducked over the road and waited for Lefty stepping and skipping from left to right to stop my bones getting too achy.

Lefty and me stopped at the Cubans on the way home and there was fish and coconut stew in a giant pot on a back burner in the kitchen for the fighters and ragamuffins and when we took in that smell it made me dribble and we were too polite to ask for anything for free but big fat Riel didn't need no asking and served us up a huge bowl each. He gave us hard greasy beautiful bread crusts too and as we ate one of the coaches came over and pinched the flesh on Lefty's back and then did mine to see how much fat we were packing and he pinched about four places. It was a common thing and we took no notice and we just kept eating the soup and bread and watching a TV high on the wall which was showing something in Spanish about love and dancing. Jesus came and sat with us but drank only black coffee with careful little sparrow sips from a tiny cup. The coach said some stuff in his Cuban Spanish to another man and Riel and Jesus and they nodded. Then the coach gave us the thumbs up, nodding and smiling . . . 'Lean . . .' he said in English, 'very good to be lean.'

Jesus smiled. 'He says you are lean. Good and lean.'

Lefty looked at. 'He said we're lean. Good and lean.'

'I know he did Lefty, he was speaking English.'

Jesus laughed and slapped Lefty on the thigh and shaking his head he tore off a piece of bread and dipped it into Lefty's soup, which was the Cuban way of saying Lefty was one of them and fully accepted like a Cuban, and I wanted him to dip it into my soup too but he never did. When he stood to leave though he gently pinched my cheek like an old aunty.

We walked the rest of the way home and Lefty asked me straight out if I had found Melody's pad and I was embarrassed that he knew me dropping out of the run was so I could dog-eye her place and I hadn't been totally straight with him and I told him what I found and he liked the sound of it. I told him about how it was like a secret cottage in some storybook and I didn't know the names of the flowers but he made me describe them in every detail and even their smell. As I told him and painted the word picture for him he told me their names and I didn't know if he was truthing or making them up to sound smart and tease me, but they were good names like Little Lady's Pockets and Peachy Pink Prickle Pods and it was a nice walk home with aching legs and a full belly and a heart full of hope.

Twenty-One

I went back to that cottage after lights out and saw a flowery Vespa scooter had been bumped up the steps and through the gate and that proved beyond question that Melody Grace lived there, and I should have left but I couldn't help having a peep and even though I'm not a pervert peeping made me tingle just a bit.

Inside the cottage a lamp was lit, throwing soft golden light and I could smell wood smoke and see faint trails of smoke against the dark sky where she had a fire going inside. The road was still busy and cranes were still moving logs over the way, all lit up with big white floodlights but it was quiet inside the fence and all around the cottage and I realised the high wooden fence and heavy foliage acted as a sound break, muffling the noises of the evil engines and all the world. I wanted to peer inside the windows but knew if I was caught it would be the end of us because I would be a peeping Tom and she would surely think me a pervert (which I am not) and look at me with contempt and I knew a clever plan was needed so I could bump into her accidentally on purpose and strike up a conversation and win her trust and then her love.

I trotted home slow and snuck into bed and decided Johnny would know how to bend the situation my way because bending situations was his speciality and maybe he would swing by before sleep did and I hoped he would.

Later Johnny sat on my bed in just his yellow and black polka-dot boxers and Leon joined him in camouflage pyjamas with little dead ducks embroidered on the collar and they listened to my dilemma and Leon said, 'You don't need a plan, you need a process', and Johnny nodded and blew a professional quality smoke ring. 'A good hunter don't trudge the woods, he waits where he knows the prey will be. A watering hole, a rutting spot, or a lair. You got her lair.'

'You do boy . . .' Johnny nodded. 'You do. And her rutting spot.'

'He does. And now you wait, morning and night to plot her movements. See the prey, plot the prey then on the third seeing, drop the sights between the eyes and put a slug in the forehead. See the prey, plot the prey, drop the prey. Unless you're using a bow, then you go for the heart and lungs shot, straight behind the front legs.' He poked me in the ribs. 'Bang.' And he took Johnny's smoke and drew hard.

'I don't want to kill her!'

'I know. But hunting's hunting. Don't matter if you're killing the prey or fucking it! Not that I've ever fucked prey!'

'That's not true,' Johnny said and he reached to take the cigarette back and Leon stubbed it sharp on Johnny's hand and Johnny squealed and jumped back and Leon flicked the butt at him and Johnny leapt off the bed as the butt bounced off him and tiny red smotes lit up the dark. We all got busy patting them out before my bed went up in flames and the two boys stood like gaunt white spectres as I searched my bed for embers and patted it all over. Johnny grabbed up the nub of cigarette and finished it.

'So to recap,' Johnny said softly, licking his hand. 'Go watch, see her once, plot her twice, move on three. Don't wait more than three unless you really have to, prey can change routines like hunters can. One, two and do the job. Like dancing the three-step.'

'What's a fucking three-step?' Leon said.

'A hunter's dance hombre. A bit more than a two-step, a bit less than a four.'

They giggled like little girls and wrapped themselves in blankets they took from Humphrey and went to bed.

After that Lefty and me ran her way a couple of times a week and with the evenings light and warm Johnny and me cut that way to the beach on our sunset trips and thus I kept watch on her place all hours and I tingled the whole time and couldn't think of nothing else.

See her, plot her, and bang . . . I just wasn't sure what the bang bit would be. To see her, that would be enough for now.

Twenty-Two

Roses smell like peaches and not many people know that and I learned it unexpectedly and you don't often smell flowers that clean. Usually in my limited flower experience the scent is just heady or heavy or just out of reach on the wind or carried on the sweet air in the rising heat of an early morning or a lot of flowers on flower stalls, and flower shops don't even smell at all but the roses in Melody's narrow garden smelled like peaches and soap. Them roses and some really colourful tiny button-like flowers whose name I'll never know wrapped themselves around the cottage in a tight belt of colour and scent and the summer wasn't even properly come yet so I knew that when it did the air there would just explode and with nowhere to escape in the high solid fenced garden the air would be heavy and sickly sweet and beautiful. I reckon it would be so heavy I might not be able to breathe and that's the garden you want if you have a garden at all, and to suffocate under the scent of those flowers would be a sweet death.

And insects. I never knew there were so many flower-loving creepy-crawlies. Lines of ants, tiny black and red and green strands of fine unbroken cotton thread marched up stems and over stalks and leaves and petals, and big shiny beetles polished as new pennies sneaked clumsy and funny over the dirt. There were even bugs I couldn't hardly see and I only knew they were there because they glittered in flight.

Come high summer the colours of the garden would erupt like the scent so you could barely stand to look at it and I just knew it. My eyes would be overcome and I would have to squint to see and when I told Lefty about the scent of roses he sniffed the air like he was there and nodded like he knew and told me green ants tasted of lime juice. I never knew that either and I could wash in them roses if they were soaked in water and I believe I would drink green ant juice instead of limeade.

At the back of the garden were runner beans strung up a back wall under the steep bank and in two homemade wooden troughs were plants neatly separated from the flowers and I knew they were important because they were alone in the troughs but they had no fruit so I identified them by clipping leaves and running to ask Mister Sesay one lunchtime because he was a lover of plants and growing things. Mister Sesay raised trees and bushes and shrubs in barrel tubs which he rented out to business functions for just enough money to cover the effort and he was fascinated by my cuttings and examined them like they were the most precious things he had ever seen. I told him where I got them and he was concerned and told me it was unsafe to spy on fairies and he was serious and I summoned up my courage and after he told me the plants were tomatoes and strawberries I asked him about the note he left for me that morning long ago at the Lincoln Valley Boxing Gym, and I asked him what was tilting at windmills and when are windmills giants and I said I didn't understand and he smiled and showed me a thick book and he read it with me a very little every day after and explained it and he told me sometimes monsters come as windmills, so tilt, he said, tilt, and the man in the book tilted, too.

I spied so much I came to know Melody Grace's home like it was my own and it had two bedrooms off a lounge and kitchen. In the lounge was a large old sofa made out like a patchwork quilt and sat facing it was a big ancient leather wingback armchair in deep brown leather. There was an old piano hand-painted white with more rows and chains of flowers painted all over it and entwined in vines of green with the lid up over the keys and sheet music set up and piles more on the top of it with a piano stool and in one corner of the room a cello and before that was a music stand and small wooden stool and there was hardly room left to move in that room.

A fireplace was painted white and the walls and ceilings were white too and the floor was stripped and varnished wood. In the fireplace was a potbellied stove well blacked and next to that a basket overfilled with little pale wood logs. That's all I could see in that room but it looked perfect and light and slight and fresh and alive.

Through a tiny window on the other side I could see into a small bedroom and I could see a sewing machine and fabrics and an easel and canvases and a telescope pointing straight up through a skylight. In one corner were piles of deep cushions.

The windows to what must have been the main bedroom were French doors but there were thick net curtains hanging and I could no way see inside.

Sometimes I just sat a while and read in her garden and never saw no harm in it and never got seen either and then one late afternoon Lefty and me ran to the beach and shadow-boxed as pollen and sand came in a storm from the west and over the bay from the pine forest across the island, sweeping the vast beach with witches and banshees riding high on its yellow front. The pollen was a yellow oily smear across the sky and the dust, heavier and looser, rolled beneath it. The sand rolled under it all like a wave and we shadow-boxed defiant in its face and waited for it to come.

'Run fools! Run!' A girl's laughing voice cut across the air and I knew its sound as soon as I heard it and turned to see Melody Grace on top of the beach by an old hut the lifeguards used in high summer. She was laughing at us and had pulled her scooter over and seemed to be dancing foot to foot in excitement and she pointed at the coming storm and I could see she wore blue jeans ripped at the knees and an army parka.

'In here!' she called, backing away into the hut and my heart had stopped beating and the sun hung motionless and the storm waited patiently and all time paused as stars fell and supernovas exploded and Melody Grace herself was calling to me. Lefty sprinted past me towards the hut and slapped my backside as he went and I followed and it was Melody Grace herself, calling me, and angels swooned.

By the time I reached the hut the storm was whipping my legs with sand and the full power of the wind was building at the end of the beach and picking up the sand there into twisted genies and the ocean was blown flat and being stirred grey and I decided I had to be cool and I had to be chilled and play this calm and mature, just like it says in the *Book of Cool*.

I followed Lefty into the hut and Melody laughed and her eyes lit up the gloom like torches and she glowed and was lit from within and she dusted sand off us like she had known us all our lives.

'Hello,' Lefty said and reached out and shook her hand as he sat on a bench built into the timber wall of the shed and I sat beside him and smiled at her real polite.

'Hello yourselves boys!' she laughed. 'Are you mad? I saw you dancing! That storm will whip you raw! That's why I pulled over. It will blow me off my little shit-mobile no trouble!'

'We were shadow-boxin', not dancin' . . .' Lefty corrected her gently. 'Is different.'

'Ah . . . hang on, I know you!' She looked straight at me. 'The boar slayer! How'd you do Mr Slayer? Do you remember me? From the day at the river?'

I looked at her and pretended to think, playing my hand cool like Luke and I bit my lip and made a deep thinking face and then Lefty laughed. 'Does he remember you? You's Melody Grace eh? I know you by his descriptions! He been lookin' for you half a year or more! All we bin hearing for half a year is Melody Grace this 'n' Melody Grace that 'n' he been so love struck he needs a doctor's medicine! He got your wedding planned, your kids named and he even been spyin' in your windows!' Lefty looked at me and nudged me. 'You must have sand in your eyes if you don't see who it is, it's Melody Grace herself right here in front of you!' He slapped my thigh. 'God is good, eh?'

I had never seen Lefty look so happy and I looked from Melody Grace to the floor and stayed looking at the floor because there was nowhere else to look and no defence and no explanation and only shame and there was just *fuck* and that word fits everything real snug. *Fuck.* I started to pick my palms and they bled real fast and I didn't even know I was doing it and then Lefty realised he had maybe said too much and Melody didn't speak at all and I saw she was gently biting her bottom lip. Lefty was honest and true and one of the dumbest people God ever put breath into.

'Actually, I gotta run.' Lefty stood up.

'The storm,' I said.

'It'll toughen me up and besides, I got a call comin' up at the house.' And he went straight out into the stormy dark and wind and never looked back and I knew he never had a call coming because nobody ever called us and the phone didn't even work and the door banged shut behind him as he left. 'Captain Oats?' Melody Grace whispered, and I shrugged and she shrugged.

I stared back at the floor and was examining the grain in the old timbers when Melody Grace suddenly plopped down heavily beside me and right next to me. 'So . . . It was you mooching around my house?'

I stared harder at the floor. *Fuck.*

She poked me in the ribs and then she held out her hand to shake hands and when I didn't move she reached down and took my right hand in hers and shook my hand. 'I'm Melody Grace and it's nice to meet you again . . .' Then she laughed gently and softly.

I didn't speak or even look up. Her hand was soft and strong and tiny and I stared at the floor and observed an interesting combination of knots and grain barely visible in the gloom.

'Cat got your tongue?' She nudged me again.

'I don't know what to say.'

'You're saying plenty.'

'I'm not saying nothing.'

'Anything. You're not saying anything. And you're saying plenty. Trust me. Anyway, words are overrated in the pantheon of communication.' I watched her from the corner of my eye. 'You know?' I didn't know. 'First we communicate with what we *feel*, and *show*. What we see but not *just* what we see . . .' she made rabbit ear signs with her fingers '. . . but *how* we see.' She tapped her heart. 'And *how* we dress and how we move. What we show the world. That's the first, then *scent*, how we smell. What our scent says is so important. Then comes tone, how we sound, the noises we make. Then lastly comes words. *What* we say. You have to stop seeing with your eyes and this . . .' she prodded my forehead. 'See with your soul, speak with your soul. Close your eyes and see the whole everything. Get it?'

I didn't get it so I looked at the floor which was just about the only safe place to look.

She took my chin and turned my face to hers. 'Watch!'

Melody Grace jumped up and mimed and posed and strutted around and made me guess her mood and her intentions in a game of charades in the near darkness. At first I was embarrassed but she was real insistent and wouldn't stop until I joined in and we laughed and she took off her parka as the hut warmed up and she got hot with the acting. She wore a button-up blouse and her jeans were low cut and tight. I had a go at acting just like she said and she directed me and guessed right every time.

'Stop looking at my boobs,' she said. 'Your eyes are on my boobs. *Eyes*, look at my eyes.'

'I wasn't looking *at* your boobs Miss Melody Grace, I was looking *for* your boobs!' and I realised I was doing Cuthbert's voice.

Melody's eyes opened wide in mock shock and she leapt up and punched me in the gut playfully and her knuckles were surprisingly hard and she threw me onto the bench.

Then she leaned over me so her throat was close to my face. 'What do I smell like?'

I sniffed. 'Skin.'

Melody frowned.

'Nice skin. Ladies skin.'

She frowned more. 'Not Channel?'

'I don't know what that smells like.'

She spoke into the darkness like she had drifted off some-where. 'Maybe I should use more. It's so bloody expensive though.' She sounded like a little girl and stamped her foot and huffed, 'It's French. Classic.'

'I didn't watch your place to be a pervert, just to see if it was where you lived.'

'We won't talk of it again.'

'No.'

'But stop it now?'

'Yes.'

'It's a bit yucky.'

'Sorry.'

She sighed. 'So, you wanna hang out?'

I didn't move. She ruffled my hair. Fuck! 'We will then!'

'You're a good actress.'

Melody smiled. 'Thank you, Kind Sir, but I know. One day I'm going to Hollywood to get a job as a waitress and live really poor and work my way up. My career plan is Homeless Beauty, Tired Waitress Beauty, Desperate Junkie Beauty, Porn Star, Superstar!' She giggled.

'Really?'

'No. Not really. I hate drugs. And porn pays really poorly and you can't wash it off.' She sighed again more heavily and sat back next to me with a surprisingly heavy thud. 'I don't know. Hollywood seems so far away. Sorry if I hurt your belly.'

'Where is it, exactly?'

'Kind of above your groin and under your chest . . .' she poked my belly . . . 'Just there.'

'Hollywood?'

Melody waved her hand in the air vaguely, 'Oh . . . Over there, somewhere. Far away. Light years. Maybe I can get a boat there someday, like a stowaway!' She laughed at herself. 'In a barrel in the hold or on a jetliner.'

'Will the Wizard go with you?'

She frowned. 'Wizard?'

I realised I had used a term that existed only in my head, 'The man you were with at the river?'

Melody laughed gently, 'Why do you call him a wizard?'

'I just thought he looked like a wizard. Is he your boyfriend?'

She recoiled. 'Eeww!!! No, he most definitely is not! And just because he has grey hair and a gnarly wand, doesn't make him a wizard! His name's Dave, he's OK, but he's just someone I know . . . so no, he won't be going anywhere with me! He exists here, in this place alone and no other!'

I took a pack of cigarettes from my joggers and offered her one. She screwed up her nose. 'They're filthy.'

I went to put them away but she stopped me, 'I'll have one though. Let's be filthy!' And she smoked luxuriously, like a movie star.

When the storm was fully passed, evening had settled in and she gave me a ride home taking the dark back streets because I didn't have a helmet. Everything, rooftops, roads, cars and the rubbish bags and papers rolling lazy along the road in the last of the winds was covered in greasy yellow pollen and sand and I held her around the waist and she felt perfect even through her army parka.

At Fell we pulled over on the drive at the top of the back quad and the lamplight was orange so Melody looked like she was made of solid bronze and her multiple headlights lit up the building where lights were burning from the windows and lit the walls cold white and she revved her engine before killing the coughing, rattling old scooter. I stood beside her as she stared towards the bunker that was Fell House and I saw it through her eyes using my soul and it looked monstrous and dilapidated and brutal and safe and home but she didn't see the safe and home part and how could she? To her it was neither. Her voice was hushed and timid. 'You live here?'

I nodded and every undraped window filled with the pale white and brown and black or yellow bodies of a hundred boys and they were naked to the waist as they prepared for bed.

'*Lord of the Flies* . . .' she whispered. 'The building weeps . . .' She looked at me with pity.

'It's Fell.' I sounded a bit uncertain and proud too and I was ready to defend the old place. 'Its long name is Feallan House but we just call it Fell. And the sign says Fell. See, there's a sign . . .'

Lefty came to the back door and looked like he had been sucked through a jet engine. Running home through the storm had even ruffled his hair and that ain't easy with an afro. He waved and then Leon and Johnny appeared at his back.

'I think I should go . . .' Melody Grace started her scooter and the air was smashed with its noise as she turned it in the drive and I still didn't move so she went around me and stopped again and leaned over and kissed my cheek and red love hearts floated and popped from every window and filled the sky.

Melody shouted into my ear, 'You and me. A gang of two! Tomorrow, same place same time!' And she roared and choked and cackled into the night, her scooter's noise bouncing off the walls in the quad like explosions, and I was ten feet tall.

Twenty-Three

Melody Grace was true to her word and met me the next night and many more after until we had a habit formed. She seemed lonely, which was impossible for someone so beautiful, but she was as keen to spend time with me as I was with her. I told her stuff about me including a lot of secrets and she played piano for me as I sat and watched enthralled and bewitched. Once upon a time she wanted to be a concert pianist and practised eight hours a day when she was a little child but the money run out and her parents split up and she read somewhere how poorly paid concert pianists were so she gave it up and went waitressing. There was a musical instrument seller on the other side of town called Musical Mike and he did her a special deal she said and she got the piano and cello very cheap and for next to nothing but she never said what the deal was and I never asked because it would be plain impolite. When she played piano I could listen all day and all night, which was a good thing because once she started playing she would play hours straight off and she was in a trance and worked each sequence of notes like the strokes of a paint brush making a picture and she went on and on layering the notes over each other and she could play every note perfect and all of them, too.

Melody said if becoming a Hollywood superstar didn't work out she would like to open a café and play piano there and then we talked about cafés and what made one better than another and I made out like I knew when in fact I had no clue. She said we would open at night like a speakeasy from the old days. She would cook and play piano and sing and I would tend bar and Lefty could do the door and play saxophone. Lefty didn't know how to play saxophone but Melody said we would get him lessons because being big and black meant he should play sax. He could play a bit of ukulele but she didn't think that had the same vibe. Melody bought two big scrapbooks and wrote my name on one and her name on the other and said we should fill them with ideas on a café and pictures and menus and drawings.

One Saturday morning we went to the market to buy vegetables and strange grains and seeds and she wore a short white dress with lace inlays and you could see right through it to her lacy bra in the sun, and on her head she wore a fascinator like a nanna would wear but on her it looked perfect and classic and stylish and she taught me to make cakes.

We kneaded flour and dropped in raisins and chopped dates when we made scones and we got messy and laughed a lot. I iced a cake and tossed a salad using balsamic vinegar and toasted granola with oats and nuts and berries and dates and maple syrup and desiccated coconut and we only cooked with cold-pressed extra-virgin olive oil, which is a funny thing because olives can't have sex anyway, and coconut oil which is a miracle oil you can use for cooking and wound healing and moisturising your skin to stay young as well a spoonful a day for general good health and mental wellbeing and ease of motions and aching joints, and Melody used a substantial amount of coconut oil and made sure I did, too.

I told Mister Solomon Sesay everything I knew about Melody Grace and he gave me a book of poetry and before I knew what happened he brought a flask and two cups and we were sipping tea in a deserted corner of the yard and I was telling him everything and he listened and smiled and nodded kindly. He said it was a good thing I wasn't spying on fairies no more and he suspected she was at least part human and maybe that would keep me safe. He was the only adult I trusted with my tale because he read poetry and he didn't laugh at me or play down my love and he told me what flowers to pick for her and how to take my time and not rush so I didn't frighten her off.

He said I was lucky and blessed and he envied us and he said, 'There is a place I read about and saw photographs of, in New England, USA, where autumn comes and turns everything to golden fire and it is the most beautiful thing I think I have ever seen. But it only lasts a week. For one week the trees blaze and light up the world and then it's over and things change and this is like youth and love and life. It is short and if you can find a way to make it blaze then do it so, for all you are worth.'

And he asked me to write it down about Melody Grace in a diary because one day when the dust covered my memories and my hair was thin and grey and my joints were stiff and sore that journal would warm my soul and make me smile again like in my youth, and Mister Sesay told me that. Later that day he gave me a thick notebook and a pen and that notebook had a brown leather cover and fine heavy paper and was made in Africa like he was and he was proud of that fact. He told me there was one commandment only and that was to forgive, I should forgive her, he said, whatever else I did, forgive, and I knew that would be easy. I could forgive her anything, everything. If she killed me I would forgive her and still welcome her to my fire in the Summer Lands.

I told Melody about Mister Solomon Sesay and she asked me to describe him and how he sounded and smelled and she said he was an ancient African prince of a mysterious tribe but she said not to mention her to him again, just in case, and what we had wasn't for sharing she said. Melody Grace had a tiny brass statue of Buddha on a low table by her bed and two little brass bowls from Tibet all enamelled with turquoise and blue and orange and little brass-handled ladles that made the bowls ring and sing and vibrate beautiful and deep and she went to her bedroom and knelt down in silence breathing deep and then made that bowl sing for about five times and then she threw it against the wall real violent and noisy and huffed a bit, then she sat with me all sweet and happy again and said, 'Ohm, gong and move right on . . . it's a Buddhist enlightenment thing.' And I knew I mustn't tell people anything about her again because it made her angry and darkly clouded her enlightenment.

Some nights we ate together and Melody Grace had a special way with food. She didn't eat much and always seemed to dwell on every bite so mealtimes were a new experience and slow and sometimes confusing and she slowed me down, telling me to *see* the food. She told me to savour every morsel and *appreciate* it and imagine what it had taken to get it to my plate . . . 'Ask yourself,' she said, 'what journey did that carrot take, what hands did it pass through, what cost? Ask how the pig died, the fisherman froze in the great southern seas, how the back of the vegetable picker ached and her hands bled from picking the cabbages and lettuces and spring onions that people scoff down without thought and they don't even look at the sweet perfect little onions. The journey of the coffee bean to an espresso . . . fuck!' She swore so suddenly I jumped. 'Its epic and it warrants serious *serious* contemplation. The great sin of our age is blind and thoughtless consumption! Do you have any idea how much this product . . .' she waved a spring onion in my face '. . . this food people scoff down should really cost? If its true cost was known, nobody would be fat! It would be like a golden onion.'

I thought a golden onion was a variety I had never heard of so I asked her, 'What's a golden onion?' And she frowned and told me it was an onion made of gold and I felt stupid but she touched my nose with her finger and we laughed and she punched me in the belly.

One day Melody took me to a handmade soap shop where every smell was like a taste and every scent of every land on earth hung there like an Arab bazaar heavy with spices and even the hammered copper platters holding the nuggets of soap seemed to have a taste that settled metallic on the tongue. Melody told me an Arab bazaar was about the most sensual place on Earth and she would take me to one someday and said Lilly would love that shop and she bought some small lumps of soap in different flavours and told me they were for Lilly and she even bought a big padded envelope to send them in and paid the postage. I knew Lilly and Melody would be best friends one day and I decided I would write Lilly a letter to put in with the soaps and tell her all about Melody Grace and maybe Lilly would be her bridesmaid when we married, but I didn't tell Melody that bit.

Twenty-Four

The next holidays Tommy No F got arrested for stealing a pair of running shoes and his defence was that they stole him. He just tried them on and they ran off. Never trust running shoes he said and after that he wouldn't go near climbing boots because he was terrified of heights. He went to juvie for a few days while he awaited trial and they sent him back to Fell after but those days in juvie he shared a cell with a musical kid who taught him F and gave him a tattoo and when he came out a week later Tommy did the longest community service in community service history because they sent him to work at the petting zoo and he made special friends with a small monkey and he didn't want to leave there. He said he was institutionalised and asked Leon to kill him so he could come back as a monkey and Leon said he would do that for sure but not quite yet.

That was the holidays the wind went round to offshore and the surf kicked up in a bay just south of the town beach and I went there each morning and the surfistas let me ride their waves and one gave me loan of an old long board and sometimes I rode all day long and half the night and surfing is like sex. Almost.

I dived down when I wasn't trying to catch a wave and held onto rocks to brace against the current and enjoyed the peace and quiet and solitude and watching the surf roll and cloud in a cauldron high over me and I was still and silent in the cooler clearer water and it was like being in the deep waters of the lido.

Melody was working most of that holidays because a lot of people had come to town for the sunshine so my time with her was limited and I was sad for that but we made carrot cake in her kitchen and she looked tired sometimes and not as healthy and bouncy as before but I figured waitressing all day must be exhausting and she wasn't exactly young. I told her to rest up more and think about her health because the poster says your health is your wealth and she just giggled. I saw her stripped down a couple of times at the beach when we shared a cold shower outside the toilet block after swimming and her body was firm and lean with heavy breasts that were perfectly shaped and even under her bikini top her nipples were long because the cold water made them erect and hard and her breasts were large but didn't droop at all. Her bum was perfect and her legs straight and nice shaped and she had broad shoulders and was actually quite blocky and solid and she didn't have the sparrow-like quality of Lilly but she was perfect in a different way and it's strange how women can do that and you can see one who is perfect and then see another who is completely different and perfect, and another who is different again and perfect again, like perfection in women is very very flexible. Melody Grace was twenty and a half years old and a real formed and proper woman of some distinction and her body was so much woman and sex and beautiful shapes that just ran into each other. Even the way she bounced tiptoe from one foot to another under the cold water was perfect and she didn't even know how beautiful and perfect she was and her boobs jiggled and her shape under her bikini bottoms was like a peach and her hair was ringlets even when it was wet and hung and bounced like coils of deepest copper. When she saw me seeing her she looked down and away and averted her eyes. *Melody Grace*, I just kept saying her name in my head. Perfect.

Some mornings I ran to the beach and got there just before dawn where Melody meditated and did yoga before the ocean just as the sun rose and she let me sit and copy her and a light rose up over my life and I was happy.

That was the same holiday Leon took Johnny and Lefty and me to the holy golden arches and told us over a massive cheese-burger with bacon and cheese and onion rings and fries that he was joining the army and he didn't need permission from his parents or school and nobody could stop him on account of today was his birthday and he was eighteen and we didn't know whether to celebrate his special day or mourn his going-away news and we just said nothing and chewed real slow. He said he wasn't joining the national army because they didn't get to fight much so he was joining the Foreign Legion which is in another country and made up of pirates and ragamuffins and warriors of no flag. He said he was signing up for twenty-five years and I saw those numbers sink into the dark black swamp in my mind where everything that didn't make sense gets swallowed in wet black sludge. It was for ever. Lefty and me and Johnny had no words and my burger stuck in my throat after that and I had to force the meat down with the banana shake and fries and strug-gled all the while and didn't even enjoy the apple pie or the date and banana cake or the sundae or the fizzy cola.

That night we drank too much whisky and tried to make a happy night for him but it was tragedy time and we laughed and cried and danced and just kept drinking and talking until all the lines blurred and the pain went away and Lefty and Leon and Johnny were asleep and I was deeply deeply numb and very sorrowful. I wanted to go to Melody then because she was my perfect place but couldn't walk well because my balance was shot and I wouldn't even get down the stairs and the booze made the world spin so I tuned the radio looking for Lilly to tell her I was coming for her soon and I knew it and soon, but all I got on the radio was music. Marionettes danced for me as the music played and carried on even after Ems went to sleep and I told them about how Leon was going away to the army for ever and it made me sad and they didn't say much but they listened intently and held their tiny wooden hands over their hearts and mouths in horror and bowed down low after as their master snored and huffed in sleep.

I won't forget that night not even until I forget my own name and how to tie my own shoes and button my fly.

In the morning I took a cold shower and ran to find Melody and I told her about Leon going away to join the Foreign Legion and she was sad and thoughtful and did a gong for him. We hung out all day and laughed and whispered and danced and every touch was startling and every nerve in my body was super-charged with life and for that whole day she made me happy and helped me forget my friend was going away for ever. The whole world is a magical mysterious place when you're in love and your love is with you.

I asked her to come to Fell House while it was quiet and the holidays and see my birds and that evening an hour before sundown she came to the roof and we bundled her up so she got pushed and pulled onto the roof with Lefty above her pulling and me below her pushing, but she was pretty strong and hauled herself up like a strong boy could and we only made it harder with our help but we had to help because she was a lady. She took it all with a smile and she held the birds properly tender and cooed and nuzzled them real natural then she sat cross legged on a crate as we flew them against the setting sun and I could tell she was impressed and she asked lots of questions and was honestly interested even in what they ate and how much they pooed and how often I cleaned their loft and everything. Then as they lifted up and wheeled into the sky she was silent and stood up to watch and as they tumbled she gripped my hand and I saw Lefty smile and stand back a little and Melody silently tiptoed from foot to foot in excitement like she did under a cold shower but slower.

I passed her the feed tin and she rattled it like I showed her and the birds came straight home and she was even more impressed at how good I had them trained. She looked like a little girl in a fairground and as we started to climb down through the hatch she said, 'Do you want come over the hill to the west coast for the day? You and me? Tomorrow? Maybe stay the night?'

I looked at Lefty because it meant I would miss training and that was like missing breath but he shrugged and nodded and said, 'We could run the dunes. Good fitness! I never even been over that hill before.'

'Not you Lefty, sorry. Next time though? We have to ride my scooter all the way.' Melody said it so sweetly he couldn't take offence no matter what and he grinned. 'I'll cover for you.' He smiled but already I felt guilty and it was like abandoning a teddy bear and that sits heavy on any man.

I slipped hand over hand down through the hatch and dropped the last little bit then looked up in time to catch Melody as she released her grip early and I saved her with a manly catch so she landed soft.

We sneaked softly through the bathroom door and there stood Swindell in the half dusk and he looked huge as a giant and for a moment we all froze and didn't breath and our hearts stopped and he turned every which way like he didn't know what to do as I stood before him and Melody Grace followed me and Lefty followed her, and we were petrified and when he stopped dancing his little jig he was glaring at me full of darkness and rage and smug because I was caught bang to rights and he had a great victory over me. Melody tried to slip past us all but he caught her wrist and spun her back to him and then he saw her properly and his face kind of morphed and changed and he choked a little and turned away and back and away again and dropped her wrist and she shrunk and backed around him and out and Melody Grace didn't stop at the door and she bolted and I ran behind her calling her to slow down but she wasn't slowing down and she ran from Fell House and mounted her scooter. She looked afraid and upset and small and I couldn't figure it because she was a grown woman and he couldn't hurt her but she was red-faced and turned on the scooter and gunned it.

'Go away!' she shouted over the engine noise. 'And come to my place at six tomorrow morning if you're coming and if you don't come, fine!' And her voice was hard and she rode away and I was lost about what had happened. I expected Swindell to punish us and scream and shout and stamp but as I walked back into the house to get the abuse and maybe smack him up for grabbing Melody's wrist he walked out fast and straight past me smiling and chuckling to himself in his little-girl laugh and just about skipping and Lefty came after him and he looked puzzled, too. We watched him go and he didn't even look back. He was wringing his hands and sweating just a tiny bit and looked way too happy and he didn't say a single word and Lefty and me sat a while pondering then Lefty said he wished he was coming to the bay too because he didn't want to get the trouble all on his own but he knew he couldn't fit on that scooter and he knew I had to go. He said it was biological. 'But you don't stay away too long. Just one night in case they come looking.'

And I agreed. Only one night.

Twenty-Five

We went to the west coast beach on a road that took us over the mountain on a road woven into it like a rhythmic gymnast's ribbon. Melody had lied to Lefty and we didn't ride her scooter but took an old hippie housetruck she had the loan of from a friend. It was no Skyline but it took the hill well and in a couple of hours we were looking down the other side on a great wide plain that swept over farmland and orchards and vineyards and forests to the endless surf-smashed beaches of the west.

We stayed on that road a long time and passed an estuary filled with a million black swans and just black swans, so you never would think there was a single white swan on Earth, and that road went on a long time until it ran out in a tiny town called Larkswood. It was so hot in Larkswood the tarmac road was melting in places and sticky and stank that beautiful tarmac smell and clung to my tennis shoes. A lone little terrier mad with the heat and wide-eyed chased a scrap of paper down the middle of the road and stopped dead to stare at me for an instant and we had a moment of bonding and he wanted to know if I was going to chase his paper too and I was surely tempted but knew if I did there would be no stopping and madness is like that. After Larkswood was a gravel road ten miles long and after that was a walk of an hour over huge dunes that could have been in the Arabs' desert and then beaches and coves opened up with rock archways and pools and pillars rising from the ocean where baby seals swam on their backs and rolled with the joy of being fat and at home in perfect water as their mums watched and rollers crashed in with set after set after set of perfectly sculpted deserted surf.

We didn't take surfboards over those dunes but Melody had fins and we bodysurfed in cold clear water so fresh it softened the skin and so powerful it near ripped off your shorts. Melody came up again and again with her bikini top half off clutching at herself and trying to straighten up and laughing like a little kid with beautiful snot running down her nose. The sun shone, the waves crashed and birds wheeled overhead and it was a paradise like any heaven so I knew God once walked on that beach.

A few hours of surfing and rolling and diving in that cold water under the hot sun and I was exhausted. We sat on the beach and got nicely burnt and tingly then we walked back to the van drained in blissful perfect peace and the walk back was longer and slower.

There were more benches lining the main street in Larkswood than I'd ever seen and the old woman in the only café said it was because a long time ago someone had placed a bench in the street with his family name cut into it and a competition had begun so every man and every family ended up putting a bench in that long empty street and naming that bench for their own and of a sunny Sunday every family would take its place and try to lord it over the next. They also painted a pedestrian crossing and hung up stolen traffic lights even though there was no traffic to stop. They had an air-raid siren too and an entrance sign to a subway station but no subway and not even a bus ran through it and the old woman was proud and laughed like a mischievous schoolgirl as she told it.

We ate ice cream after with coconut and real fruit boysenberry in waffle cones and as was the tradition in Larkswood we each sat on a different bench so we shouted our conversation. We laughed real belly laughs and watched two old women race each other in mobility carts and cuss each other then smile sweetly as they passed us and waved polite as you like then cussed again soon as they were passed.

We ambled slowly, arm in arm, back to the truck and there was nobody to look at us or see us and the old café woman told of a spot outside town where she said we should camp a night and we rolled slowly that way and there we found a place where 200-year-old wisteria trees covered a small meadow in purple and pink blossoms like electric neon rain falling from deeply twisted trunks and tortured arms that draped us in colours as fine as lace and soft as satin and took our breath away and made Melody Grace gasp. And there we stopped the night. Melody said she loved this place more than any she had ever discovered before and it was now her official favourite spot and I wondered what would happen next because there was only one big bed and she was looking romantic and the wisteria was working magic.

The sun set but it was still hot and the night broke open in so many stars we pulled the mattress onto the roof of the van and stared at them and the way they lit up the blossom of the trees. I had never seen so many stars and usually when I looked up all I saw was the top of my skull but now I saw the universe. It was like someone had blown silver-white dust into the sky and it just hung there suspended by magic. There was a shooting star that made us both catch our breath and the moon was a crescent of white gold and seemed to know our names and hang there just for us and Melody said we were seeing light that had taken a billion billion years to reach us and the whole Milky Way was draped over our van, then she rolled into me and raised herself up on her elbow and her body was close to me and touching and she kissed me and she taught me to make love. Her body was heavy and firm all at once. Her breasts were a woman's breasts and round and settled lower but firm and full and when she was nude they were all I could see in all the world and her nipples were dark and hard and long and her shape was like a figure eight and her legs strong and straight and her bum firm and she was heavy lipped and perfect shaped and warm and very wet. She groaned softly and purred and slowed me down and she said love was a crop sowed fast but best reaped slowly and that was romantic and she had to slow me and calm me because I was trying to taste everything all at once and I was panicking and I was afraid that right at that moment of perfect pure experience one of those fucking meteorites was coming my way and just as I was about to make love to my perfect love I would be fucking atomised. I knew it.

Mad Louis once told me that God has an intimate relationship with poor people because every time they turned their backs he fucked them in the arse and I knew if I was God it would be funny to drop a meteorite on that van just as Boy Wonder was about to get his rocks off with Princess Perfect and I prayed *Not yet Jesus, not yet. If you gonna kill me kill me in an hour I beg you. Half an hour even . . . five fucking minutes . . .* But then I thought maybe Melody Grace would save me because no God however warped and dysfunctional or comical would want to hurt something so perfect as Melody Grace who was most definitely made in the image of something holy and divine and godly.

Melody shushed me and slowed me more and took my hands and guided me and kissed me. She swept over me and washed me like a warm soft wave made of pink and white marshmallows and licked and teased and I could see into her watery eyes and see right back to the beginning of the universe and right forward to its end and it was all perfect and all of it was somehow wrapped up in a woman's shape and fed by her breasts and watered by her eyes so I knew right then that God was a woman. My mum used to tell me stories of how women shaped empires and fed armies with their breasts and how women were the most holy and sacred and strongest and most resilient of all beings and how every name that ever was remembered was born of a woman and named by a woman and fed by a woman and how one day I would understand that everything perfect in the world was woman, and right then I understood two things for sure: first my mum was right and wise and clever and second, never think of your mum when you are doing what I was doing right there and then, and I told Melody what my mum had said and she paused, then laughed and told me to shut up and not think of my mum and she pushed my face down and I drank.

The night was perfect and exhausting and I was raw and alive and the next day we kept doing it and swam again and late in the day we realised we were really hungry so we collected pipis by driving our feet into the sand in the shallows until we felt their bunches and then dived down and scooped them up and we went for mussels and scallops too. Melody caught a cray and we boiled the whole lot and ate stale hard grainy bread that was left over in the van, picking off bits of mould, then sweetened our mouths with berries from the trees and we drank red wine and cold water from a stream. It was just about the best meal anyone ever ate. Then we made love again and then Melody said it was enough and laughed and touched my nose with her finger and her eyes looked happy and sad all at once and she looked so young and so old and we drove home in silence and it was like driving back to the end of the world as we crested that mountain.

I prayed and prayed it would end then and Jesus would send a meteorite on top of me because I knew it wasn't going to get better and it couldn't get better and it could only get worse and it would get worse.

'I love you,' I blurted out as we got into town.

'Don't.'

'Do you love me?'

'Don't,' she said again and smiled softly in the dark van and car headlights lit her up as she leaned over to kiss my cheek.

'I do and I can't stop.'

She shook her head. 'It'll pass.'

'It won't. I know it won't.'

'I know too, and it always does.'

'It won't. And you love me too. I know it.' I tried to sound cool but I was talking dangerous stuff and I knew I could scare her off but she didn't look or sound scared and I wanted to buy her something as a gift but I had no money and I wanted to spend all the money in the world buying her everything her heart could want.

'If you still love me in a year or two, or three, look for me.'

'Look for you? Where are you going? You live here.'

Melody said softly, 'Love fades, and yours will too . . . or you will hear things you don't like or a schoolgirl will turn your head. And that's OK. Remember that. It's OK.'

'You're wrong. I won't stop loving you. Love's in my nature. My sister Lilly always said so.'

'Ah, Lilly . . . She sounds lovely.'

'She is . . . You'll love her!'

'Love love love . . .'

'Love love love . . . I won't ever stop loving you and I won't ever leave you!'

Melody groaned then sighed then said, 'You'll find me then, so relax Romeo. It will be whatever it it will be . . . But I have to go away.'

There was silence and I didn't know how to fill it or what to say or even what she meant and after a while she looked at me. 'Are you alright?'

'No . . . You're coming back though, right?'

Melody Grace didn't speak.

'I thought we were going out now. Attached?'

She sighed again and it was a big, almost aggressive noise. 'We are . . . attached. But it isn't about being attached or not attached, not to anything or anyone, that's way too simplistic.'

'What is it then?'

'Maybe it's about being attached to everything and everyone. So it all matters. Wherever your focus goes it matters and you love it all equally even if you love it differently and I have to go somewhere else because somewhere else has taken my focus and because sometimes a place turns toxic, you know? But it doesn't take away what we shared.'

She looked at me to see if I grasped what she meant but I didn't and I didn't want to and she saw it and I said, 'So if everything matters the same there's nothing good especially and nothing bad? That doesn't seem right . . . but if it's true, why go anywhere? Why not stay right here with me?'

'That's not what I meant. There are bad things just like there are diseased trees in the forest. They might not have started out diseased but they become that way, just like people don't start out bad, but they become bad and maybe bad can be called diseased. *Dis- Eased*. Think about the word. Look for the root. So you cut them out of the forest or the whole forest becomes diseased or at least the trees around them do. It doesn't mean we hate the diseased trees, we just fell them in the hope some part of them can come back strong or that part of the forest can recover. Problem is we all stopped cutting them out. You have to prune!' She laughed to herself, 'Prune . . . I'm pruning.'

'So if it's diseased you should cut it down . . . people too?'

'You can't cut people down so easily. But most people live in a world of chaos.' She slapped the steering wheel. 'Discordant! It's like a *discordant* orchestra where all you hear is noise, do you understand the word discordant? Sound over sound so you can't hear the rhythm or the tune or beat, just noise and more noise. You can't even distinguish one instrument from another, so however beautiful it all is when it plays in harmony, as *discordant* noise it crushes you and confuses you. It disorientates you and it's toxic and it kills you. Am I preaching? I don't care . . . Listen for the rhythm. That's where peace lives. Everything else is disharmony! Sorry if I'm preaching . . .' She breathed and her eyes bored into me. 'Search out harmony in everything you do Romeo. Or else don't, just dull yourself to the chaos and get numb and get old. Your choice. But me, I have to go away. I just have to . . . because I have to. I'm following the symphony.'

And I knew it was done and she had worked it all out and I didn't have the words to parry her and straight away I stared at her trying to freeze her face in my memory.

Then softly she said, 'Come find me . . . if you love me like you say.'

We were pulling up at the back of Fell House and all the light in the world was going out and I was going back in the dark and I was scared and the loss and fear and grief roared in me like a lion.

'Look for me at Baelo Claudia in Cádiz at sunset on the summer solstice when the stones are turning pink and the statue goes to electric blue with the fall of night. And the sunset is so red the whole world goes pink, even the air in front of our faces, so we're breathing pinkness like an old lady's aura, like a rose garden exploded filling up every molecule. I almost wanted to say mollusc but that would be the wrong thing. Molecule.'

She sounded like a perfect poet. 'I will! It sounds perfect. Where is it?'

'Cádiz.' And she pointed to a picture postcard pasted to the roof over the driver's seat and it was exactly what she just described and it was a magic miracle that its picture happened to be right there like she had conjured it with her words and words are like that. 'Se llama Cádiz,' she said.

'I will!'

She yanked up the handbrake with manly vigour and kissed me and let her lips dwell on my cheeks and her face touch mine and stay there so her soft sweetness lingered, then she sounded like a child. 'Thank you for the day and the night and the company and thank you for loving me, it was pure and it was wrong and you are too young and shit, you're just a kid and I could go to jail, but I don't care and thank you for reminding me what peace is supposed to sound like. Really.' And she was like the fairy of the river on that first day and her eyes were liquid pools and I wanted to fall into them like you fall into death complete and for ever and with no way out.

Suddenly all the cool in the world deserted me and I lunged for her and clung onto her and she laughed in pity and then she got firm with me and she had to peel me off and push me away and all my cool bravado was gone and I was pathetic and not ashamed to be that way and she peeled the postcard off the roof lining and pressed that postcard into my chest and my hands clung to it and she pushed me out of the van door and she kissed my hand as she pushed it away and she said, '*Vaya con Dios. Hasta*

Cádiz'. And I watched her drive away and saw a tail light was out as I strained to catch a glimpse of her silhouette and all my guts went to sickness and my hands went to my face and held my head and I gripped my head so hard I hurt myself and love ain't like it is in the movies. In the movies Melody Grace would have spun that van around and come back to me but in real life she just kept going and I was all ended and walked slow and weak and weeping into Fell. I knew right then that God didn't need no meteorite to flatten and kill people because He was way too mean and brutal and cunning for that and Mad Louis was right and somehow I had turned my back.

Twenty-Six

The height of summer came late that year and ignited the world like it did all the ages ago in the lido and I expected a plague of black flying ants too.

At night we slept with all the windows open and no covers and prayed for wind and one hot night I dreamed and couldn't put a name to the old black and white men and delicate fragile women and fat aunties I see in that dream and maybe they were dream people looking for someone to own them and claim them and give them the life of memory. Maybe there is whole army of dream people who come at night to comfort those who don't have anyone real any more and that night they came to me.

I saw my mum and dad and sister and I saw them in sunshine and colour.

My mum was dancing in a field like a happy dervish in a floral dress and the sun in her hair and her feet bare and toenails painted, but I don't remember seeing her dancing like that in life so maybe I saw what should have been instead of what was and maybe its her waiting in the Summer Lands for me to come and sometimes things get confused in me. And my dad. I dreamed of my dad.

I told it to Johnny he thought the heat was making for strange dreams and the next night he brought a big bag of ice and we lay down on wet towels on the bathroom floor with a cold shower running and we covered ourselves in ice cubes and rubbed them all over each other. I even had ice cubes on my eyes and Johnny swaddled his balls in them and squeezed one up his backside. I didn't do that but I slept better that night and felt cool to my core and I didn't dream once.

I wrote Lilly a letter about my boxing and my Fell friends and Melody Grace and I tended my birds and went to school and tried to focus on two weeks' time when Lefty had a bout. Everyone was expecting big things from Lefty and he was starting to feel the pressure because Tawhaki got a football scholarship and went without hardly a word and that's how thunder always goes, so he just wasn't there one morning and with Big Ben gone all the talk was about how Lefty was gonna win titles.

Lefty and me considered it possible that Melody Grace might change her mind and come home once she realised how much we missed each other and every day I went to her cottage to see. Weeks passed and I went every day and looked through the windows and sat waiting on her steps and I tended the garden and pulled some weeds and watered the flowers and made sure her scooter was OK and not getting too dusty or stolen and I wiped down her window frames and swept her doorstep.

Then one day her scooter was gone and when I looked inside through the window most of her stuff was gone too except the piano and cello and they looked ruined and shabby and all the magic was gone and everything white was grown grey and I panicked and I knew she wasn't coming back and I sat down on her back step and cried. I smashed my fists into my chest and face and head and I wanted her back even if she wasn't my girl just so I could maybe catch a glimpse of her sometime or see her passing on her scooter and she didn't even have to see me but just be in town so I could see her and others could see her because she was so special she made everything and everywhere and everyone better, and I sobbed. I sobbed for Melody and for my dad and my poor mum and my Lilly and for Davy and my Mad Louis all full of bullets and holes and rotting in the ground and I sobbed because it was lost and I couldn't find it nowhere. I felt all the pain in all the world like I was raw and open and I couldn't bear it not one second more but the sun hanged motionless in the sky and the moon couldn't rise and she wasn't with me and I couldn't take away not one bit of all the pain and hurt and it hurt so much right from the beginning of time until the end of time and all the pain in all the world was in me and I was sobbing like a baby and I could feel hell rising all about me with fierce giant dogs to eat me up and I howled, and the back door opened and I looked up and expected to see them big dead mouths ready to gobble me up and drag me to the underworld and I see Dirty Dick Dave looking down at me all blurred and puzzled.

'What the *fuck* is wrong with you kid?' he asked, then he recognised me and slid down beside me. 'Ah . . . ah. OK.' He sounded softer. 'Fuck fuck fuck . . . you got it bad, eh Slayer?'

I tried to get a hold of myself but I was shaking and my guts were convulsing and a river of snot ran over my mouth and I must have looked really bad because he put his arm around me and pulled me tight to him. 'Stop it now. Shush shush shush. Get a grip boy.' And I did. Slowly I caught my breath and stopped the sobbing and wiped my eyes and nose and he pulled me in real tight to him and we sat like that a while. He lit a cigarette and passed it to me and I started to cry again and he took it back.

'Ah fuck, she's a heartbreaker for sure, son . . .'

'She (*sob sob*) said (*sob sob*) she (*sob sob*) was my girl (*sob sob big sob*), she ain't is she? (*sob sob wail*). My heart is broken you know! (*sob sob*) She ain't coming back is she?'

He sighed and smoked deeply and put me in a gentle neck lock. From inside his jacket he pulled out a cloth and wiped my nose for me and then I took the cigarette and he let me.

'I don't know Slayer. But honestly I don't think so, she ain't the coming-back type.'

'Where is she (*sob, tremble*), do you know?' I took the cloth and assumed responsibility for wiping my own snot and tears. 'I got some things for her I can send.' I lied and I offered him the smoke back but he waved it away.

'No. No I don't. And I'm sorry you're hurting boy but it comes to all of us I reckon. If you live long enough life, everyone in it will disappoint you or break your heart or tear your guts right out or shit over you, or you will do those things to other people or yourself or most likely all three will happen. Sorry and all that but that's the way it is. Welcome to life on Earth. You just have to cowboy up.'

'She's my girl though.' I looked straight into his eyes and my breathing rattled.

'That she is son. You and me both . . . But that don't mean you're her boy, if you get the difference? She's like one of them little ballet dancers in a music box that goes round and round to *Swan Lake* when you open the lid.'

I couldn't see it and he saw I couldn't.

'She spins and turns to her own tune and she isn't really real. She's just an illusion, entertaining for sure but she won't tell you or show you anything about herself or let you see anything other than that mesmerising perfect little dance that fucking well hypnotises and bewitches every man who sees it.'

'That's not her. She told me stuff.'

'Really? What did she tell you?'

I thought hard and then harder still so my brain got pain. I felt like every cell in me knew every cell in her and that every mite of my existence was entwined with every mite of hers and I knew nothing much except her name. I didn't even know where she came from. 'She said that she was going to be an actress in Hollywood and she was an uncommitted non-conformist Buddhist and she played piano.'

Dirty Dick Dave smiled sadly. 'See? She ain't real. Who the fuck is a Buddhist?'

'She is real.'

The man shook his head. 'I gotta go to work. Let her go boy, like a good wet dream. She ain't and never was and never will be real. I just came here to open up for the music man to take back his stuff and even now I can see her perfect fingers on those piano keys and it ain't none of it real but that's OK, perfect's never real. People like her just ain't for people like us. People like us, we don't get to dance to *Swan Lake*. People like her, someone turns the handle and music tinkles out and we're captivated and hypnotised but we can't keep her going. And to be fair, if we could it would get boring, eh? If she was like us she would be ruined and if we were like her we'd be wearing fucking tutus and bringing home boyfriends just to pay the fucking rent. But look, she left this. You have it, go on, take it.' It was one of her tiny Tibetan bowls and I took it like it was sacred and holy. 'And you did really good son, and it meant something, a man can tell. That little day up the river was a week's paid work for me and it meant nothing to her. For me it was worth it, almost a whole day with her . . . just her company. You, you had it all and for free which means it meant something. You two were special. Brief,

217

but special. And maybe the most special either of you will ever know, brief and intense and pure. You tasted love, boy, so be fucking satisfied. You got lucky or blessed, or both.'

We walked into town and he said nothing I heard then he peeled off at the trot into the biggest hotel the town had where he said he worked the kitchen at night washing dishes. I watched through the window as he went straight to work with his head down, grabbing an apron and gloves and some weedy man shouting at him that he was late. I was sorry I made him late and sorry he washed dishes and seeing him like that was sad even though washing dishes is the single most important job in any commercial kitchen and that's a known fact.

Twenty-Seven

We drove five hours in an old mini-bus with me and Lefty plus three other boys, Coach Petey and Dom, his assistant coach, and one of the boy's mums, and all the boys were bang on weight except Lefty who was fighting as superheavyweight so didn't have to worry, but we agreed not to eat nothing so we wouldn't tempt or tease the boys who were making weight and even I honoured the deal even though I wasn't fighting because I couldn't be matched. And we were all good and stuck to the fast except Lefty and halfway there he pulled open his bag and took out half a bakery and a chocolate factory and he ate everything. He even sucked up the crumbs and he described every taste of every morsel and smacked his lips and giggled.

Lefty went to sleep and he had sugar round his mouth so I nearly licked his lips but didn't because I thought it would look bad to the others. We arrived late in the city and it was dark when we arrived and not much was happening but we pulled into a big drab motel Coach Petey always used on fight nights and got straight to bed five in a room.

The contest was in a social centre about three miles from the motel and it was a single-storey shitshack surrounded by wrecked buildings that hadn't been fixed up yet since an earthquake years before but it was decked out with flags and posters and everyone was real pleased to see so many fighters arrive and feel so much good energy come to their wrecked and forgotten neighbourhood.

At 7am the boys all weighed in and made weight bang on and we got a feed and the fighting started at 2pm and broke at 4 for two hours then started again for the evening. Lefty fought at 3pm and won, then was in the final at 10pm and it was a day of glory.

Before the fights Lefty was afraid and shaking and he asked me to pray with him which I did and we knelt down in the changing room before he came out and he prayed saying, 'Please God forgive my opponent and protect me and him and turn the fucker to dust for me when I just beat him and beat him and beat him down. And let me beat him down and down and down and don't let me be ashamed by losing and don't let me die or get brain dead or nothing bad and help me kill that fucker deader than dead and help me make his nose and face flat like a fucking butterfly and—' He would have gone on more but Coach Petey was sitting in the corner and stopped him because the other boy was wrapping his hands by the door and looking pale and sick and Coach Petey pulled Lefty up and told him God probably heard enough and to just say Amen and Lefty did what he was told. God was listening good that night because he near enough answered everything Lefty asked for and after the fights the fighters hugged and kissed and raised each other's hands high because glory and honour is to the fighter win, lose or draw and that's the ancient code.

We ate all the way home and stopped at two different fast food places before we even got out of the city then pulled into a service station and topped up with bad food and fruit too and Coach Petey paid for it all even though he was no rich man and he was nearly in tears and said it was the best night he ever had. It was a pleasing journey home on bloated stomachs and sore hands and

I was sorry I hadn't fought, too, and Lefty was grinning all the way even when he slept, but he had hurt his wrist in connection with the second fighter's elbow and was in some degree of pain but he said the trophy he held onto more than made up for it and every now and then he just beamed a more massive smile at me in the darkness and rubbed that trophy over his injured hand like it was magic, which it might have been.

We drove through the night straight and I could see nothing from the windows but my own face looking back and after we ate and sang and ate some more and we slept and stopped once for a toilet break in the bushes and got back to Fell a bit before 5am and nothing was different and nothing moved and it was all normal and quiet but both Lefty and me knew something was up. It was like we smelled it in the air even though there was nothing to smell and maybe the tiny vibrations in the atmosphere were unbalanced or upset or the house itself whispered to us but we knew, both of us, tired and bruised and elated and exhausted and puffed up with glory as we were, that something was changed and something was wrong. We stood in the cold greystone dawn and looked at the building and my gutbrain made my whole body twitch and Lefty got it too and he stowed his trophy in his kitbag for safety then led the way and I followed.

We walked softly softly up the stairs and Lefty led me into my dorm and it was relief to hear the heavy breathing of the boys.

Leon and Johnny were in my cube, fully dressed and fast asleep, but Leon woke up the instant I walked in and he nudged Johnny awake.

My eyes worked out their full shapes in the dark and Lefty threw open the curtains so the light lifted and he punched on the reading lamp set into the wall and in their arms were six dead pigeons.

Both boys were sickly white and Lefty gasped and dropped his bag hard to the floor and Johnny flicked off the light and we stood in grey light and no light and folded into each other.

There had been a culling while we were away and it was a sorry story, as cullings always are.

They came led by Swindell just after we left for the fight and smashed the pigeon loft and killed the birds by wringing their necks. They were pests Swindell said and the men were backed by teachers and the headmaster and his assistants and the men went through the trees after and killed the quail and rabbits and bush turkey and possums and hedgehogs and everything else we had always kept safe, and Ms Biggs stood and watched and told the boys it was necessary and it was ecology, but really it was murder and a strike at the guts of Fell House and every boy living there and even Ms Biggs didn't stay for the all of it.

Carlos was gone too, taken straight off by social services because the headmaster said it wasn't safe for him with so many stairs, as if the stairs had arrived suddenly the day before, and he said he feared for his wellbeing which was unfounded slander and Swindell had confiscated his radio and looked for mine too but mine was with me and after that I hid it good in a hollowed-out school book, and Swindell had broken the valve set in a big search of the whole house and smashed every valve to dust. Our boy Carlos was alone in a strange place with no radio to banish the voices and nobody to tell him he belonged and was important and no one to listen to his stories, and the story went that the men laughed as they killed and Swindell giggled and I can't say it's true but it's what I was told.

Twenty-Eight

Three days is the time it takes a soul to travel the cold empty worlds of darkness before it finds itself in the Summer Lands and this is called the Passing and three days is the Grieving. After that time when the soul is purified and safe with the ancestors you can start to live again and build a future without your beloveds or if there be just cause, plan your revenge on their behalf, and Doris confirmed it was so and it was agreed by all. Mister Solomon Sesay agreed too and said he was sorry for me and sorry for all my birds and the furry creatures of the woods. When I was alone I clenched my fists and chewed my own forehead and I tried to put back the pigeon loft but it was matchwood and I stroked stray feathers and people let me do it without interference and then another layer of armour went on and was buckled and burnished and we made a pyre and burned the bodies of the fluffy and feathered and let their spirits rise to the sun and moon and stars as smoke.

I woke after those three days and nights of passing and I could see my pigeons free and tumbling and wheeling in the clear air against the blue skies and rolling white sunlit clouds of the Summer Lands and I see the quail running after their mother and the rabbits hoppity hopping along the river and right down in my guts I knew they were all safe and although I was cursed with the pain of remembering, I could breathe again.

Then I carefully took that pain of remembering and I took the pigeons and the creatures of the woods and put them all with Melody Grace and all the other things whose memory made me weak in a hole right there beside my left foot, and it was a deep dark hole with no bottom and just darkness and coldness, and it swallowed up all the things that made pain in me and everywhere I went the deep hole was. You put something down that hole and it don't matter no more and don't come ever back. It's where you put painful things and things you don't or can't care about no more. A lot of things go down that hole and stay gone except Sun was still hanging in my eye and the pigeons were still warm in my hands and Melody was gurgling and burbling and bubbling and she wouldn't stay quiet or properly gone and that deep hole was too full and overflowing and I told Mister Sesay all that and he said, 'A great poet once said, *Tis better to have loved and lost, than never to have loved at all* . . . I think this poet was African at least in his heart on the day he wrote that.' Mister Solomon Sesay claimed for Africa everything he liked or was impressed with or respected and sometimes he said that all the people in the world came out of Africa, even white people before they got bleached by the sickness of evil and greed. He said Africa invented music too and dancing and ice cream. Then he said more poetry to me and he talked a long time and he told me I must not discard my love and I must reach out and pluck her from the abyss and undiscard her or she will gurgle at me for ever.

'Keep breathing and you will endure,' he said. 'And the pain, it will lessen. I promise. And even for these deeds done against your brother pigeons the anger will lessen. I promise this too.'

But I had come to another place in my thinking and I said to him, 'I don't need anything to lessen. I won't let it lessen.' I sounded strong and I liked that I was in control of my voice. 'I'll feed it and remind myself of its shape every day and every hour.'

Mister Sesay laughed softly. 'Why? I'll tell you, I know. Because it's yours. It's always the way with poor people, they will cling to anything that is theirs because they have so little. Even pain and suffering they cling to.'

'I am going to kill Swindell,' I said. 'Over and over until he's dead twenty times', and I looked at the tattooed black man beside me and he looked right back and didn't blink and he knew I meant every word and saying those words made a con-juring and I could feel it and Mister Solomon Sesay looked away and a moment later he looked back and he was changed and he wasn't my teacher then but a man of black and deadly stillness. He breathed deeply then he patted my knee. 'Killing him won't change anything or bring anything back as it was. You know this, yes? And where do you stop? How many have harmed you or are harming someone else right now? How many will you kill? One? Ten? Ten thousand?'

'As many as it takes to make me feel good. That's all.'

He looked at me for a full minute without speaking or blink-ing and that's a long time and I fought with myself so I wouldn't speak first and I won.

'That is all? It's not all. It's a big thing, killing. Even when you kill bad people, small people. Even white people. And it won't make you feel good.'

'Maybe. Maybe I don't care.'

The evening covered our faces with shadows so we bled into each other and were like one inseparable dark shape.

'You will kill this man for killing pigeons?'

'That's a good enough reason . . . They never hurt anyone and didn't even shit on cars. And he done more than that. He grabbed Melody and that's why she left and even he didn't I don't care. I'll kill him just to kill him, pure and simple, for Sun, and not just him. All of them. I am going to be a killer. A natural born killer.'

'You are no natural born killer. All killers are made, every one, and cannot then be unmade. For all your troubles you have not hurt anyone and that makes you an unwritten paper, an unblemished canvas. Once you change that and you blot the paper you cannot unwrite it. And you are too young and too good to deliberately blot your paper and you have choices just as your Melody Grace had choices and Swindell the Pig has choices. The choice to, and the choice not to. You have not yet chosen and not yet acted, so you are blessed. You are young. Do not say these words again.'

'I *will* kill him.' I stared into his eyes looking for a response and even in the dark I saw he didn't blink or shrink away from the idea. 'I want to make him suffer and hurt and I want to kill him slow so I see him die right there in front of me. In my own bare hands.' And when I heard the words and felt them in my mouth I felt good and strong and what I was hearing was brought into life.

I think Mister Sesay smiled and maybe he thought I was a kid talking out of anger and injustice and maybe I was but it didn't feel like it, it felt like I was speaking the whole gospel Jewish Jesus truth. Like saying it made it real.

I stood up to go but still he just watched me and his eyes were boring into me from the darkness so I couldn't walk away and I stood staring at him like he stared at me and the African and me were on new ground.

I wanted to break out Lilly and find my gurgling Melody and we would bring retribution and revenge and war against everything and everyone and there was no end to it and no sense to make of it, and I stood there and all that I told Mister Sesay. I told him I wanted to destroy *them* and *it* and *the whole fucking everything* and I had a calling and a fate and it was burning me up and I waited for him to react and condemn me and I expected clean adult disapproval or mocking but he nodded slowly and reached up and took my hand and pulled me to sit back down. 'Sit sit sit,' he said gently and I sat. 'You are drowning in tears . . . and who is *they?*'

I didn't know.

'Name *them* . . . and, what exactly, is this *whole fucking everything?*'

I couldn't name them or describe the everything. He sighed. 'Perhaps I underestimated you. You have shapeshifted perhaps, but your shape is not yet formed and your thinking not clear. You must concentrate now and make sure you form yourself otherwise *they* will form you and shape you in *their* image and you will be sad and uncompleted and diluted and filled with poison until you are too old and weak to change. You do not know who *they* are but I do know this and will tell you. *They* who you mention are real, and the *everything* is the lies and deceptions and evils, and perhaps you are called to arms like a shining warrior and I will ponder this. I did not expect this.

'But let me enlighten you. We are on our own. You, me, all of us and there is no cavalry coming to save us. No General Custer. I used to think it was just black people who had this problem but maybe it is not just black people. You are we, we are *us* and those not *us* are *them.* You understand this? *Them* are powerful and numbered. *Them* believe they are the pinnacle of social development and evolution. You understand pinnacle . . . ? Good. If anything reveals the otherwise, *them* adopt it and alter it, so Shakespeare stops being for the vagabonds and poor and roughians and wretches and becomes polished and out of reach and unintelligible. You understand *unintelligible*? I will explain sometime. So even Jesus Christ becomes one of them. The *arrogance* . . . So yes, perhaps you should want to destroy it all. You should want to burn the whole thing down and you should not even seek to build anything in its place. You can't be both destroyer and builder. Destroy it if it is of man, and let God create the new world. This is the meaning of holy war. Embrace it. But to feel this way does not mean you have to *act* on it. If you act you will only destroy your own self. This holy war is best fought within yourself and within your own heart. *Inshallah. Amen. Fingers is crossed* . . . whatever is your saying.'

'So I will be a coward.'

He laughed gently. 'Not a coward. Not a coward. You tilt at windmills. You are no coward. But you are very young for such matters. Too young.' He held my hand like I was a child and I liked it and let him. 'I tell you what I wouldn't tell others because to tell others would be casting pearls before swine. You know this saying? It was Jesus saying.'

'Jewish Jesus or Cuban Jesus?' I whispered.

Mister Sesay frowned, 'Who is *Cuban* Jesus?'

'He lives in the café. The Cuban café. He's my friend. He's full grown.'

'And he is called Jesus?'

I nodded.

'Is he *the* Jesus?'

'No. I don't think so . . . he's Cuban.'

'Strange . . . I must visit him one day and test him. Is he amenable to visitors?' I didn't know what amenable meant so I nodded. 'Anyway, the Jesus I speak of is the Jewish one . . .

the Nazarene. We, you and I, have lost very much that is very dear. Too dear. Too much. My only peace is that I am not loved by anyone so I cannot hurt anyone when my death comes. That pain I could not wish for anyone. So much sadness. Forever sadness. You know this too . . . For a long time your compass has been broken and demagnetised . . . you understand this term, demagnetised? I will explain properly in school. You are not one of *them* but they will not stop hitting you like so much clay to try to make you like them. Like teapot or ashtray. I used to wash in bleach until I bled raw and I hoped my skin would go white because whiteskins seemed to possess the whole world and one day I think you will wash in bleach too and it will not help. Believe me. Trust me. But let me tell you, above all *them* fear that you might be strong enough to not want to be *them* and your strength will come for them in their nightmares and one day maybe you will be there standing a giant over them in the night and you will leave nothing spared. Not one stick of straw or blade of grass. *Nothing*. If it is written for you, you will raze their world down to ashes. You will bring the light of the great fire into their darkness like a terrible falling star . . . *Inshallah.*'

He released my hand and it dropped to my lap and then he leaned in and stared into my eyes really close. 'Do not let them sully you. Above all, do not let them sully you. And killing the fat man is disproportionate to his sin . . . I will educate you. This is the way of revenge. If he offended you with his tongue, punish his tongue, if he looked upon you with disrespect punish an eye or two, if he used himself against your beloved castrate him, if his hands were raised against you, let your punishment be upon his hands, you see all this is satisfactory and not overreaction, but his life? This is a big price indeed. Once you kill you cannot cry back the dead and when you cry for them you disturb their rest and you want the dead at rest, believe me. Trust me in this. I have great expectations of you and I know you will carry yourself tall and you are brave. But be just too, and proportionate.' His hand went to the back of my neck.

'For now just breathe and step one foot before the other and move on. As you grow older things get taken away bit by bit. We change bit by bit and the world changes but we do not have to be afraid. We just keep going forward one step in front of the other. Left, right, left, right. Like soldier. Do you know why they teach soldiers to go left right left right? It's not so they look pretty on the parade ground, it's because once you learn it and it becomes your nature you can keep going even when everything else fails and you are ground down and lost and barbarous. Left right left right, like soldier. This is our secret . . . I know this of which I speak because I was a soldier in my homeland, in Paradise, from when I was no higher than a grown man's waist, and from now on, I will call you Soldier. Now straighten up and stick out your chest and pick up your chin Soldier and start to march. You understand? And speak of this to nobody except me.'

'Did you kill people?' I sounded small and stupid . . . 'In Paradise?'

Mister Sesay was silent and I could hear only my breathing and not his, he was so silent he might not be there at all. It was a long time before he said, 'By gun, and knife and cutlass. But they killed me more.' Mister Solomon Sesay sounded far away.

He rose and walked away into the darkness leaving the roof and the night and me and his feet made no sounds on the black gravel and he made no sound as he passed through the door and I knew on that roof that night that Mister Solomon Sesay had shapeshifted and I just wasn't sure what into.

The weather broke late that night and thunder tore the skies and I prayed lightening would strike the roof and bring it down and kill me and everyone in the rubble and destroy the whole world, but the roof stayed on and the world survived and for the next few storm-smashed days the roads flooded and I spent my days with the African teacher and he told me that before gold is gold it must be torn from the filth and rock and much must be smashed and many rocks broken and great heat brought to bear and then flows the golden blood, and if I was to walk on the golden path I needed to smash and break and boil and throw my old self into the furnace.

He said gold comes from pain and death and that makes it rare and for that it is valued.

Majid showed me a book of golden writing and intricate golden shapes and he read it backwards and it was God's words and Majid said that's why it was golden and why it must be honoured and Mister Sesay said all gods were to be honoured and once when he was a boy soldier they desecrated a sacred grove and late that night one man, healthy and strong and fit and hard, sneezed, then another and another and in thirty minutes half the squad and every man who had been into that grove had sneezed themselves to stone cold death. Mister Sesay was careful from that day never to offend gods of any name and he was mortally terrified and suspicious of sneezing and he warned me against desecrations and the infections of the sinuses.

Then a month later I went to see my Lilly.

Twenty-Nine

The Cubans heard about my history in the way café people hear all secrets and sent word calling me to the café one evening and for the first time they treated me like I was fully Cuban, and kind fat Riel and Cuban Jesus sat Lefty and me down and fed us till we were busting then they grilled me. Jesus wore a topknot in his long oiled hair and heavy gold chains and was covered in tattoos of Mother Mary and the saints and wore a singlet even though it wasn't hot.

I told them too much but they just kept listening and I wanted to tell more. Lefty listened all the while like he had never heard it before and sometimes if I missed out something Lefty nudged me and reminded me of a point of detail that seemed to him to be important to the tale. He even told them I had rubbed my cock raw inside Melody and they high-fived me when he said that and shouted to other men in Spanish. I told them about the Fell boys they laughed at my stories and raised their eyebrows and when I told them about Sun hanging himself and the things Swindell said and the pigeons and Carlos.

They were mean-eyed when I was all done, it was late and a whole group of people were listening, and Jesus said to me not to tell it again and he told me he would take me to see Lilly because she had been unvisited too long and left too long without seeing a friendly face and her loving brother and that wasn't my fault but now they knew of it they had a responsibility to remedy it and that's what he said and they wanted to help me. Jesus said from now on Lefty and me were to eat there free for ever and train there anytime we wanted. He said we were home and they were our brothers and family and I walked back to Fell House with a dance in my feet.

On the school break Riel got permission for Lefty, Leon, Johnny and me to be away from Fell House for a few days and Jesus drove a long time north through the shorter days and lengthening nights and we went all the way to the juvenile penitentiary. Jesus had written permission on a special form from Corrections to take Lilly out of jail for a few hours and he had forged papers that showed he was an adult relative. We collected Lilly in the morning at eleven and had to have her back by four that same afternoon and she was allowed to be with us only on account of her good behaviour.

It was cold that day and smelled of ice and snow which was too early but still real and I shivered and was scared to think I was going to see my sister again. It had been so long and maybe we were changed and maybe we wouldn't be the same.

Jesus showed the people in the prison the papers of approval and after he got looked over by the guards like he was a bad smell Lilly came out of the big gate and into an inner courtyard where we were to meet her and we saw each other and she wasn't changed one bit and all my fears went away.

She was pale and looked cold and her denim clothes and a heavy grey sweater were too big for her and her hair was tied back tight but she looked stunningly, classically beautiful and delicate and filled with grace in that cold and soulless place and even its evil pointlessness hadn't damaged her to my eyes. When she came out to me she walked like a model on the catwalk and stood looking at me for a while just an arm's length away and her lips looked white and trembling, then she reached out a delicate finger and touched my nose and my face and lips like she was a blind woman feeling me and I was taller then and she had to reach up where before she reached down, and Jesus took the boys away a bit of distance to let us have space and Lilly cried then I cried deep and sobbing and we hugged and hugged and held onto each other. Feeling her in my arms was like feeling all the good, living, beautiful things that ever went before or were yet to come right there with me and all the aches in my body and pressure in my head went away and I felt warmth, real human godly holy warmth, and breath and life all there entering me from her tiny thin body, and I had grown and was bigger and stronger now and she felt tiny and frail and her hands went over my shoulders and arms and chest.

We stood like that until the others came and guided us out to the car and we couldn't let go of each other so they pushed and squeezed us into the back of the car and didn't say nothing. We drove out from that stone block and hateful place and went ten miles to the local town and got hot chocolate with marshmallows on top and cinnamon sprinkled all over them and cakes with icing and raisins and custard cream inside and then we went to a wild deserted beach where the waves were huge and confused and made of grey and black and green marble and their white foamy tops sprayed over the beach and foam floated high in the air and the wind bit hard into exposed flesh and there were caves filled with fine rivers of icy quartz in the cold. Lilly laughed and played with the spray foam and Lefty and Johnny made her laugh and giggle so hard she had to hold her sides and we all did, even Jesus and Leon, who didn't laugh easy.

One of the caves was full of half-burned candles in little pots and old jars nestled on rocks and ledges where Johnny reckoned the town's lovers went to get away from the world and it was magical and smelled of hope and Johnny lit all them candles and the walls of that cave was shiny like ice and slime covered it and little trickles of cold water ran down the slime but they reflected golden and silver with a million tiny mirrors of crystal ice and quartz, and Lilly sat there with candles bouncing light around her and everyone who saw her perched like a pixie and talking with a voice like a songbird fell straight away in love with her. Johnny couldn't even speak he was so besotted and Lefty stared like he was seeing angels. Jesus looked pleased with what he saw and he and Leon left us there a while and Lilly talked about jail and told me she wrote every day even though I only ever got a few of those letters and I told her so and she snarled inside so I saw it on her face and it was a look I hadn't seen on her before. Later Jesus gave her the address of the Cuban café and told her to send her letters there from now on and I would get them then and nobody at school could take them, which was a really mean thing for a school to do. Lilly told that jail was like a magical land filled with magical creatures and good friends because Lilly could always see beauty in everything, even a rusted-up iron fence and prison wire and mean routines.

I told her how I listened to her on the radio at night and how she kept me safe and took away my fear and she smiled gently and put her finger to my lips and told me to keep it our secret. She said it was our own personal thing and made me promise not to tell anyone about it ever again. I told her Johnny had listened, too, and when she looked at him he shrugged bashfully and she went over and kissed his cheek and he blushed up in that frozen golden room.

Jesus came back with rum and cigarettes and giant French stick loaves filled with every food you can make shaved down thin and tasty and we smoked and drank and ate and you never seen a woman look more perfect with mayonnaise on her chin and jumper and her belly swelling up with too much food and then it was time to take Lilly back and all the drive long we didn't talk a word and when we got to the jail Jesus was strong with me because I was weak and I couldn't let Lilly go. Leon sat in the car and just stared at the world but Jesus and Lefty and Johnny broke us apart back at that prison gate where the guards took Lilly and my friends took me, and as we parted we kissed and kissed and her tongue flicked between my lips and we tried to swallow each other and be one with each other and the pain was so whole and too whole and Jesus whispered to me over and over that this was not the day to do dumb things. He pulled me away and told me to let her go because it was a thousand times harder for her than it was for me and then he got strong and told me to stand strong and tall and show her her brother is a man, but it near killed me when the gate slid closed and she was gone again and there was so much I never said and she never asked and I knew I wasn't going to leave her there for another lot of years because if I did that we were both of us dead. I was coming to get her and she knew it and Johnny and Leon and Lefty knew it and Jesus knew it too and it was my duty.

A guard led her inside by her arm that was broke back when she got arrested and she turned to look at me and I saw her smile and wave but I knew inside she was crying and dying and as the gate closed her strength slipped and I heard her cry out and Jesus caught me in his arms and looked me dead-eye and told me she was doing good. He promised me she was doing good and the time would come to help her but it wasn't here yet and I would make things harder and worse if I went stupid now and he told me to be cool and he shoved me into the car and was strong and he held my face and looked right into my eyes and he smiled and spoke in Cuban and then he told me in English, 'Boy be cool and relax . . . your guns will be hot soon enough.'

Lefty took a hold of my belt and pulled me close to him and Johnny slid in the other side of me so I was boxed in tight and couldn't break out and we drove back fast to Fell, which seemed all at once to be a royal palace and a holy place and a safe place. I cried and Johnny and Lefty cried too and Jesus shook his head and smoked cigarillos with Leon and drank rum straight from the bottle as he drove us two days home and Johnny and Leon shared the drive and we said we would break Lilly out one day soon and we all agreed except Jesus who didn't say nothing on it.

Jesus was a good man but everyone who saw him stared at him and people didn't like him and didn't like no Cubans but they didn't know them like I knew them. In them days Cubans were not so popular but Jesus transcended hatred and fear. Men envied him and babies loved him and women wanted him and I could tell just by seeing how they reacted when he was in front of them and this made him a king and little people hate kings and all them same little people kill the kings in the end and bring down the heroes and they don't care that once all the great oaks are cut down all that's left is scrubby, thorny bushes and nettles, and Melody taught me that, and eventually nobody remembers what a great tree looks like so they never know how poor their world has become and that's called the decay and the weak call it progress.

We stayed the night at a motel run by a sweet old lady and her even older mother who was so old that as we stood there and booked in she licked her thumb and tried to wipe Jesus's tattoos off his hands and neck like they were dirty marks and he just stood there and let her do that while he did the business with the younger old lady. He was patient and had been around old people all his life, so he knew old people always licked their thumb to wipe you clean like you're a baby and it don't matter how old you are and there ain't no point resisting. The younger old lady gave us a discount on account of Jesus being smeared by her mother's spit and let us all sleep in one room, dragging in a put-you-up bed on wheels and not letting us help so it took ages and nearly killed her, and because I was smallest I got to use it. It was better than the car is all the good I can say for it and we ate fried chicken and ice cream and donuts and I felt fat as a cow.

I dreamed vivid that I was on the bank of a river and a wild white horse came galloping at me and I stood my ground and let him rush me and he went around me and came to me and I lay down and he lay down with me, then we slept and when we woke he carried me across the river and I looked back at everyone I knew and they were all on the other bank far away and didn't even see me going. I thought it was pretty mystical and maybe I was going to die and the horse would be taking me to the Summer Lands and I told the others and they just shrugged.

Soon after we got back there was a short little letter from Lilly waiting at the Cuban Café and it was sweeter than coconut cakes and filled with love and lots of thank yous for visiting and chains of her usual flowers drawn in pencil pastel shades with butterflies. She said Johnny and Lefty were beautiful and Jesus was like a magical mariachi and Leon was scary but sweet too.

Lilly didn't seem changed but I knew she was, just as I was, and our meeting was like a blinking of time when our old selves long buried and twisted could speak to each other and play together even if it was just a game of remembering and not real.

What we shared was bigger and stronger than what we were and the past is like that and overpowers the present because the present is weak and small in time, but the past is long and solid and even if it's dark and haunted it's still there real as it ever was. People say live in the present, but the present is just the tip of the spear and without the spear it's nothing and it can't even exist and in her letter she put a tiny photo of our mum and it took my breath away because I had forgotten and Lilly wrote for me to keep it safe and I put it away after a few days because looking at it made me very sad so my throat closed just seeing her. Lilly didn't ask after our mum which meant she either knew something I didn't and wasn't wanting to speak of it or else she had forgotten. Forgetting is something to fear because it's so final and too easy and once you forget you don't even know what you've forgot, so it's like it never was and that's what them old people sitting alone on park benches and staring confusedly straight ahead are staring at, the mist and the hell of forgotten things and faceless shapes with no edges and barely any form and only jumbled voices and noise. Discordant.

I know this is true: To live and be forgotten is worse than never having lived at all and that night I used the edge of a razor to cut my mum's name and Lilly's name into the inside of my bicep nice 'n' neat like artwork so I wouldn't forget. There was so much more I wanted to cut into myself but it hurt too much to cut everything into me and when he saw it Lefty got cross with me and dressed the cutting really careful like a nurse and that night was a good old night, and Moby felt the love and danced for the first time in ages and we all got drunk and licked sugar from his breasts, and two marionettes performed until the early hours and then I listened to Lilly on the radio and some Johnny Cash who was singing about the man coming around and just then Lefty came and sat on my bed and put more cream on my arm and a bandage.

Lefty had took to opening his bible at random times and saying that whatever passage his eyes lit upon was advice from the Good Lord Almighty and he opened that good book and read with his lips moving but not making sounds and then he pondered a while and then he read again and then he said it was going to rain a lot and be *deluge* and he had to build a fucking big boat, and that's his swearing not mine or the bible's, and he seemed daunted and went quietly to his own bed and then I closed my eyes so tight the blackness spun and hurt and squeezed my head till it was tiny as a golf ball and the names in my arm stung and I slept.

Thirty

Two Saturdays after seeing Lilly I was on the roof at day's end when darkness came down and a golden light lit the sky and set fire to the underbellies of clouds and the trees blazed orange and bronze in the cold air. Darkness crept over the earth like dark relentless water and I just sat and smoked and was content and waited for the other boys to come because Saturday night was scheduled traditional getting-drunk night and we were promised a very rare and expensive tequila Leon had liberated and it was a special and exquisite brand, so he said. Lefty came first and then Johnny and we didn't speak a word or even a hello and we just sat and waited and Leon came last of all and looked us over like a general looks over his troops before a battle.

'Glad you could make it,' Johnny said and passed him a smoke.

Leon smiled. He pulled a bottle of tequila out from under his jersey and a dark rum too and unstopped the tequila and slugged before passing it to Johnny and as we drank we were light as supernovas and young again and we all laughed too much and too easy.

The tequila went one way and the rum went the other and as a bottle passed I slugged it and passed it on and I swallowed deeply and was warmed and comforted. Once it was properly dark with just a single molten hook in the western sky like a last kiss and the tequila was drained and the rum was three quarters gone, we all slowly and stiffly rose to go inside and find a victim to bully or rob and the rooftop door crashed open and Swindell almost fell through it onto the roof with an excited shout and panting slobbering breath and his big old flashlight swept its cold light over everything and he so was loud and sudden he made us all jump and startle so I near dropped the bottle I was nursing. It wasn't so dark with the moon risen and the stars opening up and orange light from the lamps that lit the path beneath Fell, but he put his long chrome flashlight beam straight in our faces one by one so we had to look away like naughty little kids and I thought it would all come to nothing because we were kids caught on the roof and nothing more and I hated him but that was all. He wore a walkie-talkie clipped on his belt and went to take it off and call it in but he saw the rum and snatched the bottle from my hand and I let it go too easy and he raised it up like a trophy and giggled and guffawed. Leon went to lead us past him and suddenly Swindell put that light into Leon's face and Leon stared right into it without blinking or flinching and Swindell was boasting about what he was going to do to us and Leon reached out and gently guided the beam of the torch downwards and out of his face and in that moment the air changed and shifted and in that reaching out he crossed a line and just that gentle act was all it took to tell my spider senses and gut brain that a new game was on us and a new journey into some dark poisonous forest was begun, and it wasn't a game I wanted to play or a journey I wanted to take but there I was and there it was and we were playing it and walking it and all I could think was fuck.

Then Leon took the torch from the grown man's startled hand with unexpected ease and put its beam in Swindells face and Swindell let the torch go before he even knew what he had done and Leon took the rum from Swindell's other hand and passed the bottle to Johnny who slugged it and set it down. Leon washed the torch beam up and down Swindell before leaving it in his eyes again and Swindell screwed up his face and he was ugly as an ugly person's baby and he went to snatch the torch but Leon slapped his hand down and I think I groaned.

Leon leaned towards his ear and asked, 'Are you, by chance, possessed of a firearm?'

Swindell looked at him and then at the rest of us. 'Of course I'm bloody not!'

'No . . . ? Then you have made a grave error of judgment,' Leon said and I reached out my foot and crushed the butt of my cigarette so Swindell couldn't report us for smoking as well as drinking and I don't think he saw it.

Swindell's anger and authority fired up and he remembered he was an adult and we were kids and he had authority and we had none and he tried to grab the torch but he was clumsy and Leon was swift and teased him and moved like a matador and Swindell was the bull and again and again and again Leon tempted him with the torch and then the rum and hard words and the man flubbered and was making threats and spitting fury and I could hear he was confused in his anger but he stopped trying to grab things and started to pace and predict our short futures, and as Swindell paced on the roof ranting and raging Leon scratched his nose real calm and cool and was smiling and openly drinking the Captain Morgan. Then as Leon got bored and bent to sit the bottle down Swindell came in fast and strong and explosive and unexpected and he moved unnatural swift and snatched his torch back and knocked Leon backwards and Leon would have gone straight off the roof but he skipped light and moved his feet like a boxer bouncing right on the edge and regained his balance just on that lip and was saved. It took my breath away and stopped my heart because we reached and lunged to save him but were too far away and it was so close and too close and Swindell was reaching out to save him too and his eyes were wide with the horror of sending a boy off the roof, then Leon was safe there was a moment of stillness and relief and thanks-be and he walked forwards and all our eyes met in relief. Then too fast to see demons leapt from the shadows and came starving upon us and we were all of us possessed, then Swindell was real mad again and we surrounded him like jackals and he swore at us with proper foul language and we snapped at him and teased him and Johnny pulled down the big man's trousers from behind and his pants were round his ankles and his balls hung low halfway to his knees and we howled at the spectacle all puny and white and hairy and horrid under the moon and Swindell roared like a bear and tugged up his pants and pushed and shoved us and swore at us and grabbed me by the collar and swung me around so I went flying like a skittle and we laughed as he roared in rage and humiliation and manly fire and he would have killed us right then and he came on and Lefty hooked him in the jaw in reflex and Swindell sat down and thudded like a sack of potatoes dazed and hurt and shocked to his soul, like all men are the first time they get socked in the jaw. His torched clattered and rolled away and he stared up at us and in the dark I could see the whites of his eyes and it was confusion and fear on him like he was a small child and it was stunned, dazed, silent pleading and we were all frozen in that act and we were doomed and dead and done and he felt his mouth and frowned and Johnny and Lefty and me stood over him and Leon picked up the sacred torch and came and sat beside him. Lefty looked scared and shocked at his deed and whispered, 'Sorry, Sir', and Leon patted his big back and told him not to apologise.

Swindell reached absently for his torch but Leon didn't give it to him and played its beam on the man's face then Swindell looked at Lefty and regained some sense. 'You're fucked, boy!' he snarled. 'All this was worth a few days' detention and maybe bye-bye to one of you, but you, you dumb fucking gorilla, you're going to the cops for this! This is assault!'

Lefty looked shaky and not bouncy like he would have been if he delivered that sweet punch in the ring. And Leon sat tighter beside Swindell and lit a cigarette and Swindell looked straight at him. 'What are you doing?'

'Smoking . . .'

'Smoking is prohibited on school grounds. That's in section 2a. A detention and a letter home! At least!'

Leon was amused. 'A detention and a letter home . . .' He patted Swindell's knee and blowing smoke into the night he said, 'You reap what you sow you old fat gluttonous pig fuck. You cherry-picking bloated insult of a human being . . . Lefty, who said "*It is better for him that a millstone were hanged about his neck, and he be cast into the sea, than he should hurt one of these children*"?'

'Jesus said that Leon, it was Jesus. Proper Jewish Jesus not Cuban Jesus they's spelt the same but you say them different.' Lefty nodded proud that he knew the answer.

Leon put the torch beam back in Swindell's face and stood up. 'Well, he was one hard core bastard, eh? A fucking millstone fatman . . .'

Swindell rubbed his jaw again. 'Morons.'

'Shall we kill him?' Lefty whispered. 'He was mean about Sun and has been mean to everyone and took away Carlos, too. And killed the pigeons and we ain't got no heaters on account of him and my mattress springs cut me every night. And my blankets are very coarse.'

Swindell almost choked. 'Your blankets are very coarse? *Coarse*? Where the fuck did you get *coarse*? And kill him? *Kill* him? What are you bloody talking about you dumb fucking ape?'

'You're a bad bad man.' Lefty sounded disappointed.

Swindell sighed deep and tired. 'You're all fucking morons. My Christ . . . Just go to bed all of you and tomorrow one of you will hang, at least one. So get some sleep before you make it worse.'

'He's lying,' Lefty said. 'No one's gonna hang, eh boys?'

Johnny smiled kindly. 'No Lefty. It's a figure of speech. He means we're in real deep trouble.'

Johnny took the bottle and swigged, he passed it to me and I swigged.

'We could torture him . . .' Johnny smiled.

Leon shrugged. 'We do that anyway. But . . . we can't let Lefty hang! Fuck. We ain't even in trouble. If he says anything we say we got into a tussle with him 'cos he was making the boy there suck his cock . . .' He leaned low over Swindell. 'You tell anyone about tonight and we will all witness and swear that you were making him suck your cock and lick your ginormous saggy bollox, which we can unfortunately describe in minute fucking haunting detail. That gets out and you'll wish you *had* died here tonight. You'll be one they fucking hang, *Sir*.'

'You sucking his cock?' Lefty asked me.

'No Lefty, it's a cover story.'

Leon got so close in Swindells face it was like they were touching. 'You understand? And don't come back to our house

246

again . . . oh, and be fucking nice to people.' Then Leon snatched the walkie-talkie from Swindell's belt and went to throw it from the roof but stopped and looked at it and tested the weight and examined it closer and laughed to Johnny. 'It's a fake . . . a fucking toy!' and Johnny laughed and Swindell squirmed pitifully and reached out and Leon handed it to him.

Swindell tucked the walkie-talkie back in his belt and held out his hand for his torch but Leon tossed it towards the edge of the roof and it bounced and rolled but stopped just short and its light washed back at us all and Mr Swindell rose wearily and went to pick up his torch and he was dead silent and knew we had won the night, and Johnny and Leon and Lefty started to walk away and I followed Swindell and picked up his torch for him and handed it to him and he took it without a word of thank you, which is just plain impolite.

I looked into his eyes real close and I saw the moon and stars and city lights behind him and he smiled and steam rose from his ears and he took a big deep life-filled breath and one of the boys called to me and in the darkness and shadows Swindell looked flushed and alive and relieved and almost young even though he was still sweating and panting like he was on top of a young beautiful woman with deep watery eyes and copper ringlets, and he was one inch from the roof edge and had his back to it and my hands came up and my feet were balanced and he saw me and his eyes changed and widened and I saw myself and I saw my hands go forward and felt my muscles coiled and my hands were on him. He was soft in my grip and I felt my fingers pull his flesh into my tight fists and I wanted to bite and eat his face and I was ready to explode and I pushed an inch and had him and tensed and then I was trapped and frozen and it was like my hands were blocked from doing the act and I could have pushed him right off that roof and he would be gone and it was so easy and I should have pushed him and I don't even know why I was blocked, but it was like a metal band was about me and locking me like a statue, and I could have just done it so easy and every cell in my body said push him and he falls and he is on the edge and just a feather touch and he is gone and I had dreamed of this moment and planned this moment and promised the dead this moment and sworn this act and then, and then, I couldn't push him. I held him strong and I clenched his coat into one fist and his throat in the other and I wanted every cell and muscle and sinew in me to push and push and I pulled instead.

I stood there in front of him and I just stood there and in my mind I saw I pushed him and he didn't scream and when he landed it was three floors plus the basement and his weight landing flat made the building shake and I heard his bones crack. His face stuck in my mind as he went over. His eyes and his living sparkle.

Leon walked to the roof edge watching me real close and he didn't take his eyes off me and didn't get between me and the edge of the roof and he was looking at me the whole time and then he took my hands off the man and took me by the shoulder and led me through the door and down and didn't say a word and my boys looked at me like mutes and Swindell didn't move the whole time and he knew for certain that he just saw death and for some reason death didn't want him.

I went down and then outside to where my mind saw Swindell was laying and it wasn't very nice because his arm was folded under him and one leg pointed the wrong way and looked like no leg should ever look and he was bleeding heavy from his head but he was still breathing with little bubbles of blood around his mouth and I couldn't help looking at him but had to look away and back and away and back and part of me was panicking and part was really calm like a natural born killer and his eyes were open and he blinked and his eyes looked around but he didn't seem to know what he was looking at. And I made believe the boys stood back shocked and pale and dumb and Lefty looked ashen and tearful and I could see him clear from the lights of the house, and from that other world of innocence and schoolboy pranks and harmless youth I could hear music and boys talking and someone playing piano just a few feet away in the prep room and nobody knew the fat man was there but I saw myself knelt next to him taking care to avoid the blood and gently I put one hand over his mouth and pinched his nose with my other hand and I told him it was OK and he was fine. His chest bucked and he looked wild-eyed but didn't move much and I think his back was broke and the feel of his skin and face and breath and sweat and blood and spit wasn't very nice at all and he was sweating but cold and his skin was rubbery and I held him firm but not roughly and he died quick.

Then sudden as a gunshot I knew things were different and I had fallen and I was no hero and I was a gutless coward like everyone else because Swindell lived when I could have ended him and right there his life should have ended in a broken body and deadened brain and the hand of a child over his mouth and nose, and my chance was gone and I couldn't do it and I hadn't done it and I was in eternal shame. I let myself be led away and I was a disgrace.

The ripples from such cowardice are like a black sludge virus that changes and destroys everything it touches and cowardice is the greatest sin a person can commit even if it's not always the greatest crime, and it lingers on you like sickly scent and I wanted to scrub it off but it don't work that way and I couldn't scrub it off no matter how much I tried and I tried hard.

And I was ashamed and I was impure and I felt soiled and low and base so I washed and I washed and showered and cried and scrubbed myself again and again like I was baptising myself over and over and Lefty pulled me from the showers and I was raw from scrubbing and bruised from punching myself in my own face and he read me from his good book and soothed me with Sudocrem, which heals all wounds, but I was changed and that was for ever and I was so small, like an ant but not as strong.

In the next days Mister Sesay watched me with snake eyes and called me one day to stay behind in class and he took me back into his tiny unwindowed office. As I sat in the low light and mustiness of that room I realised my hands were scabbed and sore where I had been picking them and it was a nervous habit and maybe I was trying to pick off my cowardly skin and Mister Sesay turned a chair and sat facing me and looked at me and looked at my hands and for a few minutes we stared at each other and then I started to cry and I told Mister Sesay everything, shame and all and how I had betrayed the dead, and I told him about the names in my black notebook of people to kill and how I had failed to even kill one and how I had washed and scrubbed.

'This book of yours . . . is my name in this book?'

I nodded and caught my breath. 'On page seven.'

'Page seven is good,' he said.

I wiped my nose. 'Why is that good?'

'I too have such a book and you are on page three of my book. As I am a far superior killer than you, you will not reach your page seven. Assuming you even start on page one . . . In truth you are less than a convincing or productive killer. Why am I in your book?' I shrugged because I had forgotten his crime and he smiled and ruffled my hair and afterwards he sat in silence with me again then took my hand and he whispered, 'This is murder you have wanted done . . . murder is not a good or sensible act and you are not a coward for not killing a man. Not a coward, you hear me? You must understand that killing is not honourable. There are many ways to skin the goat . . . Killing is base and not sophisticated or educated or imaginative, especially pushing an fat old man from the roof. Where is honour in such a thing? Where is glory? You want to be a hero but there are many ways to be a hero. Remember this always. Many ways. The mother who works fourteen hours a day to feed her child alone, is she not a hero? Poor and tired and still beautiful and filled with grace? A father wounded and shattered and lied about, who battles and bears pain and agony and sadness without murmur and with great dignity. A man who fights to raise his son and free his daughter, is he not a hero?'

I caught my breath as an image flickered in my mind and I turned it away. 'Your father was a hero, was he not? I would say so . . . To endure such pain and torture and not cry out, to dine daily with death and see death grow bold in his presence and poverty grow in its shadow and yet not shrink or hide or whimper. Is this not hero enough? I would be proud of such a father. And the mother, so strong for so long. Brave and fighting in such darkness and working fingers to the bone and holding fast against such fates and caring for so many beloveds, and all as her world crumbles until she no longer knows her own face but still she loves. I would be proud of such a mother as this. An eagle soaring over mountains is not brave or heroic, he is just an eagle doing his business, but a sparrow soaring over the mountain, this is brave and heroic. This is truly tilting at windmills. You are the child of soaring sparrows. I would be proud of such heroes . . . See them . . . I see them and I see you. You are not a coward.'

I stared at Mister Solomon Sesay and I knew he was a crazy man and I saw that sparrow fluttering wide-eyed and terrified and its little wings going ten to the dozen like it was plugged straight into the mains and his little sparrow brain doing flicker flick flicker, flicker flick flicker wondering what the fuck was going on and I wondered who the teacher saw before him and I saw that sparrow falling and falling and as the ground came up I closed my mind. I went to leave but Mister Sesay pulled me back and I was angry and my anger boiled at him and I saw a crashing sparrow and a wounded and bruised man and a frail and unbreaking woman betrayed by her mind and tortured by demons beyond her controlling and they were smiling in my memory and filled with love and I had refused them and I was ashamed of myself and I remembered how evil swarms people with plague and pestilence and poverty and their strength is stolen and how they rise and rise, but how God fells them down with all their power and life sucked out and I saw it. I hated God with all my might and I swore I would storm heaven one day and slaughter him and all his angels and I lashed out at Mister Sesay but he caught my hands and he pulled me into him. I bit into his shoulder but got no flesh and just a mouthful of coat and he let me and I told him I would kill Swindell and I would eat his face and his heart and his liver and I would storm heaven and I will kill God and all his angels and turn his sunsets black and to ash because He was not righteous or holy or just and Mister Solomon Sesay hushed me and shushed me and calmed me and I trembled and slowly, slowly Mister Sesay brought me back.

'You are good boy. And no bleach and scrubbing. Look at me . . . five years I scrubbed in bleach . . . industrial strength commercial grade, and I am still an underpaid and unvalued black man!' He grinned and tried to make me smile and he wiped my tears with his thumbs and looked kindly on me and I tried to smile for him but it made me cry more. Then he said 'It seems we never stop grieving, child. But we must find ways to celebrate the days of our beloveds. They are still here, just changed. They are on the evening wind and warm sun and the soft rain and they watch over us in the night. They are in the air we breathe. Maybe in some way in their passing they become even closer to us, more precious and life giving. Inhale deeply, child, and breathe them in. The Lord sees you. Allah sees you. Rejoice in his everlasting company. You will understand one day. Heaven is not for storming. You are not a coward. I see you. And you will see yourself. You will understand one day, and one day you will see. I make this a promise.'

Mister Sesay and me discussed many things over the next weeks, tucked in the back of his classroom in break times between lessons and sometimes after school, but we never talked of the ghosts and phantoms and dream people again and if I saw them in my imaginings I sent them away and didn't know them yet.

And without telling anyone where I got them from I took Mister Sesay's teachings back to Leon and Johnny and Lefty and they nodded in agreement and wonder at my wisdom.

Swindell faded from sight after that night and maybe his humiliation and his toy radio and sagging balls done for him and he didn't want to see any of us again and his passion for teaching was most likely undermined and taking a man's passion and laughing at his humiliation was a killing of sorts but I didn't feel proud or satisfied.

Leon took us shooting and told us he had his passport and tickets and was going away real soon and any day now and everything was set and he told it as he put bullets through playing cards at three hundred yards.

That same night we got near dead drunk and when we were getting that way Leon spun the bottle as we all sat around and when it spun he said whoever the bottle pointed to when it stopped had to give us a name and that name would be killed stone dead this very week. Hearing him say that we were all silent but Leon smiled and spun the bottle fast and he said they had let me down and I was the only one who had been willing to kill and heroic and willing to do the ultimate deed and he said, 'That's why he has wisdom now, we've all heard him, his mind has been opened', and the bottle spun on and I couldn't tell them Mister Sesay had been tutoring me and reading books with me and teaching me to tilt at windmills, and the bottle spun and it stopped and the darkness of the room closed in and the soft yellow lamp light seemed far away as the bottle rocked gently and its noise was like a heartbeat. It pointed to Johnny.

Johnny sighed real deep, sat up straight and spun the bottle again. The only noise in that room was the bottle spinning and rocking on the wooden floor and it slowed and slowed and again it stopped on Johnny like an invisible hand just made it happen. After a few soft breaths he reached out to spin it again but Leon's hand fell on his and stopped him. Johnny closed his eyes. 'Ms Biggs,' he said.

Leon nodded. 'That's a righteous choice. And it's justified. At the weekend then. we can't wait longer or I'll be gone away, so, how? You get to choose.'

Johnny opened the bottle and drank, then nodded like a voice in his head told him it was OK. 'Let's hang her. For Sun', and we all agreed and the deal was done and I went to bed drunk and a marionette came to me and whirled and posed and played a mandolin and a mandolin isn't fruit and I didn't know that.

Thirty-One

Leon spent the next couple of days staring silently at the world and packing and staring more like he was etching memories and he looked both the saddest and the happiest anyone had ever seen him. He laundered and pressed his best clothes above fifty times and gave away things to boys who might use them and he took me and Majid walking back into the forest and hills and showed us where he buried guns and ammunition and explosive dynamite and he called it his camp. He made me strip down his rifle with a blindfold on and I had to recite all the things he had taught me about shooting and blowing stuff up.

I felt water in my guts because Leon leaving was big change and I didn't like change and it weakened us and we were still fighting so in some ways it was like I was being betrayed, but I didn't say nothing because if someone wants to leave you have to let them go and if they come back they are yours and if they don't they never was and that's profound and I seen it written on a poster.

Johnny went and bought a really nice length of rope from a boat chandler's, thin as your thumb and soft and flexible but strong enough to hold a couple of ton or more, and it had a little bounce in it too so it wouldn't snap when her body hit the bottom of the run and maybe wouldn't jerk off her head. Johnny had it all thought through and I was impressed by his diligence. The rope was yellow and burgundy and I thought Ms Biggs would like it and it would look quite pretty on her. Lefty buried himself in his bible and doubled up his training but he wasn't much fun because he was real broody and intense with not many words or smiles and he was solemn and his bottom lip stuck out.

Ms Biggs often worked late in her office on the first floor of the college main building right by the top of the stairs. Those stairs were marble from when the college was fine and proud and over the stairs was a landing with solid brass hand rails right by her office door. Almost certainly she would be in there with a heater on and a low light burning as she looked through files and reports for some way she could harass someone no matter if they were student or staff, because she liked to feed on innocent weaker people and needed to cause trouble and pain and it's just the way she was. Sunday night she calculated her pain calendar for the coming week and our plan was ABC and we wrote it in the back of the little black book-of-soon-to-be-dead-bastards. We would set up the noose and rope and she wouldn't know and she would come out for Leon real easy if he showed up at her door and from then it would be simple and quick. Leon would feign needing her advice and pretend he was suddenly reluctant to confide in her and walk away into the darkness of that landing and she would follow him and try to get him to talk and we would come from the shadows and grab her fatness and throw the noose over her head and throw her over the balcony and she would swing and jig to her well-deserved painful-as-fuck death. Or else her neck would snap and she would go quick if the Good Lord Almighty chose. I thought maybe God would make her linger a good few hours because as far as I could see she really was Satan's own personal fuckbuddy.

That was the whole of the plan and even though there wasn't a cloud in the sky the Good Lord sent deluge upon deluge that night.

Leon had the long rope coiled across his body like a bandolier and the noose already made and we all wore black and moved silently and we got in a side door of the school and locked it behind us.

It was dark in the corridors and moonlight lit up the tops of the walls through the high windows and the top edges of all the ancient photographs that lined the walls were lit silver. The boys in those photo frames were all gone now but they stared down at us like a curious and cold audience judging everything we did and they measured me every day and looked down their noses at my efforts and even my very existence. Other boards were long panels of rich dark wood and had names etched in gold of student leaders and prefects and athletes from long ago and in any light they lit up shining in gold leaf. I sometimes stopped to look at the names but always tried not to remember any because they were all dead, and carrying dead names when them names aren't your own people is a sure way to get haunted and dragged down. Sam's name wasn't there and I knew that already because I had searched.

But Hamish Taunton's was and I saw it for the first time in that darkness and it made me stop dead stiff in my tracks and I never had seen it before and if I had it would have stopped me anytime and even on a bright sunny day. The boys came back when they realised I wasn't walking with them and Johnny hissed at me, 'What's up with you?'

I pointed at the name in the moonlight. 'I seen that name before,' I said.

'Course you have, all of them. You walk past them every fucking day!'

'No . . . Him . . . Hamish. I mean I met him once. On my way to Fell when I first came. He gave me sweets. Rhubarb and Custards. At the airport.'

'Fuck off.'

'For real.'

'You still got them Rhubarb and Custards my brother?'

I shook my head. 'Long gone.'

Johnny looked at Leon and I quickly told them more about the boy at the airport who had been real nice to me and Leon then put his finger to my lips to shush me.

'What are you fucking reading?'

I pointed to the board. 'There, Hamish Taunton.'

Leon and Johnny looked at the board and each other and Johnny went to speak but Leon stilled him with a raised hand. 'So what? He didn't say his name was Hamish fucking Taunton did he?' Leon asked.

'No, he wrote it on a piece of paper.'

'So maybe it was one of his ancestors or his granddad or maybe Hamish Taunton is some famous name he's heard of or passed down through his generations? No matter. You never met anyone on that board because that board is a hundred fucking years old.' He reached into his jacket and took out his zippo which was brass and engraved with his initials and a circle with the crosshairs of a scope on the back and he lit up the plaque on the wall so we could see it better. The golden name became like a magnet and pulled me in closer like it had breasts and erect nipples.

'I ain't heard of him,' Lefty whispered so loud we all looked to see if his voice brought Ms Biggs from her office.

'So what?' Johnny asked,

'So he can't be famous!'

'Because you know every famous name in the fucking famous name dictionary do you?' Johnny was fighting not to sound fed up but he sounded it anyway.

'No . . . I ain't even got that dictionary,' Lefty shrugged. 'But what if it was a ghost?'

'Like Sam?' I whispered.

Leon snuffed his lighter. 'If he was a ghost, he wouldn't be boarding a fucking aeroplane would he? When people are dead they're fucking dead. They don't hang out in airports handing out fucking sweeties to transient little shit kids, do they?' Leon walked on and we followed. Lefty was trying to get him to stop without speaking so he tugged on him like a little kid tugs on his fast-walking mum and then Lefty grew up in a split second and spun Leon to face him and in the darkness the boxer looked mean and moody and dangerous and his shoulders were up and poised and he said his mind was made up. He said he searched the Good Book before and couldn't find no justification for killing the woman bitch as she was and now he was worried she would come back as a ghost.

Leon and Johnny whisperingly and urgently detailed every sin Ms Biggs had committed and the way she had driven out so many boys without good cause but Lefty shook his head, no. He agreed fully she was a bad person and a bitch and nasty and mean but that didn't warrant a hanging and I kind of agreed but I never said a word because I was thinking of Hamish and ghostly Rhubarb and Custards.

Leon kept on at Lefty and Johnny crept to the office and was scoping it out and spying inside and Leon settled Lefty by shushing him over and over and then he whispered, 'This ain't like smoking, you know? You don't just quit. It's what Jesus wants. It's good work. Godly work.'

'I don't think so Leon. I don't think Jesus wants this.'

'There's no wriggling out of this Lefty. There's no *And I don't want to, shit*!'

Lefty shrugged, 'I do want to shit.'

'What? You want to what?'

'I want to shit. Really bad. A proper shit.'

'What?'

'Shit.'

'Shit? Now? Right now?' Leon looked from Lefty to me and Johnny crept back to us. 'Are you kidding me?'

Lefty shook his head. 'I need to. Badly. Very badly. Not normal badly. Very badly.' And his face screwed up like a little kid and he looked panicked.

Johnny whispered to Leon, 'Maybe he's right, maybe Jesus don't want her dead . . . She ain't in her fucking office!'

Leon laughed and was dismayed and whispered to Lefty, 'It's OK mate, it just so happens, it's all off anyway.'

Lefty looked hard at him trying to see if he was being tricked. Leon nodded,

'You're lying.' Lefty said, and he clutched at his stomach.

'I'm not lying.'

'So I bought that rope for nothing? I paid good fucking money for that . . .' Johnny protested.

Leon laughed. 'You don't hang someone just because you bought a fucking rope!'

'Well fuck!' Johnny grumbled.

Johnny went on mumbling and grumbling about how much that rope cost and what a waste of money it was and what else he could have spent that money on and what kind of *intelligence outfit* were we operating that would send us to a kill zone with no enemy present and Leon ignored him and put his hand on Lefty as the big boy bent a little and held his stomach and groaned softly. 'I'll do you a trade Lefty. You deposit that steaming smelly shit you're holding onto right there outside her office, and we let her live . . . Deal? For Jesus.'

Lefty looked horrified but bent over more. 'That's disgusting, Leon. I ain't gonna do that. I'm a warrior, warriors don't shit outside doors!'

'To save her life? And it looks like you gotta go real bad . . . seems like a Christian act to me . . . go on. She won't ever know it was you. Go on . . . do it . . . you gotta do it anyway . . . Why waste it? Take a shit and save a life, big guy!'

Lefty swayed and groaned and ran and stumbled and staggered crouched and gut clenched through the dark towards the golden light of that deserted office and right outside the door he dropped his track pants and pulled them right off and he crouched and instantly exploded like mortar fire and distant deep core earthquakes and I actually felt the floor vibrate under my feet and wondered what the hell he had eaten and hoped to God I hadn't eaten it too, and Johnny and Leon and me were in awe of such a deposit and Johnny gently took us both by the tail of our jerseys and pulled us backwards further into the dark of an alcove and kept pulling us and he held us as we watched and I screwed up my face and the scent came over the air and Johnny glided us more and more backwards into the blackness and the office door opened and Ms Biggs stood over Lefty and Lefty looked up at her and said *hello*, just like that.

Unseen in the dark we bit deep into each other to keep from being heard as we swallowed the scene in awe and horror and wicked jubilation and flapped our hands in sheer delight and time fled and all the ghosts too and then came the greatest most terrible scream I ever heard as Ms Biggs' brain finally processed

262

what she was seeing and smelling and feeling and she would never forget it and neither would I and she was scarred deep to her soul and she was panting and clutched her huge heaving bosom, and Lefty stayed crouched and she whacked him on the head with a pile of papers she was holding and she dropped them as she struck and Lefty reached out and picked them up and they were stained now and dripping yellow and brown and black and Lefty tried to help and do good and he handed them up to her and kept one sheet and tried to wipe and then she blew again and again and Lefty was whimpering and Johnny whispered, 'I lied . . .' and Leon actually fell down with utter and silent delightful ecstasy.

The light from Ms Biggs' office was low and warm and spilling golden like Christmas Eve through her windows and half-open door into the corridor and from our hidey hole I could just see through the crack in the door and I could see she had a golden silk scarf draped over a lamp and that office was real fairy-tale cosy and she screamed and bashed Lefty and his arse squelched with yet more offerings and I heard him whimper more and Ms Biggs tried to hit him without getting too close but she trod in some of that awful pooling shit and for an instant she was surfing and then falling, and then Ms Biggs and Lefty were embraced and flat out and sliding and we wanted to stay but we would have got caught for sure so we scurried out unseen and unheard and unsmelt and in pain at holding in so much happiness, and it was all so perfectly perfectly perfect. I swore I would take her name out of my book because Ms Biggs was going to be smelling that shit and feeling it on her skin for ever and she would be tortured by this night for ever and ever Amen and Hallelujah! And I laughed until my face froze with cramp and then I cried and was all overcome with happiness and joy.

Thirty-Two

We lay down on the front field in the damp night grass trying to recover, but my laugh had hurt my body and I couldn't breath and we crawled to the bushes and Leon gave me the fine and fancy yellow and burgundy rope and I hid it under leaves and dirt and we sneaked on our bellies and it was just about the best night ever there was.

Then Lefty came into the moonlight and stood at the top of the long steps looking out over the field like he was searching for us. He looked burnished and even in the darkness I could see he was holding his track pants and boxers in one hand and was all naked from the waist down to his white socks and trainers and he was breathing heavy, and his clothes hung unnaturally heavy in his hand like they were wet but it wasn't water and I swear I could smell the clinging evil liquid shit even from one hundred yards.

Johnny, Leon and me clung to each other and Lefty came down a step or two sniffing the air for our scent.

'He can't see us . . . not from there . . .' Leon whispered.

'No chance . . .' Johnny's voice wouldn't have disturbed a deer at ten yards but Lefty paused and tilted his head and turned his eyes to us like a demonic robot and he focused and lazered right into us as we flattened harder into the earth, 'No. Fucking. Way,' Johnny hissed. 'Super-fucking-natural . . . .'

Lefty raised his pants high towards the moon and shit ran off them and dribbled down his arms and I saw it clear as he saw us and we shivered under his sight.

'You three gonna wear this for a fucking fucking week!' Lefty bellowed like a rutting stag and he took off leaping down the steps six and eight at a time and ran straight at us, and we screamed and yelped and tried to rise and run but we were all tearing each other backwards to give Lefty a sacrificial smearing victim and we fell and staggered and he came on like a bull and thundering out biblical verses and unseemly abuse and I think he was possessed right then and we staggered into graceless and dishonourable flight.

We ran blind and desperate and still Lefty closed, and we ran one whole lap of the field with him chasing us and getting nearer like we were in some Satanic 400-yard dash and we were panting and losing and then Lefty doubled over again and we stopped and caught our breath and he stared at us and I don't think he was one bit happy. Lefty pushed down his belly pains and stood up tall and he came on again like he would kill us all, so we broke off that field and in panic we ran straight towards the lights of town and Lefty followed. Then came police sirens and adult voices and flashlights in the trees all round and Leon shouted, 'Run home Lefty. Cops cops!' But Lefty wasn't following us no more and we were safe through the hedges and trees and settled to a nervous walk and Leon said he would buy Johnny and me a burger and sing Lefty's name loud in honour, but best not go back to the house just yet, he said, in case the big boy slaughtered us all, and we all agreed.

Leon was good to his word and bought us all burgers and chips and pickled onions and after we sat exhausted by happiness and bad food under a street lamp on the corner near a long set of stone steps that led into a park. We were smoking and retelling the story and keeping low and every now and then one of us would laugh as the memory of what we had seen came into our minds and then we would all laugh and we killed an hour that way until we saw Lefty pass us real slow and all cuffed up and head down and bloody in the back of a police cruiser. He looked up as he passed and saw us in the shadows and he looked like he was hurting and had been crying and it wasn't OK no more, not by a long long way, and it wasn't funny no more either.

We went back to Fell in shadows all the way and not talking and we went straight to Leon's room to form a plan to save Lefty, and Majid, cloaked up in a deep blue robe and his face covered like an assassin, was sitting on the bed in the light of a single candle and beside him was Mister Solomon Sesay. For a few moments we had a silent unbreathing standoff and Mister Sesay stared into me and I couldn't read him.

Silently Majid held up his hand to Leon and passed him his brass-engraved zippo. For the first time ever I saw Leon look shocked and just for a second he was fully stunned and I saw his hand go down and tap his empty pocket and then he stood taller and took the lighter and looked at it and slipped it into that same pocket. 'Thank you,' was all he said and he reached out and flicked the light switch so a single overhead bulb lit up cold and white and he took two steps to the window and closed the curtains.

The room was immaculate with everything lined up perfect and neat. The bed was made and sheets turned down and there wasn't a mite of dust in that room so you felt guilty just breathing, and Leon didn't like people in his room.

There was a bedside lamp and an oil-filled radiator plugged in at the wall but nothing of home and no photos and no ornaments or clutter and a single long holdall under the desk. Leon bent and turned on the bedside lamp at the wall then flicked off the overhead light so the warmth of the lamp was freed. He snuffed the candle and with the coming of the lamplight the mood seemed to ease a little.

'You were spying on us?' Leon asked. Majid nodded.

'I didn't see you . . . good work . . .' Leon looked grudgingly impressed.

Mister Sesay put his hand on Majid's shoulder and patted him but Mister Sesay wasn't one bit smiling or looking proud.

We never mentioned Ms Biggs to Mister Sesay because he already knew and we went straight to the part about Lefty being arrested. He listened without blinking and said he would go to the police station and get him released or find out what he was being held for. 'And when I have him I will bring him home to here, but then, once this dust is settled, we have no more dealings. As soon as the spotlight is passed you are passed with it from my eyes. All of you. Each and every one of you. You made the boy Lefty debase himself to spare an innocent if unpleasant life and all was seen and heard and now he will be severely punished and the hatred will rise against him and he cannot hide and he cannot deflect it. They will see his blackness and his crime and they will feel justified in their hatred and you are not friends, you are abusers. I am ashamed to know you. And to hang the woman? Really? Is this just? No!'

And I was cut in two by his words and then cut in two again so I was quartered and the black teacher didn't blink and we hung our heads. He told Leon to dress quickly in his best number ones and meet him on the lane out back. Leon nodded because he understood something I didn't.

Leon and Johnny and me washed and brushed up really good and were angelic and shiny and looking fine and innocent like kids in a painting or a choir and we all went to the car, but Mister Sesay was cold to me and as the others got into his old battered rustbucket he sent me away and being sent away made me bleed inside. He said Leon and Johnny were from solid farming families and the cops would know their names and know they had family weight, but Majid was an Arab and I was a poor, hated runt from a family of highway robbers and pirates, and Johnny tossed me a pack of smokes and me and Majid sat on the roof and blew smoke rings round the moon while the African teacher took two shiny white boys to a racist cop-shop to free a black boxer who just shit an Everest outside a white lady teacher's office. I reassured Majid that Lefty was a good and solid Christian and Majid said that explained everything and we were fucked for sure.

It took three hours to get Lefty bailed to Mister Sesay but in the end he came home.

The cops who picked him up said when they approached him and cornered him he fought them and pulled a knife, so they beat him in self-defence and stuffed him in the car where he shat all over their back seat and squirted it up the windows. They made it bigger than it was once they realised he was a school kid and they had overdone the bashing and he had bloodied one of their noses and dropped the other with a body shot and he was hurting from blows and words and injustice and the deluge that was the purging of his bowels, but the police report was clear and precise and they even found a knife on him which he never would carry and drugs he never would use and Ms Biggs made a report about the vandalism of her office but withdrew it when she heard the amount of charges Lefty already faced and heard he was beaten up.

Lefty never told anyone we were with him that night and he said it was just a prank and he was sorry for what he done, and I begged him for forgiveness and so did Leon and Johnny, and Lefty said there wasn't nothing to forgive and he said it was his own fault but he was deeply sad.

Afterwards Mister Sesay's car wasn't starting in the car park back of Fell and he was killing the battery because he wanted to get home and was impatient and still angry. I heard the trouble and knew its starter motor needed a hammer blow because my dad's old Singer had the same fault and I remembered it and the sad sound of the slow clicking death. Quickly I grabbed up a hammer from the cleaners store and ran to get there before he fixed it so I could help and be a hero and win favour, and I sought out Mister Sesay but he got out of his car and started to walk away and I chased him. I asked him how had I offended him so much and he didn't even answer me and he kept walking and pulled up the hood of his old coat to cover his head and I thought I should bury that hammer in the back of that hood and how easy would that be, but he read my mind and spun and looked at me and I thought he was going to hit me or cry or both, and he was angry and holding in the anger and I hadn't seen him like it before and he was tight in the mouth and I was sick to have disappointed him and afraid to be losing his cloak and his friendship and my teacher walked away without a word and I stood and watched him and then I fixed his car and it only took a single hammer tap.

We helped Lefty undress and I got him into the shower and he was brave and smiled until the warm water got on him then he cried and I heard him. I think trying to do the right thing and always being beat down hurt him more deeply than I could know and seared his actual soul and I let him cry and just stood outside the stall holding his towel and at least he didn't shit again and he said he couldn't figure it out and he didn't recall what he ate that could cause it but maybe it was the deluge and God done it to him and I thought maybe he was right because that shit sure was biblical.

Then Lefty slumped down in the shower and I got in the shower with him and knelt beside him and let him cry all over me and he said the Lord was sad with him and he was ruined and lost and that shower ruined my best number ones but I figured I wouldn't be wearing them again any time soon.

Johnny came a while later with fresh towels and his best clean and pressed flannel pyjamas with tiny armadillos on and tigers and we got the big boy to bed and Majid watched over him.

Afterwards I drank gin with Leon and Johnny and we didn't speak. When I went to bed and hoped I wouldn't dream I didn't and the next few days and nights passed in a rush so cloudy it was like seeing through ice.

I didn't sleep much and didn't eat much on account of Lefty's shit still troubling my mind and definitely didn't talk much, and especially not when anyone was around to hear, and all I was thinking was poor Lefty was in trouble for saving a life and Leon was going away to wipe out nations and Mister Sesay hated me, and all that made me poorer and weaker and sadder and broker.

When the gin ran out we drank bourbon we confiscated from the younger boys and those younger boys were going all wrong and with no significant adult supervision they were drinking and carousing and their behaviour was sometimes appalling, so we taxed their weed too.

Johnny and Leon hunted one last time before Leon went soldiering, and brought back pig and goat, and the Fijians fetched up lobsters and on Leon's last evening we had a party. It was a good party and wild and by the end we were banging drums and making music and dancing in a big sweaty group, and Moby was wearing a belly dancer's outfit and veils and a golden headband with a jewel in his forehead and he looked beautiful and Majid was dancing with him and clapping and laughing and it was just about the biggest and wildest party anyone ever saw. We were like rich kids at Christmas and no adults even came close and Lefty looked happy and like his worries were gone for the night.

As we went to bed Leon embraced us one by one and I knew one day loneliness would eat me up and I would be lost in it like Jonah and it seemed like all my life I was made of sand and took the shape of everyone I got blown up against but I had no shape of my own and however hard I clung to that shape it always went away and the winds came and I was nothing again. I couldn't stand the thought of losing my friends one by one to the world and I was deep tired and drunk and I should have slept sound and long but my dreams were all messed up and I woke up scowling a couple hours later and I was scowling so hard my face hurt and I was too hot in the cold dorm.

Thirty-Three

Sam was standing in the darkness looking down at Humphrey, but just after I woke he turned to me and his wounded face smiled. 'He's a butt ugly little fucker, eh? Looks like a fucking gargoyle. Scared of life that one. I can smell it.' He knelt beside me and stroked my face with the back of his hand and it wasn't so cold but it was very bony and his skin was hard and thin, 'Not like you . . . You're so, so brave. Mad as a fucking hatter though, aren't we? You're pretty too . . . not like ugly boy there.' My face stung and I knew straight away I was bruised in the mouth and jaw and all my face and someone must have hit me in my sleep.

'You seen yourself lately?' I went to sit up but my sheets were jammed tight under the mattress and tucked in hard so I was pinned down flat and helpless.

'Now, you know that just isn't fair.'

'Help me,' I hissed at him but he shook his head. 'Did you do this?'

'Did I do what?'

'Pin me?'

'No.'

'Well, unpin me!' But Sam shook his head again.

'You've been busy. Too busy. You've become a bad, bad boy. Anne with an E won't like what she sees, Cutherbert!'

'Let me out of this!'

'No can do. Wriggle fool, from your feet up, like a worm.' He wriggled a grotesque demonstration.

I gave up and stared at the dead boy. 'What do you want?'

'Already got it. You're awake. I just wanted you awake. Awake, alert and making sense. Or a reasonable proximity.'

'Why?'

Sam smiled then and even in the soft-lit dark it wasn't pretty. 'I'm helping you, I guess. A humanitarian act. Actus a humanitarium.'

'School must have been bloody dull when you were a real boy.'

'Hmmm . . . I am thinking it would have been more interesting had you been around. I can say that in Latin too.'

'Don't bother.' I breathed deeply to get a grip. 'Do you know Hamish Taunton?'

Sam thought for a moment and his good eye wandered back into memory but he said nothing.

'His name is on the wall. Old.'

Sam shrugged and his shoulders looked loose. 'There are a lot of names on the walls. Sometimes they come back for a look around and a yarn or a smile or just a reminder I guess. Now get up you prick! Death came and can come again if you hurry and you should *not* be in bed. Tonight is an exciting night!'

Sam went to leave my cube and almost fell over a marionette who had arrived unseen and unheard and was standing watching frozen and silent and curious and Sam jumped almost clean out of his dead skin and almost landed on Humphrey when he saw the little wooden head tilted just so and his little white wooden face impassive and filled with gloom. The ghost composed himself and stared down at the little man and the little man folded his arms and drummed his fingers and he didn't change his expression not once.

Sam shivered. 'That's very disturbing.' He looked up and saw Ems peering over the top of the wardrobe as pale and silent and bug-eyed as the puppet and Sam shivered again. 'That too. Skilful, mind you, extraordinary but disturbing. Fuck!' And he went from the dorm like wind and I was left staring at Ems. I tried to get free again and made a big effort to illustrate my predicament and at first the marionette tried to help but he couldn't grip the sheets properly in his tiny slippy hands and I realised I was miming to him and not talking, which is weird too and the boy dropped silent as an assassin and tugged me out of my sheets and I breathed and sat up and it was a massive relief and must be that way for a baby getting born and getting free of his mother.

'Did you pin me?'

Ems bit his lip and looked afraid and I knew the answer even before the marionette shook his head.

'Do you know who did?'

He nodded.

'Who?'

He ran away and I flicked on the reading light.

I looked across at Humphrey and he was pinned, too, and as I swung my feet out of bed I collided with the big army jerry can full of diesel from Leon's truck and nearly broke my toes on it and seeing it there I could straight away smell the fumes of that oil even though the can was still sealed, and I was scared. This was a bad picture indeed.

I dressed on the run and quiet as I could and went to Lefty and charged into his room putting his light on as I went and he was pinned and I woke him. He punched and heaved his way out as I pulled back the sheets and a coarse grey prison style blanket that had been added over his normal bedding and I knew those blankets only got issued on the coldest night to the coldest boys and I had spares but he didn't and he grabbed my face and looked at me hard. 'Who hit you?' He was angry and for the first time since getting out of bed I felt how bad my face stung and his grip made me wince and I realised the bruise in my mouth and jaw was deep and someone must have hit me really hard in my sleep and I felt the full pain for the first time. I wondered again why I didn't wake up and wondered if I was so tired or if I'd been so drunk or the punch had knocked me out cold and maybe that's why I didn't wake up and didn't remember it and my teeth felt splintered so I pulled away from his hand and told him I didn't know.

We went to Johnny and he was pinned, too. Majid was pinned. Which meant we were all pinned and we whispered urgently and I told them about the can of diesel and that one thing raised the horror and alarm but we didn't know what was happening and none of it made sense. Ems appeared in the gloom and took my hand and dragged me towards Leon's room and we all went and all of us were thinking Leon was pinned and we ran. At Leon's room Ems stopped and stood aside as we burst in to free him and crashed the door open without even knocking, and Leon hated people entering his room without knocking but we didn't care right then, and we burst in and he wasn't pinned.

Leon was sitting on his bed by the light of his lamp and wore his camo' hunting clothes and boots. He was checking a short-barrelled semi-automatic rifle and had fitted a muffler to it and he gauged us and me especially and really snake-eyed me and then went right back to checking his gun and snapped in a magazine and laid the gun across his lap cool and calm as you like. Then he looked up from his gun like he was inviting us to talk and happy to see us and he smiled and in that light I thought he could be a movie star. His cheekbones were high and sharp and he had eyes like a cat and a strong chin that was manly but not brutal.

He was wearing sand-coloured army boots and his camo trousers were tucked into their high tops and his boots were laced perfectly and he looked good and tight. He hadn't flinched when we crashed his door and it was like we were expected.

'Decided not to knock, did we?' He leaned closer to see my face and I saw my reflection in his window and saw my lip was split and my jaw was bluing in a big bruise and my tongue was searching for split teeth. 'That hurts eh, boxer boy?' He winked and studied me hard and something unsaid hung there and then I said, 'We were all pinned. All of us. We thought you were too. We came to help you. And your jerry can is in my cube.'

'Well, thank you kindly . . . but knocking only takes a second.'

Lefty stepped towards the window and was filling the room. 'We thought you were pinned.'

Leon sighed, 'Someone said that already. And I'm not.' He went back to his gun.

'How come we were all pinned and you're not?' Lefty asked and there was silence all round.

Leon clapped one hand against the butt of the gun and it made a dead thudding sound.

He looked dismayed. 'Fuck . . . I don't know Lefty, *did I pin* you? Actually the question should really be *how* did anyone pin you, one by slumbering victim one? Not exactly alert are you? Even with the drinking and shit, that's poor form boys.'

'Why the jerry can?' Johnny shifted his feet a little like he was nervous. He scrubbed his face with his fists, trying to focus through tiredness and alcohol. I knew he was thinking a jerry can by my bed and all of us pinned and a loaded rifle and our

276

friend fully dressed when he should have been asleep and him being a good shot too was a recipe for *close the gap*. That's a rule of fighting I learned from my dad. Close on a gun, run from a knife. We started to close, just tiny bits and maybe just the balance in my feet changed and I couldn't say I moved but my weight shifted to the front foot and I sensed Johnny's did too because we knew it ain't no good running from a sharp shooter like Leon, not when you this close. But Leon was a fighter too and he knew our weight shifted and he picked it like he would the changing tension in a deer's muscles just as it leapt to spoil his shot. He smiled a crooked little smile and nodded just a tiny bit.

'Why the can?' Johnny pressed him and smiled all at once. 'And the gun?'

Leon smiled a small smile. 'Actually, if you take the time to scope it out there are cans on every floor.'

'You were going to burn us,' Lefty whispered and his voice trembled like an autumn leaf about to fall. 'All of us?'

Leon leaned back against his wall and he looked at me and I didn't have a clue what was happening but he was cold and beautiful and scary as hell and I had never seen him so cold and distant and I was afraid and he didn't even blink and he didn't take his eyes off me.

'Sam said Death was coming,' I said.

'Sam?'

'The ghost.'

Leon chuckled and sat up straighter. 'Of course. Silly me. Well, dead boy Sam should know I suppose . . . and we wouldn't want to disappoint Death would we?' He took a huge breath and sighed. 'So since we're gathered here with fuel and lighters and no bedtime reading and the old drunk boy fucker is asleep in his house . . . Why not light him up? That would make me happy and be a fitting leaving gesture and might just satisfy Mr Death himself. With any luck? Although I suspect nothing will satisfy him eh?' He looked at me hard. 'What says you?'

'Why burn the headmaster?' Lefty asked.

'Why not?'

Majid looked from one to the other of us. 'He is this boy fucker thing. But you cannot kill everyone,' he said.

'Yes he is, Majid, well observed. And he isn't everyone, he's just one. And so far we've hardly been a murderous fucking success, have we?' Leon was looking at me like I would support him and he was measuring me up and down.

'And us? Would you kill us too?' Majid sounded like a kid. He was almost sixteen but right then his voice lacked manly maturity. 'What did we do to deserve this fate? Why would you do this? We are friends . . .'

Leon ignored Majid and stared at Johnny and there was like a hundred years of memories in his eyes. Ems slipped back out of the room and Leon's gaze went far away and then to Majid. 'Death came and he thought I would be sleeping like you were but I was wide awake and we talked and he said to me what more glorious end could there be than the fires of a great Viking hall? A great and fierce pyre. A great forest of sparks and embers rising to the moon and stars . . . No Majid. I would not kill you. And now I am tired of this somewhat overcrowded and fucking weird tête-à-tête. Get dressed properly and let's go burn the headmaster.' Leon looked at me again, 'Yes? No? Or fuck off back to bed. I don't care.'

Johnny was frowning so deep you could surf on his forehead and when he spoke he whispered, 'You were going to burn the house down with us in our beds . . . a Viking pyre for the glorious death?' It was stunning and true and not possibly true and I twisted inside at the thought and the horror and his voice was cracking and Johnny had tears on his cheeks.

Leon stared a bit longer and Majid twitched and Leon whispered something under his breath and looked at me sadly like I could help him, but I couldn't, and then Lefty shifted and the rifle came up swift and smooth and without Leon seeming to move and it was on me so I froze and we all did and then Leon had nothing on his face at all.

'Leon.' Johnny's voice was soft and he was reaching out. 'Leon . . .' His voice trailed off and it was several breaths, three four five, before Leon moved and nobody else moved first because he could have killed two of us before we closed that gap, but when Leon did move it wasn't to shoot, it was to rub his eyes the way you would if you were crying but he had no tears and he coughed a sobbing sound just softly and his noise was a dying musical chord with all the tremors lost and sad. It was the first time I ever saw him show emotion. 'Maybe it would be better. Viking style. All of us. We would always be together then. Brothers. We are so fucking messed up. Death isn't coming, Death's here bold as brass and we didn't even know.'

His own words seemed to make him angry and he stiffened and I knew I was looking straight at madness and madness isn't a monster and it isn't a stranger and it's right there in the room and just a twitch away from all of us always and it can have high cheekbones and almond eyes and a strong jaw and sometimes it just comes from the corner of the room like a coil of soft smoke and you can't stop it or fight it or waft it away, but Johnny was brave and edged forward, hushing Leon gentle, and his body was relaxed and his voice was low and velvet soft.

We had fallen off the world and Johnny stepped towards the bed gentle and slow and brave and stalking and the gun swung and was levelled at his chest.

Johnny took a pigeon step closer and Leon wiped his eyes again and there were tears now but he kept his right hand on the gun and his thumb knocked off the safety, but Johnny didn't pause or wait and he slid right up to the gun so he was almost touching it and knelt down but didn't grab for it or wrestle or nothing like heroes do in movies and on his knees he was on the same level as Leon and the end of the muffler was right between his eyes. My best friends were eye to eye with only a loaded, cocked, muffled short-barrelled semi-automatic between them and it was poetic and romantic and intense and beautiful and I was excited.

Leon closed his eyes and I thought he was going to shoot but two things happened at once. First, Ems appeared at the door with the marionette and the marionette was still in his pyjamas and they tiptoed over to the bed, and at the same time, Johnny leaned past the gun and Leon let him and Johnny hugged him and pulled him close and the gun barrel drifted away and down as I heard Leon whisper close to Johnny's ear and Johnny nodded and then they spoke in the most hushed and softened voices as only hunters can and I couldn't make out a single clear word.

Lefty moved first and waved me and Majid to join him and we gathered around Leon and Johnny and Ems and all of us swallowed Leon in a hug and somehow without me seeing it Johnny slid the rifle away and dropped the magazine out and made it safe all in that great hug of love and we all cried on Leon and even the marionette laid his head on our backs and I loved Leon then with all my heart.

We left Johnny and Leon to talk quietly and I went to nurse and fix my face and afterwards Majid and Lefty collected the fuel cans and emptied them in the drains and we all sat with Leon a while and he seemed tired right to his bones, but Majid was watching nervously and he was filled with caution and fear and whisperingly I told him Leon had said sorry and that we were safe and he was true to his word.

'And you believe him? And I am to believe you?' Majid asked.

'I do,' I said, 'I believe him.'

Leon smiled at me as he heard us discuss him and our whispers were loud compared to his own and Majid said, 'But you people believe there are fairies at the end of the garden and trolls live under bridges and even elves help the shoemaker. I have read it in your history books. And in unicorns. So with respect to you my friend, I will stay awake tonight. Maybe I think I will stay awake for many nights to come. Maybe all of my nights.'

'My uncle's seen unicorns,' Lefty said, and after three or four breaths Leon started to laugh with his head hung and shoulders hunched, but as he laughed he looked up and tears ran from his eyes and he pulled Lefty into a hug and Lefty didn't know why.

Later we left Leon with Johnny again and afterwards I never slept straight away because I was deeply sad that my friend was going away and I wanted him to stay and I was jealous that the world would have him and I wouldn't have him no more. I wondered whether Majid was right and there were fairies at the end of the garden and trolls under the bridges and I was worried Leon might burn me dead in my bed, and that thinking would keep most people awake and on edge.

I owed Sam my life and told everyone who would listen but they hushed me gently and later Johnny came and took them one by one and they went to see Leon and nobody drank whisky or smoked weed and then Johnny sat on the table in my cube and watched over me and halfway through the night Majid came and brought Mister Solomon Sesay and he was tense and he touched my face gently and they stayed by me and all my friends stayed close to each other and they watched over me, which was reassuring, and they kept me safe and made me feel important and loved.

They sat up all that night and tucked me in bed real tight and made sure my radio was playing and it was a lovely night to just doze because every time I looked, someone I cared for was caring for me and nodding to me in the dark until finally a deep sleep came to me and brought dreams of beautiful fires licking and flickering right up to heaven in a blaze of fingers and tongues, and the Boy Fucker Headmaster was burning alone and shunned and Fell was ablaze and children were screaming, and my spine tingled and it was a great Viking pyre and a glorious glorious death. And I dreamed we were all together for all time and our ashes were mixed and mingled on the wind so we were one and nobody could separate us and we were fire and life and death and smoke and I slept deep and sound and peaceful and blessed.

Thirty-Four

Next day just after dawn, Leon left his room and the house with his clothes and a few possessions and his favourite knife and rifle in a big military kitbag like he was a soldier already and we lined up on the front quad to give him a send-off and the house piper was dressed in full Scottish ceremonial garb and a kilt and played 'Scotland the Brave' and we stood as close to attention as best we knew and formed a tunnel of branches like Leon was Caesar reborn. He looked brave and sad and I was sorry we had stopped him burning our world down in the night because in my nose was the smell of an old dead damp fire and the only way to purge that smell is with a new hot living flame.

We were making great noise and ceremony befitting a Roman parade and chanting Leon's name and hugging him and throwing confetti and the headmaster and his midget assistant showed up at the top of the steps below Fell but stopped right there under the trees and we got silent and stared at them across empty unfillable space, and Leon was like a god and an Achilles and compared to the gods and heroes the headmaster and his midget were feeble chickens, but chickens can bring down gods of any name by pecking and pecking and pecking until the giants and heroes and gods fall in despair at the whole fucking futility of a world owned and ruled by chickens, and the best solution I could think of started with a single spark.

'We came to wish you farewell and safe travels,' the head-master smiled. 'I heard you were leaving us today?' He waited for a response but Leon was silent and the headmaster went on, sounding less sure, 'If you ever want a recommendation, you just have to ask. You know that . . . You've been a fine example to others. If you have time, come to my office and I can write you a reference now?' His midget assistant tried to smile and stretch his body up to be mansized but he scowled instead and was still tiny and then he looked down at his tiny baby feet and his feet were going hoppity hoppity hop because he was anxious.

Leon sounded like a full-grown man and didn't smile when he spoke and we all heard him and he was cold. 'Keep your letters headmaster, you and I are done, Sir. Before I woke this morning, I dreamed of you. Both of you!' and it sounded like words of love so the men looked uncomfortable and unsure and they didn't know the gravity of what he said but they were smart enough to know there was some hidden meaning and there was silence and stillness and then the silence and stillness was ripped apart as Moby screamed out a warble like an Arab woman and waved his hands in the air and shimmied at them in beautiful feminine defiance, and the fake men turned away and left with hatred on their faces. Leon spun back to us, raising his open hands palms up to the skies, and with that our noise and ceremony struck up again much louder and more powerful than before and Moby screamed and warbled and shimmied so much he near fainted and got everyone pounding and leaping as the drums erupted up and up and up. He was wearing thick blue mascara and lip-stick and blew kisses for Jewish Jesus and for a while longer the ceremony went on and one by one boys came forward to shake Leon's hand and even boys whose names I hardly knew and who kept out of our circle completely stepped in and said goodbye and we were brothers bonded in sad separation. Then we ranked up and Johnny led a war chant and it was the most powerful war chant I ever heard or done and we were red-chested and sweating and puffed by the end of it and Moby had a touch of the vapours, or so he said.

As Leon marched around the outside of Fell House towards the lane above the car park the noise died down and boys drifted away to breakfast and morning chores or back to bed with last calls of good luck and goodbye and after the noise was gone and boys faded away Leon looked brave and strong and a long way from the demons of the night before, but there was water in his eyes and ours too. He said he would become just about the best sniper anywhere in the world ever and he said his name would be sung and he would have 1,000 kills, not including innocent people or those whose faces he dreamed, and he made me swear to keep the book of soon-to-be-dead-bastards safe and he told me that he would still help me break out Lilly and all I had to do was shout, he said, and he would hear me and come, and I did a rebel yell so loud my lungs cracked open and he nodded, yep, he said, that would do it.

The piper played him up the lane and through the back streets to his truck and that boy did a good job and we were proud of him and Johnny drove Leon to the ferry and there he jumped the bus and he rode north to the airport and from there he said he could fly and bus some more until he reached his destiny. I shook his hand and hugged him, then kissed him gently because my mouth and whole face was sore and he said he hoped it healed soon. When he was gone it seemed like a great emptiness came upon the world and all the demons and harpies gathered on the rooftops and in the trees and knew we were weakened and they watched and waited.

Later that day things got even sadder because at breakfast Lefty got a letter and it said his court date was just a week away, so I went with him to see Mister Sesay and when we couldn't find him we went to the Cubans for advice and took them good dark rum and we ate food with them and as the men sat around drinking we told them of the court date. They listened and thought a lot and talked a lot and smoked and drank the rum and then Jesus told Lefty to run because on top of everything else, a black man cannot shit in a white cops' car, righteous an act as it was. He said he could help him set up home and get work and fight pro and Jesus said he knew a place where Lefty could live safe and make a good life and not be downbeat or beat up on account of the colour of his skin. He said there were places like that where you can be black and not hated or trod down or lied over and he knew where to find them and how to get there, but if he stayed and went to court Jesus thought he would go to jail for sure. He said Blacks are like Cubans and they don't have to do anything wrong or make no crime to go to jail.

We went to Mister Solomon Sesay's house later that same day and we took seeds for sunflowers and a baby tomato plant we got for pennies and knocked on his door and he let us in and took us through to a tiny stone courtyard at the back of the house and it was quiet and private and shaded and he watched me close and asked me if I was all right and I said I was and he smiled and said that was good. We asked Mister Sesay for his advice and we told him what Jesus had said and he put his arm around Lefty's shoulders and told him it wasn't so and there was no such place in the whole wide western world where the colour of his skin wouldn't matter and the Cubans were wrong and if he ran he wouldn't get far enough and the police would bring him back and things would be worse for it. Mister Sesay said he would go to court himself with Lefty, and me and Johnny would go, too, and we would see that a fair hand was played. Mister Sesay said he was a teacher and an employee of the government and he would demand it. The cops would give Lefty a lawyer and his social worker would come and he would maybe get off completely on account of having a night of near mortally challenged bowels and if he didn't get off maybe he would get a fine which we would all pay. Mister Solomon Sesay said if you run, you can never stop running and eventually you have to because you run out of road or breath or luck or money.

Lefty got four years in prison.

The judge said he was guilty of resisting arrest and assaulting a police officer, and defecating in the car was called wilful damage, and being poor and having a knife and drugs and being black and a fighter and refusing to beg . . . and them last things weren't on the charge sheet but they were his real and only crimes and Lefty kept saying sorry.

Lefty hung his head low as he was took away. We didn't even get to say goodbye properly and I felt ashamed that day and I didn't know why.

Mister Solomon Sesay didn't speak after, he looked like all the air was sucked out of him and he stared straight ahead, but I hated right deep to my core how the lawyers from both sides and the social workers all walked out together to get lunch like Lefty didn't matter at all and his whole life was smashed to pieces in under an hour and he was innocent and all them adults were liars and they knew it and still went to lunch and later when Mister Sesay did speak he told me he was sorry for being angry with me before and that none of *them* were innocent and all of *them* should die.

'I will kill them all,' I promised and it was an oath and he accepted it.

Mister Solomon Sesay sighed deeply. 'By your saying. But you should know you cannot and will not win this war. None of us can and knowing this you will still fight it?'

I nodded, I would still fight it. Mister Solomon Sesay held my face in the palm of his strong hand. 'That is the right answer, because only a coward fights a war he knows he will win. To fight when you know you will lose, this is righteous. To charge when there is no hope and all hope is gone and to face this and not be broken or bowed down, this is righteous. To walk in the valley of the shadow of death even when you fear evil, this is righteous. So puny little boy, my son, be ready to embrace Death when he comes because I think he comes too soon. But not today. Not today. *Insh'Allah.*'

That night I dreamed so many faces coming at me and it was like watching them ride a soon-to-be-fucking-dead-bastards merry-go-round and I woke up dizzy with Johnny back in my bed and a candle burning on the table beside us.

'What do you want?'

'That's no way to greet a friend,' Johnny said and nudged me to make more room.

'How long have you been here?'

'Long enough. I woke up and couldn't go back to sleep. I was dreaming.'

'Me too. Faces.'

'Me too . . . Who did you dream?'

'Loads. Everyone.'

'Everyone? I dreamed of everyone, too!'

I sniffed up gently and slunk under the covers because it was cold and whispered, 'Maybe Leon did the same before he left? Maybe that's why he was going to burn us all? Righteous. Maybe it's written? I don't know.'

Johnny nuzzled into me and pulled me tighter. 'It wasn't him dumbo. He saved us. It was you. It was you and he stopped you. He told me. He was terrified of you. He said you're the death dealer and you are pure and we should have to either kill you or leave! He busted your jaw with the butt of his gun! That's why we all sat with you all fucking night and Mister Sesay came . . . not just love, buddy, terror!'

I looked at him for moment and tried to understand and then it was so silly I giggled and he giggled too, just softly and gently, and I slid under the blankets and tried to remember but couldn't.

'Will you kill everyone?' Johnny asked and followed me into the warmth.

'Probably not. But it would be good to actually make a start.' And our bodies were like they were glued together.

'Seems a bit overwhelming,' he whispered. 'Seems to me bad people are too many and no sooner you kill one bad egg than another one will pop up. Bad people are like the fucking hydra.' He stroked my hair.

We touched and I wanted to touch more but I was too tired and I yawned so hard my jaw almost dislocated and I winced and Johnny laughed.

Johnny was nose to nose with me. 'I think maybe we were lacking sufficient and significant adult supervision at a critical juncture in our development.' He sounded very young and like he had drifted away and I realised something had shifted and he was looking for me to guide him and I was the leader. He snuffed out the candle and snuggled in. 'Is there a plan? In your dreams?'

'Go to sleep . . . there's a plan.'

'Tell me? I won't sleep if I don't know.'

'Break out Lefty, break out Lilly, find Melody in Cádiz, find my mum and kill every other fucker who gets in our way.'

Johnny nodded. 'Can't we just go home? Go hunting . . . play football?'

I hadn't expected that and it sounded sweet as honey and I wanted it but it wasn't mine. 'I can't. They won't let me. You can go home though. If you want to. You got a nice home. Good people there.'

'You could come with me?'

'They'll find me. They'll bring me back here or send me worse places.'

'You could go live with the Cubans. In that place they told Lefty about. That place sounded cool. We could all go there?'

'After I got Lefty and Lilly and Melody back then maybe we will go there. Not yet though.'

'How will we eat? How will we get money?'

'I don't know. Rob banks and trains?' We were stroking each other like cats.

'Like Bonnie and Clyde?'

'Like Bonnie and Clyde. Jessie James . . . Butch and Sundance.'

'Can I be Bonnie? I'm tired of being Butch,' Johnny asked softly, and then he kissed my nose and he was back sounding stronger and he kissed my mouth and I tasted him and we slept.

But he wasn't back and in the morning he said he was going home for a few days and he said his parents needed help on the farm and he was taking Valerie too. It was kind of code speak and when he was telling me he wasn't even looking in my eyes and everything had come to nothing and everyone was gone away and maybe that's how it always goes.

Before he left, Johnny gave me some money and Valerie gave me a list of girls who would look after me all the way up through the country in a secret network of beautiful and morally bankrupt wahines.

At the back of Fell Johnny and Valerie waited, dressed tidy and washed shiny like the most innocent people in the world and Johnny's mum and dad arrived in a big four-wheel drive all clean and new and took him away. His mother was a nice lady and she smiled at me as she waited to take her boy and I wished right then she would have took me too but she didn't and then I knew I was the untakeable and that's a stain you always wear.

Johnny and me shook hands with manly grips and no hugging or kissing and his mum and dad watched and Valerie turned her eyes away to give us privacy but his mum didn't and I held onto his hand and we looked right into each others eyes and I knew this was a big parting and a big deal and Johnny knew it, too. His hands were bigger and stronger than mine and calloused and I would miss them and my nights would be poorer without his hand to hold and I knew that holding his hand had got me through many nights and then I thought maybe if he died before me I could cut off his hand and keep it safe in my bed as a comfort to keep and hold and soothe me and I thought I should ask his mum for permission but decided not to right then because it didn't seem to be the opportune or polite time and some things are better left for another day. Valerie kissed my cheek and her lips were so soft and beautiful and lovely and then Johnny started to cry and he threw his arms around me and he whispered in my ear over and over, 'I'm sorry.' And he sobbed and I never expected that and he didn't even care that his mum was watching and she pulled him away and Valerie helped her and Valerie was crying, too.

I didn't really breathe much the rest of that sad day and it started raining and with the light failing I walked through town and lost myself in the dark mournful misery of Cutter so I would get fully wet and cold and it added to my misery, which is exactly what I wanted.

In the late hours that night Sam came and woke me, blowing cold breath on my eyelids, and when I woke he held his finger to his lips to silence me and beckoned me silently and I followed him and he beckoned again and we went to the bathrooms and he turned to me in there and tried to smile but he looked cold and very unwell and faded and the stone floor was cold under my bare feet and I was sleepy still but almost glad to see him.

'You're lonely?' Sam whispered and his breathing rattled and hissed. 'Everyone has gone? Nothing good lasts, eh? There's a lesson right there. Even your Hillbilly mate Johnny gone back to the farm (*hiss rattle, hiss rattle*), not a hillbilly at all was he? More a Hill William. He was just playing at being an outsider. Not like you and me. We are *The Fell*, pure.' Sam looked past me and around the room as if he was afraid. His breath smelled sweet and stale and sickly and I followed his gaze wondering what could make a ghost fear.

'You can stay . . .' he rattled, '. . . here. You can *stay*,' he hissed.

'I know. I am. For now anyway. I don't have a choice.'

'No, I mean you can really stay.'

'I am staying.'

'You'll leave . . . soon. I can tell. I've seen it a thousand times. The Arab too.'

'We all leave. We have to. We grow up. Not yet though.'

'No, we don't have to. You can stay. Like me. I stayed.'

'Well OK, maybe not you but the rest of us . . . we leave.'

'Stay. Be like me. We could have such fun. Real fucking funny fun. And no one can hurt us.'

I know I frowned because he came closer and studied my frowny forehead. 'The other world, outside, the other side of the foggy meadow, you don't want that. You want to be here, with the boys. Fell boys. Home for ever. You and me.'

And I understood right then that Sam was afraid and so lost he clinged to Fell House with his very last echo and I shook my head and frowned harder and he traced my frown lines with his finger. 'Listen to me . . . you were left like me, you were untaken, and it will never get better than this. You and me, we don't need *them*, we don't need anyone. You will never be leaner or stronger or more handsome and you will never have these days again. It's like the head-fuck-master always says in assembly, these are the best days of our lives!' Sam was desperate and urgent and he wasn't threatening but pitiful and trembling and I didn't speak but he heard me. 'No . . . Don't say no . . . I have something for you. Just for you, special.' He took my wrist in his hand and his hand was gentle and I thought his fingers were elegant and fine and I never did notice that before and he led me round to where the showers were and there was a chair alone on the stone floor and over it, hanging from the rafters, was a rope, burgundy and yellow and pretty and fine and narrow as your thumb with just a little stretch in it so your head won't come off and at the end of the rope was a noose. 'End it now. End yourself. Not end, transition. *Transition* . . . I can help you. Guide you. Brothers. Family. You miss family? I miss family. If it can't get better quit while you're ahead, isn't that what they say? Quit now. Come on . . . we make a good team . . . you and me. Brothers for ever. Fell House. The Fell boys. The Fell . . . It's so *so* easy. And your beloveds waiting in the Summer Lands. Think of them . . . Transition . . .'

Fear came up in me sudden like bile and vomit and I pulled my hand free of his grip and I knew what he was suggesting and I knew it wasn't right or good and he was speaking out of fear and loneliness and dread and it was so easy and so tempting and all I had to do was reach out and touch the rope and the rest would follow, and I stepped towards the chair and the peace and the emptiness and the solace and the sun on my face of the Summer Lands, and for an instant I saw myself there and I buckled when I saw it and Sam grabbed my arm and I shook him off. I ran out of that room so quick I was falling over myself because there was a terror in that room that night and I knew if I gave Sam just one tiny nod or one moment of possibility, death would swarm me and Sam would bring it to me because everyone lonely or sad or afraid or confused or lost is followed close by death, with suicide whispering in their ear sweet promises of peace and rest and lies, and I told myself I must not be the hanged man, I must not be the hanged man, I must not be the hanged man, and over and over I said it like it was a mantra so it was seared into my brain. *I must not be the hanged man.*

'We can be Bonnie and Clyde!' he called and I ignored him and slammed the door behind me and behind me I heard him weeping and I felt sorrow for him and pity and hatred and I said it aloud and only I could hear, *I must not be the hanged man*, and I slapped my own face and pushed my fists into my eyes and said it again and again until it was all my mind knew and there was no argument.

After that I stayed out for a few nights and the Cubans gave me a bedroll and blankets and I slept on the floor of the gym with a couple of young Cuban fighters who didn't have a home. In the night they swept the café and scrubbed the surfaces and washed up and in the mornings they prepared food, chopping salad and vegetables and kneading dough, and I helped them. It turns out kneading dough is quite therapeutic and I told Jesus about Sam and the rope he gave me a rosary just like my mum gave me once and I remembered her and I was safe then.

Between the Cubans and Coach Petey and the boys at Lincoln Valley I was OK and I still had a bed at night and food in my belly and Majid and Ems and Moby and Tommy and even ugly Humphrey, but The Fell brotherhood was a candle about to snuff itself out and that leaves only darkness and I knew the time was coming and I crept back into the house to taste it a while before the end and this was brave and manly even if not everyone was happy to see me.

Slowly Mister Sesay warmed again but his smile was weaker and he had to force his face to do it and one day he sat with me and walked with me and talked small talk and then he gathered himself up and asked me to please find out more from the Cubans about that place where skin colour didn't matter and he said he could teach there maybe or just fish for his supper and mend broken stuff and when he spoke his excitement grew as he painted a word picture of the place and put himself in it and when he said to *please* find out I was sad. Mister Solomon Sesay was a warrior and a teacher and a samurai but his heart was broken and I never did ask the Cubans about that land because I didn't want him to go away and I knew that land was just a kids' story like unicorns and flying fish and splitting atoms and little green Martians and glowing worms and humming birds.

Thirty-Five

Majid was sure that if you waited long enough, whatever was meant to be would reveal itself. He prayed at me every time we hooked up in some mumbled words and he said he was blessing himself against me and asking Allah to save me and he said it wasn't the right thing to do but he stayed close like a true friend and hopefully Allah forgave him because loyalty is holy and Majid said it was so. He said being with me meant he might have a garden in paradise, but I think he was my friend and maybe he didn't like to admit it on cultural grounds.

Then I got a letter from Lefty and he said he was OK and settling in just fine. It was written in the most beautiful hand-writing I ever did see. He said there was an English teacher there in the jail teaching him to use words better and his cousin was in the same jail and was looking over him and they had a good gym and mostly the people were straight and true. He said even the prison officers were mostly decent. He figured he could still be the champion of the world one day and he would train real hard and read more and turn his disappointments to his advantage. He told me he was in 'good health' and said 'I hope this letter finds you well' and that I should *show fortitude*, so Moby decided his English teacher must be a hundred years old at least, and Lefty sent me a concise thesaurus dictionary and a pamphlet about the visiting rules which looked much the same as Lilly's. He said we should each learn a word a day and grammar too because he said *grammars makers manners* and he asked if I would be on his visitor list and no one else was and maybe I could visit in the coming long holiday. He told me I should look up Kaleidoscopic, Equidistant and Panacea, and when I wrote back I had to put them together in a sentence, but it was a trick because I looked them up and there ain't no such sentence. He asked if I could send his bag, gloves and wraps and boxing shoes and the photo of all us boys taken in front of the house in our best number ones for the school year book. We took that photo way back and he had his copy laminated and I did what he asked and Cuban Jesus paid for the carton and got me a proper paid part-time job cleaning up and making coffee and doing jobs out back of the café, which paid real folding cash money, and Jesus gave me lots of tips about how to survive and even do well.

I even started to walk more softly and smile at adults more often and some days I even did school work and said thank you to teachers so they were shocked and told me I was welcome. I tried to use more words from my dictionary and I surprised them teachers with some of the vocabulary I used in my schoolbooks and my use of correct grammar and punctuation too, and punctuation has nothing to do with being on time. If you don't believe me, look it up.

Mister Solomon Sesay and Coach Petey and the Cubans all offered to take me in for the holiday because they had kindness in their hearts and all I needed was permission from the headmaster and they all wrote to him making the same offer and they were true and solid friends. Everything was possible now and the ingredients of my life were mixing up nicely so my world became *kaleidoscopic*, and Majid and Humphrey still watched me sleep most nights and sometimes Moby did too and he ate a whole bag of broken biscuits when he did his watch and made little belching and snuffling noises all night which I liked to hear, and I would hear him sucking up the crumbs and singing to himself and I loved that noise. Food was his *panacea* and he was mine.

Thirty-Six

Real close to the end of the year the headmaster called me to his office and I had to take my bag too, which straight away was a worry because when a boy got a note like that often he didn't come back and as I left my classroom other boys looked afraid for me. I knew I had no say over what happened next and it wasn't going to be good news, so I walked like a gunslinger and that's what you do when you ain't got nothing else, just like Jessie James. Outside the headmaster's office was an alcove and in there were three hard chairs. The headmaster liked to leave people sitting there a long time so their fear got to them and by the time they went into his room they were already broken and defeated and I sat a while and took out a book and opened it on my lap and just about took a nap until he called to me through his half-open door. He always told us in assemblies that his office door was always open as if that was an invite and a sign of trust, but the gates of hell are always open too so it don't mean shit and I knew he wasn't going to call me in for anything good.

When he called he just said, 'Come!' but I didn't go straight in or let him know I had heard his call and he couldn't see me because his desk didn't oversee the alcove and I made him call me again and again, saying the word 'Come!' louder and louder like I was a badly trained dog and in the end he got up to come and see if I was still there. Then I made out I hadn't heard him because I was too engrossed in my book and he made a big deal of hobbling on that perfectly good leg and in a cabinet beside his desk he had them medals that he never even won and he bought them in an antique shop and he tried to look old as if looking old gave him more authority.

He coughed under his breath and studied me for a moment, easing the fake pain in his good leg, and took my book from my hands without asking but gentle as a friend and turned it to look at its cover but it didn't have a cover because it was all worn and torn away and that's how I found it in the small lonely library in Fell House. Then he looked surprised like he knew the book well enough to call its title just by what was written inside but he never did, and I didn't want to ask because that would make me look dumb but I wished he had said it because for a long time I wanted to know its name. I thought he might keep it or bin it just to be mean but he handed it back and it didn't matter too much if he had kept it because I knew by heart the bit that mattered because I made myself learn it and it was beautiful.

He invited me to enter his office once more and I smiled like that kid in a Jewish Jesus movie again and I followed him, carefully putting my book in my bag and stroking it before I let it go. Its pages were thicker than new books and worn so much they felt like brushed-cotton pyjamas and it smelled like an nice old man's living room and just a bit musty and just a bit warm but the opening page was filled with vagabonds and deadbeats and love and that's what always got me and I read it over and over.

The headmaster's office was big with a ceiling so high you could stand on your friend's shoulders and still not touch the hanging lights unless your friend was tall as Big Ben and even with a real arch and whip in the whole body I doubt you could hit the ceiling with spit even if you was a champion gobber.

That office had huge windows looking over the football field front of school and three deep green leather sofas arranged around a low table. His desk was in the window so the light would spill in over his shoulders as he worked and there was a giant fish aquarium with a whole army of sharp-moving super-colourful little fish, each one *equidistant* from the next.

When he saw me looking at it he smiled with pride and satisfaction and said he had kept fish for thirty years and was an expert. He said his tank balanced itself and he didn't have to clean it because it was ecologically perfect and he was over proud of that tank even if it was a biological marvel and I was thinking the worst thing I could do to upset him the most and break his heart would be to upset the ecology of that tank with an oil spill or infusion of urine, but then I thought them fish hadn't harmed no one so I would let it pass. For now at least. The way he looked into that tank I reckon he loved them fish more than any warm-bloodied person and he started on about the social habits of the fish . . . social habits of fish. You know you're in trouble as a human being when you want to talk about the social habits of the fish sitting in a glass tank in a teacher's office. I wanted to kill him right then just for being so boring and maladjusted: (Dysfunctional. Disturbed. Abnormal. Psychoneurotic. Bonkers).

He went back to his desk and let me stand there looking at his fish and he said other people were coming and we waited for them to arrive but he didn't say who was coming and all he said was they were important and they were late. I made out I was real interested in the fish just to keep him happy and give me somewhere to look and in truth they were kind of fascinating. He made a big act of remembering something and handed me a letter he had been holding for me and he sat in his big leather chair and worked at his desk with me stood by the door and he didn't even offer me a seat which showed a lack of class (civility, breeding, cultivation). I opened that letter real sly in case he was watching and my whole body jumped and twisted with electricity because it was from Melody Grace and though it was short it was perfect and lovely, and right in the heart of the paper it was written on was a dried pressed flower from the pink wisteria tree we made love beneath and I knew she must have collected that blossom on that same night and kept it safe till now and that was just about the most romantic thing a girl can ever do.

She said she was missing me with every breath and her heart was in a thousand pieces so each piece could fit through the eye of a sewing needle and she was sorry she had had to leave. She said the town of Cutter was too small and people were saying bad things and sooner or later the waters would poison and meeting me made her know she wanted pure things back in her life and she begged me get older quickly and she said she would be waiting and hoped I would come find her like a knight in armour on a great white steed, and I knew I would and I stood taller and straighter. I waited until I knew the headmaster wasn't looking and I smelled the paper and it smelled of her and I kissed the letter and put it inside my shirt close to my heart and touching my skin and I hoped it would take me to her and I was sure it would.

Just as I put the letter safe the headmaster looked up and stared at me. 'Everything OK?' he asked and I said it was. 'A good letter? Good news?' he asked and I said it was, thank you, and he went back to his work, but I could tell he wanted more information and I wasn't going to share and he didn't like that.

There were huge pictures on the office walls of old-time head-masters painted in oils and framed in gilded wooden frames with brass name plaques under each one saying their names and dates and those old men were all in robes and looking real important and stern and pretty cold and I bet they all limped on good legs. The man behind the desk was waiting eagerly to be one of them and he was waiting for me to ask why I was there and what he wanted and who was coming and stuff like that, but I knew better and every now and then he looked up from his work to see if I was going to speak but I didn't. Every time he looked up at me I smiled that big sweet smile and after a while longer he got up stretched and moved to the sofas and invited me to sit opposite him and for a moment I panicked and thought I should have smeared chocolate on my butt and he was making a move on me, then quick as I panicked I calmed because no way could he pick me in his office in daylight with the door open, no way.

He placed a diary and a jotter pad in front of him on that low table and laid a fancy golden pen neatly across them then he pushed a cut-glass jar of mint suckers across the table and nodded to me and I took one.

'Congratulations on your boxing. I hear you are a champion in the making?'

I nodded. 'Thank you. I hope to be.'

'Do you like it here?'

I nodded cautiously because he wasn't my friend but he was sounding friendly and I knew that kind of play would work on a lot of boys but not me and I wasn't going to give him nothing. He motioned for me to take another mint and although taking two is bordering on being impolite I did so because I had been legitimately invited and they tasted really good and about as good as a mint ever did. He smiled. 'I've had promising reports on you from staff lately. Well done.'

'Thank you. I am trying to enhance my academic credentials.'

He smiled. 'Are you now? Since you arrived it's been a hard and trying time and for that I must apologise. Not at all conducive to enhancing one's academic credentials. You must think what a mad place this is with all the behaviour problems and Sun's passing and your friend going into detention. It's never happened before. Not in my time or anyone else's. It's been incredibly trying. I don't know . . . This is a small school really, in world terms, and a small town, excellent of course, world class even, but so so small, don't you think?'

I gave a cautious nod just to be polite.

'And you think you are so much bigger. Don't you?' He smiled like a snake. It was a sudden turn but I didn't react. There was an edge in his voice like a tiny droplet of venom had come onto his tongue and he was savouring it and deciding whether to spit it out or swallow it, but either way it wasn't good for me. 'I know. But you're not so big . . .' Then there was contempt in his eyes and a sneering hatred as he looked me over like he was looking at pure garbage and I don't think it was deliberate or intentional but coming from some real deep down place. 'You're not so big at all.'

Then I spoke despite myself. 'That's because I'm still a kid.'

He tapped his pen and he fixed me with slanty snake eyes trying to read me but I didn't give him nothing that I could feel so he huffed a deep sigh. 'You would think so . . . I'm just a teacher. I came into teaching because I wanted to help young people. Kids. Like you. Well, maybe not *quite* like you . . . I'm a good teacher too, but now, now I don't teach, I just manage. I move things around, like a chess master. I could have played footy, you know? But I chose to teach. Just as well I suppose, I'm a little small to play football.'

'You're big enough. Mr Harker is small.'

The headmaster laughed a little and his eyes lit up blue and for an instant in time he looked like a good man and that's how he fooled people. 'Yes. Yes he is. Don't let him hear you say that though!' He took a mint and unwrapped it slowly and deliberately and sucked it like it was the sweetest thing on earth. He actually seemed to be *thinking* about sucking it and doing it with mindfulness and consideration, so I felt guilty that I crunched mine up straight off and decided if I got another dip I would suck it slow. He seemed to read my thoughts and pushed the heavy pretty jar to me. I declined from polite etiquette but he insisted so I did as he had done and unwrapped that hard round mint real slow and kind of placed it on my tongue and just let my spit get to work on it, but then despite my best intentions and Buddhist mindfulness my mouth went berserk and betrayed me and crunched and crunched because my brain so much wanted to get to the taste explosion and free the fine sweet grainy sensation secluded within the hard-boiled shell.

The old man laughed. 'That's how I want to eat them, too.'

'Why don't you then?'

He thought about it. 'Because then they wouldn't last. I wouldn't really savour them.'

'They're sweets. They're not meant to last . . . crunch it!'

Right there he thought about doing it, I could tell, and he was thinking of letting go and letting his jaw and teeth destroy that bad boy and I thought to myself if he crunches that mint, just once, just one go at crunching it, he will be saved and he will be human and I will let him live because I just knew sitting opposite him that he would have to burn one day and the spirits were singing with the joy of it and I could hear them clear. I could even see how to do it. I could smell and feel the flames and they warmed my face and he screamed a long long time and that's how I saw it. Flames right up to heaven, cherry cherry red.

Crunch the mint . . .

But his eyes glassed over again and he didn't crunch it, he restrained his mouth. 'You see, so much is small. This town, this school, this office, and me of course . . . but you, you are smaller still. And just as I won't crunch the mint I won't crunch you. Not because I'm weak but because some things are worth savouring as you eat them, dissolve them, and turn them to nothing.' He smiled pure evil and twisted and in that smile I knew he wasn't a well man and burning him would be a mercy and right then two people appeared at his open door grabbing his attention, a man and a woman, and being polite they knocked to enter even though the door was wide open and he beamed at them and was transformed and waved them in and stood up and I did too. I could tell he was alarmed that his smart mouth might have been heard but they didn't hear and if they did hear they didn't mention it and they smiled broad and clean as Mormons and we all shook hands and he invited us to sit and his face was kindly again and tired and waiting to be captured in oils.

He said their names but I didn't put them in storage because he flicked me a cold warning look that took my attention and I sat down to listen and not speak.

The woman was my very own personal, dedicated, bleeding-heart do-good social worker and she talked to me like she knew me and we had met before but I didn't know her face, and the man was from the Justice Department, but it wasn't called that, and they were the guardians of my future or so they thought, but they weren't called that either and that would have been a cool title, but they didn't have a cool title and they weren't nothing much.

The Social lady smelled of talcum powder and asked how I was and if I needed anything and how I was doing and if everyone was being nice to me and she spoke about how I come through a troubled time but how they were getting such good reports on me and what a shame it was that my friend Kellen was now in jail and had gotten into trouble and done such a terrible thing, and I thought for a minute then because I wasn't used to hearing Lefty called by his real name, and when one of them said something the other nodded agreement and they took turns to say stuff like they knew me so well, each one being sweeter than the other. This is called the *softening up*.

The headmaster nodded and agreed with everything the woman was saying and he said I was doing well and how popular I was and how he and I met often to talk over things, which was a plain and straight out lie, and he told it so well I almost believed him myself and I was impressed that his lies sounded more sincere and honest than most people's truth. He told them how he was trying to stop me crunching the mints we shared so often and they all laughed because he had such a nice and kindly way with him and was so fatherly and uncley and he played the role so well.

The Justice man asked me if I liked mints most of all and I nodded politely and careful and I said I liked them best of anything ever but not half as much as the headmaster liked cherries, and I did my kid in a Jesus movie smile and the look the headmaster sent me was acid sudden and cold and deadly and the Guardians of my Future shifted like their arses just got hot but they didn't say nothing. The headmaster composed himself and smiled again and said something about the benefits of fruit and they all cooed and nodded and he grinned at me warm and kindly as a circus clown.

The woman started saying sticky-toffee-treacle pudding stuff about me and he was pouring on the custard, then the Justice man started saying less positive things, not about what

I was doing but the company I was keeping. He was saying the boxing scene wasn't one they could support and how a Cuban they suspected from *intel* was a criminal had taken me to visit Lilly with forged papers and the headmaster was nodding to that too and agreeing with him like he suspected it all along, and it dawned on me that he had made his way in life by never making a stand or having an opinion and he just made people feel clever and smart and right so they wanted to be with him and he agreed with whoever was talking, and sitting there I saw him plain.

The Justice man went on talking and everyone went on agreeing with everything he said and it was all just words and nothing in it and I promised myself to keep quiet and was doing well while the vanilla lollipop just mouthed more about the Cubans and how Jesus was this and Riel was that and the café was no place for a child and so many Cuban children were in the *system*, and while he was talking the woman and the headmaster looked all pain and pity and the worst thing was this guy had to keep looking at his notes to get everyone's names right. He was saying his *office* weren't happy and the headmaster was saying he agreed and they could keep me confined to the grounds because they had *a duty of care*.

I didn't get worried because the headmaster was just agreeing with someone because that someone was talking and it meant nothing so I just stayed cool and linked my fingers on my lap and nodded and kept eye contact to a polite level and made out I was interested and slowly I went into a meditative state and I was ohming in my deep mind. They were saying I would be sent to another site for summer because the school couldn't supervise me during such a long break this year being they were short of staff in Feallan House (he said it *Fee-Allan*) and they were sorry it meant I couldn't live with Coach Petey or work in the café and it was so nice of Mister Sesay to offer to take me in but he wasn't equipped to look after me and they said his name wrong and they had to be mindful of the cultural difference and of course I couldn't go to the Cubans . . . *hahaha* they all laughed so clever and witty and the Justice man looked wide-eyed at the headmaster, who looked the same back, and the woman looked so proud of him because he was so smart and so so funny, and he wrote in a notebook open on his lap.

I rolled with it and it wasn't important and it was all just words and they were sending me away for the summer but I was coming back and they didn't like the Cubans but I knew the Cubans didn't care and I didn't care neither. I knew if the Cuban boys were there in that office the Justice man and the headmaster wouldn't be saying nothing bad no way and the dried-up Social woman would be wetting her knickers and opening her legs for Jesus (Cuban Jesus, not Jewish Jesus, although Jewish Jesus would be fucking her hard come Judgement Day, and I just knew it) and I was cool and I was in control of myself and it was going well. The Social woman said they would usually send boys like me to a special farm near the city in the south and I knew that city because it was where some of the boxing bouts took place and I knew people all round that city through my being a fighting man and she was saying boys on that farm could work with animals and learn farming skills and I was thinking that would help my strength and fitness, but then just when she had painted a picture I wanted to be inside she said that in my case it was better I went to a lonely west coast town for the summer because the *known prostitute* I was *reported to associate with* was thought to be in that southern city and she skipped bail there and Justice and the headmaster nodded like dumb rocking horses and Social do-good woman nodded and even I nodded.

Then the words landed in my Zen-elevated brain and I was puzzled because I had never known a prostitute and I thought I would like to say, 'I don't associate with known prostitutes . . .' or something real mature and effective but it wouldn't make any difference and I knew this was no parlay and this was a lecture on my immediate future and it was taking dark turns, and the headmaster muttered to the woman but I missed what he said and she smiled and said something back, and the headmaster said something else and I heard the woman say the word *Twenty Dollar* and she scrunched up her face and they all three belly-laughed and I heard and saw the name *Twenty Dollar* echo through my head and turn over and roll around so my inner eye looked at the word from every angle and my ear heard it in many voices and I lost control of my face and a frown came hard over me.

I had to be bigger than them and rise above their words and slanders and lies. My dad taught me the eagle doesn't chase the fly . . . I forced myself to stay controlled and humble and I breathed deeply like Buddha and I composed my deep mind to help me ignore them as they talked about the woman I loved and who I was sworn to for all eternity and who loved me back the same way. I was an eagle, they were flies. And I was deep under the cool sparkling waters of the lido and all I could hear was silence and my own heartbeat and I held myself there as they called my beloved a known prostitute and they were being so fucking self-righteous and smug and no one cared that Melody Grace played piano and cello and grew roses and made carrot cake with real fucking carrots and was going to be a movie star and was a true-born fairy girl so pure and holy and lovely and I saw her dancing foot to foot in the face of that storm and calling to Lefty and me that night on the beach, and the woman was speaking under her breath and not opening her mouth to form words but she was still talking about '*Twenty*' and I was underwater and Mad Louis was there and he smiled at me under the blue water and tiny bubbles rose and played all round us and I smashed that Social bitch so hard in the mouth her jaw just disintegrated and two of her lower teeth went airborne and hit Justice in the face with a whole spray of spit and blood and I was shocked how her jaw just mushed and splintered because I was used to hitting boxers and they didn't mush that same way.

It was a slow motion movie and everything went slower than a wild flower opening for a summer dawn and the men recoiled and the woman erupted and her teeth rolled through the air and her head spun and in that paused time I could have reached out and caught them and took them back into her mouth and if I had a rewind button right then I would rewind the whole thing and not hit her even if she had it coming with her phoney kindness and concern and self-righteousness, but instead I reached out and grabbed a handful of those delicious crunchy mints that light up your mouth and threw the thick heavy beautiful cut glass jar straight through the aquarium glass and as the whole tank full of ecologically perfect water and sharp little shocked-as-fuck-and-soon-to-be-dead fishes hit the carpet, I ran.

And I kept running.

Thirty-Seven

I ran to Fell House without breaking stride, leaping up the stairs and steps and sprinting up the slopes under the trees so my lungs were bursting and burning and I grabbed my stuff best I could, throwing it all into my backpack and folding my clothes just roughly, and I got changed into mufti and stashed my uniform in my bag because you never know when you might want to look like a schoolboy. I folded Melody's letter real neat into a square and slipped it in my pants and I was fast and quiet but as I went to leave the dorm I crashed straight into Moby and Majid. Already Majid had heard what had happened and he bolted to catch me and Moby was already in the house hiding from a maths class and eating white sugar on white bread sandwiches with lemon curd and they stood there looking full of alarm. Moby was trying to swallow the tasty stodge so he could talk but his mouth was full and there was sugar all round his lips and he was stuck.

'The police will be coming,' Majid said, and Moby nodded furiously and I stared at the Arab, and there was concern there and deep softness. I went to push past them but Majid caught my arm,

'You go where?'

'I don't know. The gym? Maybe Jesus.'

'Cuban Jesus? Not Jewish Jesus?'

'Cuban Jesus . . .'

'That's good then. But they will be looking for you,' Majid said and Moby swallowed hard and laughed, 'No shit!' He went to throw away the rest of the sandwich and thought better of it.

'They're going to send me away.'

'You think?!' Moby said and Majid scowled at him. Moby licked some sugar from the crust of the bread in a nervous reaction and his tongue moved fast as a lizard.

From the window behind them I saw other boys streaming up the path to Fell, all running and panting, and I knew word was out. Tommy came next into the dorm, 'Cops are in school already, they got a sniffer dog too! It's OK though because our stink will fucking kill it! We're out there running everywhere. Can't track in all that! Seen it happen before when they sent up a drug-sniffing beagle bastard in my first year. It tripped out so hard it thought it was a fucking squirrel.'

Moby laughed and bit off more sugar bread. 'Just hide out a while until they're gone. All the boys will be up here soon and we'll just get in their way.'

It was well-meant advice but it was all wrong and I knew it because they could seal up the building and search all night and all they needed was enough people and after what I'd done they would bring everyone and everyone's mothers. I needed distance and I told him I needed to run and right now.

Then Moby nailed it. 'Tommy, put on some of his kit, take a bike and ride into town and we can all see you go! A decoy!'

'And where do I go?' I asked.

'The woods, the forest, the bush, or whatever all that green shit up the hill is called. Wait till dark. Then run . . . somewhere. I would run with you but I can't run and I'm too fucking fat to hide, but my ample breasts will be awaiting your return to nourish you, my noble, noble traveller. Behold.' And he pulled up his shirt and exposed his bosoms and he spoke softly and with love, 'For the wind is in the palm trees, and the temple-bells they say: Come you back, you British soldier; come you back to Mandalay!' He pulled me into him and whispered, 'The carnival is over . . .!' and Majid frowned and pulled me away and I didn't know if Moby's plan would work but given my limited options it was my best bet and Tommy was already stripping and grabbing anything of mine that wasn't packed and then he hugged me and ran with Moby waddling behind.

I stood back from the window and Majid held my hand and we watched as boys emerged from the trees and stairs and came from school in all directions and Tommy grabbed a good bike from the shed and we watched him tear off through the trees and north towards town with Moby screaming that I had taken his bike and I saw Moby punched himself in the nose so he fell down and bled and other boys took up the shout that I had hit the big belly dancer and about five other kids ran past him and whacked him too just for effect and they were laughing and he was furious, and bad as the situation was it was funny to see. And the boys ran back towards school again and shouted to the teachers and cops and the yapping dog on the long lead and at the far end of the steps I saw three policemen and that dog and little Mr Harker and the fat assistant principal and they heard the shouts and saw the boys running and Moby wailed and when he was in plain sight of them he fell down clutching his nose and just then at the foot of the track where it met the road Tommy must have broken cover and hit the steep downhill because to a man they all peeled off and went the wrong way and chased him for all they were worth and ignored Moby who staggered down the steps. All except Mister Solomon Sesay who stayed on the path in the distance and looked right up to my window and he nodded just once, slow and strong, and then turned and slipped his arm under Moby's to support him and walked him towards school. Fell boys came and went and ran into each other and shouted and made the most of the fun and I loved those big-eared odd-shaped boys and I felt tears on my cheeks and I stuffed my precious transistor radio and the headphone in my bag and I slipped out of the fire escape down the stone spiral stairs and into the woods.

Majid said he would meet me at the camp where Leon stashed his guns after nightfall and would bring food and water and I needed that darkness to come soon and it couldn't come soon or deep enough. The town was one road in and one out, so the cops could close it up easy, but I also knew they would only do so much for a slug in the mouth, even for a good slug on a woman. Soon enough something else would happen in town and the cops would be taken into a whole new mess and not have time for a kid like me and in the scheme of things I would keep.

I guessed I would be safe at the camp for a couple of days and things would settle down in that time so slipping town would be a cinch and while I waited for Majid I turned over a rotten log and took up a folding spade Leon kept there and dug up one of the duffle bags, the one with a short-barrelled level action .44 rifle and 12-gauge pump and a semi-auto long gun and loads of ammo and a travel first aid kit and a good live knife and then I covered all signs of it again and stashed the spade back under the log so I could come back another day and get the other stuff.

I had cut my knuckle when I hit the woman and cleaned it by sucking and licking it hard and getting my tongue right into the cut and I opened up the little green pouch of first aid and put antiseptic cream into the cut because cuts from teeth can go real bad real quick then I slipped a band aid over it to keep out the dirt.

Sooner than I thought Majid arrived with all his kit and he was panicked and twitchy. The moon was up but it wasn't full dark and I was just making a bivvy spot for the night but Majid said no, he said the woman was in hospital and still not woke up and the headmaster knew the cops would stop actively looking for me soon as the next thing took their eye, so he told them I was a suicide risk and the counsellors agreed, which was a real dirty clever trick because it meant the cops would be everywhere, including the deep woods and with dogs and maybe even volunteers and a chopper. A suicidal kid isn't something they can ignore and no cop wants to find a school kid hanging or with open veins, so I was now top priority number one with fucking stars over it and would stay there until they found me and I had to respect that trickery and cunning and I knew I was going to burn that highly combustible drunken headmaster like a fucking sparkler soon as I extricated myself from the pickle. But not yet. Right now I needed distance.

Majid gave me a mountain of sandwiches of white bread and heaps of butter and thick with white sugar and peanut butter and jam and a bottle of water and one of homebrew gin. The sandwiches were a nutritional disaster and Majid shrugged when I looked at it. 'Moby done it,' he said, and I guessed it would give me a lot of energy and then a sugar coma but it was better than nothing and I was grateful.

The night darkened and we packed up our bags and strapped them tight on our backs so nothing would rattle or bang just like Leon and Johnny taught us and we ran for the Cubans but took the higher forest tracks so we wouldn't arrive too soon. We needed it properly deep dark before we got to the lights of town and better still we needed some drunks on the streets to keep the cops on edge.

Some of those tracks skirted the town like veins and Majid went ahead to scout and kept running out and coming back and reporting what he saw, but after some time I was deeply disappointed because there were no cops anywhere and no dogs and if they weren't looking now those dogs would lose any chance of scent by sunrise. Clearly the mercy and compassion and pity for a suicidal kid didn't extend to searching after dark or up the tracks. Even Majid was surprised and as an Arab he was well accustomed to nobody caring for his wellbeing.

We stood on a wooded crest looking down across town and we could see the main road in and out and there were no red and blue flashing lights and no search parties in the trees and no sign of anyone and no chopper or barking dogs. 'I thought they would search harder for a Christian boy,' Majid whispered.

'Me too . . .'

'Perhaps it is because I am with you?' he said and I agreed it probably was.

'Perhaps they are thinking if they save you they will save me too?'

It made sense.

Just to be sure, we ran a circuit of the town staying hidden by shadows and darkness of the trees then went through the unmetalled gravelly back alleys that smelled of dog piss and cigarettes and the rotten eggs and vinegar of meth.

The Lincoln Valley Boxing Gym was close and the lights were on and door open and boys were training and I wanted to get in there and train and be a kid without a care in the world and I edged closer and closer drawn in by the perfect music of someone hitting the speedball inside. A young fighter was skipping on a boarded pallet outside and he was lit by a single orange street lamp and hooded against the night. I'd only ever seen someone skipping there in the hottest summer night but tonight the air had a chill and the young man was wrapped up warm and skipping beautifully with a poetic lazy rhythm he could likely keep going all night if he wanted. I recognised him without even seeing his face. He was well sweated up and his sweatshirt and hood had damp patches that showed black in the orange light and he was older than me and a proper grown man, but he was always friendly in that distant way grown men can be to kids. His name was Manny and he must have been nearly twenty-one or even twenty-two and was singing as he skipped in a rhythmic kind of chant and I couldn't make it out, but as I crept closer he must have seen me or sensed me because his voice went a bit louder but he never lifted his head or looked my way. 'Stay away, there's cops inside . . . stay away, there's cops inside . . .' went the soft low chant and I was still, and hissed, 'Why? For me?' And he carried on still without looking up from his hood or changing his beat. 'Stay away, there's cops inside . . . the bitch you hit has fucking died . . .' and he repeated it again and again in a rhythm like an American Army marching song and his feet skipped in time with the words and then he sprinted doubles on that rope and my heart stopped and something sunk in me and I peeled away and ran back into those shadows in a half-crouch like I was a soldier ducking a sniper's bead.

I don't know how long Manny had been skipping under that light in the chilly night air but when I looked back he was gone and his job was done and I was grateful and I was scared and small as a dormouse and I trembled. My hand throbbed from my cut knuckle and I bit it and it was the only thing I was feeling and I wasn't like before and I was changed and didn't know myself then. I was in a mess of a situation and couldn't think of an out and I felt sick and numb and I couldn't go into the

Lincoln Valley Boxing Gym and hit the bag and be a boy and that was for ever and I wasn't ready for that. I would have run in panic and begged the universe and all the gods to take it all back and thrown my filthy worthless self under a truck and I couldn't breathe but Majid gripped my hand and wrapped his arms around me smothered me and he held me tight and I cried into him. Majid told me I was transformed and transformation is like that and the butterfly can't climb back into the safe secret scabcase and you can't get back inside your mother's belly and transformation is scary. Majid whispered to me that transformation is how the oak is grown and gold is made and the hero is created and he told me to remember and he told me to compose myself and he said I was discordant and I must hear the symphony and I slumped down and he knelt and held me still. We stayed right there for a long time and slowly my wings unfurled and I breathed and I was a killer and I had blossomed and become whole and slowly the chords separated and I heard the music and this was called *facing the music*.

Majid looked at me straight. 'Will you want the bleach for scrubbing?' he asked and I said no, no bleach and no scrubbing, and we jogged back into the alleys and went to find Cuban Jesus and I was a killer, bare handed and hunted and the kid Billie and Jesse and Sundance and Clyde and Mad Louis had all been where I was on the day of their first kill and it wasn't nice and it wasn't cosy and I didn't want to be in that club but it ain't a club you can ever leave.

At the Cuban café cops were everywhere and the café had no music playing and a couple of their fighters were hanging around the front door just making small talk and lounging and staring at the cop cars with menace and it was a scene of heightened tension. Majid stayed back while I took up a position under a flatbed and watched like a hunter would watch and I see Jesus drove past in his car with its windows down and he cruised real slow so I knew he was out looking for me and on another night I could just slide right in but tonight a police bike gave him a tail. The police weren't looking for a suicidal kid no more, now they were hunting a juvenile suicidal woman killer and I was ticking too many boxes and I knew they wouldn't leave off and the little pickle had become a giant Moby-sized jar of onion relish.

In the distance I heard Island boys shouting abuse at cops near Skinny Joe's and the noise reminded me of Fat Vinny and his family and the days so long ago I had near forgotten and right then I was back there just for a perfect precious blink and straight away I knew there was no *back there* and no road went that way. Then I thought time is a strange thing and viewed backwards it is nothing and just a heartbeat and all those people and noises and smells were with me again and all in an instant and all the wounds were open and happiness too. How can anyone learn anything in that single moment that all past time lives in and where every past day is like a single past second? But then viewed forward, time looked like a lazy for ever road winding through forests of dreams and swamps and traps and I wished I could visit Mister Solomon Sesay and get the answer to time because I knew he would have it but no road went that way either. Right then I was on the edge of being smart and learning something but I couldn't wait for that wisdom to land in my brain because I had to move and it missed me and likely it squashed a bug or lit up an ant and now there's some fucking ant lives in some ant palace talking wisdom shit to loads of other ants and it should have been me and instead I was running.

Majid and me shifted on a while and took cover in a ditch and I saw Majid was pale and afraid and he looked small and determined and loyal and I said he should go back to Fell and get clear of all the trouble and it hurt me to say it and my heart stopped in my chest when I knew the loneliness that was coming, but if I hadn't said go he would have stayed with me and knowing that felt good. We held onto to each other one last time and he kissed me and I told him I would find him when I came back to burn the headmaster and he swore he would be waiting with petrol and we would go to Cádiz and I swore a solemn oath.

I saw us then, in Cádiz waiting for the pink summer solstice and Melody would come and we would live for ever in peace in a tent in the desert and I told him and Majid nodded solemn as a monk and passed me a card with golden Arabic written on it and he kissed it and held it to his forehead then he quickly scribbled his father's address in Arabia on the back and said, 'If I am not there when you come back for me, I will wait for you in my own country and we can join together with Mister Sulaiman Sisay as holy warriors, and we will burn down this bad world. For love, my brother. And if by Allah's will we are not to be holy warriors, we can drink tea. Peppermint tea.' And I was to look for him in the desert lands of the great Algeria where the Sahara is and he said it is not so far from *Qadis* and he said pass the card to any local and he would make me safe and Majid would serve me sweet figs and peppermint tea in tiny cups of fine white china on trays of copper inlaid with turquoise stones and we would wear robes of azure, which is the colour blue. It sounded just perfect and that was something to look forward to and I thanked him and he was gone like smoke on the wind and he was the last to leave me. I don't even know if that country he said about is real but if it is I like to think there will be sweet figs and tea like peppermint in tiny cups waiting for me there. And my Arab brother. Inshallah. Inshallah. Inshallah.

Thirty-Eight

Skipping a town when everything is sealed up and cops are seeking you down is not easy except for one thing: the laziness of adults and their complete lack of imagination, so that's two things.

I knew the bus station was closed for the night and there was an old security guard who sat the whole night in a glass box in front of the booking office and I'd said hello to him on the nights we crept out to buy a late-night burger and he was a nice old man of limited movement and interest and even less enthusiasm and he didn't care any more than he needed to. The morning buses would take their leave from 5am and it would be dark and cold like 5am always is and I would be on one. I couldn't rightly pick which one because their numbers and destinations hadn't been scrolled up, but I knew the first buses to leave would be on the front row and they would be long-distance rides heading for the far south or the west or maybe for the ferry and the north or even the crowded east coast seaports, and I could to hide out with the pirates and vagabonds and drifters and grifters and I could get a name for myself there. I didn't really care and it didn't much matter because all routes led well out of town and that's where I needed to go and once I was out I could change rides and hide and breathe and wait and get to know my hands again because they looked and felt foreign and strange and like they were not my hands any more, and that's common once you kill with your hands like I did and I read it once. It would take a while for them to come back to me . . . *Hush, hush, hush*, said the voice.

I knew I could ride in the luggage hold underneath the passengers and those holds were deep and dark and up the front there was a narrow stretch that you couldn't see into if you opened the lift-up luggage doors and just looked inside lazy, and you had to get right into the belly of the bus to see in that alcove and it would be cold, dark, frosty and five in the morning and that's where laziness came in because no one was coming to look in that hold.

I rolled out my bivvy bag and snuggled into that hidden stretch and dusted it first to get the dirt off the rubber matting and closed off my nose to the stale smell. I loaded the short-barrelled .44 rifle and put my headphones in to listen for Lilly and I went to sleep.

I dreamed I was a child again running in the meadows and trees and the lido fields and smelling hot tarmac and splashing in the cool waters and then seasons jumped and it was Christmas morning real early and the sun wasn't risen and the fire was lit in the grate and glowed orange and the fire was warm and promised magic was to come and I stood on the stairs and peered into that room and it was perfect. In my dream I missed my father's arms around me and I missed my mum and her delicate softness and strength and love and her belief in the fairies and her perfect grace and how she loved and protected me, and as she reached for me I woke and the driver loaded up with a dozen suitcases and the quiet early-morning tone of sleepy people drifted my way, then the driver gunned that engine alive and we lurched out of the station and on to the great wide road to freedom.

As we left town I got teary because that brutal old butterfly of Fell House and the strangled and strange little town of

Cutter had become all the home I had and those boys were like my brothers and I did feel sorry for the woman who died and I hated her too for dying like that and putting me in this mess. I swore to not be so quick to anger again and I made a note to myself that if you kill make sure you kill cold rather than hot and that's a learning right there. Staying busy is important too so when you kill you don't go brooding afterwards and right now I was busy getting away which is why my mind didn't go to regret and sin and self-pity and after a while I started to consider what hobby would be a good one for a killer, but that's not so easy as it sounds when you ain't a hobby person. I started to make a mental list of possible handicrafts because I knew I was a natural born killer and I wasn't planning to stop and I liked the visual effect of crocheting and its silky texture, so that was a possibility and I pondered.

The bus made a few turns and I sensed we were heading south and that was perfect and then the bus pulled over and its brakes were groaning and hissing then it jolted to a stop and I heard police radios and voices outside and that wasn't perfect at all. My heart was racing so I had to control it with my mind again as the police searched the topside and a cop chatted to the driver like old and good buddies and I nursed that rifle and got ready. I could hear yapping and they opened up the hold and chucked in a dog, but the policeman himself didn't even bother to look down where I was hiding or even slide a suitcase across and the dog came over in the dark and snuffled me as I rubbed inside his ears and he licked my face and went away again and I was grateful and in my mind I could see the policeman's happy ruddy face and big belly and chubby podgy hands and I was really glad I didn't have to unload in his face and kill him dead even though killing policemen is not a sin even if it is a crime.

I rested my rifle and made it safe and did an ohm and gong and everything was kind of working out fine and I was moving on up. I hoped wherever the bus dropped me would have ice-cream shops and a surf beach, because with the holidays so close hiding on a surf break would be easy, and a boxing gym, it should have a boxing gym, and I could hold out for the summer and then liberate with expediency my friend Lefty and my Lilly and then go look for Melody Grace herself and there were butterflies and bluebirds all over that picture. Maybe the summer would disguise me and maybe I would grow taller and maybe I would live under the boardwalk or pier or in beach huts and wherever I was going it would be OK and *flicker flick flicker* I could feel a plan taking shape. I really hoped there would be a surf break and a gym and it was all good and that's no lie.

I had to stay positive and the shroud of lonely was on me heavy, but I pushed it away because I knew good things were coming and I was visualising and I was warm and I had food and the bus rolled easy towards the mountains and bays and the engine hummed and voices drifted down from passengers talking and laughing and I plugged my magical hold-in-your-hand radio back into my ears. A sweet kind lady sang to me about 'Morningtown' and sunlight speared through the gaps around the luggage door and lit up floating dust like my own miniature universe and I beheld it in wonder and awe and I was grateful.

If you're happy and you know it, clap your hands, and I clapped until my hands went numb.

Acknowledgment

When I was initially asked to add acknowledgments, I baulked. Not because I don't appreciate those who helped bring *The Fell* to life, but because it is part of a longer story, and one which many people have fed and watered and to do it right, I have to go back a bit.

The Fell developed over a number of years and at some distance along my journey as a writer. That journey began with my mother, Kathleen, who filled a small house with many children and our dark evenings with stories of strange lands, adventure, escape and the magic of the sea, of whaling ships and pirates. And my father, Cliff, who filled those same evenings with stories of the city, of people belonging and standing strong and fighting your corner. He was the formidable champion of the underdog and fought giants with a passion. The two of them wove us into an enchanted land and filled our crowded house with books and though for me school never figured large, learning always did. Books and learning were sacred in that house. A house filled with little formal education but mountains of intelligence, wisdom, compassion and hope.

My older brother Terry, wrote first and believed writing to be a real and possible thing. He was also the first in our whole wide family of many houses to go to university.

And my sister Debby, who whispered stories whether anyone was listening or not and acted every sentence. She terrified me.

There was a teacher once who told a troubled teenage trouble maker he could write and fed him paper and let his every lesson in her classroom be a creative one. I don't remember her name, hopefully she doesn't remember mine.

I found writers, playwrights, poets and artists glittering in the dark alleys and backstreets of London and some of those writers were household names in households long since quiet. Mostly though, they were penniless and impoverished and despite this, they held on to a belief that if they were good enough, their hour would come. They inspired me. They were *real* writers, and it was all possible, just like Terry said. They told me to write and never stop. Keep the faith, they said.

And then came Donna, who believed from day one and never stopped. We married when she was 18 and I was 20 and lived it up on nine quid a week. I couldn't type but Donna could. I couldn't spell either, and she was a living breathing spell checker. I couldn't dance but she danced all night, and I wrote and all day she typed with never a single complaint.

I was compelled to write and stories burned in me and when I was writing I wasn't in trouble, and since trouble found me easily, writing became a life raft and I clung to it, and Donna clung to it too.

As each novel or play or film script ended I thought my hour must soon be upon me but the clock ticked and the hour didn't come. I made short lists in writing competitions, and theatres occasionally gave me space to develop in, but never audiences. Agents gave me time but never a contract, publishers gave me nothing . . . There was something missing, so I went in search of whatever it was to UEL as a sulky, surly half educated, mature student, and in the dying body of their revolutionary school for independent study I met Malcolm Hay. He was a man who loved a challenge and he made me shape my questions and channel my thoughts, made me read, and made me learn the craft. He was like a sculptor and his partner Toni was a director of energy. Words were powerful to them, and never to be wasted. I met other writers there, we were rough and raw and straight from East

End streets and through them all my hour came tantalisingly close . . . the minute hand was trembling but still it didn't quite tick over.

And then of course came Harry, my saintly son, who listened to my tales and shared stories and made me laugh with clever insights. Calmly, he believed, and like ice in a glass he knew it could be cracked and he would not tolerate a non-believer. I watched him grow into a man, and still young he outstripped my maturity and wisdom and he encouraged me as I once encouraged him. And Hannah, my daughter, always riding unicorns and fighting dragons in magic lands and always seeking company there. She had faith and certainty, because the volcano knows if you pour forth enough lava, all must yield. They let me play out my stories and tolerated with great patience and humour my many tales and fantasies. They never dismissed my ambition and believed it was only a matter of time. *Time* and *only* are often paired in youth.

They are heroes and warriors and they believed if the hour won't come, rip it from the wall.

Thank you to Bruce, who tried, Chris, who tried, and the fiction editor of a big five publisher who rejected *The Fell* with such enthusiasm and accolades and such praise, I was inspired and compelled to push on. She wrote the most enthusiastic and uplifting rejection any author could receive, made me cut the novel by half, and rejected me! It was confusing, but it reinforced my determination.

And I thank the boys of many names and many flags who, like the crew of a pirate ship, weathered storms and fought battles, loved and lost and fought on and will fight on still. They gave me far more than I ever gave them. None of them or their stories are in this book, except perhaps as echoes and shadows, yet all of them are in me.

Finally I would like to thank the RedDoor team for their enthusiasm, talent, courage, patience and kindness. And for giving a writer the chance to rip some semblance of that hour from the wall.

Non illigitimus carborandum . . .

Book Club Notes

When and where do you think The Fell is set? Is a sense of time and place evoked?

How old do you think the narrator is?

Is Mister Solomon Sesay a positive role model and mentor? At any point did you change your opinion of him?

Are the boys and girls in the story heroic? If so, why? If not, why not?

What role does sexuality play in the novel?

Is the relationship between Melody Grace and the narrator, a positive thing?

Is the drug and alcohol use by the children supportive or destructive? Discuss.

What stood out as a memorable passage or piece of dialogue?

What are the main and recurring themes addressed in The Fell that resonate with you?

Did you find any aspect of the novel shocking or disturbing?

Do you support the narrator? Does this change over the course of the novel?

This novel is rooted in a brutal physical reality, but also fantasy. How do these concepts explain the behaviour of the characters? Where does fantasy first penetrate reality in The Fell?

Which novel or novelist would you compare this work to?

The Fell is aimed at adults, but should this story also be read by young adults?

Find out more about
RedDoor Publishing and
sign up to our newsletter
to hear about our **latest
releases**, **author events**,
exciting **competitions**
and more at
reddoorpublishing.com

YOU CAN ALSO FOLLOW US:

 @RedDoorBooks

 RedDoorPublishing

 @RedDoorBooks